REASONS TO MEET ANNIE VALENTINE,

Celebrity Shopper

'You'll be rooting for her as she battles family
life . . . and the scary world of telly, while never looking
anything less than fabulous.'
Heat

'A woman who was making makeovers hip long before
Gok Wan came on the scene.'
Sunday Herald

'The world of TV fashion makeovers is given
a hilariously warm send-up.'
Daily Mirror

'More heartwarming than an expensive round
of retail therapy.'
Daily Mail

'A brilliant read that'll be popular with fashionistas!'
Closer

'A sassy little number'
OK!

'A rollicking tale'
Glamour

Celebrity Shopper

Carmen Reid

BANTAM PRESS

LONDON · TORONTO · SYDNEY · AUCKLAND · JOHANNESBURG

TRANSWORLD PUBLISHERS
61–63 Uxbridge Road, London W5 5SA
A Random House Group Company
www.rbooks.co.uk

First published in Great Britain
in 2010 by Bantam Press
an imprint of Transworld Publishers

A CIP catalogue record for this book
is available from the British Library.

ISBN 9780593066287 (cased)
ISBN 9780593062982 (tpb)

The Random House Group Limited supports The Forest Stewardship
Council (FSC), the leading international forest certification organisation. All our
titles that are printed on Greenpeace-approved FSC-certified paper carry the FSC logo.
Our paper procurement policy can be found at
www.rbooks.co.uk/environment

Typeset in 11.5/15.5pt Palatino by
Falcon Oast Graphic Art Ltd.
Printed and bound in Great Britain by
Clays Ltd, Bungay, Suffolk

2 4 6 8 10 9 7 5 3 1

Celebrity Shopper

Chapter One

On-screen Annie:

Purple and white dress (Mango)
Blue wooden wedge sandals (Chloé)
Mighty beige control pants (Spanx)
Belt? Yes? No? Can't decide (Topshop)
Heavy-duty anti-perspirant (Mitchum)
Heavy-duty anti-shine powder (Clinique)
Heavy-duty hairspray (Elnett)
Total est. cost: £530

'I think you're going to cry . . .'

'OK, here's our shooting schedule for today,' Amelia said, opening the file in her hands and bringing out two sheets of paper neatly stapled together.

Amelia, in her white ankle-grazer jeans, chiffon top and pink suede wedges, may have looked as if she was about to go clubbing, but she was the most ruthlessly efficient PA Annie had ever met – which was of course why Tamsin Hinkley, producer and boss of Hinkley Productions, employed her.

Our shooting schedule!

Annie still felt a little inward thrill when she heard those words. Appearing on TV still wasn't ordinary; it still didn't feel humdrum, typical or routine in any way at all.

For years Annie Valentine had worked as a personal shopper in The Store, one of London's most glorious fashion meccas. Somehow, even though she wasn't willowy thin, or under thirty, or married to a famous producer, she had managed to swap shop life for a TV-presenting job. Well, OK, her first TV-presenting job had been a thankless, penniless grind, but now . . . now she was filming her second series of *How Not To Shop*.

The first six-episode series had been a surprise Channel 4 hit, steadily climbing the ratings charts to become one of the most popular slots on Wednesday night.

A second ten-episode series had been commissioned, Annie's generous wages had increased and now she was beginning to feel like a real, live, genuine TV star. She got fan mail! People waved at her in the street! Taxi drivers asked her: 'Ain't I seen you on the telly or something?'

Just like its presenter, *How Not To Shop* was girlie but ballsy, frivolous but with feeling. It was a chatty but inspiring Girls' Night In.

Viewers didn't necessarily watch at home alone. They rang their sisters and their girlfriends, opened a bottle of wine, brought along a bucket of popcorn and watched Annie together.

Annie did makeovers on the show, yes, but always with a twist: what to wear to your ex-husband's wedding, what to wear to ask for a promotion, what to wear to tell the plumber that his work was terrible and he wasn't getting paid . . .

The show also featured a high-street sweep, with Annie picking out all the best things from the mainstream stores.

Plus, she did little thought-provoking strands, including a regular 'Women and Money' slot. She didn't just want to be on TV encouraging women to part with their hard-earned cash, she wanted them to be careful and clever with it too.

Annie tried to understand money, as did her partner in the slot, Svetlana Wisneski. Svetlana, a multipily married millionairess, would sashay on to the screen draped in a super-label dress plus jewellery worth ten times the average salary and huskily begin with something like: 'Is a *w*-ell-known Russian saying: "Spending is short, but earning is long." Don't throw away your money, my darrrrrrrlings, choose and use your assets *w*-isely.'

After twenty-plus years in England, Svetlana had finally learned to pronounce her 'w's properly, but she tended to over-exaggerate them.

Since Annie had been signed up to do the programme, she'd gone through a series of radical changes. Her once trademark bright blond ponytail had been lopped off into a tousled, face-framing short cut which highlighted her delicate features, ready smile and friendly eyes in a different way. Annie had always been devoted to fashion and dressed to impress but now there was more clever camouflage work involved. Her figure, ever more curvaceous than she would have liked, had now curved right out of a size 12 into the dangerous fashion territory of size 14 and *beyond*. This had everything to do with her biggest change of all, the knock-out change, the one which had redefined her the most: she'd gone from being a mother of two to a mother of four.

Annie still wasn't sure how it was possible to be so busy and so tired at exactly the same time. Without her partner Ed currently taking an extended paternity leave and dealing with just about every aspect of family life, there was no way Annie could be the star of her own television show.

Right now, Ed was downstairs coping admirably with breakfast for the thirteen-month-old twins: Michael and Minette. Or Micky and Minnie as Annie's thirteen-year-old boy, Owen, had christened them as soon as he'd heard their official names.

'So what are we going to wear on screen today?' Amelia asked Annie.

Annie closed her eyes, not to help her think, but to let make-up girl, Ginger, apply a careful coat of shadow, liner, and then mascara for the benefit of the camera.

'These are the shoes and I think you're going to cry,' Annie replied. She pointed past Amelia to a pair of high wooden wedges adorned with a wealth of straps and buckles. 'You're going to be soooo jealous.'

'Oh, to die for . . .' Amelia agreed, 'but that's as far as you've got?'

'The red dress?' Annie asked hopefully.

'No!' Amelia replied, flipping through her file until she came to the outfit schedule. 'Been worn four times already; even the viewers who think it's great you wear things again are beginning to worry.'

'I love that dress, it's so flattering,' Annie sighed, and then ventured: 'The orange?'

'Too like red,' was Amelia's verdict. 'How about something blue? Or purple? Shall I look in the cupboard?'

Annie wanted to say no, because she didn't like people – even people as smart as Amelia – to leaf through her carefully chosen things. But this was her 'office' wardrobe. There was a clothing allowance for the show (as Annie constantly reminded Ed. Yes, but she definitely subsidized it, as Ed constantly reminded Annie).

The BlackBerry on Annie's desk, right beside her hand, began to ring. Actually, it began to trill, buzz, bleep, shuffle and jump, because she kept her phone on every possible setting so that despite the noisy chaos which tended to surround her – both at home and in the studio – she didn't miss a call . . . well, not so many calls anyway.

'Hi!' she answered cheerfully, seeing the name of her sister Dinah on the screen. 'How are you doing? I'm sorry it's been—'

'Exactly one week since you said you were going to phone me right back?' Dinah sounded unusually frosty.

'I've been busy,' Annie protested. 'The telly . . . the babies . . .'

'Annie Valentine, you know perfectly well that you have a full-time, completely saintly nanny partner on hand twenty-four hours a day, so don't you dare give me the I-was-too-busy-with-the-babies line,' Dinah snapped.

'I'm sorry. I should have phoned before,' Annie apologized.

'Yeah, you should have.'

Annie decided to change the subject. 'How's work?'

'That's what I've phoned to tell you. I've been laid off and I'm just gutted . . .' Dinah began.

But the words didn't get nearly as much of Annie's attention as they should have done because, just then, Amelia held out a monstrous shiny purple wrap thing which Annie must have bought when she was drunk or maybe blinded by the glare of the sun – what other explanation could there be? Plus, the call-waiting signal began to bleep in her ear.

'No, no, no. No way!' Annie exclaimed, which was right for Dinah, but she was actually talking to Amelia about the dress.

To Dinah, she said: 'Babes, will you hang on for one tiny moment? Just for me? Pleeeeease. I'm expecting a call from my boss any second.'

She pressed a button.

'Annie!' came the warm, fruity voice of her best friend, Connor McCabe, actor.

'Hello, honey,' she greeted him.

'We're supposed to do lunch,' he reminded her.

'I know, I know, I've been terrible. How many times have I put you off now?'

'Three. One more refusal and that's probably it, I'll have to strike you from my contacts book.'

'Connor! We go way back, doesn't history count for anything?'

'Errr . . . no.'

'I knew you when you weren't famous,' she reminded him.

'I can now say the same thing about you,' he reminded her.

'I'm not famous,' she immediately protested, mainly because the idea of being famous was terrifying.

Annie loved doing the TV show, she loved the programme's growing success, but she tried to think of it as doing what she'd always done in the changing rooms of The Store: giving people good advice about how to make clothes work for them. It was just on a bigger scale . . . the latest viewing figures were close to two million.

Annie didn't want fame. Imagine having photographers posted outside your front door, there to snap you on the way to the supermarket all covered in dog hairs and baby sick. Imagine being sniped at in gossip columns. Or having to endure your bikini shots on a magazine cover. It was too hideous even to think about.

Annie had decided that if she didn't act famous, if she still went on the underground and still hung out in the same places with the same people as she'd always done before, then she couldn't possibly become famous. Fame was a nasty, inconvenient disease that she didn't want to catch.

Whereas money . . . now that was a different matter altogether. Annie wanted all the money that could possibly be had, because to her, money represented security. She'd not had nearly enough of it for most of her adult life and somehow, even though she was very well paid, she still didn't seem to have enough now.

On her desk, buried under all the other cuttings, magazines and bits of paperwork, was Annie's bank statement for this month, greeted as usual with horrified shock. It wasn't just the clothes, it was the mortgage, the school fees, the groceries, the taxis, the gym subscription, all the multiple expenses of life. If you worked hard, you seemed to have to spend just as hard. Maybe she would cancel the gym subscription . . . it had been five months since she last set foot in the gym.

'So when are we doing lunch? I need a date,' Connor insisted. 'I want to go somewhere incredibly cool and show off to everyone who's anyone that hot new telly star Annie V is my oldest and dearest best friend.'

'Aha, so it's not about me, it's all about you,' Annie pointed out.

'It's always all about me!' Connor told her. 'You've known me long enough to know that.'

'True . . .' Annie was still shaking her head at Amelia's dress options. She was also sucking in her cheeks as instructed by Ginger, who was now dusting on rouge.

'How about a week on Thursday?' she suggested, glancing about for her planner, but unable to locate it. 'I don't think there's anything happening lunchtime that Thursday; I'm sure I can get away for a couple of hours. Where shall we go?' She did manage to locate a Post-it note on her desk and a Biro to scribble down the details.

'I think we have to go to De Soto's; it's where all the Soho power people go these days. It's the place. The powerhouse.'

'OK, you book the table and I will see you there a week on Thursday, one p.m. I will call you immediately if I have a problem with that. Love you,' she added.

Connor hung up and Annie flicked back over to Dinah's call, while instructing Amelia: 'Yes! That one, that will work with the shoes, we'll open it right up, put a white vest top underneath, very fresh, very summer-is-on-its-way.'

'It's February,' Amelia reminded her.

'I know, darlin', but we have to give people hope. Hope is what we are all about.'

She spoke into the phone: 'Dinah, babes?'

The line was dead.

'Oh no,' Annie said out loud.

Annie would have called Dinah straight back, her finger would honestly have hit redial, straightaway, but just then Ed popped his head round the door and all activity in the room ceased, because he had Micky and Minnie in his arms.

'Hello, my babies!' Annie gushed.

'Hey, cuties,' Amelia had to join in.

'Awwww,' Ginger added.

Micky and Minnie were perfect. They were chubby, giggly and drooling. They crawled, they wriggled, they had delicious, chunky rolls of fat on legs which they waved about delightedly at nappy-changing time.

Their dark blond hair curled on top of their big heads and they had pearly white teeth that winked with every smile. Minnie had Ed's sparkling blue eyes, Micky had eyes that were a hazel green-brown, and apart from this one difference, it might have been hard for even family members to tell the twins apart; although, obviously, they were dressed as a boy and a girl.

The dressing of the babies was something of a little 'discussion topic'. In fact, the sleeping and eating routines of the babies, the reading material for the babies, the feeding of the babies, the placing of the babies' cots and so on and so forth: these were all little 'discussion topics' for Annie and Ed.

Annie had been a mummy twice before (to Lana, now seventeen, as well as Owen). Ed was entirely new to the game. He was the over-anxious first-time parent, whereas Annie, who had a whole TV career taking up quite a portion of her time, tended to be relaxed. Maybe sometimes just a little too relaxed.

Such as when she fell asleep with Micky in her arms and dropped him off the sofa and on to the dog, Dave. Or when she re-heated a bottle of defrosted breast-milk and gave Minnie food poisoning. Or what about when she walked home from the corner shop without the pram? She hadn't realized until she'd put on the kettle and then gone upstairs to look for the babies in their cots. *That* was a moment she'd never forget.

'Annie?' Ed asked her now. 'Do you have a second?'

'Ermmm . . .'

Her face was done, but there were still nails to file and paint just as soon as she'd been buttoned into the purple and white dress which had been given the Amelia seal of approval.

'I think we need to talk about the whole builder thing again,' Ed said, narrowing his eyes the way he did whenever he was worried.

Any moment now and he would push back his messy (in a good way) tangle of brown curly hair and then she would know that he was really agitated.

'The builder is going to be fine, really fine...' she rushed to reassure him. 'I've spoken to two other people he's done work for and they were both totally positive.'

'Yeah, but do we really need the work done?' Ed asked. 'It's not as if we don't have enough going on. And it's very expensive.'

'Ed!' She looked at him with a touch of exasperation. 'We will all enjoy having a fantastic new bathroom. I promise you.'

'Yes,' he was prepared to concede, 'but huge new windows for the kitchen?'

'Loads more light,' she countered, 'plus, they are triple-glazed, so even though they're bigger, the room will be warmer.'

'Hmmm . . .' He still sounded doubtful. 'But the cupola? Surely we do not need a cupola slap bang in the middle of a roof that we paid a complete fortune to repair?'

Ah, the cupola. The cupola was going to be much, much harder to argue for, she had to admit, as she stripped down to her strict and controlling mega-underwear.

'While we've got the builders in anyway,' she began, 'we might as well get everything done that we want to get done. We don't want to go through all the mess and upheaval all over again.'

'You said that the last time,' Ed reminded her. 'It's only three years since the house was entirely "remodelled" . . .'

'But it's dark and gloomy in the hallway; if we let in more light, by putting in some windows . . .'

Some windows . . . She was talking about a copper-domed turret, she was soooo playing it down here, but this was her little indulgence. She'd worked unbelievably hard, right through her pregnancy, back in the studio two months after the birth. She'd earned that cupola.

'If we put in more windows,' she went on, 'think of all the money we'll save on lighting the hall.'

'We're making a hole in the roof, Annie.'

'But it's so well insulated,' she protested.

'That's really nice,' Amelia broke in cheerfully, 'maybe with a chunky belt?' She was pretending to tune out this domestic disagreement, but really she and Ginger were lapping up every single word.

'Yeah, I have a good belt for this,' Annie agreed, before turning to Ed once again. 'Babes' – she gave him her biggest, most soothing smile – 'I think you're a bit tired. As soon as I'm back this afternoon, I'll take the babies and you have a nap. You'll feel much better when you've had more sleep.'

She didn't add: *and so would I, but it's completely impossible, because these bloomin' babies are the worst sleepers in the whole world.*

'All right, all right,' Ed conceded. It was hopeless trying to talk to Annie like this anyway: him with his armful of baby, her with her army of helpers.

Despite having a baby in each arm, Ed still managed to use his foot to give the door a huffy slam on his way out.

The door slam sent a blast of air across the room, scattering papers across Annie's desk and sending the small yellow Post-it over the edge and down to the floor, where it settled behind a neatly stacked pile of *Vogue* magazines.

Chapter Two

TV boss Tamsin:

Pink merino tunic (Whistles)
Purple satin skirt (Miu Miu)
Purple over-the-knee boots (Russell & Bromley)
Pink tights (John Lewis)
Chunky gold necklace (Tiffany)
Total est. cost: £1780

'Don't we pay you enough?'

'Oh. My. Goodness. What do we think of the new, improved, interview Rachel? We like her, we like very much, do we not?' Annie said, beaming at the camera.

Rachel's smile flickered for a moment, then she went back to looking nervous under the hot glare of the studio lights as she stepped carefully over the cables and wires and made her way towards Annie and the great big looming black camera.

Rachel had been filmed earlier in the interview outfit she'd chosen for herself: a sober grey trouser suit and white blouse with her blond hair falling over her shoulders.

Now she was wearing the interview outfit Annie had picked for her: a black fitted cardigan, a beautiful silk skirt patterned in sober grey, gold and black and a pair of black suede boots. Her hair had been pulled back into a loose up-do and she was wearing an elaborate gold and black necklace.

'How do you feel looking like this?' Annie asked her.

'Good,' came the reply, followed by a shy smile.

'Professional but memorable and really personalized,' Annie told both Rachel and the camera. She put her hand on Rachel's arm and faced her gently towards the lens. 'The problem with anonymous suits is that every other person up for the job will be wearing an anonymous suit, so even if you say all sorts of amazing things, it's hard to stand out. But this' – she gestured to Rachel's lovely new outfit – 'is unique and different and feminine.

'OK, my top tips for the career girls out there.' Annie smiled, full beam, at the camera. 'It's all right, you don't have to leave your personality at home, it's fine to be a little more *you* at work. I'm not mad about super-smart trouser suits with messy hair. I would rather you dressed down a little but made sure your hair was groomed. That's more chic and professional. Sober colours are fine, but they can still be in a dress or a skirt, no one says you have to wear suits all the time. Michelle Obama wore a cardigan to meet the Queen. It was white cashmere with sparkles, yes, but still a cardigan.

'The more skin you show, the less power you have. So sandals, cleavage, even sleeveless tops are a no-no if you're aiming for the penthouse office upstairs,' Annie went on. 'Obviously if you work in fashion or the creative arts, you can wear whatever is so hot it's cool, and if you have a uniform – hey even pole dancers have a uniform – the accessory is your best friend.'

She paused to let this message sink in, before telling her viewers: 'Next week, we're going to have Katy Flinn, head of recruitment agency Flinn–Power, here to talk to us about what to wear to work. Because it's interesting! The rules are changing all the time. Work is changing all the time. Shake yourselves up, girls!

'OK, Rachel, you do a twirl for us. Oh, isn't she pretty damn smart-looking? Right . . .' The camera zoomed in close on Annie's face. 'It's nearly time to say goodbye, but I'm just going to squeeze in a little email feedback.' She turned to a laptop perched on a desk just to her right as an assistant led Rachel silently out. 'Petra from Derby.' Annie shook her head at the screen. 'Petra, Petra,' she tutted. 'Petra thinks I am too cheeky about anoraks and sensible shoes.' Annie raised her eyebrows at the camera, gave a little wink, then she read out: ' "I live in a part of the country where it is chilly and rainy. Anoraks are a necessity! They may not look very exciting but we need them. I wear comfortable, sensible, waterproof shoes that I could even hillwalk in if I had to. There's nothing wrong with this. Please stop telling women to swan about in flimsy dresses with their feet stuffed into torture devices. It's total rubbish." '

'Petra . . .' Annie looked up at the camera and shook her head again. 'It is not all about dressing for the worst-case scenario. I promise you. Where is the fun in that? Is there a Mr Petra? Does he like anoraks and sensible shoes? Anyway, in case you're wondering, I could hill-climb in three-inch heels and a dress, carrying a very nice handbag, looking like a lady who lunches at The Store. Easily. Training . . .' Annie added and with that she stepped out from behind the desk, showed her high wooden wedges to the camera and proceeded to give a little skip and hop.

'Believe me,' she assured the screen, 'without my heels, I

don't feel dressed. I feel like a little fat frump. I'm convinced nothing exciting will ever happen to me if I'm not wearing interesting shoes. So there!' She stuck her tongue out cheekily.

'OK, time to rewind and review,' Tamsin began. She leaned back in her chair and looked at Annie. The show producer and her presenter held a regular brief meeting when filming was on to catch up with problems, bounce new ratings-boosting ideas about and to bond with each other.

Annie genuinely liked Tamsin and was learning so much from her; Tamsin really liked Annie and was learning plenty right back.

'Too much focus on work going on, maybe?' Annie dived straight in with her thoughts. 'We did Rachel's interview outfit this week; we've got Katy Flinn in next week. Are we getting a little too heavy?'

'No, I don't think so . . .' Tamsin assured her. 'Next week's other items are sexy lingerie for all shapes and sizes and the best of the discount fashion websites, so I think that's fluffy enough. But will you phone Svetlana up and see when we can use her again? She's very popular. And by the way,' Tamsin added, 'you look exhausted. There's only so much concealer Ginger can put on your face without using a trowel.'

'I am absolutely blooming shagged,' was Annie's response to this. 'If those babies don't learn to sleep soon, I am going to die. Is it possible to die of tiredness?' she wondered.

'Well, yeah,' Tamsin warned her, 'you'll drive your horrible green mini-van into a brick wall and that will be the end of the Annie Valentine show and all its potentially lucrative spin-offs.'

'Don't talk about the mini-van,' Annie groaned. This was the single worst thing about having four children. Her trusty black Jeep, which had served her so well for so many years, had been sold off to make way for the hulking great super-sensible VW Sharan. A seven-seater! She felt like a bus driver whenever she got behind the wheel of that thing.

'But talking of the lucrative spin-offs,' Tamsin went on, 'I know you've got a talent agent now, putting you up for personal appearances, but what is this chitter-chatter I hear about an Annie Valentine fashion line?'

'No, no, nothing like that,' Annie was quick to answer. 'Don't worry, I'm not going to humiliate Channel Four with some tacky tie-in that upsets all their advertisers.'

'So what is the source of this intriguing gossip?' Tamsin asked, pushing her long hair behind her shoulder and fixing Annie with a serious look.

'Ermmm . . .' Annie felt a little nervous now. It was one thing plotting away at meetings with agents and sub-agents and marketing division heads, but sitting here in Tamsin's all-white, girlie but professional office, having to spell out the ways in which she planned to sell her soul, was just a little nerve-racking. 'Well . . . so long as it's OK with you, I'm going to collaborate with a handbag company,' Annie admitted. 'I've looked over some designs and I'm going to put my name to an "Annie V" handbag.'

'A handbag? That sounds fine.' Tamsin looked pacified. 'Just make sure you really like it, otherwise you might feel a bit silly.'

'Of course!' Annie agreed, relieved because plans for the handbag were further on than she'd made out.

'Don't we pay you enough?' Tamsin wondered.

The question pricked Annie's conscience. Hadn't Ed asked her this just the other day? He too had wanted to know why she needed a talent agent and a handbag collaboration. Wasn't what she earned with the TV show enough?

'Why be satisfied with enough when there is plenty more to make?' she'd asked him.

He'd shaken his head and asked if she'd considered how much time it would all take up.

Annie felt Tamsin's eyes on her. It felt hard to explain that she didn't think she would ever have enough. She would always want more. And anyway, where was the fun in life if you weren't chasing more?

'I'm happy with the pay . . . for now,' Annie answered, shooting Tamsin a wink, 'but I don't want to have all my eggs in one basket. I've been sacked twice before and I think it's good to have a back-up.'

'Maybe you should save some money as a back-up, Annie, instead of tearing your lovely house apart.' Now it was Tamsin's turn to shoot Annie a wink.

'Ouch!' Annie replied.

'OK . . . the hillwalking rant? Are we really going to leave that in?' Tamsin asked.

Annie looked at her blankly.

'You know, Petra from Derby?' Tamsin jogged her memory. 'Anoraks and sensible shoes and you going on about how you could hillwalk with three-inch heels and a handbag.'

'I could!' Annie insisted.

'Well, I'm just warning you now, there might be a campaign to get you up a mountain in a pair of Manolos.'

'Bring in on!' Annie smiled. 'Might be a ratings winner.'

'Hmmm . . .' Tamsin glanced down at the tiny silver laptop on her desk and frowned. 'I've had some worrying news. Viewing figures for last week are good, still close to the two million mark. Channel Four sound like they want to sign us up for a third series,' she said carefully, 'but . . .'

Annie anxiously met Tamsin's eyes. *'But?'* she asked, feeling her heart leap into her mouth. Maybe it was silly and irresponsible of her, but she hadn't considered for a moment that there wouldn't be a third series. She thought she was on an endless upward trajectory; she thought she was a big success.

'There are rumblings, Annie . . . rumblings about bringing back the show but putting a much bigger celebrity in your place to really grow the audience. Myleene Klass is apparently "interested". I doubt they can afford her and I'm going to do everything I can . . .'

But Annie could barely make out the words of reassurance that followed. The thought of *How Not To Shop* just carrying on without her . . . it hadn't even occurred to her! The thought of being 'replaced' just as she'd thought she was arriving . . . It was terrible. Devastating. And what the bloody hell would she do instead?

'For the two last episodes of this series,' Tamsin was telling her now, 'we've got to think of something amazing, barnstorming! We have to end the season with all our viewers clamouring to have you back. That's our mission, girl.'

'Right,' Annie said, barely managing to whisper the word. She felt as if she was going to be sick.

Chapter Three

Svetlana in her office:

Very tight cobalt blue dress (Issa)
Very high green and blue stilettos (Prada)
2.4-carat diamond ring (last ex-husband)
22-carat gold rope necklace (same)
3.5-carat diamond earrings (first husband, deceased)
Silk underwear (La Perla)
Total est. cost: £78,400

'He say "no"!'

'Ya. Is great idea. No? I put big heap of money in, Harry put money in but we still need more, so I think of you. You big, clever, rich man . . .' Svetlana Wisneski was on the phone, using her most charmingly persuasive voice.

She was always on the phone these days because her daughter, Elena, was working her very hard.

Svetlana Wisneski had in fact become Svetlana Roscoff over a year ago. But she still liked to use the name of her most recent ex-husband because she was mildly famous through him and she liked it that way. Igor Wisneski was one of the richest Russians in the world: a gas baron. Svetlana was still the mother of his two and, as yet, only sons and heirs and although she'd suffered a very public divorce, the silver lining to the cloud was the multi-million-pound divorce settlement she and her barrister-turned-fourth husband, Harry Roscoff, had wrung out of Igor.

Well, that was then and this was now. Post credit crunch, post stock market crash, it turned out Igor's fortune had been downsized from billions into millions, so Svetlana's settlement and monthly maintenance had shrunk accordingly. For nearly a year, Svetlana had raged and tried by every means possible to squeeze more money out of her ex.

It wasn't as if she was penniless. Very far from it. She still had her beautiful four-storey house in Mayfair: no. 7 Divorce Settlement Row, and Harry was undoubtedly wealthy. But Svetlana had been *super-rich*. She'd been the wife of a billionaire. She had been used to limitless oceans of cash, all the luxuries life could offer and never once having to consider the cost of anything.

When she'd realized she could not wrestle any more money from her ex-husband, she and her devastatingly clever daughter Elena had begun to develop another idea.

The phone still at her ear, Svetlana turned her feline grey eyes to Elena. Her daughter was at the computer tapping furiously with her elegant hands. Just as Svetlana loved to phone, Elena loved to email. She emailed and emailed and surfed the internet all day long, looking for clues, tracking down information, building up her data. Inside that beautiful blond head, uncannily similar to her mother's, was a big brain, hungry for knowledge and success.

Elena had spent the past year at business school. Yes, up until now she had studied engineering, but she felt that a business qualification would stand her in good stead.

Svetlana and Elena's relationship had not begun in a very promising way. Svetlana had given birth to this unplanned and inconvenient daughter twenty-three years ago in Ukraine and she had paid distant relatives to bring Elena up. Then, at the age of twenty-two, Elena had arrived unannounced on her mother's doorstep and demanded to be taken in.

At first Svetlana had been horrified, but now the mother–daughter relationship was growing much closer than either of them could ever have expected.

They really liked each other. They got on. They enjoyed the same things and shared the same goals. Svetlana felt as if she had learned so much from her fearsomely independent daughter. Before meeting Elena, Svetlana had thought the best way to have plenty of money and security for herself and her children was to marry a rich man (she had done this four times now). Now, she was quietly impressed with Elena's many enterprising money-making ideas. But this latest one, this was the biggest and definitely the best.

This time Svetlana was jumping in with both expensively shod feet and as much cash as she could lay her beautifully manicured hands on.

'Ya,' Svetlana said into the tiny little silver phone again, 'my daughter and I will be personally in charge and we will make this work. Ya, is slightly risky. But these are risky times. No? Igor always say only losers avoid failing.'

Svetlana listened carefully to the reply to her pitch, then she clicked the phone off in frustration.

'He say "no",' she informed her daughter. 'Tcha!' she exclaimed, pacing the small, expensively decorated office several times in her high heels.

Even at home, Svetlana liked to dress up. Maybe, because of her previous full-time husband-keeping job, Svetlana liked to dress up *especially* at home, whereas Elena was at her desk in sober clothes because this was work and, when she was working, she liked to look professional.

Elena did not stop to hold an inquest about the failed phone call, she merely looked at the list on her desk, pointed to the fifth name down and said: 'Next.'

'Oh, I don't know about him ... I don't like him,' Svetlana whined as her eyes fell on the name. 'I don't think this will work ...'

'Mama,' Elena said, the word coming as easily as if she'd been calling Svetlana this all her life, 'we need another thirteen thousand pounds. That's all. We have sixty-two thousand in the bank already. Once we have this money we can press go. We can start up this whole wonderful business. So phone! Someone on this list will say yes. You are so good at getting wealthy men to say yes,' she flattered her mother, 'that is why I give you this job, because I know you are going to win! Now get on the phone.'

Just as Svetlana opened her phone once again, it began to ring.

'Ah, it's Annah!' Svetlana said enthusiastically, spotting the caller display. 'Maybe she have more work for me on the television.'

Elena rolled her eyes: 'Another three-hundred-and-fifty-pound appearance fee, no? We not raise big capital like this!'

'Annah!' Svetlana gushed, ignoring Elena's remark, 'Annah, how is your show and when can I next be on it?'

Annie was delighted to tell her that Tamsin wanted to film a Svetlana slot just as soon as Svetlana was available.

'Ya! I know just what we do next: we call it "Raising capital for girls". Now, do you have some money you'd like to invest in my new business?'

'What?' was Annie's surprised response to this. She had heard nothing of Svetlana's latest business plans.

'No I forget, you never have money, you have always spent it all,' Svetlana said next.

Ow! Annie couldn't help thinking. This was a little harsh coming from a woman who had relied on men as her sole method of support.

'What's your new business idea?' Annie asked.

'Elena and I are going to set up a fashion label,' Svetlana explained. 'Just dresses. We hire a designer to make two or three classic styles every season in beautiful material. Dresses to look good on every woman, Annah. Dresses you can put on and wear with anything: diamonds and heels or boots and denim jacket. Life is so busy, women want something beautiful but easy. Oh and you throw in washing machine when dirty – Elena's idea.'

'Wow.' Annie was impressed. Svetlana had great taste; if she thought the dresses were good, they were bound to be good. Elena seemed to be developing an excellent business head.

'How much are they going to cost?' Annie asked, the business head of her own asking the important question now.

'Just under two hundred pounds. Or two hundred and sixty if you want silk.'

'This sounds like a really good idea . . . it could really work! What are you going to call the label?'

'The Perfect Dress Company, because it will be!' Svetlana told her.

'I think you should put me in for . . .' Annie wondered which of her many budgets she could get the money from. The handbag deal was going to go ahead, so in a few more weeks she would have some money in from that . . . but then, didn't the builder want something upfront for materials? And shouldn't she be saving in case . . . in case of the horrible possibility Tamsin had outlined.

'Three thousand pounds,' she decided.

'Fantastic!' Svetlana replied. 'Sure you don't want to be a bigger partner?'

'Not yet. Maybe a bit further down the line,' Annie replied.

'Just as soon as we have all the capital raised, we are going to have the first dresses made up, then we launch in Paris – where else? – with the trade shows,' Svetlana explained.

'Aren't those at the end of this month?' Annie asked.

'Ya. We need the money! I have to find another ten thousand pounds in the next two days. You really give us three thousand?' Svetlana asked.

'Yeah. Put me in. I owe you . . . But can't you go to a bank?' Annie wondered.

'No. Elena say banks very, very bad. They not lend to anyone new and they want too much money back too soon. I find the money myself,' Svetlana said with determination. 'And when we launch, we do it in Paris and you come, Annah, you come with the camera and the TV programme and you show everyone what it is really like behind the scenes when you start a new fashion label.'

Svetlana glanced over at her daughter. They hadn't discussed this idea before, but it was a very good one. Think of all the free publicity and free marketing Annie's show would give them. Plus Elena could phone loads of newspapers and magazines and explain that they should write about this exciting new dress label because it was about to appear on television. Elena gave her a smile of approval.

At the other end of the line, Annie couldn't help thinking this was a genius idea. Surely this was one of the big barnstormers required for the two final, crucial episodes of the series. And she would be in Paris . . . for the shows! She would finally get to take part in that whole fashion whirl, something she had always, always longed to do.

Immediately she imagined herself at the glitzy parties, drinking champagne, rubbing shoulders with Dolce and Gabbana, getting an exclusive tour of the House of Chanel . . . It was years since she'd been to Paris and imagine being a fashion insider and sneaking a glimpse into the wonderful world . . .

'Brilliant idea,' she told Svetlana. 'I'm going to call Tamsin right now.'

Chapter Four

Ed's at home wear:

Old faded blue rugby shirt (St Vincent's lost property box)
Old faded blue jeans (Levi's)
Old faded blue socks (no idea)
Battered sheepskin slippers (Christmas, some time ago)
Plain leather-strapped watch (Timex)
Total est. cost: £65

'OWEN! Have you got a nanosecond?'

Ed had a schedule. He glanced at his watch and saw that he was running on time. That was good. Ever since he'd decided to take time off work to look after his babies, he'd found that the days ran much more smoothly if he stuck to the schedule.

To be honest, maybe it was a hangover from his day job. Teaching was all about the schedule. You had to be at your lessons at exactly the right time. Bells went off regularly to inform you just where you were in the day. If he was honest about it, Ed would have to admit that he found bells and schedules quite comforting.

Now that the twins were a little older and the fog of looking after tiny, unpredictable babies was finally clearing, Ed was truly enjoying his new children, the schedule and the many extras: the story reading, flashcards, baby yoga, baby Mozart . . . Ed was determined to be the perfect parent. These children were going to be the brightest, most creative and most talented children ever.

Breakfast was at 6.30 a.m. (unfortunately). Even after months and months of this, it still felt criminally early every single morning. Snack was 9.15 a.m. Nap the first ran from 9.30 to 11 a.m. Lunch was at 12 noon. There was another snack before Nap the second from 2 to 4 p.m. Now, at 5 p.m., Ed was planning to cook supper for the babies, which they would eat before going for a bath and then bed at 7 p.m. He would also get supper for the rest of the family started. They would eat later, at about 7.30 p.m.

That was the schedule.

Unfortunately feeding, bathing and putting babies to bed while trying to get another meal on the go was always the point in the evening when Ed could no longer manage by himself.

The good news was that upstairs, lurking in their bedrooms, were Annie's two older children, Lana and Owen, who were perfectly capable of feeding or dressing babies, stirring pots, adding ingredients and all number of other helpful things. The bad news was that they were often sulky and unwilling. They made excuses like: they had homework or music practice or friends coming round, or they were just 'too busy' with 'school stuff'. They whinged. They asked for treats or bribes and, quite honestly, Ed sometimes felt he'd be better off getting on with things on his own than involving the two of them.

Owen wasn't quite as bad as Lana. Sometimes, when Ed had a moment to himself, he worried that Lana hadn't bonded properly with her new siblings. But mainly Ed was far, far too busy to worry about anything other than what he should be doing next and what did the babies want now.

'OWEN!' he shouted up the stairs. 'Have you got a nano-second? Just a very quick job.'

There was silence. Then Ed heard a door opening two flights up on the attic floor.

'Awwww . . .' came the moan. 'Milo's coming round any minute.'

'That's fine,' Ed said, trying to sound as patient as he could, 'I just need you for a few minutes.'

There was a pause while Owen weighed up the pros and cons of having an argument and decided that it probably wasn't worth it, so he began to bound down the steps two at a time until he was down at the bottom of the stairs.

'You rang,' he said jokily to Ed.

Ed smiled back. He had a twin on each arm. This was a pose Owen was now very familiar with: Ed usually had at least one twin on one arm at all times.

Owen was looking too terrifyingly teenage, Ed noticed with a lurch. He was tall for his age and his shoulders had broadened out almost overnight, so he no longer looked so gangly and skinny. His thick, sandy brown hair flopped about all over the place, but he laughed in the face of regular trips to the barber's. Instead, he preferred to just keep on trying (and failing) to push the overgrown mop out of his way.

'I need ten whole minutes of baby-free time,' Ed informed Owen, 'while I put the chicken casserole together, then I am happy to take them back and put them in their bath . . . while you and Lana peel some potatoes?' he suggested optimistically.

'Lana?' Owen raised his eyebrows. 'Good luck with that.

C'mon, hand 'em over.' He opened his arms to his baby brother and sister.

'Have you got them?' Ed worried. 'Are you taking them upstairs?' he worried further. 'Are you sure? Be careful on the stairs, won't you? You have got them properly, haven't you? You won't take them somewhere where they can eat Lego off the floor?'

'Yeah, yeah, yeah . . . and no,' was Owen's nonchalant reply to these questions.

Micky and Minnie were safe with him. He rounded the corner of the stairs and decided to duck into his mother's office. That was a nice enclosed space, he could shut the door, the babies could crawl around and he would keep an eye on them while he took a peep at the official Annie V website.

Owen was proudly in charge of his mother's website. She trusted him to post her updates, answer any uncomplicated email with simple replies and flag up the more complex requests to her.

As Owen switched on the computer and logged on, keeping half an eye on Micky and Minnie as they crawled about the office floor looking for interesting things to explore, he had to admit that he was enjoying all this responsibility.

Here he was age thirteen, in charge of two small babies and a website. It puffed up his chest and gave him a feeling of power.

About ten or so short emails downloaded, all along the lines of 'Annie, I love your show' to which Owen would answer with one of his mother's kind but standard replies. Then there was a request from a jewellery designer who was hoping her bracelets could be featured on the programme; Owen would forward that on to his mother's personal email account.

Now, using his mother's email address, Owen composed

a message of his own to a well-known supplier of top-notch camping and hiking equipment.

Two arctic sleeping bags, a duvet coat, one portable camping stove, waterproof trousers and hiking boots in size 7: these were the items he requested from the company, saying that the show was 'considering' an outward-bound special and would be 'requesting' items from several camping companies to 'compare'.

Just as he was about to power down and find the M and Ms something more exciting to play with than the dust bunnies they'd discovered under the radiator, an email dropped into the in-box.

'No!' Owen warned as Minnie picked up the bundle of dust with her tiny forefinger and threatened to put it into her mouth.

'Dear Annie Valentine,' the email began, distracting Owen once again from his baby duties:

> I hope I'm not being rude but I'm a massive fan of your show and I'd just like to ask you a couple of questions. When is your birthday? How old are you? Where were you born? Are your parents still alive? Where did you go to school? I'm just being curious. Look forward to your reply, Vickie P.

Owen didn't give much thought as to whether he should or not. He just hit reply and bashed out:

> Hi Vickie P, thanks very much for your message. My birthday is in July. Let's just say I'm thirty-something. I was born in Bow, east London. Think that makes me a Cockney officially. My mother, Fern, is certainly still alive. No idea about my dad. I went to school in Hackney then when I was fourteen I went to a posh girls' school for four years. Thanks for asking, lots of love, Annie xx

Then he pressed send.

'Micky!' Owen called out. He sprang from his seat and went over to look at his baby brother. 'What is that?' he asked and managed to get his fingers on the little bit of yellow poking from Micky's mouth.

Out came a very soggy, very well-chewed corner of paper. It looked like the remains of a Post-it note; Owen wasn't sure, but it was the right sort of colour.

If it had been a Post-it, then two-thirds of it was gone, along with whatever may or may not have been written on it. Ah well. Owen gave a shrug; it couldn't have been that important if it was down there on the floor.

He popped the remaining piece into the bin and picked Micky and Minnie up again. 'C'mon, let's go play bouncy bouncy on the bed.'

Both babies erupted into giggles at the prospect of this wild game.

Chapter Five

Lana in her room:

Black skinny jeans (Topshop)
Black and white stripy tunic (Warehouse)
High-heeled black wedges (Dune)
Bead bracelets (borrowed from Greta)
Total est. cost: £75

'It's just a bag of sodding potatoes!'

Lana heard the *ping* of a message dropping into her in-box and put down the history book she'd been pretending to read for the last ten minutes.

She didn't need to open the email to start smiling because she saw at once who had sent it: Andrei.

Lana was always pleased to hear from Andrei. Even though they'd spilt up ages ago and he was now at university, she still sometimes felt as if he was the only person who *really* understood her. Lately, he had become the person who had the most time for her. Now that her entire family revolved around the twins and her best friend Suzie was going out with Jules and Greta was totally obsessed with exams, no one in her immediate circle seemed to have time for all of Lana's concerns the way Andrei did.

The only anxiety on Lana's part was that there was this girl, Sophie, whom Andrei mentioned often. Lana wondered if she was supposed to understand something about Sophie. Was she his girlfriend? Would Lana mind if Sophie was his girlfriend? She knew she shouldn't, because after all she'd finished with Andrei so long ago . . . but she suspected that she would mind.

So maybe that's why Andrei wasn't spelling it out, he just mentioned Sophie here and there, so as not to hide her, but not to shove her down Lana's throat . . . so to speak.

How you [*Andrei's email began*]? You weren't v. happy yesterday. Did French class go OK? Did you get your essay mark? I bet it's not that bad! Here, we get weeks and weeks to write something, but every single person, every single student I know, seems to leave it until the night before. Then total essay meltdown follows, you stay up till 3 a.m. and hand in something utterly rubbish the next day. How anyone is going to get a degree at all, I have no idea!! Spk soon, A xx

Lana read through his note several times. She wondered when he was next going to be in London. It was ages since she'd seen him. The last time, he'd looked different, older. It was as if he'd gone away to uni and then been put into a time machine: gone for a term, but back looking two years older.

She couldn't decide exactly what it was; maybe the fact that she didn't see him in school uniform any more, only in his studenty outfit of T-shirt and leather jacket. Plus he'd learned to drive and had this battered little car now.

That seemed so grown up, so way cooler than all the

other boys in her class. Lana was at the very top of the school now. She was going to sit her A-levels this summer. 'This summer' sounded as if she still had loads of time. In fact it was almost March and the exams began at the end of May.

Clever Andrei had managed to get into Cambridge and Lana had a feeling that no matter how hard she studied, she was never going to be able to join him there . . . but still, there had to be hope. That was why she was spending a lot of time in her room trying to memorize entire textbooks. But it wasn't exactly fun.

Although Lana could hear Ed calling her name from downstairs, she began her reply to Andrei, tuning Ed out completely.

She couldn't believe how much Ed and her mother expected her to help out. They were the ones who'd decided to have those babies, weren't they? Lana had definitely not been consulted. If she had, she'd have said what a completely ridiculous idea. Her mother was nearly forty, she was swamped by her TV career, what on earth did she need *twin* babies for?

Anyone could see that Ed was a total novice to the whole thing. He went about checking his watch the whole time, wondering which end of which baby to attend to first.

Lana found the babies an unbelievable inconvenience. And they woke her up in the middle of the night! Didn't they realize she needed as much sleep as possible? She wanted to do amazingly well in her exams.

She opened a new message and took a long time to think about her reply to Andrei.

'Hi Andrei,' Lana began finally.

French was OK. Essay mark was fine. So much boring studying still to do, so many boring exams to sit. I can't wait for it all to be over. I still don't know what I'm going to do next, but I think there's still a bit of time left to decide. Help! If I'm going to go to uni, I know my mum wants me to work for a year so I can save up some money. I like the idea of going to work. As long as she doesn't drag me into her TV business. Can't think of anything worse. Funny how just about everyone in my class wants to be famous and now that my mum is actually on TV, I can't stand the idea! I'm just waiting for her first appearance in one of those celeb magazines. 'Annie V has bad hair day' . . . But will she let me leave home when I'm working? That's what I want to know. I can't think of anything more boring than having to stay here and help out with the boring babies. They are still waking up every night and crying the house down. It's exhausting! I have to go. I can hear my dad shouting in the hall for me. Wonder what chores I am supposed to do for him now? L xx

Lana hit the send button and yelled out a reply to Ed.

But just before she went downstairs, there was one more thing she wanted to do. Logging on to her mother's website, she clicked on the schedule for the next show. She liked to be prepared for the teasing she got at school. One time, she'd walked in completely unaware to be met by a volley of laughter.

'Shopping with your teenager', one of the girls had read from Annie's preview schedule. 'How to avoid every mother's worst nightmare.'

'Oooh, Lana, did you star in that episode?' The teasing questions had come thick and fast for the rest of the day.

Lana skimmed through the items for the next programme and couldn't see any potential minefields ahead: 'Dressing for work', 'Choosing an evening bag', 'Best of the high street' . . . Oh no . . . there it was, the really embarrassing item all her classmates would be talking about for the rest of the week: 'PMT shopping: how to avoid the pitfalls'.

Why did her mum have to do this stuff? Why couldn't she just have stayed at her job with The Store? Hadn't that been embarrassing enough – helping other women, including lots of mothers of St Vincent's pupils, to buy their clothes?

The mothers had no doubt wondered how this glorified shop assistant could afford to send her children to one of the most expensive private schools in London. But then they'd had no idea how hard her mum worked, both at her day job and on her many sidelines.

'LANA!' she heard Ed bellow from the foot of the stairs.

'OK, OK,' she shouted back. She stood up from her desk and hurried to the door.

'It's just a bag of sodding potatoes . . .' she huffed to herself. Did it really matter whether she peeled them now or in fifteen minutes?

Chapter Six

Post-bath babies:

Non-bleached, biodegradable nappies (Oko)
Layer of baby moisturizing cream (Green People)
Red organic cotton baby grows (Piccalilly)
Blue and white organic sleep bags (Green Baby)
Total est. cost: £49

At ten to seven there was a flurry of activity at the front door. Annie burst in, unburdened herself of her many bags: laptop, carrier bag crammed full of trial pots, tester items, prototypes, ideas for the show. She kicked off the deathly uncomfortable shoes, massaging her aching Achilles tendons as soon as she came down from the towering heel heights, and rushed first to the kitchen to kiss Lana hello and then upstairs to see the rest of her family.

'Owen, hi!' she aimed up the attic stairs at Owen's door. 'See you in a minute, got to do baby bedtime first.'

'OK!' came the cheery reply. Owen wasn't worried. He had things of his own to do in his room now, such as: play air guitar; find new hiding place for laundry mountain.

'My babies!' Annie exclaimed, swooping into her bedroom, kissing and cuddling everyone in sight.

Ed, Minnie and Micky were all treated to a barrage of affection.

'I've missed you,' Annie said, scooping the clean, pyjamaed babies out of Ed's arms and into her own, 'I've missed you, yes I have!'

She kissed the fat cheeks and snuggled her babies against her. The twins were always delighted to see her. That was the very, very best thing about little children; they were always so pleased to see you. Before the babies had arrived, Annie had almost forgotten that undiluted pleasure. Older children had other things on their minds, other worries, other issues, but little children just needed to see Mummy and they were thrilled. Blissed out. Nothing was better.

Annie couldn't resist nibbling under her babies' chins to make them giggle.

'Don't get them all excited,' Ed warned, 'it's bedtime.'

'No worries,' Annie replied, 'I'm sure I'll see them many more times before morning.'

'You never know,' Ed replied, ever optimistic that maybe tonight was going to be the magical night that this legendary event would happen and the babies would 'sleep through'.

He'd become obsessed with the idea of 'sleeping through'. It was like the Holy Grail, the pot of gold at the end of the rainbow; he'd begun to think it couldn't possibly ever happen or really exist, but he dreamed of it, wished for it, felt that if only he could add some magic touch, maybe his dream would come true.

Annie, wrung out with sleeplessness, had made many dark threats about 'leaving the babies to cry' but Ed ignored them all. His children were treated with nothing other than devoted love and respect. If they needed him, if they cried out in the night, he was always, always going to respond. He couldn't imagine it any other way.

'Say night night to Daddy,' Annie told the babies, 'he's going to make dinner and I'm going to snuggle up with you.'

Micky and Minnie shared a big cot at the foot of Ed and Annie's bed. Annie was certain this was part of the problem; they should have their own cots and their own room, which she was sure would give everyone a better night's sleep. But Ed wouldn't hear of it. His style of parenting was all about love, warmth, sharing and cuddling together. What a soft-hearted daddy he was turning out to be, Annie thought to herself with a smile. His twins were going to run rings around him. They already did.

With one baby in each of her arms, Annie lay on the double bed and began to sing gently to them. Old, old songs, ones her mother had sung to her and she'd sung to Lana and Owen. When she couldn't remember the words, she made them up, enjoying just crooning quietly to her twins.

She loved feeling the chubby bodies grow still and heavy in her arms, loved to watch their eyes go dreamy and fix far away in the distance. Now, both babies were putting up a momentary struggle with their heavy eyelids but then their eyes were shut, long lashes curled against their cheeks.

Still singing, Annie put them both down in their cot, patting them gently before she stole out of the room.

In the kitchen, Ed was chopping carrots while Lana peeled potatoes. This was a chore she had begun reluctantly, but now that Ed was talking to her about school, desperate to hear all the latest gossip, she didn't mind it too much.

'So tell me about the Easter concert,' he was saying with interest. 'What are they planning to do?'

As head of the music department, Ed would usually have been heavily involved with the planning of the Easter concert.

'Well, I'm only hearing this from Suz,' Lana began, 'obviously I'm not involved, but I think it's bits of *The Messiah* and stuff from *Jesus Christ Superstar.*'

'*Jesus Christ Superstar*? Good grief!' Ed exclaimed. 'Has Pinkie gone stark, staring mad?'

'Pinkie?' Lana had to ask.

'Er ... yes. That's my *private* name for Mr MacPherson. You don't need to know that and neither does anyone else at St Vincent's.'

But Lana was already giggling. 'That's good,' she told Ed, 'he is very pink. In fact, he's always pink. He's either sunburned or incredibly worked up about something.'

'*Jesus Christ Superstar*! For St Vincent's parents?' Ed was still trying to come to terms with this news. 'Has he run it past Ketteringham-Smith?' he asked, invoking the name of the headmaster.

'How would I know?' Lana replied.

'It's only two weeks away ... I should warn Pinkie. It could be hideously embarrassing; he could get the sack.'

'For *Jesus Christ Superstar*?'

'Ketteringham-Smith will be horrified. He'll want holy music all the way. That's the St Vincent's tradition. You can jazz things up a bit at the summer concert or even Christmas, but messing with the Easter ceremonies ... he will not like it one tiny little bit. Why didn't Owen tell me about this? I've not heard Owen practising anything from *Superstar.*'

As he said these words, it occurred to Ed that for some weeks now, he hadn't heard Owen practising his violin

46

at all. In fact, the only sounds coming from Owen's room had been loud music blasting from his iPod speakers or that bloody electric guitar Annie had given him for Christmas.

He'd been meaning for ages to ask Owen how his violin was going, but the babies sucked up so much time and so much energy that he'd either been too busy or too exhausted to remember.

'Owen is in the concert, isn't he?' Ed asked Lana.

Lana turned back to her potatoes and gave a shrug, determined not to land her little brother in anything. 'You'll have to ask him,' she said.

Ed went immediately out into the hall and was about to shout for Owen to come down, but he remembered that the babies had just gone to bed, then there was a small *brrring* at the doorbell followed by the scamper and flurry of fur that was Dave, the small, wiry and extremely noisy family dog, rushing to sentry duty.

'Shush!' Ed grabbed hold of the dog and held his muzzle shut to demonstrate. 'No barking,' he said, but as Dave was almost deaf, this wasn't very effective.

Dave issued two or three sharp little barks as Ed let Annie's mother Fern in the front door.

'Suppertime?' Fern asked brightly.

'Yes,' Ed confirmed, 'come in, take a seat. We're nearly there.'

Fern had been living in the basement flat of Ed and Annie's house for almost two months now. She'd been diagnosed with the earliest signs of dementia over a year ago now and the illness was progressing erratically. Sometimes she would be totally lucid, capable and normal for days, even weeks, but then if she got stressed or emotional, a cloud of confusion could come over her which was bewildering, not just for Fern but for everyone around her.

She was currently starting a new course of medication to keep the illness at bay and Annie had persuaded her mother to move into the basement flat until they could all be sure the treatment was working for her.

Ed and Annie didn't mind Fern living with them one little bit; the person who really minded was Fern. Every day, she wanted to have the conversation with Annie about going home and, every day, Annie did her best to avoid it.

Ed walked with Fern towards the kitchen. Although it had only been a few hours since he'd last called in on her, he still asked: 'How are you doing?'

'Oh, fine,' she told him, 'I've spent all afternoon looking for . . . Lana!' she interrupted herself. 'Black and white stripes?' She was referring to Lana's top. 'You just need a mask and a swag bag, then we'll know you're a robber.'

'Thanks, Gran,' Lana said with a smile. 'You just need a walking stick and plastic pants, then we'll know you're an old lady.'

Ed froze in horror at the cheek of this remark, but Fern exploded into laughter.

Several minutes later, Annie and Owen came downstairs and soon the family's evening meal was in full swing.

'Have you heard from Nic?' Annie asked her mother, referring to her other sister.

'Nic, yes . . .' Her mother paused, forkful of chicken in mid-air. 'She's going to come and see us as soon as she can and bring little Tara with her. Today has been a very good day, by the way,' she added, 'no white mists . . . well, not that I've noticed anyway; obviously if you go out into the garden and find my underwear hanging all over the bushes, then we'll know otherwise. I've been looking for . . .' She tailed off.

For a moment there was a little pause. Everyone was aware that Fern couldn't remember what she'd been looking for, but they tried not to panic. It didn't necessarily mean anything scary.

'Oh, never mind,' Fern said finally, 'it'll come. Tell us all about the TV world today.'

Annie did, not mentioning a word about the threat she was under because everyone around this table so depended on her. Lana and Owen's school fees; Ed's unpaid sabbatical; Fern living downstairs in their basement flat – if Annie lost her job, it would affect everyone very badly. Better to just work on and keep it all to herself. Focus on making those two final episodes amazing.

Mouth full of salad, Owen butted in with the information that a jewellery designer had emailed Annie and wanted to be featured on her show.

Before Annie could reply, Fern looked up and blurted out: 'That's it! Jewellery! I've spent the whole afternoon looking for . . . for . . .' but then she was groping about; whatever word or idea had glimmered in front of her had disappeared again. 'Oh!' she cried out in frustration. 'I can't bloody well remember.'

As she turned her face back down towards her plate, it didn't escape Ed's notice that both Annie and her mother had tears in their eyes.

'Owen?' Ed remembered, desperate to change the subject. 'How's the violin? What's your part in the Easter concert?'

'Uh oh,' came Owen's reply. Desperate to change the subject himself now, he threw in: 'And when are you and Mum getting married?'

'Uh oh . . .' came Annie's response.

Chapter Seven

Annie ready for bed:

Saggy PJ bottoms (La Senza)
Saggy white vest (M&S)
Pink maribou-trimmed mules (Agent Provocateur)
Frownies (Boots)
Crème de la Mer night cream (eBay)
Hand cream and white cotton gloves (Barielle)
Total est. cost: £270

'Oh no . . . you can't really be thinking . . . ?'

As Annie tiptoed into the dimly lit bedroom, Ed glanced over at her from his side of the bed. He frowned, and then, spotting the white gloves she was wearing to 'turbo-charge her hand cream' (apparently), he began to grin.

'Oh no,' he whispered, so as not to wake the twins asleep at the end of the bed, 'not a mime show . . .'

'For my hard-working hands,' she informed him, also in whispers. The babies were like small unexploded bombs in the room; they could go off at any moment.

As Annie walked round the bed, so she could get in on

her side, Ed looked at her face, greased with a layer of cream and sporting those silly plastic strips that she taped to her forehead every night, supposedly to iron out her frown-lines. At least she'd stopped having her face injected with botulism . . . well, as far as he knew. He didn't put it past her to sneak off every once in a while and have little tweaks made here and there.

She lay carefully back on the pillow, face, layer of cream and Frownies facing upwards, then she placed her gloved hands on top of the duvet.

'That looks so relaxing,' Ed told her. 'You're just going to nod off straightaway, aren't you? Why don't you put in your teeth-bleaching tray as well, just to help you doze off?'

'Ed, I am so tired, I could be on a lilo at the top of a waterfall and I would sleep like a . . .' She paused. There was no point saying she would sleep like a baby because those two at the end of the bed woke up every two hours and bawled.

'Log,' he finished her sentence.

Annie closed her eyes but Ed, propped up on his elbow, continued to look at her affectionately.

'Go to sleep,' she told him.

'I don't want to,' he whispered and reached over to put the strap which had slipped from her shoulder back into place.

'Oh no . . . you can't really be thinking . . . ?' she began.

'I'm always thinking . . . there's no harm in just thinking,' he said and ran his fingers gently round her shoulder; the merest touch, but it seemed to bring the hairs on the surface of her skin to life.

He touched the side of her neck with the same very gentle, tickling caress.

'I'm not doing anything,' she told him, but she did nothing to move his hand away.

'Neither am I,' he replied, but his hand was still on her

skin, ruffling the downy hairs, touching the very tips of her nerve-endings and making them tingle.

When he slid the V-neck of her vest down, revealing her breast, she didn't move, just lay with her eyes closed, perfectly still.

'I'm just kissing your nipple,' he whispered, 'don't read anything into it. Don't expect it to lead anywhere . . .'

But then she felt the roughness of his stubble and his warm, wet tongue against her. Her nipple puckered up to attention and she immediately felt blood rushing from her stomach down to tingle between her legs.

Ed's fingers moved over the skin on her stomach, then walked lower.

'Just kissing your stomach,' he whispered. 'Don't read anything into it . . . don't expect . . .'

But his fingers were touching expertly, parting the skin and finding absolutely, exactly . . . the right place.

She didn't want to move and not just because of the face cream, the Frownies and the cotton gloves. She wanted to do nothing, to lie back and let him and his tingling touch slide up and down against her. Wash over her.

But then came the moment of urgency and Annie was wiping off both Frownies and Crème de la Mer with her cotton hands, peeling the gloves off and throwing them to the floor. Her vest and pyjama bottoms followed and now they were naked with intent.

Ed sat on the edge of the bed, Annie straddled over him, his hands clasping at her buttocks, her breasts bouncing up and down against his chest, gloriously getting it together in delighted defiance of all the obstacles: the unexploded baby bombs, the beauty creams, the shooting schedule, the third series angst and the sheer, grinding exhaustion.

A baby stirred.

A baby definitely stirred.

'Don't stop,' Annie whispered against his ear.

'No,' Ed assured her.

They concentrated ... this could be the only sex for weeks ... it had to be good. It had to glow in their memories as a very happy moment; something definitely worth trying to get round to again.

'Is this a good time to bring up the marriage question?' Ed whispered against her ear.

'No!' she told him. 'Definitely not. Just because you've got Owen to agree to violin practice doesn't mean it's your lucky night.'

'Pleeeeease?' he tried.

'Babes, not now,' she whispered. 'Shhhh . . .' she added, hoping this might soothe the stirring baby.

They moved back across the bed and lay as quietly as they could, Annie feeling Ed's heartbeat thud on top of hers and his blood pulse inside her.

She wiggled her hips, wanting to feel him move against her again. Needing to feel him move against her again.

He kissed her neck, slow, warm kisses from the shoulder up to the ear, which made her shudder with pleasure.

'If anyone's going to scream tonight,' he whispered against her ear, 'I want it to be you . . .'

Chapter Eight

Amelia's work look:

Batwing neon brights tunic (Topshop)
White cropped jeans (Whistles)
White wooden wedge sandals (New Look)
Orange nail polish (Mac)
Pink eye shadow (Miss Selfridge)
Total est cost: £170

'Girl, you so need more sleep.'

'Knock, knock,' Ed said outside Annie's office door. He couldn't actually knock because he had the tray of drinks orders in his hands.

'Come in,' Annie told him in a subdued voice.

He opened the door with his shoulder and brought in the tray, setting it down on the desk where Annie and Amelia were once again going through her schedule.

Annie was rubbing at her forehead, trying to make some impact on the exhaustion headache that was building up behind there. Her eyes alighted on the steaming cafetière, the two mugs, the jug of milk and the bowl of sugar Ed had just brought up from the kitchen, and she visibly perked up. 'Oh yes! Everything's going to be much better now. Ed do you have . . . the other stuff?' she asked with a wink.

'I really don't know if you should be doing this, not with coffee. You're going to be really jittery.' Nevertheless, he slid one slim, chilled can of Red Bull from his trouser pocket.

'Girl, you so need more sleep,' Amelia informed Annie.

'Yeah, try telling Micky and Minnie about that.' She looked up at Ed and saw the dark blue rings underneath his eyes too.

'OK.' Ed nodded and turned to leave the room because he didn't want this conversation to continue. He knew where it led; it led to talks of 'sleep training' and 'sleep clinics' and 'sleep rules' and he didn't want to know.

'So today' – Amelia directed Annie's attention back down to the sheets of paper in front of her – 'I'll take you over to the studio, we've got to film a few links in the morning, then there doesn't seem to be anything else in the diary apart from "Check out high street". Tomorrow, Friday, is obviously the full-on hectic all-day filming. Probably right on into the evening. We're going out of town. Remember?'

'Yeah.' Annie did remember, but she was looking at today's lunchtime gap in the schedule and wondering why it was there. She couldn't remember organizing any time off. 'So I'm supposed to be checking out some shops this afternoon?' she asked.

'Well . . . in your own time, if you are. There's nothing official down.'

'Thursday?' Annie asked out loud. 'I thought there was something else happening today.'

'There's nothing down here,' Amelia assured her. 'Anything in your personal diary?'

Annie flicked through to the right page, but nothing had been written down. 'Thursday?' she frowned. There was something . . .

Connor had arrived at De Soto's almost twenty minutes early for his lunch date with Annie.

He'd dressed carefully and taken a taxi, because you never knew whom you might run into. Well, at De Soto's you hoped that you would run into everybody. That was the whole point.

He walked up to the bar, took a seat and ordered himself a soda and lime with 'plenty of ice, please'. In the mirror behind the bar, he briefly checked himself out and felt content with the handsome, well-groomed man reflected back at him.

Connor had spent the last five years trying to come to terms with his phenomenal success as a TV, film and theatre actor. The past five months had been all about trying to come to terms with his phenomenal, well . . . 'failure' wasn't a word he liked to use. 'Hiatus' was infinitely preferable.

Three horrible things had happened to Connor all at once. His movie career, currently based on one so-so film, hadn't taken off in LA; *The Manor*, the TV series that had made Connor a star, which paid all Connor's bills, on which Connor relied as his career backbone, had decided it could get along just fine without him; then, to add injury to insult, Connor's boyfriend Hector had met someone much more appreciative of his many talents than Connor had ever been.

Connor was definitely having a very bad run. Every morning he woke up and remembered how horrible his life was at the moment; then he psyched himself up, got out of bed, showered, dressed well and picked up the phone, hoping that today was the day things would start to get better. Much of the time he managed to keep the dread that his career was over to the back of his mind. But at least once a day and about three times a night, it flooded over him.

His agent had promised to put him on the lists for as many auditions as possible.

'Theatre, TV, film . . . whatever!' Connor had advised him. 'As long as there's a cheque at the end of it, I'm there. What about adverts? Isn't there anyone who'd like *The Manor*'s cheery policeman advertising their product?'

'Well, it's a bit tricky,' his agent had admitted. 'If you were still in the show—'

'If I was still in the show,' Connor had interrupted with exasperation, 'we wouldn't be having this conversation! I'd still be in bed dreaming of how to spend the vast amount of money in my bank account.'

'How many times did I tell you to set plenty of money aside?' his agent had blurted out. 'Acting is an unpredictable career. How many times do I have to say that?'

Sitting in the bar, Connor tried not to think of how rudely he'd replied to that comment.

Never mind, today was a good day, he was wearing his favourite Armani sweater and jacket, his hair looked fantastic and he was about to be treated to lunch by one of Channel 4's hottest new stars, his very own dear old best friend, Annie Valentine.

'Hey, Connor!' He felt a firm smack on the back and turned round to see a TV producer pal he hadn't bumped into for ages. 'How are you doing?' Jay asked, pulling up the seat next to Connor's and clearly preparing to settle down for a few minutes to chat.

Connor was currently spending a lot of time prepping himself to give great answers to the 'How are you doing?' and 'What are you up to?' questions, but despite his prep, those questions still seemed to punch him in the solar plexus every time.

'I'm . . . I'm . . . fine,' he began, knowing perfectly well that it wouldn't end there.

'So what's the big project that's stolen you away from *The Manor*?' Jay asked, because obviously the trade press had not been informed that Connor McCabe had in fact been axed from the Sunday schedule favourite.

This was tricky. On the one hand Connor could lie and say it was something top secret and he couldn't breathe a word about it just yet. On the other hand, wouldn't it be useful for Jay to know that Connor was looking for something new? He might know of some good opportunities coming up.

'I needed something new,' he began carefully. 'I've been doing *The Manor* for years . . . I'm speaking to lots of people but I've not found the right thing yet. So I'm biding my time, because I want it to be absolutely the right project.'

'Ah!' Jay smiled.

Connor wasn't 100 per cent happy about that smile. There was just a little hint of something in it: triumph? Sympathy? Something he wasn't quite used to. He was used to telling people how fabulously everything was going and watching them as they tried to swallow down their jealousy and wish him well.

'How about you?' Connor added quickly.

'Just been commissioned to do a new series for BBC Four,' Jay said, giving a little wave to attract the attention of the barman. 'Nothing fancy, nothing as well paid as you're used to, I'm sure. But we are still looking for the lead, and we want to get a big name.'

'Really?' Connor tried not to sound too interested, tried in fact not to actually pant. 'So what's the series about?'

'Costume drama . . .' Jay began.

Connor perked up. 'How interesting!' He knew he looked pretty damn good in a doublet and hose. He filled a hose.

'It's a new, much more realistic and insightful look . . .'

'Yes?' Connor encouraged him. This sounded good; he imagined himself striding about in his doublet and hose, swashbuckling a little. Maybe it was Dick Turpin the high-wayman? He'd always fancied himself as a bandit.

'. . . at *The Elephant Man*,' Jay said.

Connor's lime and soda nearly splurted from his nostrils. *The Elephant Man*?

'Oh boy,' Connor had to tell him, 'you'll have a job casting a name in that part.'

'John Hurt's played him,' Jay pointed out.

'Even so . . . Who are you meeting here today?'

'Another producer,' Jay said before mentioning a name Connor didn't recognize.

'I'm sure he'd like to meet you,' Jay added.

'Thanks, I'd love to say hello,' Connor gushed.

'What about you?' Jay asked. 'Meeting anyone?'

'Oh' – Connor would at least enjoy this bit of the conversation – 'my old friend . . . Annie Valentine,' he said with relish.

'Oooh! Annie Valentine.' Jay looked impressed. 'That show's doing so well, isn't it? Totally girlie pants obviously,' he added spitefully, 'but a ratings treasure.'

'Hey! Don't knock that show!' Connor rushed to Annie's defence. 'I love that show.'

'Sir?' A waitress approached him. 'It's one p.m. Shall I show you to your table? You can wait for your guest there.'

'That would be fantastic, thanks.'

Connor was shown to his seat right in the middle of the restaurant. It was a generous four-seater table, which had been set for two. Connor seemed to remember that he'd mentioned both his and Annie's names when he'd made the booking.

The maître d' was obviously a big Connor McCabe (or maybe, he had to grudgingly admit, a big Annie Valentine) fan, having placed them so conspicuously in the middle of the room like this.

Several minutes later, Connor cast another glance at his watch. Surely she'd be here soon . . . wouldn't she?

Chapter Nine

Plain Jane:

Red trenchcoat (Debenhams sale)
Blue sweatshirt (her sister's)
Faded khakis (Gap sale)
Lace-up shoes (Clarks)
Total est. cost: £105

'You're Annie Valentine!'

Many, many miles from Soho, Annie was walking round a branch of Hobbs and looking at the clothes carefully. She was taking hangers down from the rails, feeling the material, checking out the price tags and assessing cut and colour, like the true professional she was.

She had a tiny notebook in her hand with a small pencil pushed into the wire spiral binding. On the rare occasion when Annie found an item which met all her stringent criteria, she wrote it down in the notebook. Then Amelia would phone head office, a sample size 10 would be shipped out to the studio, and it might, just might, absolutely no promises or guarantees offered, be featured on the show.

Of course the programme was sent things ahead of season, but Annie also liked to do it this way round: go to one of the less fashionable edge-of-town concessions on her own and see what was really out there hanging on the rails for women to choose.

One of the shop assistants approached Annie to ask: 'Can I help you?'

'I'm fine, thanks, just taking a good look. If I want to try anything on, I'll let you know.'

'OK.' The assistant smiled and looked at her for just a little too long.

Annie was trying to get used to this look. She came across it more often now. People would look at her and she could see them trying to work out why her face was familiar. 'Have we met before?' they would sometimes ask, to which Annie would wink and say: 'No, but I'm sometimes on TV,' as modestly as she could possibly manage.

'YOU'RE ANNIE VALENTINE, AREN'T YOU?'

Annie was startled by the woman who ran straight up to her now, shouting this out at what seemed like the top of her voice.

'YOU ARE! YOU'RE ANNIE!' the woman went on. 'I thought I saw you out in the street and I followed you in here.'

Annie was slightly taken aback. Not only had she been spotted, she'd also been followed. Even though the woman looked perfectly normal, it was just a bit odd.

'Yes,' Annie said, smiling at her fan. 'How nice of you to notice,' she added, hoping this would calm the woman down.

But it already felt as if there was something of a stir in the shop. The assistants had heard what the woman had said and so had several of the customers.

'You have to help me!' the woman exclaimed and reached out to take hold of Annie's arm with both of her hands.

'How can I help you, darlin'?' Annie asked cheerfully, trying not to worry about how strange this was making her feel.

'Look at me!' the woman blurted out. 'I need your help. If you don't help me, I . . . I don't know what I'm going to do!'

Annie looked at the woman closely. She was aged somewhere between forty-five and fifty-five. Her hair was dark with lots of grey shot through it, in a messy, grown-out short cut. She was buttoned up into a shapeless red trenchcoat which didn't go well with her chubby red face.

'What help do you need?' Annie asked in her most soothing voice.

'I need you to shop with me!' the woman exclaimed. 'I'm absolutely useless. I have no idea what suits me or what goes with what and all these girls' – she waved about the store with her hand – 'they're no good. They never help me either.' Suddenly her shoulders seemed to sag and any sense of threat totally disappeared from her.

'That's fine,' Annie assured her with a smile, 'I've got some time, so we'll do a little bit of shopping together.'

She stole a glance at her wristwatch. It was coming up to 1.15 p.m. She could easily give this woman an hour of her time. Why not?

Connor took another look at his watch. He could feel the hairs at the back of his neck prickling because he was sure Jay and Jay's producer friend, sitting two tables behind him, were watching.

Annie was sixteen minutes late. Exactly. Ten would have been OK. But by sixteen minutes, he really would have expected a call, a text, a something to let him know that everything was OK.

He slid his phone out of his jacket pocket and checked it over again. Not one single message, missed call or any sign that anyone, anywhere, had even thought of Connor McCabe for one second today.

He felt a wave of self-pity sweep over him and began jabbing at his handset in an effort to stave it off.

He called up Annie's number and heard the line begin to ring.

When he heard voicemail click in, he felt faintly relieved. She must be on her way. Maybe she was on the tube. Maybe there had been some sort of hold-up. Really, he should be feeling concerned for her, not angry.

But those eyes were boring into the back of his neck. Jay and company must surely be wondering what had happened to his famous lunch guest.

Just for luck, Connor sent Annie a text: 'U R L8!! When here? Connor'.

Then he sat back and waited for some sort of reply, or a glimpse of Annie out on the pavement scurrying to get here.

'So what's your name?' Annie asked the woman. 'You know mine, so it's only fair.'

'I'm called Jane. Plain Jane with the Brain,' she added with a false laugh. She opened her arms as if to show herself off and said: 'Can't you tell? That's what I was called in school and somehow it's stuck. The people at work call me that too.'

'Oh blimey,' Annie sympathized, 'that's not very nice.'

'No.'

'Well, you know, the 'brain' bit is good. It's just the 'plain'. We have to do something to get rid of the plain,' Annie told her.

Jane looked up hopefully. There was just a touch of something. Jane was just a little too needy for Annie's liking. Annie would have to proceed with caution here.

'Is it an outfit for work that you're looking for?' she asked. 'We should get one of the assistants to give us a hand.'

'Oh no.' Jane shook her head. 'It's just you I want. Everyone else is so nasty. But you're lovely to all the people on your show.'

'That is really nice of you, Jane, thank you,' Annie told her, but then confided, 'I can be a right old witch when I want to be though.'

Jane smiled.

'But I'm not going to be able to shop with you every time, girl, so I think we should get one of the assistants here to help us,' Annie suggested, 'then the next time you come back here, you can ask for her. I'm going to try and help you build up a little working relationship, get you used to working with an assistant. They do want to help you, honestly. I spent years being an assistant myself, Jane, I know.'

Connor fiddled with his phone. Nothing was happening. No reply . . .

'Can I get you another drink?' The waitress hovered at his elbow. 'Another lime and soda? Or would you like something else?'

'Ermmm . . .' Connor weighed it up. He was trying not to drink much. There had been times in his life when he'd drunk way too much and more recent times when he hadn't drunk at all. At present, he was trying to find a balance. He could not blank out what was happening in his life with booze; he knew that would be a disaster. He'd never get anything back on track like that.

On the other hand, teetotalism was damn, bloody, joyless hard work. Especially when he seemed to spend entire hours of every day totally stressed out of his box.

'I think I'll have a tiny tonic water . . .' He wavered. '. . . with a double gin in it, please.'

Annie had Jane in the changing room now. Her coat was off and Annie was looking at the beige trousers and navy sweatshirt underneath.

This was nothing she couldn't handle.

The phone in Annie's handbag began to bleep.

'Just one tiny second,' she told Jane and turned away to look at the message.

'U R L8!! When here? Connor.'

Annie looked at the letters for several moments.

They didn't make any sense. She was late? Late for what? 'When here?' *Where?* Connor?

Connor?

Connor!

Suddenly the fog cleared and Annie remembered with total clarity the phone call, the restaurant arrangement and the details scribbled down on the Post-it note.

'Oh bloody hell!' she said out loud.

Jane looked at her with anxiety. 'You're not going to go? Please don't go! I can't do this without you!' she wobbled.

'That message . . .' Annie began to explain, 'I was supposed to be in Soho at one p.m. to meet my really, really good friend for lunch. He's going to kill me.'

'I'll kill myself if you don't stay!' Jane exclaimed and then she opened up her handbag and took out two packets of paracetamol. 'I've been thinking about it for weeks. It's only when I saw you that I thought maybe you'd be able to help me . . . and maybe I wouldn't do it today.'

Annie was stopped in her tracks. She quickly tried to disguise the look of horror which had sprung up on her face as she wondered what on earth she should do.

The assistant hovering near the changing room with them looked totally shocked.

'Jane, I'm not going anywhere,' Annie soothed, 'you and I are going to have a proper chat. Just let me phone my friend and tell him I'll have to rearrange the lunch date.'

Jane nodded.

Annie sat down on a chair in the changing room beside Jane's and dialled Connor's number.

'Annie!' she heard him exclaim. 'Where are you? What's happened?'

'Connor,' she began nervously, 'I'm not sure how to tell you this—'

'What?' he jumped in. 'Are you OK?'

'Yes, I'm fine. It's just . . . well . . . you should have reminded me! I've bloody well gone and forgotten and now I'm in Brent Cross and I'll never ever make it over to Soho for lunch and you . . . you should have reminded me!' she repeated, wanting it to be Connor's fault and not hers.

There was a pause while a shocked Connor tried to digest the information.

'Connor?' she asked after a bit. 'Are you OK?'

'You forgot?' Connor bellowed into the phone, sending a little ripple of surprise around the restaurant.

Then he remembered about Jay and Jay's producer friend and the many other TV-related people in this place who may or may not have noticed him.

He felt himself blush as he frantically thought of a way to turn this around. He didn't want anyone to know that he had been forgotten, that would be terrible. Gossip would sizzle up all over the place: 'I was in De Soto's and guess who was there? And do you know what happened to him? Yes, really! He's so over. Even his supposedly "old friend" Annie Valentine didn't remember to turn up for him.'

The thought of this was making Connor's ears burn and eyes water.

'So this is about your dad . . .' he blurted out. 'Well, you know, I understand.'

'Connor? What the bloody hell are you talking about?' Annie asked, completely baffled. 'Don't mention my dad! Not to me, not to anyone else and certainly not in a crowded restaurant.'

'No, of course I don't mind, of course . . . these things happen,' he said, his voice laden with charm.

Now Annie knew he was playing to an audience. There was someone in the restaurant listening and Connor didn't want to lose face.

'I am so, so sorry,' she told him, 'really very, very sorry. Can you ever forgive me? Do you want to come round? Shall we rearrange lunch? What would be best? How can I make this up to you?' She reeled off the questions anxiously.

'No, no,' Connor sounded ridiculously cheerful, 'of course we'll rearrange. Please, don't even think about worrying about it. Love to everyone.'

'Connor, I'm having a hard time myself,' she added, 'they're talking about replacing me for the third series. *Replacing me!*' she repeated in a fierce whisper.

'Baby, it's brutal, bloody brutal in this business,' he whispered back, 'toughen up.' Then he rang off.

Annie stared at the phone in disbelief, but she couldn't worry about him right now; she had to go and talk to Jane.

As she pulled open the curtain on Jane's cubicle, she could see the woman looking at herself in the mirror, the packets of paracetamol still in her hands. 'Jane?' Annie said gently.

'Yes?' Jane looked round. Her eyes were moist, as if she might cry at any moment.

'I was going to pick you out a really nice dress. I thought that would be the first thing you should have in your wardrobe to get away from the "plain" tag. Dresses are great' – she warmed slightly to her theme – 'when you find the right one, you just put it on, add good shoes, lipstick, a necklace and you're done. Easy peasy.'

Jane gave her a little smile.

'Got any nice dresses in the wardrobe?' Annie wondered.

'No.' Jane shook her head. 'No dresses since I was my sister's bridesmaid. She looked really, really pretty. She wore a lovely cream dress. Mine was dark green. I looked like an ugly toad. I think she chose the colour on purpose to make me look bad.'

'OK,' Annie said gently, 'but we can't go shopping today.'

'You're going to leave me, aren't you?' Jane said, looking up wildly. 'Everybody does. I want to go shopping with you . . . I want you to have me on your show!'

'No. No, I'm not going to leave you. It's just a really important rule I have. You can't go shopping when you're this upset because you make bad decisions. Lots of people go shopping when they're upset, I know I do sometimes,' Annie admitted. 'We think clothes are going to make us feel better, clothes are going to protect us or look after us. But the opposite is true. It's the clothes that need looking after.

'You take them home, you put them in the cupboard and then they need looking after. They need to be washed and ironed. They need to be paired up with things that go with them. They need to be accessorized and taken out and worn places. They are so demanding!'

Jane sank down on to the changing cubicle's chair and began to sob softly.

'Today isn't a shopping day for you,' Annie said, putting an arm round Jane's shoulder. 'Today is a day when you need looking after. Who's the best person to do that for you, Jane?'

'My mum,' Jane answered. She began to sob. 'But she died last week.'

'Oh no!' Annie crouched down and held on to Jane's hand. 'Who shall we phone for you, Jane, love?'

Jane's face fell forward on to her legs and she began to cry freely. 'I don't know,' she managed finally.

Connor held his phone in his hand. He took a deep swig at his gin and tonic then began to text. 'I am so pissed at you. End of story.' He hit send and the message began its journey towards Annie's phone.

Connor gulped down the last of the drink and stood up. He would settle the bill. He had to leave. There was no way he was going to sit in the centre of this place and eat lunch all on his own. That would be career suicide.

He turned and saw Jay and his lunch companion glancing over in his direction. He gave them a smile and a little wave.

Then he decided to go over to their table and give his explanation.

'Something extraordinary has happened,' he began, 'Annie's dad disappeared years ago, never been heard of since, but she's had some sort of news. She wouldn't say . . . but it sounds like he's turned up again.' Connor gave a shrug. 'You can't have any hard feelings when something like that messes up your lunch date.'

'Well, no,' Jay agreed. 'Connor, this is Rob Kane.'

The two men shook hands. Rob Kane was extremely good-looking, Connor couldn't help noticing.

'Connor, why don't you join us?' Jay wondered, noticing the look that was passing between the two.

'Love to . . .' Connor pulled up a chair. 'So . . . *The Elephant Man*, huh?'

At the table next to them, Vickie Plumridge, a gossip columnist with the weekly celebrity magazine *Pssst!*, was being treated to lunch by a well-known PR. When the PR excused herself for a bathroom trip, the columnist opened up her phone and typed out a little note to herself: 'Connor McCabe stood up by Annie V. Annie V's dad! Connor McCabe with Jay Wetherford and Rob Kane.'

It was all very interesting. Vickie had been working on the mystery of Annie Valentine's father for several days now, so just as soon as Connor had enjoyed the large glass of wine which had just been poured out for him, she would go over and introduce herself.

Chapter Ten

The studio's driver:

Blue trousers ironed to within inch of life (Army Store)
White shirt ironed to within inch of life (M&S)
Regimental tie (The Regiment)
Peaked cap (Army Store)
Black shoes, brilliant with Kiwi Wax and Parade Gloss (Same)
Bluetooth phone in ear (Motorola)
Total est. cost: £140

'Your wish is my command, ma'am.'

'So Svetlana and her absolutely beautiful daughter, Elena, are planning to launch this label in Paris just as soon as they can . . . and we could be there.'

Annie had her phone to her ear and was talking at speed to Tamsin. It was nearly 7.30 p.m. and she was being driven home after a long day's filming.

'It could work,' Tamsin told her cautiously, 'it could definitely work. It can't just be PR though, it's got to be a real behind-the-scenes. We want the grit behind the glamour, the reality of putting on a fashion show and launching your own label. We wanna see Svet sweat. No, seriously, I think I like it and I think the viewers will like it. When is it supposed to happen?'

'Well . . . I don't know yet,' Annie replied. 'As soon as she reaches her investment target, she says she'll be able to get the first dresses run up in a week. She wants to be in Paris when all the other trade shows are on, to catch the wave. That's when all the trade press will be over there anyway.'

'She's going to get so much publicity, I mean she's famous anyway . . . and our viewers love her,' Tamsin added.

'Yeah,' Annie said, trying not to feel at all jealous. Sometimes she couldn't help noticing that however brightly her star shone, Svetlana's was always more dazzling. She wasn't just on TV now, like Annie, oh no. She had to go one step further and faster and launch her own label. She was probably going to be the next Donna Karan, be spectacularly rich and famous for years and years. When Myleene Klass stepped into Annie's high-heeled shoes, Svetlana would probably still be there doing her guest slots beside her.

'So in the next week or two, hopefully.' Tamsin was tapping on her notebook, calling up her schedule. 'We can't send a whole crew to Paris, way too expensive. I want to come in under budget for these episodes just to impress everyone and up the profit margins. You, Bob and his camera and maybe Amelia – because she can look after just about everything that you two can't – should go over to Paris for two days and bring us back lots of really exciting footage. Have you recovered from your shopping stalker incident?'

'Oh, she was hardly a stalker,' Annie protested.

'I've looked into the cost of getting you some security,' Tamsin added.

Annie's response to this was an astonished snort, followed by: 'You have got to be joking me.'

'No. After what happened, I think when you go round the shops for us, you should have someone with you – discreetly. Joe the driver, perhaps, he's ex-army. But we'll pay for that. Obviously on your own time, you'll have to decide what you want to do.'

'No!' Annie was shocked. 'Even Svetlana doesn't have security and she's loaded.'

'Yeah but you're a TV star.'

'I am not.'

'You are,' Tamsin insisted, 'you're a *celebrity* now. What happened with the suicidal lady was scary. What if she'd had a kitchen knife in her handbag instead of packets of pills?'

'Then I'd definitely have made the cover of *Pssst!* magazine,' Annie joked.

'That's bound to come soon,' Tamsin warned.

'Plain Jane the Brain was harmless, she was just upset,' Annie said, 'and I felt quite touched that she thought I could help her.'

Annie cast her mind back to the fraught changing-room scene. Just as she and the shop assistant had exchanged nervous glances, wondering what on earth they were supposed to do next, Jane's phone had rung. Annie had decided to pick it up as Jane had been in no state to answer.

It had been Jane's sister and as soon as Annie had explained where Jane was and how upset she was, the sister had dropped everything to come and get her.

Annie had stayed for the forty minutes it had taken for the sister to arrive, curious to see the svelte and pretty contrast who had dressed Jane up as 'an ugly toad'.

The sister hadn't been any prettier at all, which didn't

really surprise Annie. How many sibling rivalries were based on absolutely nothing at all? But you just needed one parent to express a mild preference for one child's hair or eyes or length of leg and the damage could be done.

'Don't worry about me,' Annie assured Tamsin. 'If things get really bad, I'll just start wearing a dark wig in public. It's probably time I discovered my inner goth.'

As soon as Tamsin had finished the call, Annie saw that she had voicemail. She dialled up the message and listened to it in some confusion.

'Hello, this is Christine from Everest Camping. We trust the package arrived safely. Obviously we hope you'll be able to make use of the items, but if not, please return them at your earliest convenience.'

Annie listened once again, stared at her phone in surprise and decided this must be a wrong number. Camping stuff? She'd definitely never ordered any camping stuff.

Glancing out of the window, she did a double take. There was Lana, she was sure of it, striding along, her dark hair pulled into a loose ponytail and her pale, pretty face wrapped up in thought.

'Oh! Can we pull over?' she asked the driver with a polite tap on the window.

'Your wish is my command, ma'am,' he replied, smoothly manoeuvring the large estate car to the side of the road.

Annie flung open her door and called out: 'Lana! Want a lift, babes?'

Lana looked up, her face full of surprise.

'Hello, darlin',' Annie greeted her, treating her to a hug and a kiss.

'Hi, this is nice!' Lana settled herself and her bags down on to the plush black leather seats.

'Let's travel home in style and you can tell me all about your day,' Annie instructed.

So Lana did. She began with the school news, grumbling about all the work and the homework assignments.

'Oh, you're studying so hard!' Annie sympathized. 'I do wonder if it has anything to do with a certain charming, handsome boy who is now at Cambridge?'

This caused a confused blush to spread up over Lana's face. 'I . . . erm . . . well,' Lana began awkwardly, 'he's emailed a bit . . . but I haven't seen him for a while.'

'You should,' Annie encouraged her.

'You weren't exactly very nice about him when we were going out,' Lana reminded her mother.

'Well, no, I know that. But you were much younger then,' Annie defended herself, 'and maybe I was wrong. No, I *was* wrong . . . but there was the Ed-and-the-under-the-bed incident.'

Annie turned to look at Lana; Lana turned to look back. They caught sight of the expression on each other's faces and suddenly burst out laughing. It was still the most embarrassing thing Lana had ever done: being caught by Ed under Annie and Ed's bed with Andrei in a state of . . . well, semi-undress.

'That was a long time ago,' Lana reminded her.

'Yeah,' Annie had to agree, 'but, Lana, you do know that you might not make it to Cambridge . . .'

'Yeah, yeah, of course, don't be silly,' Lana said quickly as her fingers went up to fiddle with her hair.

'And it'll be fine, not getting into Cambridge, not even applying for Cambridge,' Annie added. 'Andrei's great, but you're not allowed to make any big decisions based on him. In fact, it's probably time to play very hard to get. That always works, I promise you.'

Lana gave her mother a non-committal smile. She didn't look convinced. Still, it was nice to be in the back seat of the car, having her mum all to herself. She couldn't think when they'd last spent even ten minutes alone together just talking.

But then Annie's mobile burst into life.

A glance at the number told Annie that her sister Dinah was calling; she must have picked up Annie's long apologetic message.

'Annie—' Dinah began.

'I'm sorry,' Annie interrupted her, 'I should have phoned you back much sooner, I'm so sorry about your job and I'm a cow who should not be dropping on her own family from a great height. I'll come round and see you tonight, if you like.'

'Oh, save it, I know you're not really a heartless bitch who wouldn't phone her about-to-be-unemployed sister back, not really,' Dinah said, brushing the apology aside. 'I've just had a call from this journalist wanting to know stuff about you and our family. It was weird.'

'Who?' Annie asked in surprise.

'Some woman called Vickie . . . ermmm . . . Plummer or something? She was asking what I knew about Dad.'

'Dad?' Annie repeated, horrified. 'Why on earth does anyone want to know anything about him?'

'Well, it's a family secret – family scandal, isn't it? To a journalist anyway.'

'What did you say?'

'Well, I tried to say nothing,' Dinah said with a touch of reluctance.

'What do you mean you tried?'

Lana glanced over at Annie, wondering what was wrong.

'I kept trying to put the phone down, but she's a very persistent woman.'

'Dinah, did you give her his name?'

'Annie, she already knew that, plus his date of birth, plus the address his most recent credit card was registered to.'

'You have got to be joking.'

Chapter Eleven

Ed frazzled:

Torn rugby shirt (St Vincent's lost property box)
Baggy joggers (not exactly sure)
Socks (Hackett via Annie)
Tartan slippers (Christmas)
Total est. cost: £0

'No! I don't think that would be a good idea . . .'

'Things are a bit messy at home.' Lana decided she'd better warn her mother as they both got out of the car. 'It's not the way it usually is when you come home in the evening. That's why I went out for a walk. To get away from stuff.'

'Oh!' Annie could hardly keep the excitement from her voice. 'So the builders have started, have they?'

'Oh yeah!' came Lana's dark warning. 'They've definitely started.'

'With the bathroom?' Annie asked impatiently. 'Or with the windows in the kitchen?'

'Let's just say they've decided to do both at the same time,' Lana replied.

'Great! It will all be over so much quicker like this.'

'Hmmm . . .'

They were at the front door of the house by now and as Annie pushed it open, two things struck her at once: the strange smell and the overwhelming mess.

The entire hallway floor was thick with footprints, which looked as if they'd been created from a mixture of white plaster dust and brown mud. The trail of multiple footprints led from the back of the house to the front and then up and down the carpeted stairs to the bathroom.

Fine plaster dust was hanging in the air – well, all the dust that hadn't already settled, coating everything in sight. The stairs, the banisters, the skirting boards, the floor, even the walls seemed a shade greyer because of the dust.

But Annie's eyes returned to the footprints. They spread all over the carefully sanded and polished wooden hallway floor and crusted up her beautiful striped stair runner.

'Didn't they use tarpaulins?' she heard herself exclaim. 'Didn't they think to cover the floors before they removed a bathroom and—'

'Demolished a kitchen wall.' Lana finished the sentence for her.

'They've made a hole in the kitchen wall already?' Annie looked at her daughter in surprise. 'But we weren't ready for that. We hadn't even packed the kitchen up. Surely . . .'

Annie began to hurry towards her kitchen.

As soon as she opened the kitchen door, her eyes widened in disbelief. 'You are joking! You have got to be joking me!' she exclaimed.

A huge hole, surely far too big for the new windows, had been punched into one of the kitchen's walls. It was a gaping, jagged hole with rough edges and bits of plaster hanging from it. The rest of the room looked almost normal, except the pots and pans, the shelves, the plates, the cutlery and even the dishes drying on the draining board were all covered with a thick layer of plaster dust.

Ed had obviously not had time to tidy away one single thing before the builders had come in and bulldozed out a chunk of wall. Not even the cereal boxes had been put away, Annie saw with disbelief. They were standing in a row on the kitchen table looking as if they'd been spray-painted grey.

A chill wind whistled about the room, stirring the dust, because only a blue tarpaulin tied loosely over the outside of the hole was protecting it from the elements.

'ED!' Annie called at the top of her voice. 'Where is he?' she directed at Lana.

Lana gave a shrug. 'Maybe upstairs,' she offered.

'ED!' Annie repeated, heading out into the filthy hall.

She took the crusty stairs two at a time, pausing to gasp in surprise at the bathroom. It was a shell, stripped right back to the brickwork with bits of spindly copper pipework dangling from the walls. One pipe was dripping water on to the floor and a grubby cloth had been put underneath it to try and catch the drops.

Annie could hear one of the babies crying in the main bedroom, so she headed towards the noise.

As soon as she opened the door, she could tell that things were not calm.

The bedroom was in chaos. Mud from the stairs had made its way on to the pale carpet in there. The bed was unmade and littered with baby clothes, bits of cotton wool, two bowls of water, Babygros and vests.

Micky was standing up in the cot, his face red with the effort of crying. Minnie was lying on the bed having her nappy changed, also in tears.

'Oh dear, oh dear,' Annie soothed.

Ed looked round at her and she saw at a glance how flustered he was too. His hair seemed to be sticking up even more crazily that usual. Good grief! His hair had got so grey . . . *overnight*? How had this happened? Why hadn't she noticed? As she got closer, she realized with relief that Ed's hair too was covered in a clinging layer of plaster dust.

'I bet your day's been interesting,' Annie began.

Ed shook his head, releasing a fine cloud of dust into the air. 'Don't ask,' he replied, before adding: 'They've both got diarrhoea and Micky's bum: one great big, burning, red disaster area.'

'Oh dear,' Annie sympathized and went to pick Micky up, although Minnie was bawling for her too.

'Yes, I know,' Annie said, leaning over Minnie once Micky was in her arms, 'I'll cuddle you too, just let Daddy finish your nappy. The house is . . .'

'I know,' Ed said, shaking his head again, 'you don't need to say anything.'

'Oh, I think I do,' Annie told him, 'I think I need to phone Al's mobile number right now and shout at him. A lot. I don't think I'll really be able to calm down until I've done that.'

'The bulldozer arrived a day early apparently,' Ed began. 'Al said if he'd sent it away, to come back tomorrow, that would have been an extra four hundred pounds.'

'To him!' Annie retorted. 'He's the one who booked the bulldozer on the wrong day.'

'Yeah, but you know how it is, that four hundred would have mysteriously found its way on to our final bill one way or another, so I said yes, go ahead, we would deal with the mess. I didn't expect it to look quite as bad as it does. I mean—'

'It looks like there's been a bloody earthquake!' Annie exclaimed. 'We aren't going to be able to eat in the kitchen for a month. Stop shaking your head,' she snapped, 'you're making Minnie dusty. And what about the floors?'

'Yeah,' Ed had to agree, 'I was a bit shocked about that myself.'

'Did you say anything?'

Ed looked at her apologetically. 'It's awkward. He's a nice guy, Annie, I wasn't sure how to tell him he'd made a total mess.'

'Awkward?' she repeated. 'Have you seen my stair carpet? I don't know if that will ever, ever come clean again.'

Ed hung his head.

'I'm going to phone him right now,' Annie added furiously.

'No,' Ed advised, 'I don't think that would be a good idea. I think he switches his work phone off in the evening anyway . . . you'll just end up leaving a message that you'll regret.'

'Regret? Regret! The only thing I bloody regret is not having taped up every inch of flooring in the whole house before I let the wally in! If you want one single thing done properly, you have to do it yourself!' she exclaimed.

'Annie' – Ed handed Minnie over and took Micky back – 'Annie, let's order in some pizza, open a bottle of wine and maybe we'll all feel better.'

The loud *brrring* of the front-door bell interrupted this thought. Annie headed down the stairs, still holding Minnie in one arm. If this was Al, she couldn't help thinking to herself, she would give him a piece of her mind.

Through the frosted glass of the front door, she could make out a shape clad in blue builder's overalls. It was him. She felt her heart thud a little more quickly at the thought of having to say her piece. She would though. Look at that carpet!

She opened the door wide and was immediately stopped in her tracks by the most beautiful-looking man she had seen in ages – possibly ever.

He was in blue dungarees and the short sleeves of his white T-shirt stopped halfway down smooth, bulging brown biceps. He turned a squared jaw and chin with dimple towards her, revealing perfect white teeth as he smiled and said hello.

Brown eyes with heavy black brows were fixed on her face, apparently waiting for an answer. Had he asked a question? Annie, just like Minnie, found she had been reduced to complete silence. In fact, she hadn't even taken in what he'd said, the accent had been so chunky and unexpected.

'I Janucek, vorrrrrk with Al, I leave my tools. Is possible to collect them from yourrrrr house?' Janucek repeated.

All thoughts of a mess lecture, a demonstration of what plaster dust and mud did to polished floors and woollen carpets, was completely forgotten as Annie heard strains from the Diet Coke ad break out in her head.

'Yeah . . . course,' she mumbled, 'come in.'

Chapter Twelve

Harry dressed (down) for dinner:

Pink shirt (Turnbull & Asser)
Pink and grey Argyle V-neck (Pringle)
Grey flannel trousers (Gieves & Hawkes)
Monogrammed velvet slippers (Shipton & Heneage)
Total est. cost: £620

'To the day I met you . . .'

Whenever Svetlana arrived home, she called from the car. She didn't do keys. Keys were for women who didn't have staff.

Svetlana called before arriving at her own glossy black front door so, within moments, her maid Maria was holding it open, welcoming her in and taking her coat and bags.

'Has everyone else started?' Svetlana asked, knowing that the rest of her family would already be in the dining room.

'No, they just sit down,' Maria assured her, 'they wait for you.'

Svetlana stepped into the nearest bathroom to freshen up. There, she washed her hands, combed through her luscious blond mane, applied a fresh coat of lipstick to newly plumped lips and a fresh spritz of perfume. Only then did she emerge, ready to face her family.

As she opened the door of the dining room, she paused to appreciate this lovely little scene. It wasn't often that all of them could eat together and she wanted to enjoy every moment of the meal.

Her sons, Petrov and Michael, usually ate early in the kitchen with Maria, but here they were, looking all neat, combed and washed, their serious little faces turned in her direction.

Harry, Svetlana's latest husband, had made it back from work earlier than usual. He'd showered, changed and was seated at the head of the table.

Even Elena looked as if she'd lightened up for the evening. She was sitting beside Petrov in a thoroughly unbusinesslike pink flowered top with a broad smile on her face.

'Hooray!' Harry said, standing up as soon as he caught sight of her. 'We're all just waiting for you, darling. Congratulations!' and he pointed to the bottle of champagne which he'd had Maria put on ice as soon as he'd heard Svetlana's news.

'Fantastic!' Elena grinned. 'You have been fantastic, Mama, I knew you could do it.'

Svetlana had rung them at home as soon as she'd finished her late-afternoon business meeting.

She'd raised every last penny required. The full £75,000 was going to be in the Perfect Dress bank account by the end of the week. The champagne cork was about to pop because now, really and truly, Svetlana and Elena were in business.

Svetlana swooped down on every member of her family, kissing and squeezing them tightly.

'W-onderful!' she said, making a huge effort to pronounce the 'w' properly. 'It is just w-onderful.'

'Does this mean you're going to be as rich as Daddy?' Michael wondered.

This question made all the adults round the table laugh. Because Daddy Igor, even post-stock-market crash, was still a mega-millionaire.

'Of course, my darling,' Svetlana answered without hesitation, 'and I make you very proud, no?'

Harry reached over to lift the champagne bottle from its bucket of ice. Carefully, he eased off the cork, then filled the three crystal flutes on the table.

Holding up his glass, he looked at Svetlana and made his familiar toast: 'To the day I met you, my beautiful girl.'

Maria entered carrying a silver tray laden with the first course just as Svetlana clinked her glass first with Harry, then Elena. She held the champagne under her nostrils for a moment, breathing in the fresh, prickly scent. *Champagne, drink of champions. No?*

'So,' Elena began, needing to get back to business just as soon as the duck terrine had been served, 'we need to speak to Patrizio and begin to put together the show, huh? He thinks if we move quickly, we can still put something on in the next fortnight and catch the very end of the fashion show season.'

'Ya,' Svetlana agreed. 'I call him already, he come here tomorrow to meet with us.'

'So who is this chap?' Harry asked with interest. His new wife was still a source of constant fascination to him.

'He's very important event organizer,' Svetlana began, picking up her heavy silver-plated knife and moving in on the sliver of food on her plate. 'He put on many, many important fashion shows.'

'He will find us a venue, models and do all the organization for us,' Elena went on. 'We just have to turn up in Paris with the clothes.'

'Yes, he says he take care of everything. He want to share our vision,' Svetlana added.

'Is he French?' Harry wondered.

'No, I think he's Italian. Do you know, Elena?'

'I've not spoken to him, you have done all the talking with him,' came Elena's reply.

'So where did you hear of him?' Harry asked. 'How did you get in touch with him?'

'You told me, no?' Svetlana began, looking in Elena's direction.

'No,' Elena assured her.

'Not you?' Svetlana lifted her fork to her mouth and chewed thoughtfully. Once she'd swallowed she said: 'Not you . . . I not remember who tell me about him then. But no matter.' She gave a shrug. 'He is w-onderful. It is all going to be fantastic success.'

Chapter Thirteen

Fern at home:

Beige knit skirt (John Lewis)
Cream blouse (Mulberry via Annie)
Lace-up sensible shoes (Ecco)
Pearl necklace (60th birthday gift to self)
Cloud of perfume (Chanel No 19)
Pink lipstick (Estée Lauder)
Total est. cost: £390

'We're going to have to talk . . .'

'Who was that?' Ed called down the stairs.

'Al's guy. Forgotten his tools,' Annie called back, trying to recover from the Janucek visitation. 'Order the pizzas and I'll take Micky and Minnie down to Mum's. Wonder if her rooms are covered in plaster dust too.'

Ed, appearing at the top of the stairs, looked mildly surprised, as if this was the first time he'd thought about Annie's mother all day long.

'Is she OK?' Annie asked, recognizing the look. 'Have you not had the chance to see her today?'

'Not since breakfast,' Ed admitted.

'I'm sure she'll be fine,' Annie said to reassure them both. 'C'mon, give me Micky,' she said. Then, with a baby on each arm, she headed out of the front door and down to the basement steps to her mother's flat.

Ringing the bell, Annie felt just a prickle of nerves. Surely nothing would have happened to Fern while no one was paying attention? The builder had been around in the garden – the bulldozer tracks were obvious enough. If Fern had been in any sort of bother, she'd just have gone to Ed or even the builders for help, wouldn't she?

But what if she'd gone out? Ages ago? And no one had noticed? And what if she'd got lost?

Annie listened hard at the door and for a moment felt panicky. She didn't think she could hear anything.

The sound of footsteps came from the other side of the door.

'Hi, Mum!' Annie said with relief, seeing Fern's silhouette in the small window of the door. 'How are you doing?' she asked as soon as the door was open.

'Oh, fine,' Fern answered, but there was something of an agitated look on her face. 'Come in, bring my lovely, lovely babies and come in. I'm just trying to find . . .' She turned round, headed back into the flat and her words tailed off.

Annie walked through the tiny hallway and the compact kitchen, following her mum into the small, low-ceilinged sitting room where she sat down on the sofa with the babies. As soon as she took a seat, the twins no longer wanted to be still and immediately tried to crawl off in opposite directions.

This room looked nice now. Once upon a time, these few rooms – the kitchen, the small bedroom with doors out to the garden and this sitting room – had been Ed's flat underneath his late mother's house. Back then they had been dingy, mouldy, faded and damp, crammed full of Ed's mess and Ed's belongings. Now that Annie had taken charge of him and his inherited house, it was very different. The rooms were still small but they were neat and cosy. The fungal damp rotting through the walls had all gone. In place was whitewash, new wooden floors, a wood-burning stove and a pale green bedroom with white cupboards and long silky curtains.

'What are you looking for?' Annie asked kindly. 'You always seem to be looking for something. It's probably at home, Mum, in your house. You've not brought much with you, remember? We could go there at the weekend, find the things you want and bring them back here.'

With a sigh of deep tiredness, Fern sat down in the armchair opposite Annie: 'Give me a baby,' she instructed, watching Annie struggle to keep hold of the two. 'That way we'll each have only one to entertain.'

As Annie handed Minnie over, Fern said: 'It's my bracelet. You know the one, the beautiful woven gold bracelet. I know I'd have brought it with me. I just know it. There's no way I would have left it at home. It's very special. My mother gave it to me. I really have looked everywhere. In every single place I can think of,' she added with anxious exasperation.

'And, Annie,' she went on, 'we are going to have to talk about me going home. I know you don't want to talk about it, I know you keep avoiding me on this, but we'll have to talk about it.'

Annie looked at her mother with a mixture of great love and fear.

As Fern sat in the chair, holding her granddaughter, she looked so normal, nicely dressed and capable. Everything she said made perfect sense and she was expressing herself

91

with total clarity. But here was the problem: this bracelet had gone missing almost thirty years ago.

Annie knew the story. Her father Mick had taken it, along with various other valuables he'd stolen from the family home. Apparently, he'd planned to pawn them, use the money for some amazing new venture and buy everything back when it all worked out. But that had been the last time Fern or Annie and her sisters had seen him. When she'd discovered the theft, Fern, fed up with all his lying, cheating and scheming, had told him not to come back.

Annie wasn't going to mention one word about Dinah's conversation with the journalist to her mother. She wasn't even going to think about it. If she blanked all thoughts of her dad out of her mind, they would go away and he would stay away. That's how it had always worked in the past.

Annie could feel tears welling up in her eyes. Was this how it was going to be with her mother from now on? It was as if a computer virus had entered her mother's brain and was slowly corrupting and deleting data files, while the rest of the system carried on working perfectly.

'What is it?' Fern asked, leaning her head to one side and looking at Annie with concern.

'Oh Mum!' was all Annie could say at first. 'Are you feeling OK? Is today a good day?'

'Today is clear as a bell, darlin',' was Fern's answer to this.

'But the bracelet, Mum . . .' Annie hesitated; she wasn't sure whether she should tell Fern the truth or not. Would it upset her? Would she remember? Would she think Annie was talking nonsense?

'Yes?' Fern asked curiously. 'Do you know where it is?'

Annie nodded: 'Mick took it – years ago. He hasn't been back since. He's never brought it back.'

For a moment Fern said nothing. Then she looked away, kissed the top of Minnie's head and said quietly: 'Oh yes. Silly me.'

Annie wasn't sure what to say next and this upset her almost as much as anything else, because before, before this horrible . . . computer virus, she'd always had such a close relationship with her mother, been able to laugh and joke with her, tell her *almost* everything, confide in her and treat her like a real friend. Now she felt as if she had to tread carefully because she didn't want to risk causing her mother the slightest hurt or harm.

'I need to go home,' Fern told her.

Before Annie could make any objections, Fern held up her hand and went on: 'I know you're worried; I know you don't want me to. But I *need* to go home. It's the white mist. It comes down, it surrounds me and then it clears again. When I'm clear I'm trying to make a plan for how I can be at home and be looked after. I'm nearly there.' She paused to kiss the top of Minnie's head again. 'When I'm in the white mist all the time, darlin', then you have my per- mission to bring me back here or put me wherever you think best, but right now, while most of my day is clear, I want to be at home, dusting my own mantelpiece, watering my own flowers and waving at my own neighbours. It's where I belong,' she said firmly. 'I've lived in that little house for fifteen years. It's all paid off, it's all mine. That's where I want to be.

'You can come and see me every single week,' she added, 'and bring all the children; I want to spend as much clear time with you all as I've got left. None of us will enjoy being together when I've lost the plot.'

Annie could feel tears sliding from the corners of her eyes. She wiped them away as quickly as she could with the back of her hand. 'Mum,' she began in a subdued voice,

'I don't know how we're going to do this. I don't know how you'll—'

'I know,' Fern broke in, 'I'm working on a plan. I'm going to come up with something, OK? You're a very, very busy girl. I don't want you to worry about a thing.'

But Annie was already worrying plenty.

Chapter Fourteen

Elena at work:

Black linen shirt dress (Banana Republic)
Thin brown alligator belt (Svetlana's wardrobe)
Black-heeled tie sandals (Nine West)
Tiny gold studs (Accessorize)
Tortoiseshell hair clip (Accessorize)
Total est. cost: £170

'I do not pay upfront!'

'Now please tell me what you like Maria to bring? Tea? Coffee? Mineral water? Something a little stronger if you like to celebrate early?' Svetlana gave a throaty chuckle at this.

She leaned forward and thrust her tightly Missoni-clad cleavage forward, directly into Patrizio's line of view.

Patrizio smiled generously.

He leaned forward in his cream leather-covered chair too. His eyes darted from the sculpted angles of Svetlana's face to the objects decorating her splendid surroundings.

He had been shown into the downstairs sitting room of her stunning Mayfair home and he was certain that upstairs there was a drawing room even more luxurious and sumptuous than this one.

This one was lavish enough, with its marble fireplace, polished parquet floors and . . . was that . . . was that really a small Warhol oil on the wall over there? Just behind Svetlana's shoulder.

Patrizio would have strained to take a closer look but Svetlana's soft and fragrant hand was on his knee as she demanded his attention.

'So tell me what you can arrrrrange?' she asked, rolling her 'r's huskily.

It wasn't that Svetlana was attracted to Patrizio, it wasn't that the thought of cheating on her devoted husband had even entered Svetlana's mind, it was simply that this was the way she behaved with men from whom she wanted something. This is the way she had always behaved with men from whom she'd wanted something. It produced results – usually good – which is why she continued to use the technique.

'Because I have the very best contacts. I can still get you a slot at Le Carrousel du Louvre,' Patrizio began. 'This is where all the top, very best shows are held. You will have your own stage, your very own theatre in the Louvre tents—'

'Tents?' Svetlana interrupted. The Louvre was all very well, but *tents*? Tents did not sound glamorous.

'Ya, tents,' Patrizio went on, his own foreign accent not quite as easily recognizable as Svetlana's. His was softly Mediterranean, perhaps Italian, perhaps . . . Svetlana wasn't quite sure.

'It is wonderful what they do at the Louvre at show-time,' Patrizio went on. 'All around the glass pyramid are set out the wonderful white tents, billowing in the wind, beautiful girls, models, fashion people in amazing clothes everywhere. You will love it, Svetlana, you will feel so very at home there.'

'I've been a guest at Versace's shows in Milano,' Svetlana reminded him.

'Yes, of course . . . The trade shows are a little different from the big designers, of course. But we will still put on a magnificent display. I book five incredible girls for you,' Patrizio added. He leaned back in his chair and reached into the inside pocket of his supple leather jacket.

He had a weak chin, Svetlana couldn't help noticing. He tried to hide it with his short-trimmed beard, but the chin was small. She didn't like weak chins. They turned double too quickly. She knew. She had seen this happen with three out of four husbands.

Patrizio brought out an iPhone; he called up some images and showed them to Svetlana one by one. 'All beautiful, no?' he said of the girls.

As Maria came in with a tray set with porcelain cups and saucers, a steaming silver coffee pot, matching silver milk and sugar containers, Patrizio went through the 'simple, simple' arrangements he would make for the very first Perfect Dress show.

It sounded straightforward. Elena and Svetlana would arrive in Paris with all the sample size dresses. They would meet up with the models for a full fitting and rehearsal at the venue from 4 p.m. onwards.

'All shows over by three p.m.,' Patrizio explained, 'so you have hours and hours of peace and quiet to make whole venue yours.'

He would order flowers. A DJ was already booked for the rehearsal and the event.

'You just need to bring the dresses and invite the world.'

He flashed a broad smile at her, his white teeth standing out against his tan.

'So what will all this cost?' Svetlana asked once her many other questions about the girls, the rehearsal times, the DJ and everything else had been answered to her satisfaction.

'Not as much as you think,' Patrizio assured her. 'I know many, many people. I know how to get a good deal for my especial friends.'

Svetlana smiled; she suspected she was being softened up for the bad news.

'Twenty-two thousand euros . . .' Patrizio began.

Svetlana gasped in horror: 'For a rehearsal and one-hour show? Five girls in a tent for half a day!'

'Wait!' Patrizio urged. 'This official price, this what it should cost. But for you, my especial friend, only sixteen thousand.'

This was still a lot of money.

A huge amount of money.

Still . . . Le Carrousel du Louvre.

Five amazing-looking models. Even in the amateur phone-camera shots the girls had looked stunning.

Svetlana couldn't help feeling a jolt of excitement that it could all come together so quickly . . . so soon.

'I need the money before the show,' Patrizio went on, 'this is why I can get the price down so low for you.'

'I understand,' Svetlana told him as she took a steadying sip from her coffee cup. Weren't all the best deals made with cash upfront? 'Will a bank transfer work for you?' she asked.

'Absolutely,' Patrizio told her. 'If you can move the money straightaway' – he made a little gesture which indicated she should make the call – 'I will tell the organizer to book your slot and hire your girls.'

Svetlana reached for her mobile, but just before she called her bank, she turned to ask Patrizio the important question: 'You have all the paperwork with you, no? All the invoices, names, addresses, numbers to call?'

This much she had learned from Elena. There was always paperwork. There must always be paperwork. No paperwork, no businesses.

It was so boring to Svetlana. Paperwork was definitely not the fun side of business. Having the big ideas, setting ideas in motion: these were the things she loved to do. She thought for a moment about the wonderful show, the spectacle they were going to create in Paris, at the Louvre . . .

Svetlana and Elena's Perfect Dress at the Louvre!

Patrizio turned to the briefcase at his feet. As she saw him bring out a file stuffed with papers, Svetlana punched in the numbers to call her bank.

'I need to make a money transfer from the business account,' she told the voice at the other end of the line.

Just as she was about to ask Patrizio the name of the account she should make the money over to, he handed her a small white business card. On the back he had written out a long, thirteen-digit number.

'No name?' she asked.

'BCI Bank, Switzerland, and then this account number,' he assured her.

In the small basement office, Elena was at her computer as usual. Her hair was tied up neatly and she sat in her chair with elegantly ramrod posture. As usual, she was dealing with a flurry of emails.

Yesterday she had placed the order for the very first sample dresses and already there were hitches.

The fabrics she and Svetlana had chosen were no longer available and it was going to take at least a week before samples of the new fabrics could be sent to them.

'Where are they?' she typed back and sent the message.

'In Hong Kong,' came the almost instant reply.

Should she go out there? Would it be quicker and more cost-effective for her to fly to Hong Kong than to wait for the fabrics samples to be sent to her?

If she could see them in Hong Kong tomorrow ... approve them ... have them sent on to the dressmakers, that might shave a full ten days or so off the dress delivery times. Elena could feel her palms sweat with the effort of making a decision like this. But according to all the books by business gurus she had read, the decision-making process was the one vital asset which set *leaders* and *achievers* ahead of the rest.

Her in-box flashed with a new message: 'Have you got a date / venue / time for launch show yet? Fashion ed very keen. Will your mother do profile piece / interview? Best, McKenna'.

Elena sat up to attention at this.

McKenna was a Very Important newspaper fashion journalist. If she came to the show and did an interview with Svetlana, Perfect Dress would get the kind of coverage that would cost thousands to buy.

Just as Elena mentally composed the holding response that this email required, Svetlana herself came in through the office door.

'I book the show, Elena!' Svetlana beamed. 'This is going to happen!'

'You've booked it?' Elena asked and frowned, causing a furrow to appear on her forehead. She shouldn't do that! Svetlana thought automatically, if she didn't do that now, she wouldn't have to Botox that muscle into submission later on.

Pah! Botox! That would probably be so over by the time

Elena was threatening to wrinkle. Who knew what would have been invented by then to keep women indefinitely in their prime?

'Ya,' Svetlana confirmed, 'booked. Great deal. Sixteen thousand euros, but to get this deal I have to pay him straightaway, so I do bank transfer.'

Elena's mouth opened in astonishment.

For a moment or two, she tried to say something, but words failed her.

'Sixteen thousand euros?' she repeated when her power of speech had returned. 'For the launch show? NO! That is too much, that is way, way too much and you've already paid. Bank transfer? Upfront!' In total exasperation, she exclaimed: 'MOTHER!'

But Svetlana rushed over to placate her. 'Elena! Is going to be perfect! We have wonderful show in Le Carrousel du Louvre, beautiful girls. Patrizio book the space, the rehearsal time, the DJ, the models, even the flowers. He has taken care of all the details, we just need to turn up with the dresses. My darling, in business you must learn to delegate. Igor tell me this. Patrizio has given us a great service.'

Elena did not look mollified in the slightest. Calmly but very sternly, she told her mother: 'This is the first and the last time that you spend so much of our money without asking me. You could easily have come down the stairs and asked me. I am your partner. This is fifty-fifty. I do not pay upfront, Mother. I pay on delivery. No!' she corrected herself. 'I pay weeks after delivery, when I've already sold and banked the profit.'

Chapter Fifteen

Annie's travel to Paris outfit:

Violet silk blouse (tiniest trace of baby vom.) (Chloé)
Cream pencil skirt (Prada)
Cobalt blue 'comfortable' heels (L.K. Bennett)
Mighty beige control pants (Spanx)
Sensational black and gold patent-leather croc trim bag
(Miu Miu)
Black trolley bag (Samsonite)
Total est. cost: £1,600

'Why are you still worrying?'

Ed met Owen at the door to the bathroom; now that the builders had been in residence for fifteen days exactly, everyone was getting used to the early morning crush in the one functioning family bathroom. Not to mention the fact that heavy-duty shoes had to be worn everywhere in the house at all times, to avoid stepping in something muddy, grubby or painful.

'You need to say goodbye to your mum,' Ed reminded Owen. 'Apparently she's going to Paris. And maybe if you wet your hair . . .' he suggested, although Owen's great mop was sticking up in ways which would require a team of hairdressers to control.

'Yeah right,' Owen mumbled, and then with a weary yawn he disappeared in through the bathroom door.

Ed was trying to be as positive as he could about Annie's two days in Paris. She was only away for one night, he kept reminding himself, and although she hadn't been away overnight since the twins were born, he was going to be able to cope fine. Absolutely perfectly fine.

Although the kitchen had been cleaned up, there was still a huge hole in the wall covered with just a sheet of tarpaulin, so the room was currently as cold as Siberia. Only cups of tea, bottles of milk, cereals and toast could be made in there because no one had the stamina to stay on long enough to cook.

The new windows should have been fitted days ago, but they still hadn't arrived. Al, the man in charge of the small building team, was now shrugging at the mention of the windows.

They were special triple-glazed Swedish windows which Annie had discovered online. Apparently they were delayed, or there was some problem getting the frames the requested size . . . something was still in discussion, or up in the air or being remade . . . In short, the windows were not here and the kitchen was currently an open-plan – no, more like open-air room. Ed liked to go camping as much as the next man, in fact probably more than the next man, but looking after baby twins when you could only stand to be in a kitchen for three minutes at a time was tricky.

Plus, he had a feeling the twins were about to be ill . . . again. It seemed as if the diarrhoea had cleared up for about ten minutes before they'd started sneezing and dribbling.

'Ed?' Annie turned to him now, taking in his anxious face as he came back into the bedroom. 'Why are you still worrying? You can phone me any time. Day or night. I will have my phone glued to me. If I can't get reception, I will go and stand outside. You will always be able to reach me, I promise. If for any reason you can't get me, then the sisters are on standby, I've warned them.'

'The sisters' meant Ed's sister, Hannah and Annie's sister, Dinah. Both lived within a short drive and both were perfectly capable with babies and the dispensing of baby advice.

Ed came and stood right beside Annie. She was looking at herself in the mirror, approving of her violet silk blouse and the luxurious cream woollen skirt she'd paired with it. Not approving of the stomach straining to burst from the magic pants.

'No. I'll be fine. Don't worry about me or about any of us,' Ed insisted, determined to sound more confident than he felt. He leaned towards her and pressed his forehead against hers so she could see right inside his deep blue eyes.

'You look good,' Ed had to tell her, 'shame there's never the chance to do anything about that.'

'Shame,' she agreed, 'but I look like a fat Twiggy,' she added, fingering her hair. 'More Trunky than Twiggy.'

Minnie, lying with her head on Ed's shoulder, perked up at the sound of her mother's voice. She turned her head slightly and then with a funny sort of little cough, spluttered out a mouthful of lumpy white vomit. It mainly landed on Ed's already stained denim shirt, but several bits hit Annie's blouse too.

Annie's reaction to baby stains on her precious clothes amused Ed. He still expected her to jump up and down and freak out. But instead, she soothed Minnie with a 'There, there, do you feel better now, you poor old thing?' and stepped over to the bedside table where the baby wipes were at the ready.

Annie swore by baby wipes. No matter what kind of baby stain she'd been hit by, she firmly believed if she could just treat it quickly enough with a baby wipe, it would be all right.

'OK, there we go,' she said, wiping off the offending chunks from her blouse first, then getting to work on Ed's shirt and Minnie's Babygro.

Micky was still in the cot, fast asleep, his cheeks wibbling whenever anyone walked past his bed.

'Yes, you're sleeping now,' Annie couldn't help whispering in his direction, 'now that we're all awake! This is what you're supposed to do at night, not dance about in your cot wailing for attention. They are terrible' – this comment was directed at Ed – 'Lana and Owen both slept soundly ten, even twelve hours a night from six months. We have got to get this sorted or we are going to go bananas.'

'Don't,' Ed warned her as she peered in the wardrobe mirror at the purple circles under her eyes.

'I'm not looking gorgeous,' she told him, 'they are ruining what little there is left of my looks. And let's not even talk about my waistline.'

'Don't,' he said again, risking another hug, despite the fact that he was still armed with a loaded baby, 'you are luscious and gorgeous and the sleeping – well, the not sleeping – it's just a phase. I know this because I read it in a book.'

Ed was glued, *glued* to the baby manuals. He was in baby school; he was baby swotting. If there was a baby exam, Ed would come top. 'What is the optimal temperature for (*a*) a baby's bottle, (*b*) a baby's bath, (*c*) a baby's head?' He would know every single answer; he would get an A plus in baby theory.

Annie glanced at her watch: 'Is everybody up? Has Princess Lana been summoned from her bed? Babes, I am going to have to stop cuddling you and finish packing. My taxi is going to be here in about three minutes.'

Finally accepting that Annie really was going to leave him, leave the babies and leave the country for two days, Ed went into mini-panic mode: did she have her tickets? And her passport? And her house keys? And a raincoat?

He went over to the window to establish whether or not it was raining and, pulling back the curtain, he gasped in surprise: 'It's snowing!'

'You are joking!' was Annie's reaction. 'It can't be snowing. I've got to get to Paris!' She rushed over to the window and looked out. To her relief it was just a light dusting, nothing that would stop a taxi or an aeroplane. Hopefully.

But Ed voiced his one overriding concern: 'The kitchen is going to be completely freezing.'

'Move an electric heater in there while you make breakfast,' Annie advised him as she slipped her feet into her most comfortable pair of walking heels. 'I would stay and help, you know I would,' she assured him, before leaning in to kiss Ed and her little baby girl goodbye.

This was the hard bit. This was definitely the hard bit, she thought to herself as she brushed her lip against Minnie's delicious cheek and inhaled her daughter's slightly vomity but nevertheless lovely smell for the last time for forty-eight hours.

'Don't you dare kiss Micky and wake him,' Ed whispered, once they had kissed each other goodbye.

Annie leaned over the cot and let just her fingertip brush against Micky's forehead.

'Bye, bye,' she told them all, 'I hope the snow stops, because Al's supposed to be punching that hole into the roof today.'

Before Ed could react with the full amount of horror that this required, Annie's raincoat was on, her handbag and suitcase were in her hands, she'd kissed Owen and Lana farewell and she was hotfooting it over the rubble on the stairs and out to the waiting cab.

Arriving at the airport, Annie opened up a text from Svetlana which read: 'R u here yet? C u lunch. Paris tres belle!'

It made her smile. For two whole days, she was going to be allowed to put the babies' teething, Ed's anxieties and Al the builder's shortcomings all to the back of her mind. She was on her way to *Paris* . . . for *fashion* . . . for *TV*!

Wasn't this just impossibly glamorous? Was this not the kind of thing she'd once dreamed of doing? How jealous she'd once been of the fashion buyers at The Store, who'd travelled to Paris and Milan several times a year to watch shows and select the new collections. More than once, she'd asked to join them, but she'd always been told she was too valuable a saleswoman to be allowed to go away on trips like this.

She'd tried to argue that she should help to choose the clothes, because she'd know what her clients would want and would therefore be able to sell even more. But the three different managers she'd worked under had never been able to see it that way.

It was funny how she didn't miss The Store at all any more. It had obviously been well and truly time to move on and now she was devoted to her new job. She absolutely loved it and could no longer imagine doing anything else.

'Your flight to Paris boards at gate number twenty-two.' The check-in girl gave her a heavily lipsticked smile. 'Enjoy your trip.'

'Oh I will.' Annie smiled back at her. 'I'm going for a fashion show,' she couldn't help confiding.

'Oooh, how exciting! Which one?' the girl wanted to know.

'It's a new designer,' Annie replied, 'just launching.'

'Oh, that is so glamorous! I'm jealous.'

'Hey, Annie Banannie!'

Annie felt a heavy slap on her back and turned to see her cameraman for the trip, Rich, with a huge bag of equipment slung over one shoulder and a large, dribbling Big Mac in his hand.

'Oh yeah, non-stop glamour,' Annie told the girl.

Rich was the show's junior cameraman; obviously Tamsin had decided not to send the senior man, Bob, out to Paris for two nights. Bob's overtime bill would have been too scary. But Bob would probably have been more refined company, Annie couldn't help feeling.

'I hope you've not just left a greasy paw print on my back!' she warned Rich.

Rich leaned forward to look more closely. 'No, you're fine,' he insisted.

But now he was too close, now she could smell the onion and gherkin breath. Rich was twenty-something, a really good-looking guy, but he had all the charm of a chimpanzee.

'Isn't it a bit early for burgers?' she had to ask as he plonked his camera bag on the check-in desk and began to search through his pockets for his ticket.

'Nah,' Rich assured her, flicking jaw-length hair back behind his ear, 'sets you up for the day. That's what you need. The skilled and intrepid lensman has no idea when or where his next meal will be.'

He wasn't going to have to come to lunch with her? Was he? No! Surely not?

In fact, there was no way Annie was taking Rich to the George V Hotel for lunch with Svetlana and Elena. She would tell Tasmin that the hotel had a strict no-filming policy. Then Rich could join them later at the Louvre for the fashion-show rehearsal.

'C'mon,' she urged him once his ticket had been checked, 'we need to trot on down to security.'

She flashed a glance at her watch; just approaching 10 a.m. If the flight was on time, she would easily make it to the George for 1 p.m.

Her phone began to buzz in her pocket and, answering it, she was surprised to hear a grumpy voice demanding to know why some camping equipment hadn't been returned.

'Camping equipment?' Annie asked, 'what camping equipment?'

The woman went through a long list of items and informed her that they had been sent to be considered for approval for the Annie Valentine show.

'This is news to me,' Annie told her, fumbling in her bag for tickets and boarding card so she could get past the security checkpoint.

'With whom am I speaking, please?' the woman asked in a very frosty tone.

'I'm Annie Valentine,' Annie told her.

'Oh . . .' The woman sounded surprised. 'I didn't expect to get through to you directly.'

'I'm a bit surprised myself,' Annie told her.

'We've sent your show six hundred and fifty pounds' worth of equipment. If you're not going to feature it, then we need it back, unused. I think you can understand that.'

'No problem,' Annie told her, 'I just can't understand why it was ordered in the first place. We do fashion; we definitely don't do camping. Look . . . I'm at the airport, just about to go through security. I'll speak to Amelia, the show's PA. She'll look into this and call you back just as soon as possible. Can you bear with me? Let me try and sort this.'

The woman sighed but decided to agree.

Annie might have remembered to call Amelia straightaway, but the next thing she knew, she was in a tussle with a security guard about the bottle of perfume in her hand luggage.

The big bottle of Chanel was apparently above the maximum liquid allowance.

'What?' Annie couldn't quite believe it. 'You're going to make me leave it here? Just leave it!'

The stony-faced guard was not going to relent for her.

Once she'd handed over the perfume and walked sadly towards her gate, Annie saw something else which put all thoughts of camping equipment right out of her mind.

On one of the magazine stands was a cover which, along with Britney, Posh and *The X Factor*'s latest, had a small photograph set to the side of Connor.

Connor!

Her mind reeled. He'd sent her that stinky text but she should still have called him back once he'd calmed down about the lunch date. She should at least have tried to make up with him.

She walked over to the stand so that she could read what had been written about him on the cover.

It wasn't a good photo. The way the wind was blowing out his trousers and his top made him look huge, when he wasn't at all. He was incredibly fit and buff.

Annie read the little headline beside the snap: *Dumped* Manor *Connor piles on pounds for* Elephant Man *role.*

Oh, that was cruel.

She picked the magazine from the stand and flicked through it to find the story about her friend.

Scanning the pages, her eyes fixed with horror on a publicity shot of her own. There she was smiling back; it was a perfectly nice publicity shot taken for the start of the new series, but the words emblazoned over the picture were a different story.

Next week! World exclusive interview with the man Annie V hasn't seen for 25 years: her dad!

Chapter Sixteen

Svetlana does PR:

Pink silk shirt dress (Perfect Dress)
Purple suede-heeled sandals (Jimmy Choo)
Diamond earrings (Cartier)
Diamond and pearl necklace (Bulgari)
Total est. cost: £460,000

'So good for you and so low calorie.'

Even though she had Rich sitting beside her in the taxi to
the town centre, Annie was still excited.

'Lovely town, innit?' he kept saying until she
wanted to smack him. Annie just wanted to be left alone to
open her eyes wide and look and look and drink it
all in.

What was it about being abroad that was still, no matter
how many times you did it, so exciting? The thrill of the
other. The excitement of being somewhere else, somewhere
new where nobody knew you and all sorts of interesting
new adventures could happen.

'There's the Eiffel Tower!' Rich exclaimed. Annie turned

her head in his direction and felt a little jolt when she saw the Tower too.

She hadn't been in Paris for years and years.

Racking her memory, she came up with some glimpses and flashes from her last trip. It had only been a weekend: a crazy, snatched weekend on the way back from Prague with baby Lana and her daddy, Roddy.

They'd stayed in a plain but somehow très chic and very Frrrrench *pension*. She remembered a breathlessly giggly trip all the way to the top of the Eiffel Tower, then lying in a sunny boat on the Seine with her head on Roddy's chest and her baby sleeping in her arm. There had been a strange couscous dinner in a tiny Moroccan restaurant with brass lanterns and dark pink walls.

Roddy . . .

She only remembered the really good bits now. That's how it was when someone you had loved so much went and died on you. Your poor, frazzled, frantic mind eventually rewrote the past until all that was left was this overwhelmingly wonderful memory of how good it had been.

As if that could somehow compensate for the tragedy of losing him.

'What's up?' Rich wondered. 'You're looking glum all of a sudden.'

'No, no.' Annie was brought abruptly back into the cab; she forced a smile on to her face. 'I'm fine,' she said. 'Tired, maybe.'

She should take Ed and the babies on a trip, she thought to herself. For a little moment, she imagined leaning against Ed's chest on a boat on the Seine in the sun, with, somehow, by some miracle, both babies asleep in her arms.

She tried to never compare the two very important men in her life. She accepted that it was possible to love people equally and not have to choose whom you loved the most. After all, didn't she love all four of her children absolutely fiercely the same?

Even if it was Owen who could make her laugh the most.

She should take them all on holiday. Devote some pure, unadulterated, uninterrupted time to them all . . .

Her phone rang.

'Hi, how's it going? Is Rich with you? Is he behaving? I'm sorry it's not Bob, but just boss Rich around and he should do a good job. Yeah?' Tamsin was obviously in a hurry, firing out questions before Annie had a hope of answering them. 'So shoot two or three hours of rehearsal footage today, lots of backstage tears and tantrums. Tomorrow, shoot the whole show and we want interviews with Svetlana and Elena before, during and after, if poss. That OK? This is going to be great. The TV bosses love it. They think it's glitzy and different and empowering. Girl-power, Annie. That's what we're all about though, aren't we?'

'Absolutely,' was the only word Annie got in.

With that, Tamsin said she had to go.

The taxi was approaching the heart of the city now, driving down a long boulevard lined with trees and venerable old grey buildings.

It wasn't snowing in Paris; the leaves on the trees were further out than in London and the sun was shining with a warmth which had brought the pedestrians out in a cat-walk of spring outfits.

There were many pale beige trenchcoats to be seen, collars up and belts tied. The woman crossing at the traffic lights ahead was striding past in a blue swing jacket with blue and white striped sailor trousers underneath. Everyone was wearing sunglasses with their groomed hair.

Was there still a uniquely Parisian look? Annie wondered

as she stared out of the taxi window in fascination. Women in the most expensive areas of London looked just as groomed and glossy. And London girls had, did and would always do funky fashion so much better than Parisian girls. But still, there was a Parisian thing. No one in London would dream of wearing a Breton top like that one, just over there, under a *tweed* jacket? Would they?

As she watched another older woman walking past along the pavement, Annie suddenly thought she got it. French fashion was mature, respectable. It was *bourgeois*. This woman in her primrose-yellow belted coat, mid-heeled boots and tiny poodle on a leash was at the age it was best to be in Paris.

She was *un certain âge*. In her prime. This was when French women went chic and English women went all to seed. *Les Anglaises* started dressing for comfort, they got doggy and boggy. It was all animals and gardening and letting their hair go grey, not in a slick and shiny way, but in a mad witchy straggle.

Yes, the backbone of Parisian chic was middle-aged matriarchs looking very well put-together and important. They looked as if they had things to do, places to be and people to see, even once they had passed retirement age . . . maybe especially once they had passed retirement age, Annie thought, seeing two elderly ladies strolling out together in gold necklaces, fine coats and heeled lace-up shoes.

The taxi turned off the main boulevard and into a no-less-impressive curving side street. Annie's head began to crane. Wasn't that . . . ? Had they just passed the Hermès shop? And look, oooh, Chanel, it must have been, with an awning as shiny and slick as black patent leather and a single pair of nude-coloured Mary Janes in the window.

Tragically, there was going to be no time to even window-shop on this whistle-stop tour. It was lunch then the rehearsal and tomorrow she would spend all morning at the show and all afternoon at an after-show party. Yes, there were shops at the airport but that wasn't nearly the same.

Her face was pressed to the glass as Louis Vuitton whizzed past . . . Yves Saint Laurent! She imagined herself inside, stroking supple dresses and considering a fitting for one of the legendary, satin-lapelled *les smokings*.

She wasn't really a *le smoking* kind of girl though. If it came down to a choice between *le smoking* or a wonderful dress, she knew she'd go with the dress every time.

The taxi was slowing down and pulling up outside one of the grandest hotel entrances Annie had ever seen. She knew Svetlana's taste always ran to the ultra-lavish but this . . .

'You have got to be kidding me,' she said out loud, feeling nervous at the thought of braving the terrifying lobby this hotel was bound to have, while still all dishevelled from the plane.

She ran her hands through her short blond hair, fished out a lipstick and applied it, glancing herself over in her compact.

There was no point fretting herself to death; she would have to do.

'What happens next?' Rich asked.

Rich! He was definitely not coming in here with her.

'I get off here,' she instructed. 'I give you the taxi money and you take our bags to the hotel, then go somewhere for a coffee or maybe another Big Mac. We meet at Le Carrousel du Louvre at three p.m. *sharp!*' Annie emphasized. 'Maybe be there fifteen minutes early, just to be sure.'

'OK.' Rich nodded. 'I'll be there.'

Annie handed over a bundle of euros, smoothed down

her blouse and stepped out, clutching her large and impressive handbag against her like a shield.

The foyer of the George V was . . . *spectacular*. No other word would do. Annie couldn't think when she had ever been somewhere more lavish. Blond marble floors and *marble walls* shone back at her; crystal and gold chandeliers glittered above her head; and look, the huge vases stuffed with flowers . . . and the vast tapestries! It was spectacular.

She felt lost, bewildered . . . bedazzled, in fact.

For a moment or two she couldn't quite work out where the reception desk was amidst all the opulence of Louis Quatorze chairs, spindly side tables and wrought-gold mantel clocks. Then she caught sight of the elegantly uniformed staff manning the desk.

'*Madame?*' a sleek-haired guy turned in her direction.

At what exact moment did you become '*madame*' in France? Annie wondered. There must be a crossover period, when women in their twenties, or maybe early thirties, were *mademoiselle* sometimes and *madame* at others.

She didn't hesitate to talk in English, certain that this charming, cosmopolitan *monsieur* would be far more fluent in English than she could ever hope to be in French.

'I'm meeting someone here for lunch,' she told him.

'Certainly, let me show you through to the restaurant,' he immediately offered and stepped out from behind the desk.

The restaurant was, *naturellement*, even more awe-inspiring than the lobby. There was so much dizzying bling before her now, it was almost hard to take in.

Tables were set with rows of shimmering crystal glasses, heavyweight art loomed down from the walls, more chandeliers winked and glittered above, even more marble shone, and huge windows, swagged, draped and pelmeted in taffeta, let in a panorama of the beautiful streets and buildings outside.

There in the centre of the room, like the queen bee enthroned in state, was Svetlana, just as spectacular as her setting, with Elena by her side like a princess in waiting. On the table in front of them, champagne was cooling in a silver bucket and a huge mound of seafood was stacked high on a platter of chipped ice.

'Annah!' Svetlana exclaimed and stood up to welcome her.

Within moments, Annie was enveloped in the familiar Svetlana embrace. Perfume, soft skin, warm cleavage, fragrant hair, enormous dangling diamonds: whenever you greeted Svetlana up close, your senses were bombarded with all of these things.

'I'm sorry we start without you, but we are so hungry,' Svetlana apologized.

Once Annie had kissed Elena on the cheeks, she sat down in the chair the ever-attentive waiter had pulled out for her.

'Seafood and champagne? Is OK for you?' Svetlana asked. 'Is all I like to have when I eat out. So good for you and so low calorie.'

Looking at the two fat lobsters resting at the bottom of the seafood tower, plus the dishes of creamy mayonnaise set out on the table, Annie wasn't quite so sure how true that was, but . . .

'Delicious!' she told her friend.

The waiter poured her a glass of champagne and now she was all set to toast Svetlana and Elena's success.

'You're wearing the dresses, aren't you?' she asked, looking at the mother and daughter in turn. 'They look amazing!'

It helped of course that both Elena and her mother had

wonderful figures, beautiful faces and icy-blond hair, but still Annie could see that the dresses were good.

Svetlana's was fuchsia pink, one of Svetlana's favourite colours, with long, elegant sleeves and a flattering ruffle at the neckline and the wrists.

Elena's was more businesslike: navy with satin collar and cuffs. But the styles, the fit and the fabric looked really good. Perfect, in fact.

'Stand up, Elena,' Svetlana urged. 'Show Annie how cleverly we cut darts at the back, to shape into the waist and then out at the hem.'

Elena made a tiny scowl, but then stood up and came to stand beside Annie so she could appreciate the dress in full.

Annie took hold of Elena's hem and felt it between her thumb and fingers. 'Lovely,' she said, 'a really nice feel. Silk crêpe?'

'Ya, with just a little Lycra for fit and shape,' Elena told her. 'For winter we will do wool mixes as well as the silk.'

'This is so exciting!' Annie told them. 'So how is the show coming on?'

Elena sat back down and told Annie with another little scowl of annoyance: 'Mother has left it all in the hands of some event organizer. He has booked the venue, the flowers, the models, even the DJ. Our involvement only begins this afternoon when we get there.' She flicked a glance at her watch.

'It will be fine, I spoke to him this morning,' Svetlana told her daughter with a shake of her head. 'In business, you must learn to delegate. What you think of our hotel, huh?' She directed the question at Annie.

'It is absolutely breathtaking,' Annie assured her. 'Is your room unbelievable? In fact, can I take a little peek at it after lunch?'

'Room?' Svetlana asked, shaking her head again. 'Suite,

Annah, we have a *suite*, no one stays in just a room. How can you? There is not enough space for all the things.'

Elena was scowling again.

'She thinks waste of money,' Svetlana explained, reaching for one of the oysters on the mound and squirting it with a lemon half wrapped in gauze to ensure that no pip fell out and ruined the culinary experience. 'I have to explain to Elena is all PR, everything we do is PR. When we meet journalists and press at the show tomorrow, we say, "Yes, we're at the George V," and everyone understands we are rich, we are successful, dresses are going to be worn by rich and successful women and then it all take off, vooom.' She imitated take-off with her hand to make sure Annie got the idea.

'Cash flow, Mother,' Elena said warningly from the other side of the table. 'You know nothing about business cash flow. We had a big lump sum of capital and now we've spent all of it! The bill for the George V is going to cause a business overdraft and we've not even sold one single dress yet!'

'Yes, but how many buyers are coming to our show?' Svetlana asked.

'Forty-five,' Elena answered and allowed herself a little smile as she teased a piece of lobster claw meat out with a silver pick.

'They will buy,' Svetlana assured her and gave Annie a roll of her eyes. 'I have the big ideas, Annah, Elena does the numbers.'

'I think you make a really great team,' Annie said, smiling at both of them, trying to make this as conciliatory as possible. She took a sip of champagne and felt the bubbles melt in her throat and travel with comforting warmth down to her stomach.

Feeling hungry now, she picked off several of the juicy

fruits de mer for her plate, dolloping mayonnaise on the side, regardless of the fact that neither Svetlana nor Elena were touching the stuff.

'Now tell us all about the filming, Annah, what does Tamsin want us to do? What is her plan?' Svetlana asked.

So Annie told them, at length and in depth, and by the time the three had discussed it in full, it was well after 2 p.m. Time for Svetlana to sign for the lunch, despite Annie's objections, and for the hotel concierge to summon up a taxi to rush them to the Louvre.

As the cab pulled up as closely to the Louvre as it could, Annie was relieved to catch sight of Rich. His camera was already up on his shoulder as he captured the bustling fashion scene in full swing.

The long white tents stretching from the huge glass pyramid in the centre of the Louvre's courtyard flapped elegantly in the breeze. Bustling all around were busy and über-fashionable people. Women in sharp jackets and dark glasses were snapping into mobiles; slouchy, scruffy models were smoking by the fountain. Everywhere everyone was beautiful, even the tanned middle-aged men, in cashmere overcoats, velvet scarves and Prada shades.

'Oh, this is so amazing!' Annie exclaimed as she climbed out of the taxi. 'I need to do this every season. I need to be here,' she gushed, desperate to get inside the tent and find out which other fashion shows she could sneak a look at.

What was going to be on sale next year? She needed to know now! And right here was where she could find out. This was the beating heart of planet fashion.

Even Elena looked impressed. She let the taxi driver unload the two big holdalls of dresses and shoes from the back of the car, but then she took charge of them both herself.

One over each shoulder, she was determined to carry them alone, shaking her head at Annie's offers of help.

'Rich!' Annie called over to the cameraman. 'We're over here!'

He turned but carried on filming.

'Lovely!' he called out as the three women began to march towards him. 'The girls are in town.'

After he'd made them turn, walk back, walk towards him one more time, and then again, promising this time he would definitely have it, Elena called a halt.

'Is enough!' she instructed. 'We have to check in, find our girls and get started. There is so much to do before tomorrow.'

Rich didn't just listen to Elena, he also took a long appraising look at her. Annie saw him do it. He looked and he looked and he very obviously liked. But Elena didn't even hold eye contact with him for any longer than necessary. She didn't even seem to notice the other approving glances she attracted from so many men here.

She was very, very focused.

Svetlana, Annie and Rich – still filming – all tailed Elena as she briskly followed the signs posted up to direct visitors to the main entrance.

When she had reached the impressive mouth of the biggest billowing white tent, they stood in a little group behind her as she went up to one of the men behind the busy reception desk.

'Svetlana Wisneski and Elena Ljubicic of Perfect Dress. We have space booked in . . .' She paused to look through the sheaf of papers Svetlana had handed on from Patrizio, '. . . area thirteen for this afternoon and for our show tomorrow morning.'

*

There was a young girl standing in the reception area. She was slouching against a pole, apparently trying to blend in and not be too conspicuous. This girl had been waiting here for almost an hour now and had considered many, many times the possibility of going home. But some stubborn instinct had kept her waiting, kept her hoping, long past the point when hope should have faded.

When she heard Elena introduce herself to the reception desk, the girl suddenly stood up straight, pulled back her shoulders and felt a surge of excitement rise up inside her.

'Perfect Dress?' she asked as she came forward towards them, shyly.

'Yes,' Elena and Svetlana replied together.

'I'm Anoush, I come to model in your show,' she said, still shy and hesitant.

Everyone looked at her a little more closely. She was so small and so dainty. She could hardly have been over 5 feet 4 inches and she looked nothing like the glamazon models all three women had expected. But she was undoubtedly pretty with her mocha skin, molten eyes and halo of soft, frizzy hair.

'Hello.' Elena was the first to reply; she held out her hand for Anoush to shake. 'Is this your first show?'

When Anoush nodded in reply, Elena smiled encouragingly and told her: 'Yes, it's our first show too.'

The receptionist was tapping at the computer; then he made a phone call; finally, he turned to the three women, their brand-new model and Rich, who was still determinedly filming.

'Area thirteen is booked for today and for all of tomorrow,' the receptionist told them in clipped English, 'but not for you. Is booked for Escada. I have looked up every single other reservation and I do not have one for Perfect Dress, or Wisneski or Ljubicic.'

Elena looked through the sheaf of papers in her hands: 'But you must,' she insisted, 'we have records . . . we have an invoice . . . maybe if you look up the name of the man who made the reservation?'

The receptionist took the papers from her and began to look through them with a puzzled expression. After he had carefully examined every page he shook his head at them sadly. 'I don't know what this is,' he began, 'but this is not from us. This is not our paper, this is not our logo. *Mesdames*, this is a fake.'

Chapter Seventeen

Al the builder:

Very low-slung jeans (Lee)
Grey T-shirt (Asda)
Boots (DeWalt)
Hard hat (DeWalt)
Total est. cost: £65

'The magic touch, mate.'

'You're not having a good day, are you, mate?' was Al's verdict as he came in through the front door to find Ed holding two crying babies.

'No, not exactly,' Ed replied unusually irritably. The fact that Al was about six hours late because of some 'errands' he'd had to run and 'materials' he'd had to collect wasn't exactly improving his mood.

'Here, give us a baby,' Al offered cheerfully.

Ed looked at Al. His grey T-shirt was completely encrusted with dirt, dust, chunks of plaster and blobs of paint. He really didn't want to hand Al a baby because it would just give Ed another mess to clean up later. But it seemed rude to say no now that Al had asked directly.

'There, there, there,' Al soothed as Micky was handed over to him, 'what's all the fuss about? What's all this noise for?'

Maybe because he was so surprised to be in the arms of a total stranger, Micky stopped crying immediately.

'The magic touch, mate,' Al said, beaming at Ed, 'haven't lost it, even though mine are teenagers now. The magic touch.'

Now Ed had an overwhelming urge to punch him. But instead, he carried on scouring the hallway for the twins' beakers which seemed to have vanished into thin air although they were urgently required.

'Minnie, please shush,' he said sharply, which had no effect on the wailing at all.

What was the matter with him? He never used to be like this. He used to have all the time, patience and understanding in the world for children. Wasn't it just ironic that now Ed finally had his own children, the children he'd so longed for, so twisted Annie's arm to have, he'd turned into the kind of grumpy, short-tempered harassed parent he'd always disapproved of in the past?

'So this cupola then,' Al began. 'Think we're going to get started on that today.'

Ed was desperate to stall on the cupola front, but before he even began that debate, there were a few other issues he was going to have to air with Al.

'Al, where are the kitchen windows?' he began firmly over the din of Minnie's wails.

Al shrugged, sucked his teeth and then let out a long sigh.

'We are really, really missing the kitchen, Al. I've got two babies to look after; I need the kitchen back.'

It wasn't as if Al hadn't heard the kitchen speech before.

126

He'd heard it many times. Each time it got increasingly desperate.

'Well, those windows, mate,' he said with another deep sigh, 'what on earth you were doing ordering windows from Sweden, mate? You should have let me sort them out, I'd have had them here weeks ago. Your supplier keeps telling me that there's this delay and that delay, I've never seen anything like it.'

Al stopped there, not offering any solution or further suggestion.

'Do you want me to phone them?' Ed asked.

Al shook his head. 'Don't think that will help.'

'Do you want me to cancel the order and let you order new windows?'

'Well, I've made the hole too big now ... extra big for your Swedish windows. If I order something in now, we're going to be rebuilding that wall around 'em.'

'Well, what are we going to do?'

Another shrug from Al. 'We'll just have to wait.'

'And what about the shower? Any sign of that?' There was a definite trace of pleading in Ed's voice now.

The 'family' bathroom currently had a toilet and a sink part-connected. The shower was a jangle of pipe ends protruding from a wall of jagged plaster and broken tile. An ominous dark hole in the floor, which whiffed, marked the spot where once there had been a drain.

Yes, there was another bathroom, but it only contained an old, small bath, which – now that Owen, Lana, the babies and Ed all had to use it – wasn't the cleanest or most relaxing tub in the world.

Ed had no idea when he'd last washed his hair. He missed the shower. He needed that shower.

'Shower? End of next week,' Al announced brightly, as if this was great news.

'End of next week!' Ed repeated, horrified. 'So you won't be able to fit it until . . .'

'Beginning of the week after,' Al confirmed. 'Might not be coming in that Monday. Got a long weekend planned at the—'

'Villa in Spain?' Ed guessed.

If he heard one more thing about Al and his trips to his villa in Spain, well it would be another reason to consider giving Al a punch.

'So this roof,' Al began, heading up the stairs, still with Micky in his arms, 'I can get that done today with Janucek. I've brought in my extra tall ladder and a sledgehammer.'

Ed looked up at the sloping white ceiling, pristine, only recently repainted. He and Annie had spent a fortune sorting out the roof of this house. The idea of Al taking a sledgehammer to it was making Ed feel slightly sick.

He didn't want the bloody cupola. The cupola was pure, one hundred per cent Annie. *Think how much light it will let in upstairs and into the hallway . . . think how pretty it will look on top of the house . . .*

As usual he'd gone along with it, maybe because she was the one with the huge salary and he didn't feel he could argue. Maybe because he was just too damn exhausted to argue.

'You're going to sledgehammer up through the plaster?' Ed asked uncertainly.

'Yup, easy as pie,' Al assured him, 'then when the dust has settled, remove a nice big layer of tiling and make the hole big enough for the cupola.'

'And you've got the cupola? That can be fitted on quite quickly?' Ed wanted to establish.

'Oh yeah, I've got it,' Al told him, but looked away a little uneasily.

'Where? Outside?' Ed was keen for some exact detail here.

'Well, not here,' Al had to admit.

'Not *here*?'

'Nah. It's a bit complicated. It got delivered to my other yard—'

'Your *other* yard?' Ed's credulity was stretched to breaking point now.

'Yeah, but we'll put the hole in today and I should have it here tomorrow, should only take a day or two to fit in,' Al assured him cheerily. 'It's going to look smashing.'

'Smashing,' Ed repeated. The only thing that was going to be smashing round here was Al, smashing round this beautiful, lovingly restored Georgian house with a bloody great sledgehammer, fitting a cupola that should be here by tomorrow. But who knew for certain? Certainly not Al.

'Don't do anything,' Ed decided, 'I'm going to phone Annie.'

He was going to talk her out of this whole mad idea. This was ridiculous. It was still threatening snow outside, what on earth was he doing letting this madman put a hole in their immaculate roof?

Risking leaving Micky in Al's grubby arms, Ed turned away and went in search of the house phone, or his mobile, or any sort of method of telephonic communication at all.

After a frantic search, he managed to unearth his mobile, but the battery was dead. A thorough search of three rooms later and he finally located the home cordless phone; it beeped with low battery too because, as usual, it hadn't been returned to its base once in the hours since Lana or Owen, or possibly one of their countless visiting friends, had last used it.

Nevertheless, he punched in Annie's mobile number and then listened to the continental ring tone on the line reminding him how far away she was.

'Ed?' Annie answered and immediately sounded anxious. 'Is everyone OK?'

'Yeah ... well, slightly better than this morning,' he grumbled, 'I think it's a virus, they're just so unsettled.'

'Have you given them anything?'

'They're up to their ears in Calpol,' Ed confided, 'any more would be an overdose.'

'OK. Babes, unless it's really urgent, I have to go. This is a difficult time,' Annie told him, which was putting it mildly.

'Annie, I don't think we should do the cupola,' Ed began with urgency. 'Al's here to put a hole in the roof and I don't think it's a good idea.'

Annie gave a sigh of exasperation. 'Ed, we've had this conversation,' she reminded him. 'We've had it many times, and each time we get to the end, you agree with me that it's going to be great. So can we just fast-forward to that bit?' Her voice had dropped to a whisper.

'I don't want to do this,' Ed repeated.

'Ed, he's a great builder; it's going to be fine. Babes,' she tried to put as much warmth and love into that word as she could, 'I'm sorry I'm not there, I'm sorry I can't talk to you for half an hour, but there's a disaster going on here and I have to go.'

Reluctantly, Ed agreed and ended the call.

'Right.' Al came down the stairs and handed Micky back to Ed. With a grin, he said: 'Let's get Janucek, the ladder and the hammers in, shall we?'

Chapter Eighteen

Anoush's off-duty model look:

Striped slouchy top (Galeries Lafayette)
Denim jacket (Levi's)
Scarf (market stall)
Teeny red shorts (Diesel via eBay)
Black tights (supermarket)
Flat slouchy boots (best friend's)
Total est. cost: €60

'My mother cleans a church . . .'

Elena had screamed. She had actually screamed right there in the lobby of Le Carrousel du Louvre with some of the most glamorous image-makers in Europe within earshot.

Svetlana had refused to accept the information about the faked booking. She had first of all argued with the receptionist and demanded to see a manager; then she'd had the same argument all over again with the manager; finally, she'd punched Patrizio's number furiously into her phone.

But – to only Svetlana's surprise – the number did

not ring, because it did not, of course, exist any more.

'Where did he come from?' Elena was wailing. 'How did we get involved with him in the first place? How could this happen? Sixteen thousand euros . . .' she kept repeating. 'Sixteen *thousand*!'

Svetlana did not have the chance to answer any of Elena's distraught questions before the Elena torrent of disaster continued.

'Forty-five buyers are going to arrive here tomorrow morning, and twenty-five journalists! This is a disaster. We are *finished* – before we've even begun,' Elena wailed.

Because Annie didn't want Elena to scream again, especially as she'd just seen John Galliano in person (yes, really!) walk past the tent entrance, she put an arm around the girl and hugged her.

But she couldn't offer any soothing words or any hint of a solution.

What about her TV show? Annie couldn't help wondering. She needed this episode. She needed the barnstormer or she could be out. Still, she didn't dare to complain in front of anyone, not right at this moment anyway. But the show was already being trailed: 'Join Annie in Paris for the fashion show of the season!'

There was no way she could come back from Paris with nothing. No way at all. Her eye caught Svetlana's unusual expression. Even with the amount of Botox, Restylene and surgery Svetlana had been through, she looked upset. More upset than Annie had ever seen her.

Svetlana didn't do upset. She powered on. She powered through.

Somehow, that was what all three of them were going to have to do today.

Rich had his camera trained on the faces. He didn't dare turn, instruct or even breathe because he knew that if anyone noticed he was still filming, they would *kill* him.

Anoush looked just as stunned as everyone else.

She had waited weeks for this opportunity and today she'd been waiting hours for it to happen. She'd already been through the rollercoaster of believing it wasn't going to happen, then finding out it was ... Now, to have it snatched away again like this ... she couldn't believe it.

'We're finished. Over,' Elena was gasping against Annie's shoulder. 'I can't believe it. I've worked so hard for this.'

Annie was already frightened about what was going to happen next. She suspected that any moment now Elena was going to round on Svetlana in a fury and a great horrible screaming, shouting scene was going to erupt right here in front of their eyes.

On the way in, Annie had noticed press photographers circling the square on the lookout for celebrities going to the shows. Svetlana hadn't been spotted then, but in just a minute or two it could all blow up into a very nasty, public row and, as Elena had warned, Perfect Dress might be over before it had even begun.

At this moment the disaster was big, but it was still contained and maybe somehow, by some stroke of magic, it could be averted.

'We need another venue,' Annie said as calmly as she could.

'For tomorrow?' Elena wailed. 'Impossible! Totally impossible! This is the trade shows, everything is booked, everything is booked months and months, even years in advance. That's why I was always suspicious of this space in the Carrousel' – her eyes flashed at Svetlana accusingly – 'and where are the other models? Did he only book one? Why did he bother?'

No one could answer that.

'This is a big city,' Annie reminded everyone. She was willing her mind to think and come up with an answer. 'People hold shows in all kinds of wacky venues – on piers, up towers, in all kinds of crazy places, just to attract attention. We've got to calm down and we've got to think. Everyone, take deep breaths. And think. I'm sure we can book more models.'

For a moment or two there was silence.

Annie's mind raced. They should ask the receptionist . . . What about someone at the hotel? . . . They had to ask people. They should spew out calls and ask anyone they could think of for help.

'Ermmm . . .' Anoush made a little sound.

Everyone immediately turned to her.

She cast her eyes down and cleared her throat, but suddenly felt too scared to speak.

'What is it?' Svetlana urged. 'If you have idea . . . if you have *any* idea, you have to let us know.'

'My mother . . .' Anoush looked up at them again, eyes wide; she looked so young, maybe sixteen or seventeen, Lana's age. 'She cleans a church,' she said in hesitant English, 'it's in Saint-Denis, it have a hall and maybe they borrow you it for show. Maybe?' she added doubtfully and gave a shrug.

Elena frowned, failing to see any hope at all in this idea, but Svetlana and Annie pounced on it, desperate to find any sort of solution.

A church? In a downtown neighbourhood? *Why not?* Annie was asking herself. Why not launch Perfect Dress in a really unusual, totally out-there way? It would at least give people something to talk about.

'Can you phone your mother?' Annie asked. 'Does she have keys? Can we go there? Can she meet us there? Can we go now?'

The flurry of questions made Anoush smile.

At this moment, Elena's eyes turned to Rich. It took another moment for her to realize just what he was doing.

The camera was on his shoulder and the digital display was lit up.

Elena sprang like a cat towards him. 'Are you filming this?' she demanded. 'Have you been filming all this time?'

When he made no reply, she stalked towards him furiously. 'You have no right!' she exclaimed. 'You have no permission!'

When it was clear what was about to happen, Rich reeled back in surprise, but Elena nevertheless managed to land a resounding slap on his cheek.

Like any true professional, Rich managed to film that too.

The party of five – Annie, Svetlana, Elena, Anoush and Rich – along with assorted bags, holdalls and camera, made the journey to the suburb of Saint-Denis in a large taxi.

It was obvious as they travelled that they were moving from the glossy centre of Paris to the much scruffier outer reaches. Underpasses were scrawled with graffiti, a hotch-potch of ethnic stores and market stalls lined the streets and there was all the jaunty, noisy vibrancy of a poorer, but lively, neighbourhood.

Finally, with the help of the GPS navigator, the cab pulled up in a narrow side street outside a small church with a courtyard and a plain, single-storeyed building beside, all enclosed in a high wire fence.

As they all got out of the cab and unloaded the bags and the equipment, a dainty woman, similar enough to Anoush to be recognizable as her mother, began walking across the courtyard towards them. She opened up a gate in the wire fence and let them through.

'This my mama, Latifah,' Anoush said by way of intro-
duction. 'No English,' she added.

Elena, Svetlana, Annie and Rich all smiled and said hello.
Then Latifah, smoothing down the pink and white
cleaner's tabard she had on over her clothes, shot out a
stream of rapidly delivered information in an unrecogniz-
able language and dangled a set of keys in front of Anoush.

Annie looked at the buildings before her. The church was
an ornate, blackened old building with twiddly stone
carving and numerous stained-glass windows: very
Gothic. The church hall, by contrast, had been built
recently. It was a plain, rectangular building with small
square windows, utterly devoid of any charm or character.
Annie was no longer feeling quite as hopeful as she had
been in the taxi.

The street was OK. It was quiet with several blocks of
flats, a few shops and takeaways. It reminded her of parts
of east London, the on-the-verge-of-hip areas, the streets
and postcodes that hadn't yet made it.

Anoush's mother began to walk towards the door of the
church hall and everyone followed her. It took several
minutes for Latifah to open the door because of the two
double locks and the padlock.

'Is not so safe here,' Anoush explained. 'Robbers.'

Moments later, the party was standing in a stunningly
boring room. With its brown lino floor, shabby cream
walls and short orange curtains hanging at every window,
Annie, Svetlana and Elena knew at once that it was beyond
hope.

No way could forty-five fashion buyers and twenty-five
members of the fashion press be invited here. How
would they hold a catwalk show? Join all the wobbly
Formica-topped tables together and somehow hope the
models would balance on top of them?

Anyway, Annie reminded herself, there were no models. There was only Anoush and she was technically too small; the dresses in Elena's holdall were bound to have been designed to hit 5-feet-10-inch models on the knee.

'Oh no!' Elena was starting up again, 'Oh no! This will not work! This will not work at all. This is horrible!'

Svetlana looked at Annie. They both knew it was true.

Anoush looked horribly embarrassed. Her mother asked her a question and she answered in halting tones, obviously explaining the situation.

Although his camera was running, Rich didn't dare to put it up on his shoulder. He felt like an undercover documentary-maker in a very dangerous situation. If he blew his cover now, they would turn on him. It had never occurred to him before that fashion could be so deadly.

Anoush's mother relocked the hall door as they all stood about hopelessly in the courtyard.

'Why did we let the taxi go? How will we get another one out here? Oh, it's over,' Elena wailed, 'it's all over!'

Annie looked once again at the church. It was really an incredibly pretty building. Right here in this ordinary street, in this down-at-heel corner of town. It must have been built over a hundred years ago, when maybe there was just a little village here.

'Do you have keys for the church?' Annie wondered out loud.

Anoush translated and her mother nodded.

'She just clean the church, she not have any control of the church,' Anoush added, just to make it clear.

Latifah walked them to the wooden double doors and in the few moments it took her to once again open up many heavy-duty locks, Svetlana asked Annie: 'What are you thinking? A fashion show? In a church?' Her tone of disbelief was obvious.

Elena snorted.

'We'll just have a look,' Annie answered, 'it might give us an idea.' She knew it was desperate.

Elena's BlackBerry began to ring. When she answered, they could all tell by the false cheerfulness in her voice that it was one of the many reporters she had booked for the show. 'Hi, yes, good to hear from you, how are you?' she gushed. 'Well, I'm very busy . . . Yes . . . Preparations . . . Aha . . . Last-minute problems, of course.' They could all hear her voice break with these words. 'Call you later, OK.'

When she ended the call, she switched off her phone.

Annie followed Latifah into the vestry. Inhaling the strong scent of incense, she admired the stone font and the ornate wooden and glass panelling separating this small space off from the rest of the church.

For a moment, Annie thought fleetingly of all the brides who must have waited in here, decade after decade, smiling nervously at their fathers, adjusting their white dresses and lowering their veils, waiting in heightened expectation for the next chapter of their lives to begin.

Then Latifah opened up the connecting door and they all tiptoed reverentially into the small but unexpectedly beautiful church.

'Oh!' Elena was the first to gasp.

The sunlight filtered only very dimly through the many multi-coloured windows, landing in splashes of red, blue, yellow and green all over the dark wooden pews and black and white floor tiles. A wooden cross hung above the altar and the precious colours from the windows stained the snowy altar cloth.

The effect was like walking into a jewellery box full of unexpected treasures.

'The audience sit in the pews? The girls come down the

aisle in the dresses?' Svetlana suggested, thinking out loud. Forgetting that at present she only had one girl. Not to mention all the other hurdles.

'We squeeze the DJ over in this corner?' Elena added.

'They could even wear veils,' Annie suggested, caught up in the vision too. 'We'll make the veils in the same colours as the dresses.'

The beauty of the church overwhelmed them and now everyone seemed to forget the principal problems: they had no permission to use the church; they had no models; they had to redirect seventy people to Saint-Denis; they didn't know a DJ; and, worst of all, the show was due to start in exactly seventeen hours.

'Can we use the church for the show?' Annie asked Anoush.

Anoush just shrugged her shoulders.

'We pay,' Svetlana added immediately. 'We pay very, very good for this. Priest can buy a new . . . whatever a priest needs. Or he can go on holiday to Barbados.'

'We can't pay too much,' Elena chipped in, 'we have a sixteen-thousand-euro hole in the accounts!' She treated her mother to a glare. Lest Svetlana forget.

Anoush began to speak to her mother. The exchange took several moments as Latifah frowned, gesticulated and looked very uncertain.

Finally, she headed out of the church door.

'She go phone,' Anoush explained.

Although it was obviously a tense moment, Rich decided he would take a chance.

'Girls,' he began, 'I'm going to switch on the camera.' He was fibbing; it had been running all this time, but he wanted it up on his shoulder to get some decent shots now. 'I'll film some church interior, OK? It's gorgeous, I just want a little bit of footage. Is that all right?'

'Now?' Annie snapped. 'You have to film now? While we stand here on bloody tenterhooks waiting to see if this whole thing is going to happen or not?'

Chapter Nineteen

Micky ready to go out:

Denim dungarees (Baby Gap)
White top (Petit Bateau)
Orange giraffe-print hat (IdaT)
Fleece outdoor suit (Osh Kosh)
Total est. cost: £90

'Waaaaah!'

Dave the dog looked up at Ed. The mongrel cocked his head to the side and gazed at Ed with deep brown, mournful eyes. Ed knew what that look meant. Before the arrival of the twins, Ed and Dave had shared a simple but nevertheless close relationship.

Ed and Owen had rescued Dave from the dog home, even though Dave was ragged, middle-aged and hard of hearing. Although Dave loved Owen and was deeply affectionate towards him, his true devotion belonged to Ed. Ed had once walked him every single morning and evening, Ed was still the one who fed him and Ed even let Dave sit on the sofa, in a snug and comfortable corner, just so long as no one else was watching.

Before the arrival of the twins, Dave had felt like an important element in Ed's life. But, since the arrival of the babies, well, everything had changed. Now Dave was just a dog. A dog who had to wait his turn. A dog who had to wait for his walk to finally come round at unexpected times of the day, like 4.30 p.m. A dog who sometimes had to suffer his biscuits being carted off from his bowl by the small squawking people, a dog who had suffered the ultimate indignity, when the babies were tiny, of being tied to a lamp-post for several hours and forgotten. It didn't matter how nice Ed had been when he'd finally returned to collect him, Dave had been tied to a lamp-post for hours and he wasn't going to forget it. Every time Ed had tied him to a lamp-post since, Dave had whined just to remind him.

'You poor old boy,' Ed told the dog now, understanding the look of resigned self-pity perfectly, 'we'll go out. We'll go out just as soon as Al has finished making his hole.'

Ed was strongly of the view that as the hole was definitely going to be made, he should be in the house when it happened. He and Annie had spent thousands of pounds repairing the roof with blue slate tiles specially colour-matched in Wales. There had been weeks of listening to the workmen tap-tap careful nails to fix each slate to its rafter.

When Ed's mother had lived in the house, the roof had been so leaky that the attic rooms were out of bounds, the rooms below them had murky brown stains on the ceilings, and throughout the winter, the house had resounded with the *plink plonk* of water dripping into buckets.

Ed could now hear Al tapping at the ceiling. In Ed's relieved opinion, the tapping sounding slow and careful. Tap . . . tap . . . as if Al was gingerly and cautiously removing pieces of plaster with his sledgehammer.

Ed had been further relieved to see that for the first time since the bulldozer was around, Al was wearing a hard hat. Surely if you were taking down a section of roof that made sense? Plus, Al had Janucek with him, holding his ladder and passing up tools.

'We'll go for a walk,' Ed told the dog, 'as soon as Al's finished.'

The word 'walk' set Dave's tail in frantic motion.

Just as Ed looked back from the dog to the babies, he saw Minnie take hold of a chunky wooden block and, without the slightest intent, fling her hand backwards, smacking Micky hard in the face with the block.

His sharp 'Waaaaaaah' of pain surprised Minnie so much that she joined in the wailing too and once again Ed had his arms full of two screaming babies. He sometimes worried about the damage being done to his eardrums as two babies cried at top volume, one against each side of his head.

He soothed the twins both with his voice and by jiggling them gently.

Maybe a walk right now wouldn't hurt. Maybe he would wrap them both up in the buggy, put Dave on his lead and head out to the park.

Al sounded as if he was getting on fine. At this slow and careful rate, Ed could easily go out for half an hour or so and still not miss the grand opening of the roof.

'Are you going to be OK there?' Ed shouted up the stairs, just before he put the babies into the pram.

'Yeah, no worries,' Al shouted down from his ladder outside the attic rooms on the second floor. 'Slow progress, mate,' he added. 'I'm taking the plaster out piece by piece just to make sure the hole doesn't get too big.'

'Good stuff,' Ed called back. He buckled in the babies,

clipped Dave's lead on to his collar and headed out of the front door.

Al breathed a sigh of relief. Now that Ed had finally left, he was going to take a proper swing at this ceiling. He couldn't understand what the bloody hell was the matter with it. He had been chipping and chipping at it for ages and just tiny pieces of plaster were coming away.

'Now, Janu,' he told his workman, 'let's take a proper crack at this.' Al leaned slightly away from the ladder and swung his hammer hard.

The head of the hammer struck first the plaster and then the very old, very brittle rafter lying right behind it.

The second hammer blow split the rafter, softened by years of leaks, but the third blow was fatal. The rafter broke, splintered off in all different directions and loosened a whole cascade of tiles.

The heavy slate tiles, specially colour-matched in Wales, slid at speed through the large hole in the ceiling.

Al, clutching at his ladder but still flailing with his hammer, barely had time to say: 'What the . . . ?' before eight sharp-edged tiles rained down into his face, plaster dust flew into his eyes and he felt himself wobble and over-balance.

Janucek, despite the tiles that had fallen on to his own head and shoulders, was holding the ladder firm, but although he shot out a hand, he wasn't able to save his boss. Al fell backwards and landed with an ominous crunch.

Chapter Twenty

DJ Paul:

Oversized promo T-shirt (freebie)
Baggy black tracksuit trousers (Adidas)
Red and white sneakers (Vans)
Bowler hat (Jerry's, New York)
Sunglasses (Versace)
Gold earring (Tiffany)
Total est. cost: €390

'Quoi?'

When Anoush's mother walked back into the church, she had enough of a smile on her face for Annie, Svetlana, Lana and Anoush to feel a surge of hope.

'Did he say yes?' Annie asked Anoush.

As soon as Anoush's hurried conversation with Latifah was over, she turned to them and said: 'He say yes. One thousand euros. You can have church today and tomorrow morning. At two p.m. there is . . . mmm, for baby . . . *baptême* . . . ?' she ended hesitantly.

'Baptism, yes, but no problem. We all finished

by then? Huh?' Svetlana directed the question at Elena.

Elena had a look of total concentration on her face. She looked at her watch and, for a few moments, she said nothing as her busy mind went into overdrive.

'We are going to have to work,' she began, 'we are going to have to work so hard . . .'

'No problem,' Annie assured her.

'No,' Svetlana agreed.

'I help too?' Anoush asked. 'And my mother,' she volunteered.

The crease of deep thought that Svetlana so disliked appeared on Elena's forehead. 'I need to contact everyone and tell them that the venue has changed. We need someone to do lights—'

'I can help with that,' Rich volunteered. 'There's a guy I know who runs a photographic agency in Paris; I'll phone him, borrow some stuff.'

Elena gave him a nod. 'We need a DJ,' she added.

'I'll ask at the agency,' Rich offered again.

'Annie is going to make the veils,' Elena added.

Annie nodded, even though she was thinking: *Am I? How? What with? And where will I get it?*

'We have to make the church beautiful,' Elena said next.

Svetlana and Anoush's mother both nodded at this. Maybe this meant they would take it on.

'And we have to find more models!' Only when Elena uttered these words did her voice sound stricken.

This was when Annie decided to voice her idea: 'I think . . .' she began hesitantly, 'I think *we* should all model the dresses.' She took in the whole group with her gesture. She meant Elena and Svetlana and Anoush and Latifah and was even offering herself.

'Huh?' was Svetlana's response to this.

'We should all model because these dresses are designed

to flatter every shape, so Anoush will wear hers long, yours will be above the knee, Latifah and I have boobs, so we'll have them open to the waist with camis underneath ... d'you see?' Annie was warming to her theme. 'We want to show how good anyone can look in the dresses. Every designer loves to claim every year that they're making "real" clothes for "real" people and then what comes stalking down their catwalk? Stick insects dressed as if they're all set to be fired into outer space!'

Anoush turned shyly to her mother and began a translation. When Anoush finished, her mother pointed at herself and let out a peal of laughter. She shook her head firmly.

Svetlana and Elena were also looking unconvinced.

'We will wear the dresses, ya, but we have to talk to people,' Svetlana said.

'We can't model,' Elena agreed, 'but you and Anoush, yes, and maybe you are right: some more ordinary people.'

'Do you know anyone else who would like to model?' Annie asked Anoush.

Anoush smiled broadly and nodded. 'Friends ... and I meet one girl at the Louvre,' she replied.

'They've got to have pretty faces and like to show off, but they don't need to have perfect bodies,' Annie instructed. 'Go phone them, find them and bring them here. Does your mother maybe have a friend too? It would be great to have someone older, wouldn't it?' Annie looked at Elena, who was nodding now but in a slightly dazed kind of way.

'You do have some other sizes in your bags for the buyers, don't you?' Annie remembered, hoping she wasn't going to have to squeeze women of all different shapes into standard UK size 10s.

Elena nodded again.

'OK.' Annie pushed up the sleeves of her blouse. 'We've

all got loads to do now. I need to get netting; Svetlana, flowers! Rich, lights! Go, Anoush! Elena, start phoning! C'mon, let's go, girls!'

Annie was quite relieved to leave the busy chaos in the church and head off for one of the bustling main streets of Saint-Denis. The day was sunny now and surprisingly warm. She wondered if it was still snowing in London. It was nearly 5 p.m., Owen and Lana would long have finished school and be doing whatever else was on the agenda for today: homework; music practice; visiting friends. The babies would be getting hungry and Ed would be thinking about venturing into the battle-scarred kitchen to rustle up dinner.

For his sake, she hoped the snow had stopped.

She would bring them all a present from Paris, even though she had no idea when the shopping moment would come.

This was a busy, lively street. There were ethnic take-away shops vying with ironmongers and grocers, boxes piled with exotic overripe fruit spilling out on to the pavements, noisy clatter and the smell of sizzling oil and onions everywhere. Somewhere there was going to be a fabric shop, she just knew it.

All around streets like this there would be homes full of clever, frugal women who sewed to make the family budget stretch further. She walked on, looking hard until she spotted rolls of fabric propped against a doorway, hopefully a sign that she'd found the shop she was looking for. She ducked in through the entrance and came into a tiny room packed from floor to ceiling with rolls and rolls of fabric.

'Bonjour, madame!'

A man with the darkest, shiniest skin dressed in a vibrant

pink and yellow T-shirt smiled at her from the counter.

'*Je puis vous aider*?' he asked, making the 's' buzz like a bee with his accent.

Annie looked at him. Annie smiled. Annie racked her brain for what on earth the French word for 'netting' could possibly be.

'I look,' she said, pointing to her eyes and then around the shop.

'Yes, you look, welcome!' the man behind the counter enthused.

Annie began to rummage in amongst the rolls of fabric, cheerfully certain that inspiration could be found. Inspiration could always be found, even in the unlikeliest of places.

In fact, the shop turned out to be a netting treasure trove. There were all kinds of nylon laces and nylon nettings in all sorts of colours: pink, white, a neon green that she particularly liked and gaudy gold. Now that would look great made into a tiny little veil coming down from the crown of someone's head.

With English words and sign language, she managed to order several metres of all the material she thought would be useful.

When the man rang up the total, Annie drew her euros from the TV petty cash envelope. She would phone Tamsin as she walked back to the church and explain what was going on. She had a feeling Tamsin was going to love this. It should make for great television . . . Annie hoped.

The Tamsin phone call over and as positive as she'd expected, Annie arrived back at the church in an excellent mood to find hustle, bustle, more people and a growing sense of energy.

A fat black dude in a bowler hat and – despite the gloom

of the church – sunglasses was setting up a music deck not far from the pulpit. Annie hoped that wasn't in contravention of any religious taboos. She was a bit hazy about religion. Certain Sundays in the year had been spent in nondescript C of E churches when she was young, but her mother had never been much of a fan of church-going and Annie had followed in her footsteps. Religion was something she associated only with school, like learning Latin. For Annie, vicars were like hospital doctors, people you seemed to have to deal with only in emergencies.

Anoush's mother had a mop in her hand and was busy washing the floor between the rows of pews; Svetlana was on her phone; Elena was on her phone. Rich was nowhere to be seen; maybe because he'd gone to collect the lighting he'd promised to find.

Svetlana spotted Annie and ended her call, tucking the mobile into the tiny handbag dangling from her wrist. She approached Annie with her arms held out and once she had her friend in the embrace, she told her: 'I think maybe this could work. I think maybe we will pull this off. Everything will be saved and I think in very big part is because of you.'

Annie smiled at her. 'No,' she said gently, pulling out of the hug, 'I might have had some good ideas, but I only suggested them because I know you and Elena and, hopefully, Anoush are the kind of girls who can make them work. That's the difference. Anyway,' she reminded Svetlana, 'we're not there yet. Thank me at the end of the show.' She winked.

'I wonder who Anoush is going to bring for models? On the catwalk it is going to be you and everyone Anoush can find.'

Only now did Annie begin to feel nervous at the prospect of this. None of them would be professionals, but would have to perform in front of press and buyers. People who had seen so many fashion shows, they were totally jaded; people who knew what a fashion show was supposed to look like; who knew what a model was supposed to do!

Whatever Annie might have said next, whatever Annie might even have thought next was blasted right out of her head by the dude behind the music system.

'DJ Paul,' Svetlana shouted out at her by way of explanation.

Annie and Svetlana couldn't help smiling at each other over the noise. Suddenly the church rocked and this didn't seem quite so mad or impossible after all . . .

'Turn down!' Elena screamed above the sound. 'Or windows fall out!'

'*Quoi?*' the DJ asked.

It was true; everything in the church seemed to be vibrating, even the cross above the altar. Annie hoped the priest was nowhere within earshot, otherwise he might rush round immediately and turf them out, one thousand euros or not.

As soon as the volume had been lowered, the sound of voices could be heard in the vestry. Then into the church came Anoush and the three others she had rounded up to model the dresses.

The music came to an abrupt halt, possibly for technical reasons, and Svetlana, Elena, Annie and the DJ all found themselves staring with great curiosity at the three 'models' Anoush had in tow.

There was a small, very curvaceous white girl, probably about the same age as Anoush, maybe a school friend. She had a big smile on her face and was clearly much more extrovert than Anoush.

Behind them towered an extraordinary-looking 6-foot-tall girl, perhaps Algerian; she was much darker than Anoush, with an amazing shock of long Afro hair, dyed bright orange; she was as rail thin and slouchy as a professional model.

And behind this girl was maybe the curvy girl's grandmother: a wonderfully French-looking older lady with a silver-haired bob, sporting a cropped fur jacket.

'What you think?' Anoush asked in her shy way. 'This is Yvette, I meet at the Carrousel,' she began, pointing to the tall girl, 'my best friend, Celeste, and Celeste's grand-mère – she used to model couture. They would all like to be in the show.'

Annie couldn't help giving a clap of excitement, her mind racing into makeover mode. A beanpole, an hour-glass, a glamorous old lady . . . this was excitingly challenging. She was going to have to go and rifle through Elena's bags of dresses straightaway.

However, she was aware of the silence from behind. Svetlana, Elena and Rich hadn't said anything yet. She looked around to see that their faces were set. They did not think this was such a great idea.

'This will work, I promise,' Annie whispered at them, not wanting to discourage the party at the door.

'Is this about fashion, Annah?' Svetlana asked icily. 'Or is this about making television?'

'Good television will be very good for both of us,' Annie replied.

Annie's phone began to ring. She picked it up but only answered because it was Ed's number. If some home disaster had occurred, she needed to know, even if it wasn't exactly the perfect moment.

'Ed, is this urgent?' she hissed into the handset.

'Al's just made a great big hole in the roof, brought half the slates down on top of his head, fallen off the ladder and broken his wrist,' came Ed's astonishing news.

Annie tried to digest it. There was absolutely nothing she

could do for Ed. Yes, it was a crisis, but she was having a full-blown crisis of her own right now. Elena looked, once again, as if she might cry.

'Darlin', I love you, I know you can cope, but I have to go. I'll phone you as soon as I can.' With that she hung up. 'Come right on in,' she urged the modelling party. 'Thank you, Anoush! Thank you all for coming. Now follow me and I am going to show you all the wonderful dresses we are going to wear.'

Chapter Twenty-One

Grand-mère's own:

Black and white print dress (Sabine Boutique)
Black snakeskin low-heeled shoes (Vintage Céline)
Black alligator bag (her mother's)
Red lipstick (Chanel)
Perfume (Chanel No 5)
Total est. cost (at today's prices): €1890

'Affreux.'

An hour later and Annie was in the church hall with all four models ... battling. She was battling with dress buttons which wouldn't stay closed; she was battling with needles, thread and netting which seemed to ping out all over the place no matter how hard or how closely she stitched it. Worst of all, she was battling with a stubborn French female who did not want to be told what to wear.

'Non, pas comme ça,' Grand-mère had insisted, before taking off the sash Annie had attached to her waist and actually flinging it to the floor!

Did this happen to Jean-Paul Gaultier? No, she bet it bloody did not!

In the church, a frenzy of prep. work was under way. Latifah was still cleaning and wiping, plumping cushions on pews, polishing brass candlesticks and making the entire space dazzle. Elena was on the phone making sure every single guest knew exactly where to come tomorrow. Svetlana, the DJ and Rich were arguing about music, lighting, angles, where the models should stand, where they should walk and where they should twirl.

Annie had looked in on the scene briefly, then decided to slink back to the church hall and just keep on top of her side of business.

Anoush had been easy to dress. She'd been put into the tiny size 8 sunflower-yellow dress. After appearing in the yellow dress, she was also going to model the other size 8: a white dress with a trellis pattern in bright blue. Annie instructed her how to wear her hair tomorrow for the show and told her to bring comfortable sandals with heels and do her make-up just as if she was going out.

Then it had been Anoush's friend Celeste's turn. Her generous curves were squeezed into the two available size 12s: a black crêpe wrap and a dress in emerald-green silk. Her luscious pale cleavage oozed out from between the buttons. Despite the language barrier, she and Annie talked bras and camisoles.

What did she have at home that would work under these dresses?

Celeste offered a black lace bra for under the green dress, along with a wide black patent belt.

'Yes!' Annie got it at once. She was curvy, but she had a tiny waist, well worth defining. Celeste suggested her fuchsia bustier top for underneath the black dress.

'Yes! Pink shoes?' Annie wondered.

Celeste nodded enthusiastically.

Annie kept offering Grand-mère the chance to be next, but she waved her hand dismissively. After the sash incident, she had stayed at the rail of dresses, examining the remaining ones herself and making her own mind up about what she was going to wear.

'What about me?' Yvette sashayed up to Annie, hand on one hip, her voice throatily low and sexy.

Annie looked at her in admiration. Yvette was quite something, so tall, so bony, so downright slinky, sweat glistening through the thick layer of make-up on her face. What on earth was she doing here? Why wasn't she the star of some major designer's show back in the heart of town?

'Have you done much modelling?' Annie asked.

'I am just starting out,' Yvette replied, giving her hips a little shake. 'Modelling is boring – I like to sing. But modelling pay better.'

'I think you're going to be big,' Annie couldn't help telling her, 'you look so . . .'

'Different?' Yvette offered.

'Yes,' Annie replied.

'But different is difficult,' came Yvette's reply as she took both the bright cobalt blue and the white dress from Annie's hands.

'It's difficult at the start, but once people get used to something different, then it is big, the beginning of something new . . .' Annie told the girl and wondered if she'd understood.

Yvette fixed her liquid brown eyes on Annie's and gave her a long serious look, followed by a quick wink.

'Maybe you are right,' she said, and then turned on her heel and flounced over to an empty corner of the room, where she obviously intended to change.

Finally, Grand-mère approached Annie with a sober

navy shirt dress in one hand and a brown dress with a ruffled neckline in the other.

'*Bien*,' Grand-mère said.

It wasn't a question, it was an instruction.

Annie just smiled and nodded approvingly – as long as no one touched the red and the purple size 14s Annie had marked out as her own, all was well – so Grand-mère took the clothes in the direction of the hall toilet, where she would dress in privacy.

Annie glanced up to see Yvette, from behind, sliding into the cobalt dress. Yvette was wearing the kind of tight beige all-over control underwear that Annie could hardly believe was necessary on so bony a frame.

Just then Elena, followed by Svetlana, came into the hall. Annie felt instantly nervous, because she knew they were here for one reason only: they needed to be convinced that these models could make the show work.

Anoush and Celeste, already in their first outfits, stepped forward to be approved.

Now Rich was at the doorway: 'Can I film?' he asked, and then with a cheeky smile: 'Is everyone decent . . . or happy to be caught in their smalls?'

Yvette stalked forward in the cobalt blue.

With her orange hair frizzed out wildly on end and her lean, black limbs, she looked amazing. Like a 1970s disco panther stalking on to the dance floor for the kill.

'Oh wow,' Rich had to exclaim, his camera running, 'Paul better spin something unforgettable when you walk into the room.'

Elena had her hands over her mouth and Svetlana's lips were in a little 'o' of surprise.

'You look incredible!' Annie assured Yvette.

Yvette gave a grin, then opened her mouth and gave a

little burst of Madonna. 'Everybody comes to Hollywood . . .'

This made everyone laugh.

'What other dress she wear?' Svetlana wanted to know.

'The white,' Annie told her. Svetlana and Elena both nodded, knowing just how good that would be with her dark, glowing skin and shock of orange hair.

'Anoush and Celeste are beautiful,' Annie prompted, not wanting the other girls to be overlooked in the excitement of the Yvette phenomenon.

'Yes, of course,' Elena responded, but she was trying to work out if Yvette should come in and wow the crowds at the start or if she should be the grand finale.

'Truly great dresses,' Annie reminded everyone. 'Look at the cut, the colours, the fabric, how well they hang on everyone. The dainty, the busty . . .'

'And Grand-mère?' Svetlana wondered.

'Grand-mère is going to be an eccentric touch,' Elena worried.

'But in a good way,' Annie agreed. 'How's it going with rearranging the venue?' she asked. 'Can the beautiful people cope with Saint-Denis?'

'I think it's fine; everyone sounds intrigued,' Elena replied. 'Everyone is booking taxis to hurry them from the Carrousel and back again; no one want to miss the Armani show at two p.m., so we must be quick. Girls finished walking by eleven, so everyone have time to look at dresses, talk to me and Mother afterwards before they have to go again.'

'So this is one fashion show which can't begin an hour fashionably late?'

'NO!' Elena replied, eyes round, horrified.

Just then Grand-mère came out of the ladies' room and walked slowly and with great dignity into the hall.

She held her head high and walked with what could only

be described as aplomb. The navy dress skimmed her shape and was held in place at the waist with a slim brown alligator belt, model's own. On her legs were fine mesh brown fishnet tights and a pair of mid-heeled lace-up brown shoes. It was a totally elegant ensemble.

'That is fantastic, no?' Svetlana was the first to remark. 'I thought the dresses were only for younger, juicy women, who still have va va voom' – she jiggled her cleavage slightly at the words – 'but now I see they are elegant and chic for older woman too, no?'

'I think Grand-mère is genius!' Annie told them as they all watched her walking towards them. In the style of an old-school model, she gave them a small, considered smile, made a careful turn and then, one hand on her hip, walked away again.

Celeste began to both clap and laugh: 'Bravo, Mamie.'

'How are the veils?' Elena wondered.

'Ah . . .' Annie's eyes fell on the heap of netting at the side of the room. It wasn't proving quite as easy as she'd thought with the veils.

Annie could manage simple repairs with a needle and thread; she could sew on buttons, repair hems and burst seams, but every veil she'd made so far resembled a botched tutu, which even Yvette would not be able to carry off with style.

From the pile of netting disaster, she picked out the smallest one she'd made, or tried to make, from gold netting. This was the one which had come off the least badly, she hoped.

Grand-mère saw the offering in Annie's hands and shook her head: '*Affreux*,' came her comment.

Frightful. Even Annie could understand that.

'*Donnez-le-moi*,' she instructed, holding out her hand.

159

Annie placed the netting ball into the lined but capable-looking hands.

'Grand-mère used to make hats,' Celeste told them.

Annie looked into Grand-mère's eyes in astonishment. Something about this day seemed to be getting luckier and luckier – well, aside from Al falling off the ladder obviously. OK, and Patrizio running away with sixteen thousand euros . . . Yes, maybe she should just be thankful for small mercies.

Celeste's mamie was going to sort out the veils. She had already picked up Annie's needle and gold thread and was busy constructing something much more elaborate out of the netting.

'We should do a rehearsal,' Elena said, glancing at her watch and barely registering that it was 7 p.m.

'I think we should get some food in,' Annie suggested. It now seemed like a very, very long time ago since the small portion of seafood and a glass of champagne had passed her lips.

Now hadn't she seen a kebab shop on the street where she'd found the netting?

The very first rehearsal kicked off in the church at close to 9 p.m.

'Just thirteen hours until we do this for real,' Elena warned nervously.

It had taken this long to get to the rehearsal stage because Rich and DJ Paul had fussed endlessly about lighting, angles and songs, then fussed all over again about which lighting and which angles went with which songs.

It had taken for ever. Their fussing had brought Annie, Elena and Svetlana to the verge of frustrated tears.

Then there had been a break for the great, greasy kebabs which everyone had wolfed down, except Grand-mère who looked on disapprovingly and said that she must go home soon as it was past her bedtime.

Now Svetlana and Elena sat in pews at opposite sides of the church, while Annie stood with the other models in the lobby.

Rich's lights shone down on the catwalk – er, aisle – and then DJ Paul hit the decks.

To the thumping, rocking, hip-hopping tune he knocked out first out came Anoush and Celeste. They were arm in arm and walked down the aisle together with something of a playful skip. Annie, wrapped in the red dress and feeling a little too nervous and a little too self-conscious, walked carefully behind them, worrying about whether she should smile or put on a disdainful catwalk face.

Yvette waited in the vestry until the second song began, so that her arrival marked a change in mood. When new chords struck up, she came out in the blue dress with a fabulous purple tulle creation of Grand-mère's on her head. Elena was so impressed she let out a little *whooo* of excitement.

At a respectful distance, Grand-mère appeared and, despite the thumping bass, carried herself with elegance and poise all the way down the aisle.

The five models arranged themselves in a group to the left of the altar, the idea being they would pause here for a few moments, letting the music and the mood wash over the audience, giving a good chance for the dresses to be admired, then they would walk back along the side of the church, make a lightning change in the hall, then head back in for round two.

Annie faced Elena and Svetlana and read the surprised relief on their faces.

Now that the lights were on, the music was playing and the models were dressed up, the women in charge of

Perfect Dress could see that this stood a chance. It really might be possible for a group of total amateurs to pull off a show and convince some important people that the dresses were fantastic.

'What do you think?' Annie couldn't help asking, desperate to hear their reaction.

But before either Svetlana or Elena could answer, there was an audible crack. The music came to an abrupt halt and the lights went out, plunging the church into pitch darkness.

'Oh shiiiiit,' came Rich's pithy response, 'I think we've blown up.'

Chapter Twenty-Two

Owen at home:

White and blue T-shirt (Quicksilver)
Checked shirt (Asda)
White tracksuit bottoms (Primark)
Brown sandals (Birkenstock)
Total est. cost: £65

'It's snowing inside the house!'

Ed put his lips to Minnie's forehead. This was the way Annie had taught him to estimate a baby's temperature. If the baby's forehead felt hot to the touch of your lips, the baby was probably running a temperature.

The forehead felt hot. Ed was hardly surprised, Minnie was crying so hard that her face was red and tears were spilling from the corner of her eyes.

Teething?

Her nose was all blocked up and snotty, so Ed thought there was more to it than tooth pain. He was thinking ears: the dreaded earache, especially as she seemed to be rubbing her fist against the side of her head.

'Oh, Min Pin,' he said, holding her up closely against his face and rubbing her back, 'poor old Min Pin. Let's go and get some medicine.'

Micky set up a fresh wail too, but this was because he was still buckled into his high chair at the makeshift table in the sitting room. They were eating a late supper of mashed avocado and yoghurt, because the kitchen was far too cold to hang out in for any length of time.

Ed wasn't sure if he, Owen and Lana were going to enjoy a meal of toast, mashed avocado and yoghurt quite as much as the babies though.

Lana had been in a fury ever since she'd stepped into the house. 'It's absolutely freezing!' she'd complained. 'What the bloody hell has Al the idiot done now? Brought half the house down?'

Owen had rushed upstairs to survey the damage, even though Ed had warned him not to: 'Be careful, more might still come down. It's a hard-hat area up there!'

'Cool!' Owen's voice had drifted down from the attic floor. 'It's snowing inside the house!'

Ed measured out the medicine and, once he had given Minnie her dose, decided to risk phoning Annie.

Yes, she was busy and she was stressed, but so was he and he wanted her advice on earaches. At what point were you supposed to phone the doctor? he wondered. He'd read horrible things about burst eardrums and permanent deafness.

'Annie?'

'Hi,' she answered. She could have told him that now was not a good time; now she was in a pitch-dark church with a crowd of very angry, very baffled and quite frankly mutinous people around her, but she could hear Minnie's breath in the phone too, so Ed must be holding her right up against his shoulder.

164

She listened. Minnie's breathing sounded snuffly.

'I think Min's got a sore ear,' he told her.

Annie put one hand over her other ear so that for a moment she could block out the complaints, the cries and the threat of a fresh crisis threatening to engulf everyone all over again.

'Poor old Min, have you given her medicine?'

'Check,' Ed answered.

'Keep her warm with lots to drink. Is Micky OK?'

'Seems to be so far. Annie, how do I know if she's getting worse, though? How do I know when to call the doctor? And how do I keep her warm when there's a great big bloody hole in the kitchen wall and now the roof?'

'Oh, I'm really sorry . . .' Annie began.

Elena was crying again; even in the pitch darkness with one hand over her ear, Annie could hear her. But she needed to concentrate on her family for a few minutes. 'Ed, Minnie will scream and scream if it's really bad, that's when you call the out-of-hours service because she'll need stronger pain relief and maybe an antibiotic.'

'What if her eardrum bursts?' Ed asked. His voice was full of angst.

She tried to soothe him. 'It usually takes days to build up to being that bad. There's an electric heater in my office, why don't you plug that into the bedroom and get it all warmed up for bedtime? But are Lana and Owen going to be warm enough?'

'I don't know.'

'Maybe you should all go to Dinah's or Hannah's . . .' Annie wondered out loud, but she knew that neither sister had enough room for Ed and his four children. 'Warm up the bedroom,' she repeated. 'If the worst comes to the worst you can all sleep in there. I'm going to have to—'

'Go. I know. Are you still working?'

She laughed at this: 'Oh yeah, I am still working. Still trying to snatch victory from the jaws of defeat. Phone me later, yeah? Tell me how it's going.'

'I love you,' he told her.

And suddenly she felt tears jump up at the back of her eyes.

'This is completely bloody ridiculous,' was Lana's verdict when she heard about the avocado toast and the baby's ears and the plan to all huddle up together in the big bedroom. 'I have a mock exam tomorrow, I can't be up every five minutes all night long with the stupid babies.'

'That is a bit harsh, Lana,' Ed told her sharply. 'Things are going wrong. Things are not going to plan. We may just have to pull together and battle it out for a bit.'

'No!' Lana had stormed. 'I'm phoning Greta and I'll stay there for the night.'

Ed had just sighed in response to this. He didn't want to argue with Lana, firstly because he hated arguing with her and secondly because it wasn't really such a bad idea. At least that would be one less person to try and cater for, one less person to worry about keeping warm.

Ed, Owen and two much calmer babies ate their strange supper, supplemented with whatever could be found in the fridge, and then they listened to Owen play the violin for a change instead of the electric guitar.

'Are you just being nice though, Owen?' Ed wondered. 'Are you playing the violin for you or for me?'

'Oh, totally for you,' Owen assured him without the slightest attempt to cover anything up. 'I mean I don't *mind* the violin, but my heart is really with the electric guitar.'

Ed felt more than winded at this news. He was the one who'd first taught Owen to play both the acoustic guitar and the violin. He'd hoped that somehow the violin might win through, because Owen was naturally very good at it.

When Ed decided that it was time for all four of them to brave the bedroom and bunk down for the night, Owen went into the room first.

'It is absolutely bloody freezing in here,' was his verdict.

'Don't say bloody,' Ed warned.

'But it bloody is,' came Owen's reply.

Ed gave another long-suffering sigh. 'The electric heater is rubbish.'

'I have some things in my room . . .' Owen began.

What was he going to come out with next? 'Firewood?' Ed joked.

'No, I've got a bit of camping kit.'

'Camping kit? I thought that was all packed away in the boxes in the attic for the summer.'

Ed and Owen had spent many a happy night together under canvas. Funnily enough, their love of camping had been one of the things that had brought Annie and Ed together in the first place – but that was another story.

'Well, yeah, our kit is packed away in the attic, but I've got some new stuff.' Owen spoke with caution; he didn't want to land himself right in it.

'So what have you got?'

'Well, some really nice new arctic kit. I was supposed to test it out – for Mum's show.' He hoped this would be the end of the questions.

'Oh. Right. Sleeping bags?' Ed wondered.

'Yeah, really big sumptuous ones. You can zip them right open – you can even zip them together,' he explained with enthusiasm. 'If you, me and the babies all get into bed under the duvets and the arctic kit, I reckon we'll be all right, but we'll leave the heater on low all night.'

'That is brilliant, Owen,' Ed told him. 'Bring it on in.'

Owen disappeared off to his bedroom, and when he

reappeared his arms were full of all the things he'd managed to . . . er . . . 'source' from the Everest Camping Company. The sleeping bags and the down-filled jackets were so thick and pillowy he could hardly see over them. Then there was thermal underwear bundled into his arms and from one hand dangled a camping stove.

'I don't think we'll be needing the camping stove,' Ed told him as he dropped everything down on the bedroom floor.

'Why not?' Owen wondered.

'I don't think we want to cremate ourselves, do we?'

An hour later, the twins were fast asleep in the middle of the bed under a comforting layer of duvet and sleeping bag. Owen lay in bed on one side of them, reading a book and occasionally yawning. Ed lay on the other, so exhausted he couldn't read anything and was already dozing.

'Dad?' Owen asked quietly.

'Mmmm,' Ed managed to answer.

'You won't mention the camping stuff to Mum, will you?'

'What camping stuff?' was Ed's sleepy reply.

'You know, the sleeping bags and everything, just don't tell Mum about them.'

Sounding a little less tired now and a little more anxious, Ed had to ask: 'Why not?'

Chapter Twenty-Three

Model Annie:

Red shirtwaist dress (Perfect Dress, borrowed)
Control pants (Spanx)
Blue heels (L. K. Bennett)
Chunky gold and silver necklaces (Topshop)
Total est. cost: £180

'I don't think that was just a little fuse . . .'

It was so dark in the church after the bang that at first no one could even see their own hands in front of their faces. But, slowly, their eyes adjusted to the gloom.

'What just happened?' Annie's voice rang out in the darkness.

'What have you done?' came Svetlana's sharper and more accusing question.

'Il y a un plomb de sauté quelque part!' was the angry response from DJ Paul in the corner of the room.

'I don't think that was just a little fuse . . .' Annie said, speaking as a veteran of dodgy fuse-boxes and blown plugs.

'No,' came Rich's verdict out of the darkness over on the other side of the church pews. 'I'll try and find a torch, then I can maybe change the fuses on the lights. They probably come with spares. But that sounded a lot more serious than a little fuse. It sounded like we blew the whole bloomin' box.'

DJ Paul let out a blast of angry-sounding French, which was met initially with silence as no one in charge knew what he meant.

'Anoush?' Annie asked, hoping she could provide a translation.

'He say it sometimes happen,' she began from her spot near the altar, 'the *courant* in the building not enough for all his equipment, plus the lights.'

Then DJ Paul switched on a powerful torch, which proved that he was prepared for disasters like this and, with the beam in one hand, he began to pack up with the other.

He fired out some more sentences in rapid French, which Anoush began to translate with embarrassment: 'He's going to go now. Er, he's not going to come back tomorrow. He thinks this problem will take too long to fix and it is too much trouble for him.'

It was time for Elena to let out her by now familiar howl of despair.

Eyes adjusting to the darkness, Annie could see that Elena had covered her face with her hands. Even Svetlana's proud posture seemed to have slumped. Svetlana was not used to problems, she was used to clicking her fingers or bringing out her credit card and making every little hitch that ever dared to get in her way disappear.

There was a baffled sense of shock in the church now; no one seemed quite ready to believe that a mere electrical problem was going to ruin everything. They had come so far in so few hours: they had found a new venue and reorganized all the guests; they had found models; they had made head-dresses and veils; they'd had a DJ, even a borrowed lighting rig . . . and now it looked as if it was all going to be over again.

Annie was desperate to suggest something. Anything. Her mind was racing. Couldn't they bring in a thick power extension cable from the hall?

'A CD player?' she asked out loud. 'With batteries?'

DJ Paul seemed to understand her suggestion and he just laughed out loud at it. *'Pas moi,'* he told them with a shrug. Not me.

If anyone was going to be standing in a church playing a battery-operated CD player, it wasn't going to be DJ Paul. He had almost finished his dismantling work and Annie had a feeling that once he walked out of the door, it was going to be hopeless. Once one of them had given up hope, the feeling of doom and gloom would settle over the others and they would all walk out on this show.

'We have to think of something,' Annie said out loud, as encouragingly as possible. 'If we've got this far, we can solve this little problem. C'mon.'

For a few moments, everyone was totally silent. The DJ finished his packing by torchlight.

Once he was gone, Annie thought wildly, they wouldn't even have torchlight. They would be totally in the dark.

Then Grand-mère stood up.

'My grandmother needs to go home,' Celeste said, suddenly remembering.

'Of course,' Svetlana replied.

Celeste stood up too and prepared to follow Grand-mère.

Grand-mère walked out of the pew, but then she turned, not towards the church vestibule and door, but instead in the direction of the altar. Once there, she made a left before disappearing through the small side door.

'Where's she going?' Annie asked Celeste.

Celeste shrugged.

'Is this her church?' Annie wondered.

'Yes,' came Celeste's reply, 'she comes here all her life.'

Grand-mère shuffled out several moments later with two small cardboard boxes in one hand and a wrought-iron candle holder in the other.

The candle holder was one which had been designed to carry row after row of little votive candles.

Grand-mère set the items down in front of the altar, then she went back into the room and came out with another three candle holders in her hands.

'*Voilà, la lumière,*' she said.

Celeste was about to translate, but Elena was the one who said in English: 'Here is our light.'

Then Grand-mère walked calmly before the altar, pausing to make a little genuflection in the centre, and disappeared through the second tiny door on the other side of the church.

For a moment there was silence, then a terrifying blast of organ music reverberated round the church, shocking everyone back to their senses.

'The organ!' Annie exclaimed.

Grand-mère appeared once again and said simply: '*Voilà, la musique.*'

Celeste gave a little clap and began to speak to her grandmother in French. Then she turned back to the others and asked: 'What you think? She say she have friend who could play organ music here tomorrow.'

Elena and Svetlana appeared to be too surprised to be able to speak. They were looking at each other in the very dim light.

172

'Will the candles be enough? For taking pictures?' Annie asked Rich.

'Well,' he began, 'it's a very dark church, even in the day-time. It'll be very moody, but you know, the photographers will use flash and as for me, I'll just put the camera on the night-time setting and . . . hey, it'll be something different.'

Suddenly Elena seemed to be galvanized once again. Springing up from her hard wooden seat, she exclaimed: 'Come on, we light up all the candles we can find and we see how it look.'

Chapter Twenty-Four

The fashion buyer:

Multi-coloured knit dress (Missoni)
Simple grey wool coat (MaxMara)
Grey heeled boots (Chloé)
Aqua blue patent shoulder bag (Mulberry)
Prescription sunglasses (Boots)
Total est. cost: £2,800

'What on earth . . . ?'

'Did you survive the night, babes?' Annie asked gently down the phone when she woke up at 6.30 a.m. in her hotel room the next morning.

Unlike Svetlana and Elena, who would be waking up in the luxury of their George V suite, Annie and Rich were staying in rather more functional rooms at a business hotel on the edge of the financial district.

'Yeah, we survived,' Ed sleepily assured her, 'but I'll take Minnie for a check-up at the doctor's this morning. How about you?'

'It was a very, very late night,' Annie said and gave a

yawn as if to make her point. 'I'm just about to get dressed, put on my TV face, then Rich and I are heading over to the venue first thing to help get it all set up.'

'Put on your TV face?' Ed repeated. 'What? No make-up artist?'

'No! No Ginger, and even the multi-skilled Amelia didn't come with us in the end. Too much to do in London for Tamsin, apparently. How will I cope? No, don't worry, we're filming by candlelight, no one will get to see me in all my truly hideous detail.'

'You know you're lovely,' Ed insisted.

'Aw—' But before Annie could say something nice back, a sharp cry attracted Ed's attention.

'Got to go,' he told her, 'fighting has broken out in the playpen.'

By 9.45 a.m., fifteen minutes before curtain up, the church hall was overwhelmed with the smells of perfume, clouds of hairspray and the lashings and lashings of deodorant being used to hold nervous sweat at bay.

Annie, plus every one of her 'models', had been made up, dressed up, tweaked, teased and prepared in every way that they could think of, so now they were all peeking out of the church hall windows and anxiously watching the arrival of the buyers and the press.

In the cool light of day in the drab church hall, their elaborate plans, concocted last night in a fug of darkness, candlelight and several bottles of wine, seemed . . . well . . . a little childish, amateur and definitely unprofessional.

Look at these terrifying fashionistas walking towards the church!

Annie had been a personal shopper for long enough to know that these were very serious fashion people. They carried thousand-pound Chloé and Bottega Veneta bags.

They wore Chanel sunglasses, although it wasn't even remotely sunny; Fendi fur-trimmed coats were slung over their shoulders.

Annie could feel her heart sink, then sink some more. She just hoped no one would actually laugh outright, out loud at their poor little show.

Then she stole a little glance at Yvette and took heart once again. At least Yvette looked like a proper model. She was the real deal. A catwalk panther, about to stalk down the runway, take out her talons at the bottom and claw. Bite even.

Yvette had strapped mighty stilettoed boots on to the ends of her long legs and they made the cobalt-blue dress look slinky and dangerous. She also kept bursting into little snatches of song to gee everyone up.

Anoush looked pixieish and cute as a button, Celeste, curvaceous and gorgeous, Grand-mère of course looked *pleine de dignité* in her dress and Annie . . . well, Annie just hoped she looked on the better side of normal, even though she was wearing a red tulle veil that would have been more at home on a flamenco dancer, or maybe a lamp.

'Nervous?' Annie asked Anoush as she walked over towards her.

'A little bit,' Anoush confided. 'I hope we remember where to walk and where to stand.'

'We'll be fine,' Annie said, hoping the same thing herself. 'We just need to go slowly and then we won't trip and fall, or bump into each other. That's the main thing.'

Annie took another look out of the window and saw Svetlana laughing with a small group of guests.

Svetlana was a practised veteran of tens of thousands of cocktail parties and high-society events. She was a natural out there making small talk and no doubt telling everyone how exciting this was and how thrilled she was, building up their anticipation for the event.

Every time Annie flicked a glimpse at her wristwatch, it seemed to have jumped much further forward than she expected.

The door of the hall opened and there was Rich, camera on his shoulder: 'One more shot of backstage,' he said with a grin, 'then I need to man the action stations in there. Are we all ready for curtain up, girls?'

Annie felt a sickening lurch of nerves, but knew she had to hide them as well as she possibly could. Nervousness was horribly contagious and she wanted everyone to exude calm and sexy confidence.

'Smile for the camera,' she urged everyone.

Once Rich was out of the hall, she called all the girls together.

'Group hug,' she commanded, 'but gently, we don't want to mess our hair.' When no one seemed to know what she meant, she spread out her arms and tucked Celeste under one and stretched up to include Yvette under the other, and then she encouraged everyone, including Grand-mère, to do the same.

When they were all in the cramped huddle, she began with: 'Anoush, you translate please. We all look wonderful. We are all beautiful in our different ways. We are going to go out there and show off our beautiful dresses on our wonderful selves.'

She paused while Anoush caught up with the French version.

'*Pleines de dignité,*' Grand-mère added at the end of Annie's little pep talk.

It wasn't a bad idea, if they were all dignified, no one could laugh at them, could they?

'*Dignité,*' Annie repeated.

Elena came into the hall, looking pale with worry. The strain of being the lynchpin for this event was starting to show.

'Are you ready?' Elena asked after she'd looked everyone over with a critical eye. 'You look really good,' she added, voice full of anxiety, unable to stop herself from going over to Celeste to make a little adjustment to the short netting veil pulled over her eyes.

'We're ready,' Annie answered for the models. 'We're going to knock your socks off,' she added, sounding much more confident than she felt.

'OK, come and wait in the vestibule. I will tell you when to come out.'

Crammed into the dimly lit vestibule, Annie listened to the organ music and inhaled the thick incense that was now burning in the church to make it as authentic and atmospheric as possible.

Glancing over the other models as they waited nervously under their head-dresses and veils, she thought again of brides. How many brides had waited in this cramped space? Smelling incense and listening to the organ play as they prepared to walk down the aisle in their one and only catwalk moment, a new, strange and thrilling life ahead of them?

For a flickering moment, Annie considered the question Ed asked every so often. Would she be a bride once again? As soon as she even thought of the question, she felt the inexplicable fear . . .

The organ stopped and now the church was in silence. All the models knew that when the music began to play again, that was their cue to start the show.

In the silence, Annie thought she could hear not just her own heart beating, but the thumping of all the nervous hearts around her. Only Grand-mère looked serene. She was too old for nerves, she'd told them earlier in the day, nerves were bad for the heart.

It was simple enough, the plan for the show. Everyone was going to file in slowly, one by one, walk down the aisle, turn at the top and take their place there until the last model, Yvette, had done her walk. Then they would file out, rush to the church hall, change dresses and go through it all once again. While they were changing, Elena was going to talk about the dresses, the fabrics and the prices. Easy. So why was Annie, who was watched by nearly two million viewers on TV every week, feeling as if she might actually puke with panic?

Then the organ struck up, the vestibule door opened and before Anoush could even think about it, she walked out and the show began.

Within moments, Celeste followed, then Grand-mère, then Annie.

Walking down the aisle to the dramatic strains filling the space, Annie kept her eyes ahead of her. She felt grateful for the red veil shielding her face and her features from the crowd.

Although she didn't look at it, she could feel the audience. The church was full of the warmth and subdued hush of a densely filled space. It was packed, the aisle felt narrow because black-clad arms, black jackets, bags and blond heads were all edging in to it.

She walked carefully, one hand on her hip as she attempted to look carefree and nonchalant. All she was really concentrating on was the distance between her and Grand-mère. She had to maintain it. That was her only real job here.

Already, she could sense that Yvette had stepped out of the vestibule. Heads were turning to look at her and there was a sort of rustle of interest from the crowd.

Yvette in her shiny high-heeled boots, blue dress and orange hair, trimmed with orange net, strode down the aisle. She was a total natural who managed to convey just the right amount of disdain to the audience.

Annie turned left at the top of the aisle, took her place beside Grand-mère and turned towards the audience. From what she could read on the faces, the audience was watching carefully and paying attention, but no one was smiling or giving away the slightest sign of approval. So much for creating a wedding-like atmosphere; this was like being at a very fashionable funeral: everyone was dressed in black and looking incredibly grave.

Annie hadn't expected high fashion to be quite so serious.

But, of course, maybe it had to be taken so seriously, because everyone who didn't take it super-seriously laughed at it.

Yvette finished her walk down the aisle, twirled elegantly and came to stand beside Annie, though not too closely because the wrought-iron holder with the forty or so little candles was blazing with a surprising heat between them.

As Annie had twirled herself into position she had noticed with a flicker of worry how dangerously close to the candles her nylon netting had swished. Health and Safety wouldn't have been very impressed with this artistic little fire hazard, that was for sure.

Once Yvette had posed for a moment or two, Anoush began to lead the models towards the back of the church. As soon as the vestibule door was closed they rushed over the courtyard to the church hall to change in a frenzy of relieved giggles.

'Was it OK?' Anoush asked Annie. 'Do you think we did OK?'

'We did fine,' Annie assured her.

'I miss the DJ,' Yvette said, snatching her white dress from the rail. 'Is hard to rock to church music.'

As the rest of them dropped their dresses on the floor and wriggled into the new outfits, bras, stocking, G-strings and all on display, Yvette and Grand-mère turned away, trying to maintain some privacy despite the need for speed.

'Yvette, you are so skinny, you hardly need a body-stocking,' Annie had to say, although she was so tightly pulled into one herself that bending over was an effort.

'Oh, you would not like to see me naked,' Yvette replied.

There was no time to ask why not because head-dresses and veils had to be arranged, lipstick touched up and everyone checked over because it was already time to crowd back into the vestibule.

Pushing the door open just a tiny crack, Annie could listen in to the final part of Elena's pitch. She realized at once that every word was falling into a sea of silence.

There just wasn't any feedback. The crowd was not wowed. There was no rustle, no stirring, no whisper of interest. It felt flat and dead out there, smoky and stuffy.

Annie looked over the models huddled into the vestibule. They were amateurs putting on a pantomime and it was flopping. Suddenly, she wasn't sure if she could brace herself for round two.

Elena finished her speech and it was met with silence, not even a ripple of polite applause. As she walked up through the church to the vestibule door, to come and tell the models to begin the next part of the show, Annie could see that she looked flushed and embarrassed.

'You OK?' Annie whispered as Elena approached the door.

Elena just nodded, but Annie saw the first hint of tears in her eyes.

'Ask the organist to play the wedding march,' Annie whispered to her, struck with sudden inspiration, 'then we'll send Yvette out first, she's in white with a big veil, she's our bride, then Anoush and Celeste as bridesmaids, with Grand-mère and me bringing up the rear. Big effect, grand finale – and at least it will get it over with quickly.'

Elena made a nod of agreement and hurried off to instruct the organist to move the wedding march up to the top of the playlist.

Annie explained in whispers to the models just as the opening chords struck up.

'Yvette first, go down the aisle like a bride, Celeste and Anoush behind. Then *la grand-mère et moi, derrière*,' she stumbled in schoolgirl French.

'*Bien*,' Grand-mère agreed.

If Yvette had looked good in the blue, she looked *magnifique* in the white dress. White sandals with straps which wound up her legs had been borrowed from Svetlana for this outfit. Grand-mère had made her an elaborate veil from the full three metres of white tulle which Annie had bought. In her hand was a little posy of white flowers.

As she went out, a veiled Anoush and Celeste followed behind.

There was a little flutter of something from the crowd, Annie couldn't help feeling.

She enjoyed this second trip down the aisle much more than the first. Every one of the models seemed to. The extreme tension of walking through the church for the first time had been broken, now their shoulders lowered and their steps looked much more easy and relaxed.

As she reached the top of the aisle, Annie even managed a smile for Rich and his camera. This felt better, the atmosphere of doom and gloom had lifted and she could even spot a smile or two in the audience.

But all was not entirely straightforward at the top of the aisle. They had come down in a new order and they were now standing in different positions, which they hadn't practised before.

Anoush and Celeste had understood that Yvette should be in the centre, not at the far end of the row, so they were stepping past her and encouraging her to move up towards Annie and Grand-mère.

Yvette, in the borrowed sandals, stumbled just slightly, but instinctively put her hand out to catch hold of the nearest solid object. Unfortunately, this was a low wooden screen set out to provide a prettier backdrop. It swayed momentarily, then toppled backwards with an alarming clatter. As Yvette spun her head to survey the damage she'd done, the breezy tulle of her veil swished over one of the candle holders and ignited with an audible whoosh.

Panicked cries of alarm broke out amongst the models and the audience.

Annie's mind raced. *Where was a fire blanket? Or a fire extinguisher?*

Like a vision of calm and control, two women appeared before the screaming crowd with the necessary items in their hands.

Grand-mère was holding a thick fur coat she'd plucked from the front row, Svetlana had an opened bottle of champagne in each hand.

Just as they were about to douse Yvette, the model leaned forward and her flaming veil, along with her luscious wig of astonishing orange hair, fell to the floor in a burning heap.

Svetlana poured on the champagne, and Grand-mère dealt the fire a death blow by smothering it with the coat.

Thick smoke and an astonishingly bitter smell of burning

hair and singed fur filled the space. The audience was on its feet, ready to make a rush for the door, but the relief that the fire was out and the extraordinary sight of Yvette stopped everyone spellbound in their places.

Now that Yvette was stripped of the wig and the cropped hair underneath had been revealed, it was instantly obvious that slinky-bodied, nonchalantly slouchy model Yvette had the strong jawline and slight Adam's apple of a man.

Annie stared too.

She couldn't help it.

Yvette was just as beautiful as she had been a moment ago, but she was a he. Yvette was really an Yves, who sensed the curiosity in the room, the eyes upon him.

Snatching this little moment of fame, which was right there before him, waiting to be taken, Yvette threw his head back and gave the crowd the surprisingly polished chorus of Abba's 'Super Trouper'. It was almost loud enough to drown out Elena's whimper of dismay.

Chapter Twenty-Five

Pssst! Vickie goes fashion:

Navy-blue harem-trousered playsuit (Topshop)
Metallic silver blazer (Whistles)
Silver heels (Faith)
Purple mock-croc handbag (Osprey)
Notebook and pen (WHSmith)
Digital voice recorder (eBay)
Total est. cost: £440

'You never mention your dad . . .'

'Well, that's made selling the story to the editor a piece of cake.' The magazine columnist Vickie Plumridge turned and smiled at the journalist sitting beside her on the church steps.

The journalist nodded in agreement: 'Let's just hope the photos are good.'

'Do you think they staged it?' Vickie wondered.

'No way! Did you see the look on the faces of the other models when the bride turned out to be a guy? And the woman who owned the fur coat! She was absolutely livid!'

'Still,' Vickie couldn't help wondering, 'for two bottles of champagne to be so close to hand, and already opened . . . and for Svetlana Wisneski to be the one pouring them over the burning veil? If I hadn't just seen this happen, I'd never have believed it.'

'OK, recorders at the ready, they're coming out,' the journalist warned and tossed her half-smoked cigarette on to the step where she ground it out with the pointed toe of her shoe.

Elena and Svetlana stepped out of the church, both with bright, cheerful smiles on their faces, as if setting a model alight and nearly burning down a historic church was just another ordinary, everyday sort of thing.

At their request, Annie was standing just behind them.

'You better come out with us,' Elena had told her, 'the British journalists will want to speak to you too.'

'Hi.' Elena addressed the crowd of buyers and press assembled in the small courtyard, driven out of the church by the smoke and horrible smell.

Sounding much more confident than she felt, she went on: 'Everything is under control. Yvette is fine. Luckily, her . . . his . . .' she corrected herself, 'hair was a wig. So, I'm sorry our show ended with such a drama. But we're here wanting to talk to you now about our wonderful dresses. '

There wasn't any calling out of questions, the press pack just huddled in beside the three women and took turns to ask everything they wanted to know.

After several minutes, Elena decided to leave the journalists to her mother and Annie; she broke out of the throng and headed straight towards the huddle of buyers.

Vickie Plumridge didn't waste any time; she moved straight up to Annie with the list of questions she'd already prepared.

'Hi, Annie, I'm Vickie from *Pssst!* magazine. How are you? Did you enjoy modelling in the show? How long have you and Svetlana and Elena been friends?'

Once Annie had answered these questions, gushing as much as she possibly could about her Ukrainian friends and their 'totally genius' dress line, she was hit by Vickie's more awkward line of questioning.

'So your friend Connor McCabe. He's been dropped from *The Manor* and he's not found any other work yet?' Vickie asked, in a voice just as pleasant as if she'd said something incredibly nice about Connor, instead of something incredibly rude.

'Oh, I couldn't possibly talk about Connor,' was Annie's immediate response, 'other than to tell you he's been my friend for ever and he's a fantastic guy, a really funny, really kind, fantastic person. He's just as good a friend as he is an actor,' she went on, although they hadn't spoken since his grumpy text, 'and . . .' Suddenly she remembered the unflattering front cover photo she'd seen at the airport. '. . . he's totally buff.'

Had that been *Pssst!* magazine? The thought flashed through Annie's mind. Was this woman from the magazine that was about to publish an interview with her dad?

'You often talk about your mum in interviews, Annie,' Vickie went on, 'but you never mention your dad.

Annie scrutinized Vickie more closely.

She was young, maybe twenty-five, with a sharp blond bob, thin lips and penetrating blue eyes. She was trying to make her face look friendly and kind, but the hungry nosiness behind her questions stared out from behind the thin smile.

'I've not seen or heard from my dad since I was thirteen years old,' Annie answered calmly, determined not to show how rattled she was by this question, 'so you'll understand that he's not exactly a big part of my life.'

'Oh goodness!' Vickie was pretending to look surprised, but not succeeding very well. 'So you've not heard from him . . . you've no idea where he is or what he's doing?'

'No,' Annie said firmly, but inside she felt a churn of worry. 'Do you know something about him?' she asked sharply.

Vickie immediately exclaimed: 'No! Of course not,' but she looked down at her notebook as she said it and Annie thought there was a trace of guilt about her. 'Thank you so much for your time!' Vickie added.

Vickie?

Didn't Dinah say a journalist called Vickie had phoned her?

'Hey!' Annie called out, but Vickie's back was already turned and she was stepping away quickly just as Svetlana swooped down on Annie.

'There is someone over here who is desperate to meet my Annah.'

And that was it. When Annie next looked over in search of Vickie, she had gone.

'Mmmm. I'll have to think about it and come back to you.'

If Elena heard this line once again from one more buyer, she would scream.

No one had yet committed to a single sale. No one had told her anything overwhelmingly positive. All the buyers she'd spoken to so far could at best be described as 'luke-warm' about the dresses.

All the money was gone and, so far, neither Elena nor Svetlana had made one single sale.

As she watched the buyer to whom she'd just delivered a long and impassioned pitch walk through the chain-link fence towards a waiting taxi, the young photographer she'd noticed during the show walked towards her, raised his camera and reeled off a couple of snaps.

'I think you have enough pictures,' she told him with a slightly exasperated smile.

He shook his head and, now that she was finally looking at him, took a whole load more.

'You can't have enough photos, it's impossible,' he said eventually, emerging from behind the camera. He had a square and unexpectedly handsome face.

'And you are . . . ?' Elena asked haughtily.

'Sye Westhoven, freelance photographer, working today for *Women's Wear Daily*,' he said with a light transatlantic accent.

'The website?' Elena asked, more than a touch dismissively.

'No, the magazine,' he replied, not taking his intense look from her face.

'Do you think we'll get into the magazine?' Elena was trying to hide her excitement.

'Well, what with your burning bride and your famous mother, I'd have thought the chances were . . . hmmm . . . about a hundred per cent,' he answered.

Inside Elena's clutch bag, her BlackBerry began to vibrate, so, turning away from Sye with an 'excuse me', she snapped open the bag and answered.

She didn't hear the whirr which meant he was photographing her again.

Sye pushed his straight, dirty blond hair behind his ears, scrunched up his eye to get a better look through the viewfinder and moved round to the side of Elena once again.

He liked her face. He liked it very much. He'd looked at hundreds, probably thousands of pretty faces before and usually they didn't move him a great deal because he no longer enjoyed perfection in features. He liked a face that was interesting, one full of character, just like Elena's, with its determined little frown between the eyebrows, steely cool eyes and, by contrast, the lusciously full mouth.

He tried to keep his eyes focused on the face because if he looked too long at the knockout figure in the dress beneath . . . well, then all concentration on his work threatened to be lost.

When her call was over, Elena turned to Sye again. 'Have you taken my mother's picture?' she asked, sounding very professional.

He gave a nod.

'The models?'

He nodded again.

'The woman in the red dress, over there, she's a famous TV person in Britain.'

Sye nodded again. He was looking at her with a little too much concentration for Elena's liking.

'Then I think you're all done here, aren't you?' she asked with a smile.

He nodded, lifted his camera and banged off another frame of her.

'I think that's rude!' she exclaimed.

He did it again.

'Hey!' she said.

'How old are you?' he asked. 'Because I don't think you look old enough to be co-running a dress label.'

'That's none of your business,' she snapped back, but then to her surprise, found herself asking: 'How old are you?'

'Twenty-three,' he answered back, without hesitation, 'so now you have to tell me your age.'

'No deal was made,' she informed him. 'Anyway, you look much older than twenty-three.'

'I lead a hard life,' he replied. He raised an eyebrow, challenging her to tell him her age.

When Elena said nothing, he guessed: 'I don't think you're a day over twenty-two, are you?'

'That is for me to know—'

'And for me to find out,' he answered. He was looking at her very intently again: 'I liked the dresses, but they're not very European. More American, I think. Simple, professional, American.'

Elena shrugged and made no reply to this. She was looking at him too. She took in his thick white cotton shirt, hanging from broad shoulders, efficiently rolled up at the sleeves. He wore a woven leather bracelet on his tanned wrist . . . and now she was looking at his tanned hands, pliant and capable around the camera.

She was – she realized with something of a shock – going to have to admit to herself that she had never felt so strongly and yet so inappropriately and inconveniently attracted to someone in her whole life.

Now she didn't seem to be able to stop looking at him. She couldn't help noticing all sorts of small and enticing details. He was wearing hiking boots, for goodness' sake. How uncool was that? His grey multiple-pocketed combat trousers were grubby and hung loosely from his wiry frame.

But if she let her eyes dwell on the slim hips, she was going to lose herself. She was going to start panting with want.

The want was right there at the back of her throat, drying it out, making it hard to speak to him and definitely widening her pupils like tell-tale saucers.

'Elena!' someone shouted out behind.

She turned to see Rich, Annie's cameraman, striding towards her.

'Oh, hello there.' She tried to make this sound as disinterested and professional as she could. She didn't for one moment want Sye to imagine that . . .

But Rich walked right up to her, dared to kiss her on the cheek and squeeze hard at her waist. 'Brilliant, brilliant show!' he grinned. 'I've not had the chance to tell you how much I loved it. It was sensational, it's going to be the talk of the town. And as for the TV footage – fan-bloody-tastic!'

He hadn't let go of her.

She squirmed in his grasp, wanting to get out of it as quickly as possible.

'I've spotted the woman over there from Browns in London, she's probably dying to talk to you,' Rich added and, with a little nod at Sye, he steered Elena, before she could even protest, in the direction of a very chic, very important-looking woman.

Glancing over her shoulder back at Sye, Elena saw him give her a little salute and a wink. Then he picked up his camera bag, tied a lightweight anorak round his waist and was gone.

Elena's heart sank like a stone.

Even though her head kept telling her that she could never, ever want a man who wore an anorak.

Chapter Twenty-Six

The girl from British Vogue:

Pale pink strapless chiffon (Temperly)
Black cropped jacket (vintage, Oxfam)
Black shoe-boots (Manolos from the Vogue *cupboard)*
Total est. cost: £460

'It is so hard to break through.'

'You are absolutely loving this, aren't you?' Rich asked as he trained the camera close up to Annie's face.

She just nodded and smiled. She couldn't think of anything to say, she was too busy looking and drinking in the wonderful scene. Ever since she was a teenager, Annie had searched for fashion: in shops all over London, of course, in the racks of carefully wrapped clothes which had come into The Store at the start of every season and in the preview videos of high-street collections she now religiously scanned for her TV audience. But right here, in this ornate, chandeliered and gilded room, the George V's blue ball-room, Annie finally felt as if she had reached the epicentre, the beating heart of fashion.

Svetlana, of course, had been the woman with the invitation to this glittering fashion world cocktail party. But because she wanted company, she had swept Elena, Annie, even Rich and his camera along in her wake, merely flashing a severe look and her monumental diamond necklace at the security man who had dared to raise an eyebrow at her 'entourage'.

A quick conversation with Ed had assured Annie that the sickly babies and the patched-up roof would be fine, at least until she made it home much later tonight. So for a few happy hours, Annie planned to people-watch, celebrity-spot and generally revel in the fashion buzz.

The room was packed. Waiters were struggling to break through with their trays of champagne flutes and canapés.

Every so often in the crowd, Annie would catch a glimpse of a famous face and feel the urge to go over and congratulate them on all the wonderful work she knew they'd done over the years: every careful hem, every daring new angle on a trouser leg. She felt as if she had been studying the work of these creators for so long.

'Do you think I can just go over and say hello to a designer?' Annie asked Rich. 'You don't think that would be too pushy . . . or too star-struck?'

'Go for it!' he urged her. 'Introduce yourself to Karl Lagerfeld. I just saw him over in the corner.' Rich, in typical, subtle chimpanzee fashion, pointed.

'No!' Annie moved his hand down immediately. 'I thought I'd start maybe with Ren Pearce – you know, of Pearce Fionda? He's just over there.' She moved her eyes tactfully in the direction of the London designer. 'I think I have to, I want to invite him on to the show . . . he can talk about how to look slinky.'

'Give him a whirl,' Rich urged.

'Right,' Annie decided, allowing herself another little

swig of bubbly for courage, 'but you are definitely to keep your distance,' she warned her cameraman.

'Long lens,' he assured her, 'strictly long lens.'

In the midst of the achingly fashionable crowd, Elena was deep in conversation with a girl from British *Vogue*. They were talking fabrics, next season's colours and importing costs.

'It is so hard to break through,' the girl was sympathizing; she'd heard about Elena's struggle to start up and all the things that had gone wrong with the show. Still, Elena was almost certain that Perfect Dress was going to be featured in one of the autumn editions. She was silently congratulating herself when she felt a touch on her waist.

It was very gentle, the slightest of touches; it could just have been someone brushing past in their hunt for a champagne waiter or a canapé tray, but nevertheless, Elena turned.

There right up close behind her was Sye Westhoven, just as casually dressed as he was earlier today, despite the full-on glamour of the crowd.

'Hi,' he said, 'I thought you might be here.'

'Did you?' The surprise in her voice was obvious. 'So what . . . ?' she began, and then wondered what on earth she was going to ask him, because the incredible excitement of seeing him again had made her forget.

'I don't have enough photos of you,' he told her still with that fixed, challenging, slightly amused look on his face, 'definitely not. Not nearly enough photos.' Turning to the *Vogue* girl, he said, 'Can you excuse us for a moment? There are a few extra shots I need to take . . . outside if possible?'

'I see,' the girl said and looked Sye up and down disapprovingly.

Elena understood that look. It was the kind of look she too might have given a young photographer in a wilted white shirt and grubby combats whose hair was rumpled and overgrown and who accessorized with several Nikons on brightly coloured straps.

But . . .

She certainly wasn't shooting that look at Sye. Not right now.

Elena felt Sye take hold of her hand. Wordlessly, he led her out of the thick crowd, past fabulous women in even more fabulous dresses, past pampered and powdered fashion power brokers, through white and gilded double doors and into the cool marble splendour of the hotel's lobby.

There, they didn't have to give another single word of explanation, they just turned to face each other, Elena's hand still in his, and they began, without a heartbeat of thought, to kiss.

Kiss and kiss . . . breathtakingly hungry, startling, electrifying kisses that meant only one thing, that they were just the very start of something incredibly powerful. Kisses that ached for somewhere to go.

Annie was just beginning her weave through the crowd in the direction of Ren Pearce when she suddenly felt a hand on her arm, pulling her back.

'There you are!' It was Svetlana. 'What you think of this man? I show you. He very important.' Her voice had dropped as close to a whisper as she could manage. 'Owns two fantastic shops in London, another in Paris and one in Milano and look how young he is and how handsome.'

Annie finally homed in on the man Svetlana was steering them towards. He was handsome: a dark, strong-jawed, immaculately dressed specimen. He spotted Svetlana coming and gave a smile in their direction.

'He's not homosexual, I check,' Svetlana added through the smile she had set on her face, 'and he is single. This is very, very exciting.'

'Why?' Annie hissed at her. 'You're not single . . . and neither am I.'

'Tcha!' came Svetlana's disdainful response. 'Not for us. I think he will be perfect for Elena. They meet, he buy dresses, they go out, he buy more dresses . . . Hello again,' she said warmly as the man was now within earshot. 'Dominic, meet my friend Annah Valentine who have very, very important fashion show on television in Britain. You know how important television is to the poor British people. The weather so bad they can never leave their over-priced houses . . . but you must meet my beautiful, clever daughter. She is brains behind Perfect Dress. I am just looking all round the room for her.'

Annie smiled and shook Dominic's hand. Sadly, she glanced over to see Ren Pearce move in the direction of the door, but then he was stopped by another small group of people who obviously wanted a few words with him.

If she wanted to talk to him too, she was going to have to be quick.

'Where Elena?' Svetlana snapped, searching the room with concentration now. 'You know?' She directed the question at Rich who was standing behind her shoulder with his camera.

'No,' he answered, but he did look almost guilty because he had been wondering exactly the same thing himself. Where was Elena? He had been filming her from a distance and trying to work up the courage to ask her for a drink after the party; then he'd spoken to Annie and now he'd totally lost sight of Svetlana's daughter.

'Dominic, after the party, you come up to our suite and have a drink with us. I'm sure we find Elena and you can meet her there.'

Annie, who could still feel Svetlana's hand on her arm, supposed she was included in this plan. Now she felt conflicted. On the one hand, yes, she definitely wanted to see Svetlana and Elena's suite at the George V. On the other hand, this party was due to finish at 4 p.m., which gave her almost two whole shopping hours on the wonderful streets surrounding the hotel before she had to head to the airport for her flight.

There were presents to buy for her family, but there was also that pair of shoes at Chanel. When she'd first seen them, spotlit on a pink velvet cushion in the window, she hadn't really considered them. But now she found that they were stealing into her thoughts. At totally unexpected moments she would realize, like the solution to a puzzle, how well they would fit with that pair of trousers or how amazing they would look with that particular skirt. She had already decided that she must go to the shop, she would love to look round the Chanel shop in Paris anyway . . . she would just *ask* if they had the shoes in her size. Almost certainly they wouldn't. Then the problem of whether or not to spend five hundred pounds on a pair of shoes wouldn't really come up. Would it?

'I'm just going to speak to Ren Pearce over there,' Annie blurted out, hoping Svetlana and Dominic didn't think she was being rude. 'I just have to say a quick hello. Then I promise I'm going to come right back to you.'

Annie hurried through the crowd towards the pale-blue-clad shoulders which were definitely heading at pace towards the exit now.

As soon as she was close enough, she cleared her throat and mumbled: 'Ren, hi, I'm sorry . . . I'm such a fan I just wanted to say . . .'

The shoulders turned and suddenly she was face to face with one of the most able designers to have come out of London in the last decade.

Ren smiled – and not just a polite smile, a really friendly one.

Annie felt her throat dry up a little. 'I love your dresses,' she stumbled, 'in fact, I even have one. Purple, 2003 winter collection.'

'Yeah,' Ren was nodding, 'I think I remember that.'

'I used to work at The Store,' Annie went on.

'Oh right . . . yeah, The Store' – his smile widened – 'they took my stuff from really early days.'

'Yes.' Annie smiled and was about to say that was because she'd twisted everyone's arm and begged, but then she thought that would just sound totally pompous and stupid.

'You look familiar,' Ren said next. 'Have we met before?'

'Oh no, I'd remember that . . . no . . . I do this TV show . . .' she went on hesitantly. Surely he'd not seen it? Surely he wouldn't be remotely interested in her high-street round-ups and her dressing-for-fat-bums tips and all sorts of homely bits and pieces of advice. Surely in the high and rarefied world of fashion . . .

'You're Annie Valentine!' he said all of a sudden. 'I love your show!'

'Really?' She was completely astounded, but still managed not to let the moment escape. 'Will you come on it, then? Tell us how to bring out our inner fox . . . that kind of thing?'

'Of course.' He reached into the back pocket of his jeans, brought out a little card and handed it over to her. 'Get your people to call my people,' he said, 'and tell them I already said yes.'

Chapter Twenty-Seven

Store-owner Dominic:

Pale pink shirt (Brooks Brothers)
Pale grey suit (Ralph Lauren sale)
Pink and grey tie (same)
Handmade grey shoes (small family shop in Milan)
Total est. cost: £1,300

'Beautiful . . .'

Sye's warm hand cupped Elena's face. 'I need to take you back,' he was murmuring against her lips. 'I need you to come with me to . . .'

He had a minuscule hotel room right at the end of the Porte de Clignancourt line. He was trying to imagine how he could possibly persuade this incredible girl to come there with him. He was trying to picture Elena in that terrible little room: filled with shoes, socks, empty take-away boxes, electric wires, tripods and all the other detritus of a nomad fashion photographer's life.

Elena moved her cool, smooth hand so that it was on top of his and then she turned. He had led her out of the party, but now she was going to take his hand and lead him.

Through the marble lobby they went, towards the marble staircase.

He didn't question, just thought that wherever she was leading, he would definitely, unhesitatingly follow. What was her idea? Where was she planning to take him? Was there some quiet corridor? Some little window nook she'd spotted? He burned . . . he felt as if she was leading him up the stairs by his cock and not his hand.

On the first floor, she turned down a corridor, and then, snapping open her clutch bag, she pulled out a card. As she slotted it into the door lock, he was kissing the back of her neck and whispering: 'No!' in amazement.

As she pushed open the door and his eyes fell on the overwhelming opulence of a suite at the George V, once again with feeling, he repeated: 'No . . . Oh no!'

'Oh yes!' Elena told him gleefully.

As soon as the door was closed behind them, they were pulling, tugging, fumbling and wrenching at each other's clothes.

He opened up her dress as she slid apart the buttons of his shirt and began to tug and fumble at the buckle of his belt.

Then her cool hands were on his taut stomach, feeling their way down. She so wanted him.

Oh. She so wanted him.

He was releasing her breasts from their bra cups. He was kissing her on the mouth, then on her nipples, hurrying, hurrying, hungry and starving for her.

Her damp thong was on the floor and his fingers were feeling for her, moving inside her, her fingers rubbing and touching at the very tip of his cock.

They fell down on top of the bed.

Her mother's, she had only a fleeting moment to register.

Then he was inside, pushing, arching and grasping. Pulling her hips up towards his with those pliant and capable hands.

Her head was swimming. Her stomach, her groin, her whole body was on fire; she needed to move, to writhe, to feel him all over her.

But she forced herself to open her eyes . . . and then she saw him with a moment of clarity.

She couldn't just have sex, all raw and unprotected, with some photographer guy she'd only met today, whose last name she couldn't even remember.

'Whoa!' she said firmly and put her hands on his shoulders to push him out. 'Whoa, whoa, whoa,' she insisted.

She rolled off the bed.

The dress was still over her shoulders, but it was totally open now, exposing her magnificent breasts and slim white body, almost an exact replica of the figure her mother had sported twenty-odd years ago.

Sye looked up at her from the bed with pained confusion on his face.

'It's OK,' she told him and held out her hand to him once again, 'follow me.'

After stopping to retrieve their things, she led him through the suite to her bedroom, then closed the connecting door.

'Lie on the bed,' she instructed, sounding almost a touch fierce.

Sye did as he was told.

Elena went over to the mini-bar, and then she located a small white and pink make-up bag and unzipped it.

When she returned to Sye, she waved a half-bottle of champagne at him. 'I think we should have a little drink,' she suggested, sinking down on to the bed beside him. 'Get to know each other a little better . . .' she said, looking down at his tanned body and still impressively erect penis.

She chucked a packet of condoms down so it landed on his stomach.

'Then . . .' Elena added throatily, 'we make love.'

Svetlana, with her arm threaded through Dominic's, was heading towards Annie.

Rich walked behind them, filming hard. 'I think we're finally getting an invitation upstairs,' he said as he reached her.

'OK, I already speak to everyone I need to here,' Svetlana said, dismissing the fabulous party. She had what she wanted on her arm, so now she was done with it. 'Is time to go. We go to the suite, we order champagne, Dominic place big order of dresses, I call Elena to join us . . . we have fun. No? And Dominic, Annie show the dresses on the television programme, millions of women watch the show, we are guaranteed big success.'

'Well . . .' Annie was quick to tone this down a little. 'Close to two million viewers every week. I'm very lucky.'

Glancing at her watch, Annie saw that it was already after 4 p.m. She was trying to calculate just how quickly she could get out of Svetlana's private party. Really she just wanted to take a good old nosy at the suite, capture it on film and make sure Dominic was happily settled in and ready to place a big order, then she could get out on to the streets of Paris, just to *look* at the Chanel shoes and buy treats for her family.

She was booked on a plane at 8 p.m. this evening, so there really was not one single shopping moment to lose.

Up the marble steps they went, Svetlana and Dominic charming one another, Rich busy capturing the creamy stairs, the winking crystal chandeliers, the sheer jaw-dropping extravagance of the place.

Cool as a cucumber, a Hollywood A-lister walked down the steps in the opposite direction. He gave the camera a little wave and said, 'Hi.'

Annie was too surprised to even say 'Hi' back.

'Good hotel, huh?' was Svetlana's comment. 'Everyone interesting stay here.'

Now they were at the door of the suite; Svetlana took her key card from her bag and pushed it into the slot. She turned the handle and opened the door, which slid noiselessly over the thick blue carpet.

'Wow!' Rich was the first to whisper in awe.

'Beautiful,' Dominic added.

Svetlana ushered them in. 'This my room,' she explained, holding out her hands.

Annie could feel her jaw drop. The bedroom was amazing, from the intricate tapestry on the walls to the taffeta-draped window and the dark mahogany bed piled high with toile de Jouy pillows and bedspread.

There was a crystal bowl of luscious fruit on a dark wooden side table with a little oil painting hanging on the wall behind. This was the kind of hotel room in which even the Queen would feel at home.

Once again, Annie had a sense of Svetlana's vast wealth – even if she was down to her last few million. This was what she was used to, this was what she expected. It was so, so very different from ordinary life. That was for sure.

Through the open door on the left, the sitting room was visible with its luxurious sofas and open fireplace. But Svetlana turned to the closed double doors on her right.

With one hand on each of the enamelled handles, Svetlana announced: 'This my daughter Elena's room.'

Dominic, Annie and Rich with his camera running had all come over to take a look and they were just as speechless as Svetlana when the doors were thrown open and the mostly naked, deeply entwined Elena and Sye were before them.

Elena and Sye were so busy, so captivated and so totally immersed in what they were doing that they had heard nothing of what had been going on next door.

Half-in and half-out of the bed . . . half-in and half-out of each other, Elena's eyes were closed and the back of Sye's head faced the door.

They were making all the operatic noises which indicated they were happy – no, more than happy – with what they were doing to each other.

For a split second, Svetlana was too surprised to react. She just stood there, stock still, a door knob in each hand, trying to take this in.

Who was that man? Her brain was trying to place him, but she had very little to go on, just a head of dark blond hair, a smooth tanned back and small, taut buttocks.

He had a good body. She had to grant Elena that.

Then, suddenly galvanized, Svetlana shut the door with a slam and announced to her party: 'Maybe we go drink at the bar. No?'

At the sound of the door slam, Elena's eyes snapped open.

'Was that my mother?' she asked in surprise.

Chapter Twenty-Eight

The expert saleswoman:

Navy blue skirt suit (agnès b.)
Grey satin blouse (Printemps)
Black patent heels (Kurt Geiger)
Black seamed stockings (Wolford)
Total est. cost: £670

'Ce n'est pas un desastre.'

Annie was out on the street.

At last!

She'd left Rich at the hotel bar with Dominic and the shell-shocked Svetlana. Rich said he needed more background shots of the hotel anyway. So now she was finally out, alone, on the beautiful, beautiful shopping streets of Paris.

The nude Chanel Mary Janes were on her mind, but there was something else too.

That moment . . . that moment when Svetlana had flung open the doors to Elena's room and they had all seen the couple there . . .

Annie could smile at the memory of it now. She could even feel the beginning of a small giggle form in the back of her throat, but she felt something else too. She had a feeling which almost brought tears to the back of her eyes.

Usually she forgot about it, usually it was at the very back of her mind, like defrosting the freezer or tackling the hand washing, but sometimes, for just a few moments, as when she had walked in on Elena and Sye, it bubbled up to the surface and she had to admit to herself that she missed the sex.

She *missed* the sex. Even when you'd had children before, it still came as a shock how they invaded every corner of your life and took over your body . . . maybe for ever.

Was she ever going to feel really sexy again? Was she ever going to have the time or the energy to devote a whole afternoon to being locked in the bedroom with Ed? Would she want to be? Would they end up talking about the babies? Or the building work? Or maybe have a nice anxiety-inducing chat about the mortgage?

Was there ever, ever, ever again going to be the nail-dragging, breathtaking, toe-curling want between them again?

When she'd seen Elena, eyes shut, back arched in complete and total concentration, ecstasy, Annie had not felt horror or shock. No. She'd just felt jealous and more than a little sad.

Ed used to make her feel just like that . . . but now? Now they were more like companions who brought up children together. Very loving companions, yes, but wouldn't it be better to feel like Elena just once in a while?

Annie walked along the pavement, peering every now and then into the small, beautifully set-out windows, and wondered.

What advice would she give a client? What if someone

came on to the show and said: 'I'm too tired for sex, I'm too busy and anyway, when we have sex, I feel as if I've done it all before, we're in a groove and how on earth do I get out?'

Annie couldn't help feeling that her libido was like damp kindling; no match or scented candle was going to relight it, what she needed was a can of petrol.

She was standing in front of the Chanel window now and there were the shoes, on their velvet cushion, centre stage in the spotlight. High-heeled eggshell patent leather with a T-bar strap and a black patent toecap. A Chanel classic.

She looked at the shoes and realized that right now, she felt more desire for them than she did for her own partner. She wanted to own those shoes; she wanted to possess them and make them part of her.

This wasn't exactly a good sign. She shouldn't go in. There would be another day for buying posh shoes. Right now, she would look for a children's shop and get a little present for the babies. Maybe she also had to give some thought as to how to go about feeling sexy again.

Taking a left, she found herself in a small street walking towards an underwear shop with a mannequin in the window.

The mannequin was unusually curvaceous, dressed in a black satin basque with fishnet stockings, an eye mask and cat ears.

It held her attention.

Annie knew perfectly well that she had no sexy underwear left. Well, nothing that she fitted into anyway. She had an underwear drawer full of TV-friendly control pants and saggy bras left over from breastfeeding.

If she were her own wardrobe adviser, she'd poke around in that drawer with horror and exclaim: 'What's going on in here? Have we forgotten how to look good from the inside out? If you want to feel sexy, maybe you have to dress sexy . . . just as if you want to feel powerful, you have to put on a jacket with sharp shoulders.'

A black, strapless corset? Would that make her feel more sexy? Would that make her feel more in touch with herself than she did at the moment? Or was that too obvious? Too easy an answer?

A black strapless corset would definitely make Ed feel less exhausted. That was a fact.

Annie was standing there looking at the mannequin in the window, uncertain about whether to go forwards or not, when a woman's face appeared at the shop door, smiled at her and beckoned her in.

Ha! She smiled back, always appreciative of the talents of another good shop assistant.

'*Je ne parle pas beaucoup de français,*' were her hesitant opening words as she walked through the glass door, setting off the *ting ting* of the bell above it.

'*Vous êtes anglaise, madame?*' the woman asked with a smile.

'*Oui, madame,*' Annie confirmed.

'We parlons franglais,' the woman replied with a smile.

She was a very French forty-something, beautifully turned out in a stylish navy skirt suit with red lips that exactly matched her red nails.

That was so coming back, Annie couldn't help mentally noting, the matching nails and lips, even the matching shoes and bag.

'*Oui!*' Annie agreed.

The shop was a wonderful old-fashioned store with little glass-fronted wooden drawers and several pink satin dressmaker's dummies in normal-looking sizes decked out in delicious satin and chiffon creations.

It wasn't at all slutty, but neither was it stuffy. The

atmosphere was just right for a purveyor of quality sexy smalls. No young girl in a mini-dress trying to sell you crotchless pants in size 8 and stifling her giggles when you couldn't even get your ankle through a leg hole.

'I have two babies,' Annie began.

Annie thought Madame might understand the situation perfectly if Annie began with the babies.

'*Ah! Les bébés!*' Madame smiled. '*Quel âge?*'

'*Huit mois,*' Annie said, not sure if she'd got the right number.

'*Les deux? Jumeaux?*'

'Twins,' Annie said, wondering if Madame had understood.

'*Adorables,*' Madame assured her.

'I feel so . . . *grande* . . .' Annie ventured and ran her hands over an exaggerated big belly. '*Pas* sexy,' she added.

'*Pas du tout, pas du tout.*' The woman shook her head sadly and smiled. Annie wasn't quite sure whether this meant 'not at all' or 'not at all sexy'.

Madame gestured towards the changing room with its luxurious red satin curtain and instructed: 'The clothes off.'

Once Annie had taken everything off, save a supposedly 'sculpting' thong, she stared in the mirror with distress. This was a look she'd seen her clients give themselves so many times over the years; she always rushed in to nip it in the bud, because no good came of it.

No good came of looking at yourself in the mirror and seeing only the wobbly bits, the saggy bits, the still purplish stretch marks. No good came of it at all. But here, stripped to her pants in a Parisian changing room, she felt as if she might cry. This was horrible. Now that she had released herself from the beige spandex which kept her middle permanently under control, she looked from armpit to hips like a burst blancmange.

She would have turned around to take a look at her wobbly bum too, but the curtain was pulled briskly back and the shop assistant entered armed with . . . oh, *quelle horreur*! A tape measure!

Madame met her eyes and instinctively understood the distress. Then, just as Annie would have done if she was the shop assistant here, Madame smiled encouragingly.

'*Ce n'est pas mal,*' Madame insisted, '*ce n'est pas un désastre.*'

'*Oui,*' came Annie's reply, '*c'est un catastrophe!*'

She was measured, just as efficiently and professionally as she had measured all her clients who'd been in a state of confusion about their sizes.

As the woman told her the numbers in French, Annie tried to make sense of them, her mind reeling in further horror . . . Her waist was a hundred and something? Then she realized this was centimetres. Not inches. Her only comfort came from the fact that she didn't know how to divide centimetres into inches, so she couldn't work out how bad it had got down there.

'*Attendez,*' Madame instructed and swished the curtain closed.

Annie was left alone with the mirror and her critical thoughts once more. For so many years now, she'd been in a happy place about how she looked. She'd never expected this. This deep-seated distress, especially when she was such an expert disguiser, camouflager, dresser of good points.

But having twins . . . it was fine when you were pregnant, looking like a ship in full sail, billowing with a purpose, but now, when everyone – including her – expected her body to have returned to at least something close to what it was before, she couldn't help feeling overwhelmingly disappointed.

She hadn't shifted one ounce of the baby weight. She put

her fingers round the blubber of her stomach and wobbled it with disgust. Maybe she never would. She hated exercise, despite the offers of help from Dinah, and as for all that low-carb, high-GI, de-toxing stuff . . . she could not be bothered. She was too busy and she was too tired. She ate Ed's meals in the evening and whatever she could get her hands on during the day.

The curtain swished open once again and Madame returned, her arms draped with a confection of satin, lace, chiffon, red and black.

At the first frilly pale pink bra and matching knickers held up, Annie just shook her head. She wasn't even going to bother trying that on. It was hideous; whatever kind of underwear she bought, she knew it wasn't going to be frilly.

The next suggestion from Madame was a red satin corset with black lace trim at the edges. Madame stood behind her and hook by hook, gathered Annie in.

The effect was . . . a bit too saloon girl, Annie thought, looking at herself critically. Plus, the problem with a corset was that she couldn't put it on herself, so where was the surprise element for Ed?

Annie with many English and clumsy French words, not to mention actions, tried to explain this to Madame.

'*Ah oui, ah oui . . .*' Madame agreed with much sympathetic nodding.

She handed Annie a black satin corset with ribbons over the shoulder which cleverly became ties running down each side. Annie had to raise her arms and let it slither down over her torso. The material felt smooth and cool to the touch. She busied herself tightening the ribbons on one side while Madame did the other.

When it was pulled tight, she surveyed herself in the mirror with something just slightly closer to approval.

With the supportive boning and the sweetheart neckline,

the heavy post-breastfeeding boobs looked pale and luscious, rather than huge and shapeless. The boning held in the worst of the stomach bulge and the shiny black fabric suited her skin.

Madame suggested a little black satin thong underneath the corset and a pair of fishnet stockings. This had potential, Annie couldn't help thinking. It was very *Chigaco*, the musical; maybe she'd get some tap shoes to go with it. This could be the very beginning of feeling sexy once again.

'You mus' feel good,' Madame tried to explain in English. 'You mus' like or no good.'

A black satin corset, it was a classic: the LBD of sexy underwear.

Madame disappeared from the cubicle and when she returned, she was holding multiple packets and boxes of fishnets in her hands.

'*Voilà,*' Madame instructed, handing over the boxes. '*Essayez* . . . try dem . . .' she added in shy English.

Then Annie was alone again, looking through the handful of offerings. The first pair of hold-ups . . . too long. A second was a much better fit. She went up on tiptoes in front of the mirror and strutted a little, imagining the outfit with high heels. This felt better. This felt possible.

One box, larger than the others, was different. It was a fishnet body stocking. She hadn't tried on one of those before.

Unlacing the black corset, she decided to give the body stocking a go. *Pourquoi pas?*

She laid the corset carefully down, catching sight of the price tag tied with ribbon on to the label. Expensive . . . but then it was half the price of the Chanel shoes, and Ed would probably appreciate it so much more.

Opening the packet with the body stocking, she

unravelled it and worked out that it pulled on much like a pair of tights, so she started with one foot, then the next and rolled her way slowly up, over the belly, over the boobs, then pushing both arms down into the sleeves.

The effect was startling. The mesh was fine and small, hugging tightly to her curves. The crotch was . . . open. *Bien sûr.*

Lying on the pile of things Madam had brought in was an eight-inch-wide patent and elastic belt with four buckles at the front. This must be to go with the body stocking; obviously it would act as a sort of stomach brace.

Annie buckled on the belt just as the phone in her bag began to ring.

As she answered she stood up in front of the mirror.

The belt was genius.

'Hi,' she said into the phone.

'Annie, it's Tamsin.'

'Oh, hello.' Annie felt instantly guilty, although she couldn't think of anything she was supposed to be doing for work right now. Plus she'd already told Tamsin in detail about how amazing the show footage promised to be.

'Where are you?' Tamsin asked.

Annie looked at herself in the mirror. She liked, she actually *liked* the way her boobs looked encased in the fishnet, but she thought it was probably a detail her employer could be spared.

'I am sneaking in just the tiniest bit of Parisian shopping,' she confessed.

'Is Rich with you?'

'No, I left him at Svetlana's hotel; he needed some more background shots.'

'Oh . . . but I was just thinking, if he got some footage of you shopping in Paris, maybe that would make another

215

little featurette for us. Make your trip over there extra worthwhile.'

Annie did not want Rich filming her in her new underwear, that was for sure. Maybe at the Chanel shop? But then the thought of missing her flight out tonight, or, even worse, Tamsin commanding her to stay here another night . . . No, she really had to nip this little idea in the bud. No matter how much she wanted series three.

'Tamsin, it's' – she looked at her watch – 'nearly five thirty already, everything is about to shut here and I'm going to have to come home tonight.'

And not just in order to try on this outfit with high-heeled black boots, she thought as she looked herself over almost approvingly once again.

Elena woke abruptly from the brief sleep she'd fallen into in the warm luxury of the king-sized bed and the arms of Sye.

For a moment, she couldn't recall where she was, but when she felt the arm around her, the strand of hair brush her shoulder, she remembered exactly. Everything. Every single little thing. She felt a rush of nervy excitement.

She looked down towards the floor and saw the tumble of clothes scattered about. There too was Sye's camera; alone and unguarded, the brightly coloured strap rumpled into a heap. As quietly and as carefully as she could, Elena slid from her side of the bed.

Sye stirred slightly as the pressure of her body moved from his arm, but the exertion of the past two hours, not to mention all the late nights and very early mornings of the past fortnight, meant that his sleep was deep.

Elena picked the camera up from the floor; then, wrapping a hotel robe around her, she slipped through the doors and into the suite's sitting room.

On the table she and her mother had set up as a work-space, Elena saw her phone flashing at her angrily. Although she suspected the messages would all be from her mother, she still picked it up and checked, in the hope that maybe someone, somewhere wanted to place a dress order.

But no, the four messages were all a variation on the same theme: 'Come and see me as soon as you are finished in our room. I am in the hotel bar.'

Elena removed the memory card from Sye's camera and slipped it into her laptop, then she downloaded all the photographs he had taken of her in her George V bed.

Her eye was attracted to the many frames he'd shot of her with her dress slipping from her shoulders as she sat on the rumpled bedclothes. Although the pose was sexy, it was also extremely elegant, because the dress was a sophisti-cated gumetal grey silk. There was one photo in particular that she really liked. An image like that would be great for a Perfect Dress marketing campaign.

Once the pictures were safely stored on her computer, Elena erased each and every one of them from Sye's card. Despite her very good first impressions, she kept telling herself that she didn't know him, so therefore she couldn't possibly trust him.

Elena was just slotting the cleaned-up memory card back into the camera when she heard a voice behind her.

'Tut, tut, and I thought this was the beginning of a beautiful friendship,' Sye teased.

Chapter Twenty-Nine

Ed in bed:

White T-shirt (Boden)
Boxers (present from Owen)
Thick towelling dressing gown (White Company via Annie)
Pocket contents (tissues, breadsticks, dummies)
Total est. cost: £90

'Croak . . .'

When Annie opened the front door of her family home, the first thought that struck her was how quiet it was. Then she considered the cold.

Usually, pulling open the front door meant being hit by a blast of noise, warmth and often the smell of something delicious already cooking.

It was one of Annie's favourite moments of the day. Arriving home, she could feel her shoulders relax and her face soften into a smile as she prepared to see all her favourite people.

But today the house was silent and as cold as an empty church hall.

'Guys?' Annie shouted out. 'Where are you?'

They had to be in, it was 10.30 p.m. Where else would they be?

Now Annie could hear Dave burst into a volley of barks. It was coming from upstairs.

'Guys!' Annie called out again. 'Are you upstairs?'

She dumped her bags in the hallway, stepped out of her shoes and began to head up the stairs.

Going up without shoes on turned out to be a mistake. How could she have forgotten about all the little lumps and chunks of plaster all over the place? Now that she was on the first floor, Annie decided before going in to see her family, she would just take the few extra stairs up to the attic floor to see what had really happened to the roof.

When she got there she was astonished at the damage.

The hole in the ceiling and, above it, the roof, was at least three feet square; there was a great rotten rafter dangling down dangerously and the large blue tarpaulin which had been hastily rigged up seemed to be bulging ominously with rainwater.

A big chunk of plaster had been gouged out of the wall where Al's falling hammer had struck against it with force.

Annie might have sworn, but somehow, what with having tiny children and being on TV, she'd got out of the habit, so the only words that issued from under her breath were: 'Oh. My. Good. Grief.'

'Annie?'

She heard Ed call her from their bedroom so she left the scene of the roof disaster and headed back down to the first floor.

Opening the door, she was taken aback at the scene in here as well.

Ed was in the centre of the big bed in his pyjamas look-ing utterly exhausted, and, as an added attraction, his hair was practically standing on end with the amount of dirt and dust it had accumulated in the thirty-six hours since she'd last seen him.

Lying on his chest was Minnie, who looked up at Annie, displaying a snot-caked nose. To Ed's left was Micky, already asleep, but making the wheezing, rattling snores of a baby whose lungs are full of phlegm.

On Ed's right was Dave – up on the bed! – snuggled next to Owen, who was also in pyjamas, with a remote control in each hand. These were pointed at the small TV which Annie recognized as the one from Lana's room.

It was stiflingly hot, the *two* electric heaters plugged in beside the bed had obviously been running all evening.

The bed was piled high with duvets, sleeping bags and several large cardboard pizza boxes. There was also a white polystyrene box. Coleslaw? she wondered. Well, at least they'd been eating their greens.

On the bedside table stood a cluster of empty milk bottles and . . . *unbelievable* . . . jars of baby food with the spoons still stuck inside the remaining orange goo at the bottom.

Jars? *Jars!* Ed had obviously lost it. Ed would never, ever dream of feeding his precious, pampered babies jar food unless he was at his wits' end.

The schedule . . . the baby Mozart . . . clearly things had not exactly been running to plan today.

'Hi,' Annie said gently, 'how are you all doing?'

'Great!' was Owen's enthusiastic response. 'Totally great. We've all moved in here, apart from Lana who's moved to Greta's. We've got telly, we've got pizza, it's finally warmed up. Minnie and Dad aren't too perky, but otherwise, we are great. Aren't we, Mickster? Oh . . .'

Owen could now see that his buddy had zonked out.

Annie came and sat down on the edge of the bed. She kissed Owen on the forehead; she ran a hand over Micky's head, Minnie's hot little cheeks and finally Ed's face.

'Blimey,' was her verdict, 'so is this what happens when I go away for two days? You revert to bachelorhood – go feral? And all catch a virus?'

Ed tried to say hello or make some kind of response to Annie's arrival but all that came out was a volley of coughs so sudden it made Minnie cry.

'Oh dear, oh dear, oh dear.' Annie removed her damp raincoat, flung it at a nearby chair, took Minnie from Ed's arms and realized that she'd better get busy. 'Have we got medicine for the twins?' she asked Ed. 'Have we got honey, lemon and aspirin for you? Is Mum OK? Her lights are out, otherwise I'd have gone down.'

Ed croaked back a 'Yes' to her in reply to all of these questions.

'Can we move one heater so that Owen can at least get some peace and quiet in his room?'

'Oh!' came Owen's groan. 'I don't want to go to bed.'

Another 'Yes' was croaked at her.

Annie spurred herself into a frenzy of activity. The twins' sheets were stripped and replaced. The babies were put into fresh nappies, fresh pyjamas, dosed with medicine, sponged and finally put down to sleep.

Then Annie stripped her and Ed's bed and sent Ed for a hot bath and hairwash, despite his croaks and protests.

When he finally came back into the bedroom, he was tucked in with medicine and a hot drink.

'Maybe you're just exhausted,' she told him. 'Maybe if you could just have a really, really long sleep, you'd finally wake up feeling better.' She handed him the present she'd bought for him at the airport: a pair of hi-tech travellers' earplugs. 'Wear these,' she instructed. 'When the twins wake up, I'll deal with them as quietly as I can and you sleep. OK?'

Ed was too tired to protest. In clean, ironed pyjamas, he climbed into clean, ironed bed-linen. This was like a dream. The crying had stopped, the pizza boxes were gone, the rumpled, sweaty, hairy bedclothes and sleeping bags had disappeared.

Annie had brought order, calm and quiet back with her from Paris.

She also smelled delicious.

'Did you buy new perfume?' he asked. 'Duty free?'

Annie thought of the beautiful rose-pink packaging care-fully tied and taped around the things she had bought in Paris. On the journey back, before she'd realized how bad things were at home, she'd imagined herself showering and then, when the children were asleep, treating Ed to a little fashion show of her own.

She'd not thought at all about the roof hole, the viruses and the general chaos that awaited her.

'No,' she told him, running a hand over his still damp hair, 'I bought something much, much more exciting than perfume. I think you're going to like it.'

'Mmmm . . .' Ed said, not able to raise his head or even flicker his eyelids at her. Within moments, he was fast asleep.

Annie went out of the room and into her little office because there were three calls she wanted to make before she unpacked and showered off the long day.

'C'mon, boy,' she urged Dave, who was now trotting at her heels. He was a people dog and didn't really like to be left alone for too long.

Annie's first call was to Lana.

'Hey, you,' she said as soon as her daughter answered.

'Hi, Mum, are you back?' came the reply.

'You didn't fall out with everyone at home, did you?' was Annie's first question.

'No, I just couldn't stand it there any longer. It's absolutely freezing, the babies cry all the time and Dad and Owen just want to eat pizza.'

'I'm sorry. But it's OK, I'm back and it's all going to get sorted.'

'There's a hole in the kitchen covered with tarpaulin and now there's a hole in the roof covered with tarpaulin. The builder's in hospital and . . . good luck!'

'Janucek, he'll come to the rescue,' Annie said hopefully.

'Please don't run off with Janucek,' Lana warned in a teasing voice.

'Same to you!' Annie replied. 'How's school?'

'School is fine, I am working like a slave.'

'Good! Er . . . and when are you going to come home?' Annie asked. 'Should I speak to Greta's mum? Explain to her that you're not actually moving in on a full-time basis?'

'Fix the roof and the kitchen wall, then I'll come home,' Lana promised.

Next, Annie tried to phone Connor but when she just got his voicemail, she wondered if he was screening.

'Hey, Connor, can we talk?' she began her message. 'Have you forgiven me yet? I hope so. Love you. I told Vickie from *Pssst!* magazine that you are wonderful and so much more buff than in that horrible photo on the cover.'

Now, although it was late, Annie also wanted to call her sister.

She listened to the ringing at the other end of the phone. When the voice at the other end answered, sounding so sleepy, Annie immediately apologized. 'Sorry, sorry, babes, I know it's late, but I really wanted to speak to you.'

'Annie! And you've woken me up,' came the grouchy response.

'I'm sorry,' Annie soothed, 'I'm really sorry I've not phoned you properly for days. That bloody *Pssst!* magazine say they've got an interview with our dad running next week and I don't know what we should do about that.'

'What?' Dinah sounded shocked. 'They've tracked him down?'

'I think so. I don't know, all I've read is that some sort of exclusive about our dad is coming out in the magazine.'

'Oh God, this is all my fault,' Dinah said.

'No, don't blame yourself. It's their fault. They must have realized there was a mystery and they've gone off and done a bit of research.'

'Why have we never done that research?' Dinah wondered.

'I don't know. Maybe we've never been that interested. I don't care about him. I wish he was dead, to be honest. That would be much more convenient.'

'Annie!' Dinah scolded, but then she was a much more tender-hearted person. 'We'll talk about this tomorrow. How was Paris?' she asked with a yawn.

'It was completely, unbelievably hectic. But I was in a hotel for a night, so I got to sleep for one whole, unbroken, seven-hour stretch. It was incredible.'

'But how was Paris? The shows? Exciting? Glamorous?'

'Oh yeah, all of those,' Annie answered with sarcasm. 'Didn't you know that the fashion world is just one long fun-fest?'

'Models? Catwalks? Amazing outfits? Photographers? C'mon, I want details.' Dinah was interested now.

So Annie told her sister a little bit about the Svetlana and

Elena fiasco and how they were still waiting for their first order.

'How did Ed cope?' Dinah asked, once she'd heard enough about Paris.

'Ah . . .' Annie wasn't quite sure where to begin. 'Well, he's had a lot on. The builder made a great hole in the roof—'

'As well as the kitchen?' Dinah interrupted.

'Yeah. Then he fell off his ladder and broke his wrist.'

'No!'

'The twins have a virus or something and Ed looks like he hasn't slept for forty-eight hours and has been living off pizza all that time.'

'He's exhausted,' Dinah pointed out. 'If he was a new mum, this would be the point where friends would intervene with a nanny, a spa weekend and a hairdressing voucher.'

'Yeah, and someone would step in and sleep-train the babies. It's totally impossible. They wake up every two hours!' Annie added.

'You need to look after him a bit.'

'I know,' Annie agreed, 'or he's never going to find out about all the nice underwear I bought in Paris. It'll just be stuck in its little pink carrier bag for ever.'

'Have you got a busy day tomorrow?' Dinah wondered.

'Tomorrow, no, I get to stay at home tomorrow, for good behaviour. I was going to let Ed sleep all day, look after the babies and rally the remaining builders.'

'Why don't I come round about twelve-ish?' Dinah began. 'Billie's going to a friend's house after school. I won't have to be home till about six, so you and Ed can have a long afternoon . . .'

'Of what?' Annie wondered.

'Of you taking him out, of you looking after him, of you

getting him out of the house and reminding him who he is again!' Dinah exclaimed. 'He needs you to do all the things you did for me when Billie was a baby and I was slightly out of my mind.'

Chapter Thirty

Elena back at her desk:

Pale grey skirt suit (Reiss)
Zebra-striped pumps (Hobbs)
Pencil holding hair up (Rymans)
Unwashed white T-shirt (stolen from Sye)
Total est. cost: £290

'We just have to turn interest into sales.'

Svetlana and Elena had only been in their office for seven and a half minutes, but already the atmosphere was turning sour.

Elena had powered up her computer; Svetlana had switched on her phone. It was painfully obvious that neither of them had any good news.

The entire £75,000 start-up budget had been blown and there was not yet a single dress order to show for it.

Not a single buyer who attended the Paris show had placed an order and Elena had a horrible, sinking feeling that not one of them would.

No one had said enough nice things about the dresses, no

one had even asked questions about the fabrics, the care of the fabrics, delivery times – any of the things that would have marked them out as genuinely interested.

'This is all your fault,' Svetlana said, tension getting the better of her as she stalked up and down the office in her heels. She hadn't considered the possibility of failure. She really, honestly hadn't considered it. When Svetlana did things, she succeeded. Her life was – well, OK, apart from the divorces – one long, glittering success.

'Where were you during the cocktail party when every-one important was there?' Svetlana began nastily. 'Where were you when I want to introduce you to a man who owns four European boutiques?'

Elena didn't like the sound of this.

'You were upstairs in our hotel room, legs behind your ears with some nobody!' Svetlana spat out.

'It wasn't like that,' Elena began, blushing furiously. 'I spoke to lots of people at the party. I think we have a slot in British *Vogue*—'

'We have no buyers!' Svetlana exclaimed. 'We have a factory in Hong Kong waiting for our call, expecting us to place an order today! And not one single buyer. We have not even sold one dress. We are worse than a shop assistant. Igor always say making *first* million is the hardest . . .' she added mournfully.

'We have to turn interest into sales,' Elena said, wanting the conversation to turn from Sye as quickly as possible.

Once she had said goodbye to Sye and gone to meet her mother in the George V bar, things had not exactly gone smoothly. The store-owner, Dominic, whom her mother was so keen to impress, had already left and Svetlana had delivered a blistering lecture about the importance of selecting the right man at the right time and how Elena had failed on both fronts.

The mood in the little Mayfair office was not helped by the arrival of two newspapers, both of which carried photos of the show, but instead of featuring the dresses, they showed Yvette, the burning wig and veil, plus some fun-poking captions.

The coverage was not flattering and it was hardly going to bring a stampede of offers to the door.

'Come on,' Elena said as calmly and as encouragingly as she could, desperate to ignore her mother's disapproval, 'we will divide the buyers who were there between us and we will phone them all. Be positive. Be persuasive.'

Up until now, Svetlana had imagined that selling dresses was going to be just as much fun as buying them. But now that she looked at the list of twenty-two names Elena was handing over to her, she wasn't so sure.

This was going to be hard.

'Use your charm,' Elena instructed, 'you are a very, very charming woman.'

'You are a little too charming yourself,' Svetlana warned, but with a slight smile.

'The first person to make a sale . . .' Elena began, but wasn't sure what to offer as a prize.

'Gets champagne with lunch,' Svetlana finished the sentence.

'You think we make a sale before lunch?' Elena asked with a smile.

'Ya! I make first sale before ten a.m.,' Svetlana threw down the challenge as she began punching the first number into her phone.

As Svetlana watched Elena reaching for her phone too, she tried to forget about the bedroom scene in the hotel.

Really, she admired her daughter greatly. The girl had grown up in relative poverty in Ukraine, knowing nothing about either of her parents. She'd been clever at school and won herself a university scholarship. Only then had she tracked down her mother and come over to London, arriving in Mayfair totally unannounced.

Svetlana had somehow hoped that by paying a small monthly allowance, she was allowed to forget about this Ukrainian girl conceived by mistake. Then Elena had arrived on her doorstep, real and angry, marked not just with her mother's beauty, but also her determination. For several weeks, Elena had stayed with Annie because Svetlana couldn't bear to tell anyone about her.

But then the dam had burst, the truth had come out and . . . really, it was surprising how well it was all working out.

Svetlana felt as if she was growing closer to her daughter by the day. For the first time in her life, she felt as if she had an ally. A friend. A true friend, who knew her for what she really was and still cared about her.

Svetlana admired Elena's determination to build a business not just for herself, but for her mother too. If Elena had been anything like her mother was at her age, she wouldn't have wasted one moment trying to set up Perfect Dress, she would have been out every night at all the best places looking for the very best men to provide for her.

Deep down, Svetlana couldn't break the habit of looking for the best men, although she'd stopped looking for new men for herself, she was now looking on Elena's behalf.

But . . . Svetlana had to admit, she had been divorced three times and each one of those rich men had tried to leave her penniless. Maybe Elena's idea of building a business and a fortune all of her own was a better one.

'Hi, Tina?' Elena began her call. 'Did you have a good journey back from Paris?' She tried to sound just as relaxed and as friendly as she possibly could.

'Oh, we are buzzing with orders,' she fibbed in response

to the question about how sales were going. 'Everyone is just so impressed with how glamorous but how wearable and totally washable the dresses are. So recessionista ... everyone wants an outfit that can just totally multi-task.'

Then she listened patiently to the objections Tina was raising to placing an order. 'I know, I know, the climate is difficult, no doubt about that. Why don't you just try a handful? If they don't sell, send them back to us. You know I am so confident they will sell, I'll give them to you at a thirty per cent discount off cost price.' Elena glanced over at her mother and wondered if this was cheating. Maybe they wouldn't be drinking champagne at lunch. She scribbled '30% off cost on first six' on a piece of paper and waved it at her mother.

'Oh, wait ...' she heard Svetlana say, 'I think, just for today, just for you, I'm allowed to make a special opening offer ...'

Tina promised to phone her right back, which wasn't a great result, but despite her protests, Elena wasn't able to stop Tina hanging up.

Just as the line went dead, an email dropped into Elena's in-box.

Her heart skipping as she saw who it was from, she clicked to open and a huge photo filled the screen.

It was the photo of her with the silky grey dress slithering from her shoulder as she smouldered at Sye. Her blond hair was draped over part of her face and even Elena, her own harshest critic, recognized that she looked great. The picture came with a caption which read: 'You're stuck in my hard-drive. This pic running in *Women's Wear Daily*, if you agree. In London next week, please say you can make time to see me. Sye'.

While Elena digested the shock that she hadn't managed to wipe all the photos from his camera, her mother leaned over her shoulder and took a look at the image.

'That is very beautiful,' she said. 'The photographer take it?'

'Yes. I didn't want him to keep any pictures, I thought I cleaned them all from his camera,' Elena replied.

'Tcha,' Svetlana tutted, 'is there worse to come? More naked?'

'I don't think so,' Elena replied.

'This photo is very good, very elegant-sexy. We could use it for Perfect Dress.'

'He's given this to *Women's Wear Daily*, he wants my permission for them to use it.'

'Say yes!' Svetlana insisted. 'It's very good.'

'But I don't want to be the model,' Elena protested. 'I want to be the boss!'

'You are the figurehead. Think of Diane von Furstenburg, she always wear her dress, everyone know her, she just as famous as her dress. Say yes!' Svetlana insisted. 'Hey, I make sale. Six dresses at thirty per cent discount. Good idea of yours. Now, unless you make sale, I drink all the champagne.'

As Elena picked up the phone and punched in the second number on her list, she couldn't take the smile off her face: Sye was coming to London and he wanted her to make time!

Chapter Thirty-One

Babysitter Dinah:

Flowery flared skirt (Toast sale)
Navy leggings (Miss Selfridge)
Patent ballet pumps (same)
Navy scoop-neck top (M&S)
Olive corduroy jacket (Cancer Research shop)
Brown leather crossbody bag (Camden market)
Chunky orange beads (same)
Total est. cost: £110

'Please go away!'

Ed slept right through the twins' three night-time awakenings. He totally missed the 7 a.m. alarm clock, breakfast and even Owen's noisy departure for school. Annie hoovered up plaster dust in the hallway, changed and dressed the twins, then took them out for a walk along with the dog. Returning at 11.30 a.m., she found Ed still asleep.

But when Dinah rang the doorbell at noon, setting off first the dog and then the babies, the noise finally travelled through the duvet over Ed's head, past the earplugs in his ears and the exhaustion in his brain. Like a swimmer underwater pushing himself up towards the surface, Ed finally willed himself awake.

As he struggled to open his eyes, he felt unusually light-headed and optimistic. He remembered having the most fantastic, vivid dreams: a jumble of deep red curtains, deep red sofas, guitar music, faces from school . . . He couldn't remember many details, but it had been wonderful, so involved and intricate and far away. So very far away from greasy pizza boxes and a hole in the roof and the endless crying and whining of unhappy babies.

At the thought of the babies, his eyes finally opened properly. He lifted his head and looked at the empty bed beside him, the empty cots. Then he took a look at the alarm clock.

When he saw that it was after twelve, he refused to believe it. He shook the clock to establish whether or not it was working and watched the hand travel along for at least ten seconds before he had to accept that it really was 12.06 and he had been asleep for . . . thirteen hours.

No wonder he felt so amazingly good!

He got out of bed, wrapped his dressing gown around him and decided to venture out into the house to see what was going on.

When he padded into the sitting room, he felt almost disappointed at the calm and peaceful scene before him. The twins were playing happily on the floor; Annie was on the sofa drinking coffee with Dinah sitting beside her.

'Hi,' Ed said cheerfully in a voice that still croaked slightly. 'I've had a bit of a lie-in.'

'About time!' Dinah told him. 'Hello there!' she added with a grin.

'How do you feel?' Annie asked.

'Much, much better,' Ed confirmed, 'just husky, but

nothing hurts. So you're managing?' he asked Annie. 'Do I need to walk the dog?'

Dave, lying on an armchair, lifted his head up hopefully at these words.

'No, I've done that. Just go upstairs and dress nicely,' she instructed. 'We're going to go out for a little bit, just you and me. For the first time since . . . ummm . . . before Christmas? Dinah is going to babysit.'

'Really?' Ed looked concerned. 'Are they OK though? Are they over whatever was bothering them?

Annie nodded in reply to both of these questions. And Ed could see for himself that the twins looked much happier today.

'But do you think they'll be OK with Dinah?' As soon as the question was out of his mouth, he realized how anxious he sounded, but he hadn't been away from the twins for more than an hour or two since they'd been born.

Anxious attachment.

It was a condition; he'd read about it, but it hadn't occurred to him before that he might be suffering from it.

Annie smiled at him. 'Babes,' she said gently, 'this is Dinah we're talking about. She may be looking a little art-school today—'

'Ha!' Dinah protested.

'But she is a brilliant mummy and a baby-worshipper,' Annie added.

Dinah smiled reassuringly at Ed. 'Please go away,' she urged. 'I can't wait to be in charge of them. Look at them, they are totally scrumptious.' To prove her point, she knelt down on the play mat and tickled Micky till he giggled.

'Anyway, Dave will be here,' Dinah pointed out, 'he'll keep me right.'

Ed had to laugh at this because there was a touch of the serious watchman about Dave. He was always looking at the twins anxiously and barking when he thought they were heading off in the wrong direction.

'What about the roof?' Ed asked, thinking of another reason why he should stay at home. 'As Al was getting into the ambulance, he promised me someone would be round.'

'Janucek is coming first thing tomorrow morning—' Annie began.

'Oooh,' Dinah couldn't help interrupting; she'd heard about this phenomenon. 'Can I come round then too?'

'Shhhh!' Annie said. 'Let's not make Ed jealous.' Then, casually, she added: 'Janucek and a couple of guys are going to replace the rotten bit of beam, put back the tiles and replaster the ceiling.'

'No cupola?' Ed sounded surprised.

'No, babes. No cupola,' Annie confirmed. She'd finally admitted to herself that this was an expense too far. The cupola was going to be returned and the roof was going to be repaired as simply as possible.

'Hallelujah!' Ed exclaimed, hugging Annie round the waist. 'Swedish windows?' he risked asking.

'On a lorry, making their way to the ferry port right now . . . allegedly.'

'This is the best news I've heard all year!'

'Go get dressed,' she instructed him again. 'I'll make the plans for this afternoon. You are just to relax, rest and be pampered.'

'Be pampered?' he asked cautiously. 'You've not booked me in for some dodgy beauty treatment or something? Annie, I'm not going to spend the afternoon getting my fingernails filed or mud masks or . . .' His face took on a look of deep anxiety '. . . my buttocks waxed?'

Annie and Dinah both cracked with laughter at this suggestion.

'Go! Dress!' Annie exclaimed and threw a sofa cushion at him for emphasis.

'Now this is nice,' Ed had to agree, 'this is very nice.'

He was sitting opposite Annie in a cosy little booth in one of the achingly stylish restaurants in Selfridges department store. They were both eating something complicated and apparently 'Asian-fusion'. Ed was drinking jasmine tea and Annie had a glass of a khaki-green and slimy concoction in front of her which was apparently 'very cleansing'.

'Remember me?' Annie asked Ed with a smile.

'Remember *me*?' he answered back.

'Remember you? I can barely recognize you,' she told him with a wink.

Their first stop, once they had slipped away from home and their twins, had been a fancy gentleman's barber where Ed's curly brown mop had been washed, combed, snipped and styled, before he'd been laid back in the chair for a hot towel shave. Even his eyebrows and all those unruly bits of man hair – nostrils, ears, back of the neck – had been dealt with as Annie flicked through magazines, answered emails on her phone and tried not to let work interfere at least for a few hours.

'So what else have you got planned for me?' Ed wondered. 'We seem to be in a big shop,' he pointed out. 'I can't think why you'd take me to a big shop – unless maybe you had shopping on your mind.' He bumped his knee against hers playfully.

'Do you remember the first time we went shopping together?' she asked him, bumping right back.

He nodded with a smile in response to this. It was years ago now, before they were even together. Long, long before the joint house purchase and any thought of babies, Annie had helped him to pick out an interview outfit, just as 'a friend', doing him a favour.

And Ed, who'd only started to have an idea of just how much he liked her, had found every moment of her careful personal shopping attention totally, totally intoxicating.

'I've not been shopping—' he began.

'For ages,' she told him. 'I know. Your white T-shirts are all stained and yellowy, there are dodgy crotch holes in two of your jeans and, baby, you know I love you, but most of the time you look like an unmade bed.'

There was something of a pause before Ed said: 'Oh.'

'No, it's not that bad,' Annie corrected herself quickly.

'An unmade bed?' he repeated. 'But the babies love me,' he added, pulling a face.

'Yeah, and they'll be the only ones if you don't make just a teeny, weeny bit of effort. Ed, you're going to be back at work in four months,' she reminded him.

'Oh!' He seemed surprised at this news. 'Four months?'

Annie nodded, and then she watched as Ed's eyes slid down towards his plate.

'I was wondering about extending my leave a bit,' he began, 'I'm really enjoying being with them and I don't know if I'm ready to go back yet.'

At first Annie wasn't sure how to react to this. She felt a little surprised and yet she understood. Ed was suffering full-on new-parent guilt at the thought of leaving his precious children with someone else.

He couldn't yet work out how he was going to marry his new life with all the other parts of his old life that had been paused for parenthood.

But this was just where Annie was going to have to help him. 'You have to go back to work, babes,' she said gently.

'No I don't,' he told her, 'you earn loads of money, more

than enough for the two of us. I can always get back into teaching when the babies are older. I don't *have* to go back.'

Annie was nodding and for a few moments, she didn't say anything.

Then she told him: 'You have to go back and the sooner, the better.'

'Why?' he asked. She didn't like the almost pleading tone in his voice.

'Because you need the other parts of your life back,' she said. 'You absolutely loved your job and the kids you taught. And we have to be practical, babes, what if I don't get signed up for the next series?' At these words she felt the clench in the pit of her stomach. 'I need you to have a job, Lana and Owen get discounted fees because of your job and the school won't hold it open for you for ever.

'Our babies are going to be absolutely fine,' she went on, 'like all the other children of hard-working parents. We'll find someone fantastic to look after them. You can rush home after school to be with them every day, you can have them all to yourself every single day of the school holidays and seriously, Ed, you have to do it. I know I have to push you here. Because . . .'

She stopped, wondering how to say the next things carefully. How did she tell her lovely man that he'd got just a little over-domesticated? That he was in danger of becoming a bit boring, because he'd forgotten about his friends and how to have fun. How could she point out that, on the admittedly rarer moments when she did feel attracted to him, he was generally too tired to do anything about it?

'You used to have a cool life,' she reminded him. 'You were a pretty cool guy. You had us, but you also had school and you had so much music going on. I've not seen you pick up a guitar for ages. You never buy any new music, and when did you last go to a concert? You used to go all the time. Twice a week? And what about camping? You've been promising Owen a camping trip as soon as the weather warms up, but now I don't know if I can trust you to go on it!

'Ed, you're – in the nicest way possible – a bit over-focused. There are other people in this family, not just the babies . . . I mean Lana moved out while I was away and I'm not sure if you even noticed!'

'Annie!' Ed protested. 'It was one night, the house was freezing . . .' He trailed off and took a drink from his cup.

Annie put her lips to her straw and sipped up some of the wheatgrass / aloe vera sludge. She couldn't help pulling a face.

'We should have had wine,' Ed said, trying not to laugh at her expression, 'then we'd have been much more friendly.'

Annie stuck her hand up in the air: 'Hello there,' she said to the passing waitress, 'we'd like two *large* glasses of white wine, please.'

'After we've drunk those, I've got a much better idea than shopping,' Ed offered.

'I'm not sure I realized how much of an Abba fan you really were,' Ed said, having to lean right in against Annie's ear to be heard over the strains of 'Knowing Me, Knowing You'.

'I'd forgotten,' Annie told him, realizing with some horror that she had just drained her third large glass of wine that afternoon. 'Oooh oooh oooh oooh oh oooh . . .' She couldn't help joining in the chorus.

He'd led her out of Selfridges and up and around several side streets to a tiny traditional pub, deadly quiet post-lunch hour. They'd been drinking wine and playing cheesy tunes on the jukebox for nearly two hours now.

All sorts of songs Ed had forgotten how much he loved

had been playing, alternating with the entire Abba back catalogue.

' "I Had A Dream" . . . listen to this,' Annie insisted, 'this is brilliant!'

Finally she'd had the chance to tell him all about her Paris adventures. Yvette singing 'Super Trouper' had inspired the first foray into the available Abba selection and now Annie couldn't stop.

They were snuggled together in a dark corner, arms around each other, stopping every once in a while to kiss. It was so unusual to be alone together, more than a little tipsy, on a weekday afternoon . . .

'This is nice,' he told her. 'I haven't had you all to myself for ages.'

'You haven't wanted to,' she reminded him. 'You've been too wrapped up with the little people. Even I'm jealous of how much time you spend with those babies and I'm their mummy!'

'I've been very, very tired,' Ed told her. 'I'm not sure I even realized how tired I've been.'

'I know.' Up against his ear Annie whispered the words: 'The babies need their own room. They'll sleep better, we'll sleep better . . . we'll all feel better.'

'I know,' Ed whispered back. 'It just makes me feel sad.'

'Why?' Annie wondered.

'Because they're growing up. They're not so tiny any more,' he replied.

Annie would have quite liked to giggle at him, he was so sweet.

Instead, she slid her hands down under the waistband of his chinos and promised: 'I brought a few things back from Paris just to cheer you up, but you only get to see them when the babies have moved out!'

'Really?' He kissed her neck fondly. 'Why don't we—'

'Oh no,' she interrupted him, 'you're not going to ask me the big question again?' She moved her head away from his.

'Shhhh,' he reassured her. 'I understand,' he said, although he wasn't quite sure if he did, but he outlined his new plan: 'I'm not going to ask again until I know you're ready to say yes.'

Chapter Thirty-Two

Minnie's morning wear:

Pink Babygro (Mothercare)
Striped cashmere cardie (Brora)
Large beige blob (old banana)
Total est. cost: £85

'Waaaaah!'

The trill of her mobile woke Annie from a deep sleep. Groggily, she raised her head and looked around the room, trying to locate the phone.

The bedroom looked so different. There were no cots, no babies . . . and down there on the floor was still the tumble of French lingerie which had been peeled off in a serious hurry last night.

The underwear had definitely been appreciated to the full. It may have been a romantic night, but it had still been an interrupted night. The babies, in their new room, had slept fitfully.

Annie pushed back the duvet and got out of bed. Spotting the phone on the floor, she picked it up to answer and saw two things: it was 8.20 a.m. and it was Tamsin calling.

'Hi,' Annie answered, stifling a yawn.

'Oh, I'm not too early, am I?' Tamsin asked.

'Not usually, but this morning, it's strangely quiet,' Annie replied. 'They were up so many times in the night they're probably sleeping it off.' As she talked, she headed out of the bedroom and towards the tiny room next door where the twins had been installed. 'So what's up?' she asked.

'I've just got into the office to find an angry letter on my desk from some camping company. Do you know anything about this?'

'Uh oh!'

In a rush Annie remembered about the camping company, their phone call and her promise to sort something out. Then there was the fact that she had ... er ... forgotten.

'What does it say?' Annie asked.

'In a nutshell: they've been trying to get their things back and unless you return their stuff to them, in its original condition, or feature it on the show, they're going to take legal action. As publicly as possible. Do you know anything about this?' Tamsin asked.

Annie could hear voices coming from the other side of the twins' bedroom door. She pushed it open gently and was surprised to see Owen sitting on the floor as he read Micky a story. Minnie was still asleep in glorious pinkness in her cot.

Sweet. Annie couldn't help thinking to herself. But she closed the door again because she had to concentrate on this horrible problem.

'Annie? Do you know what these people are talking about or is this some kind of mix-up?' Tamsin asked.

With a sigh of regret, Annie replied: 'No, I know . . . well, I know something about it, but I'm sorry, I went to Paris and I forgot.'

'Oh dear,' was Tamsin's response.

When Annie had tidied up the bedroom on her return, the two thick sleeping bags on the bed had caught her attention. She hadn't seen them before and they were so new that they still had labels attached to their zips . . . that's when the penny had dropped.

The camping company that had delivered equipment to her home address had obviously been acting on Owen's orders. But she'd not had a chance to speak to Owen since then.

She took the phone downstairs, so she couldn't be over-heard.

'I think it was my son who ordered the camping gear,' she told Tamsin. 'I've not spoken to him yet.'

It was Tamsin's turn to sigh now: 'OK,' she said, 'well, these things happen. Why don't I just phone the company, tell them it's all been a mistake, we'll return the stuff to them in perfect condition and ordeal over.'

Perfect condition? Well, the sleeping bags had looked OK, but then she'd not exactly checked for baby snot with a magnifying glass, had she?

'Look, Owen's up, he's just next door. Why don't I go and ask him about it, then I'll call you straight back?' Annie suggested.

As soon as she'd hung up the call, she headed back to the twins' new room.

'Owen?' she asked, pushing open the door. 'All the stuff you got from Everest Camping . . . ?'

Owen looked up at her with an expression of guilty surprise on his face.

'It has to go back. Today,' Annie went on. 'In perfect

condition. And then we'll have to have a talk about how out of order you were.'

Owen, still with Micky in his lap, began with an: 'Errr . . .' This was followed by: 'How do you know about it?'

'Well, Owen,' Annie said with more than a hint of exasperation, 'when camping companies hand over hundreds of pounds' worth of equipment for free, they usually like to know when it's going to be featured on the programme. They take an interest, you could say.'

'Errr . . .'

Micky put up his arms to show that he wanted to be with Mummy now and Minnie's eyes opened at the exact same moment as her mouth: 'Waaaaaaah,' she called out.

Annie loaded herself up with the two babies, then she looked Owen straight in the face. 'Well? You do still have all the stuff, don't you? I saw the sleeping bags in the bedroom. What else did you get?'

'Ermmm . . . we've used some of it. To keep us warm, you know, because it's been so cold.'

'I think the bags might be OK; at least you've left the labels on them.'

'Yeah, but I might have sold the stove.'

'Sold it?'

'Mmmm. On eBay.'

'What on earth did you do that for?'

'I didn't think we needed it.'

'Well, no, but it belongs to someone else.'

'I didn't think about that. I've used the hiking boots . . . and so has Milo. He's used his,' Owen blurted out.

'Oh, good grief!'

Owen hung his head and looked very sorry, which was why Annie didn't have the heart to feel annoyed.

'Owen,' she sighed, 'please don't do this again. Is there

anything else I should know about that you've ordered in my name?'

Owen was quiet for a moment; he had to think. After some hesitation, he decided it would probably be best to be honest: 'I might have asked a guitar company for a look at a sample product or two.'

'Owen!' Annie exclaimed.

'But I'm sure it's not too late to cancel, nothing's due to arrive till next week. Then I just need to make sure that Milo hasn't—'

'OWEN!' Annie exclaimed, much more loudly this time.

'Tamsin?'

Annie had woken Ed, handed over babies, cross-examined first Owen and then Milo and was now back on the phone.

'OK, here's the thing,' Annie began. 'I think I've had a good idea. You know my joke about hillwalking in heels?'

'Uh oh.' Tamsin sounded wary.

'Lots of viewers have been in touch about that, haven't they? Daring me?'

'Lots? Yes, I think you could say four thousand emails is quite a lot.'

'Well, what if I did do a hillwalk in heels? We could do it for charity, and we'd be able to feature—'

'Some of the Everest equipment your son no longer has in perfect condition?' Tamsin ended the question herself, understanding the situation perfectly.

'You've got to admit it's an idea.'

'Why not just pay Everest for the equipment?' Tamsin suggested.

'Yeah, well, but they're still not going to be happy with me though, are they? They're always going to think I ordered those things for myself with no intention of paying or putting them on the show.'

'But, Annie, you will actually have to wear three-inch heels, carry a handbag and go up a hill.'

'Yeah!' Annie said, not sure what all the fuss was about.

'Well, if you think it's going to be too easy . . . why not persuade Svetlana to come with you? Maybe you can both carry handbags, wear dresses and coats and look . . . what were your words again? Look just as if you're off to lunch at The Store.' Tamsin was definitely warming to the theme now.

'Deal,' Annie said, sure Svetlana would come just to show off her Perfect Dress.

'Uh oh!' Ed had come into the room and caught the tail end of her conversation. 'What have you agreed to now?' he asked anxiously. 'Please tell me you're not flying to New York for fashion fortnight or maybe Alaska for Eskimo clothes week? What have you just said you'll do?'

'Oh, it's just the hillwalking-in-heels thing,' Annie replied casually. 'I've said I'll hillwalk in three-inch heels, carrying a handbag. No big deal. I'm sure it will be fine.'

Ed, who had been camping every summer since he was three, who led the school's Snowdonia hillwalking expedition every year, who really knew just what hill-walking and tenting out in the open was all about, turned to her with his mouth wide open in astonishment.

Chapter Thirty-Three

Tamsin on set:

Dark denim pencil skirt (Boden)
Cowl-necked purple cashmere sweater (Crumpet)
Heeled slouchy black boots (Miu Miu)
Total est. cost: £690

'It's absolutely bloody brilliant!'

'Bonjour, mes chéris!' Annie gave the line the best French accent she could manage and smiled welcomingly into the camera lens. 'Today we are doing French lessons. No, don't turn off! No chanting your verbs or learning your numbers, I'm talking about lessons in French style. I've been in Paris for the shows . . . I know,' she confided with a wink, 'how exciting was that! You are going to find out all about it next week, I promise, but right now I'm going to bring you French style lesson number one: coat, bag, shoes – CBS – easy to remember.'

Annie then walked towards the area of the studio where several rails, mannequins and shelves had been decked out with a delicious selection of coats, macs, handbags, boots and shoes.

'Every one of the glamorous French women I watched strolling about the boulevards wore a lovely coat, good shoes and carried a beautiful bag. Even if they were just wearing jeans and a T-shirt underneath, they looked chic, chic, chic!' Annie explained. 'And nothing has to be designer, just good quality . . . investment quality.'

She picked out several of the items in different price ranges and extolled their virtues.

'Now, two friends of mine are going to show you how the CBS makeover works. Before . . .' Annie held out two photographs.

'Just tilt them forward,' Bob instructed from behind the camera. 'Too much glare.'

'This is Jane, looking not at all French, but just you wait,' Annie said of the first photo. At the end of their first, unusual meeting, Annie had promised paracetamol-toting Jane that when she was feeling better, they would shop together and Jane would appear on the show. Annie had been delighted to keep her promise.

'This is our very own Amelia,' Annie said, holding up the second picture. 'She's going to show us how to rock a raincoat.'

'And cut,' the director instructed. 'Are they ready yet?' he called over to the wardrobe girl.

'Yes, all set to go on,' came the reply.

Bob and his camera switched positions, the lighting was adjusted and Annie's powder and lipstick were touched up.

'Ready to roll,' the director instructed and Jane came out first.

Because Annie had been at her, she looked the best she possibly could. Hair styled, make-up nice, flattering black boots and a slim-cut black coat. The slouchy bag over her shoulder and the big statement scarf were perfect Annie-inspired touches.

She looked beautifully put-together, but in a normal, attainable way. Annie always liked to use ordinary people on the show because models . . . well, they looked good in any old thing; plus, they cost money.

Annie winked at Jane to encourage her to smile and got a nervy grin in return.

'Fabulous,' Annie told her, 'all set to café-hop on the Left Bank.'

Annie put a calming hand on Jane's arm to reassure her and talked the audience who would be watching through Jane's outfit.

Then out came Amelia in pale raincoat, shiny boots and scrumptious bag.

'Where is Amelia's bag from?' Tamsin wanted to know as soon as filming on the segment was over. 'I wasn't paying attention and I want it now!'

'Oooh, I didn't know you were our audience today,' Annie said, surprised to see her boss. 'Coccinelle, if you must know.'

'You know I like to spy on you in secret,' Tamsin teased. 'Make sure you're just as good when I'm not there. No, I'm meeting someone else over here this afternoon, but, Annie, I have to tell you, the footage from Paris has been edited and it's absolutely bloody brilliant! Elena in tears, Svetlana running about in a panic, the old French lady is genius, the tranny . . . honestly, it's a shame to run it on a half-hour TV slot, it's like a film,' Tamsin enthused.

'Really?'

'Really.' Tamsin put a hand on Annie's shoulder. 'It's ratings gold. And the Oxfam hillwalk is shaping up nicely; it could be our way to end the series,' she added.

'Oxfam?' Annie asked Tamsin. 'Are you not supposed to tell me about stuff like that?'

'Another big idea,' Tamsin answered. 'We'll go on

location – Scotland, I think. We've not done a show up there yet. We'll get viewers to sponsor you online and we donate the money to Oxfam. You're going to do the hillwalk with a proper mountaineer who will wear Everest Camping's anorak and hiking boots. And we would like Svetlana to come with you. I mean, that would be fantastic: the two ladies who lunch versus the mountain guide.'

Annie could see the obvious enthusiasm in Tamsin's face. She understood that this was going to be great TV. But for the first time she felt just a little nervous about the idea of really, properly hillwalking in heels.

Ed had already warned her that what she planned was dangerous and anyway, her husband, the lovely, adventurous, just ever so slightly reckless Roddy – he'd gone hillwalking one fine weekend and he'd never come back.

'Do you know how my husband Roddy died?' Annie suddenly found herself asking Tamsin.

Tamsin looked at her with surprise. 'No . . .' she began, but her mind was working; maybe the details were coming back to her.

'He was hillwalking on a stag weekend, he fell and hit his head. Brain haemorrhage.' Annie stopped there, not wanting to add any further details.

Those terrible days spent in intensive care with Roddy on life support . . . the details were stored in a part of her mind that she tried not to access too often.

'Hillwalking?' Tamsin repeated to Annie. 'Oh no.'

For a moment there was silence between them.

'I've been a bit too flippant about this . . .' Annie admitted.

'Well . . . no . . . I mean . . . you could raise some awareness there, maybe . . . the possible dangers.' Tamsin was thinking out loud.

'You're thinking about the publicity angle, aren't you?' Annie couldn't help asking Tamsin.

'No, no, don't be silly,' Tamsin began, but then admitted: 'Yes, of course I am. Publicity is good, Annie, there are still Myleene rumbles.'

'*Pssst!* magazine have got an interview with my long-lost dad in their next edition,' Annie remembered.

'Have they? How are we going to respond to that?'

'Dunno,' was Annie's honest answer. 'Maybe we should wait and see what he says – if they really have it. They might just have bumped into someone in a bar who said they had a drink with him once.'

'What a colourful life you lead,' Tamsin said.

'So, hillwalking in heels. What's your plan?' Annie wondered.

'I'm not expecting you to scale Ben Nevis,' Tamsin assured her. 'Amelia's been speaking to a very enthusiastic guide. Plus, what do you think of the idea of using a little digital video recorder yourself? To give it a very home-made, video diary kind of feel? I mean, if we send you up with Rich or Bob in tow, then everyone knows you have a film crew with you, so there's no risk, no element of danger.'

'What kind of danger am I supposed to be in?' Annie exclaimed. 'The only risk I'm prepared to run is twisting my ankle. That's it. I don't want to fall off a bloomin' mountain!'

As soon as the car had pulled up outside her house after work, Annie knew she wanted to go and see her mum before she got embroiled with all the other members of her family.

She walked down the garden path towards the basement entrance and rang the bell. Fern opened the door just moments later.

'Hello, there you are!' were Fern's words of greeting.

'Come on in and have some wine with me. I'm having a great day.'

'Oh good,' Annie said, landing a kiss on her mum's cheek. 'What've you been up to today then? Burning all your library books in the middle of the bedroom? Gardening in your pyjamas?' she joked, only because that was how their relationship had always been; Annie had always been allowed to tease her mum.

'W-what?' Fern turned towards her, looking all hazy and lost. 'Library books? Do I have library books?'

When Annie looked back at her in distress, not knowing what to say, a grin split Fern's face and she said: 'Gotcha!'

'Mum!' Annie told her off. 'Don't do that! Don't ever do that!'

'Sit,' Fern instructed Annie as they came into the little sitting room. 'I'll get the glasses and whatnot. I have a plan, Annie, I'm very excited! And I'm feeling good, darlin', I think the pills are working.'

'Well, they did say it would take time,' Annie called after her as she disappeared out of the room.

When Fern came back, she poured them each a small glass of white wine then settled herself down on the chair opposite Annie's.

She looked unusually cheerful, which made Annie nervous. What was coming next?

'I've spent the afternoon getting Ed to look things up for me on the internet.'

That was sweet, 'look things up', as if the internet were some sort of library or glorified phone book.

'And?' Annie asked.

'I'm going to go home,' Fern announced, 'and I'm moving a toy-boy in with me.'

'What?' Annie spluttered, sending wine rushing off in all sorts of dangerous directions.

Fern just laughed. 'I'm serious,' she said, 'I've found a student who's going to come and live with me. Help with the gardening and the cleaning and make sure I don't get up to anything bizarre. He's studying nursing at the college in town.'

'He? But who is this person?' Annie demanded. 'This is scary! He could be an axe-murderer!'

'Stefano, from Chile. We're going to meet him, me and Ed, but his references are excellent. This is all my idea, Annie, by the way. You can't blame Ed for any of it. So, Stefano gets free accommodation and I get free help. It's going to work out perfectly.'

Reaching over to touch her daughter on the hand, Fern added: 'I have to go home, darlin'. I keep telling you that. I have to find a way to get home and I think this is the way. You can put me wherever you like when I've lost it,' she added, shooting her daughter the cheerful smile which was meant to cover up the great sorrow behind these words, 'but for now, I want to be in my own home. I've stabilized, Annie, I know it. I feel fine. The doctor hoped this would happen.'

Before Annie could make any reply, or could think of anything sensible to say, there was another ring at the door.

'Are you expecting anyone?' Annie asked.

'No. Must be Ed, wondering where you've got to.'

'I'll go,' Annie said, jumping up.

'No, no,' Fern insisted, 'sit, drink . . . enjoy another three seconds of spare time.'

'No, I'll go!' Annie protested.

Although she made it to the door first, she could hear her mother following on right behind her.

She turned the Yale lock, opened up and saw a leathery-skinned man of about sixty standing in front of her. He had a head of thick grey hair, cut short, and a weather-beaten face with a map of deep-set wrinkles running from his eyes. Dressed in a slouchy navy jacket and a pair of jeans, he was short but very upright, almost standing to attention. Somehow, to Annie, he looked as if he should be wearing a cap. He almost seemed to be missing some kind of headgear.

'Hello. I'm looking for Fern Mitchell,' were his first words.

'She's right here,' Annie replied, gesturing for her mother to come forward.

'Are you Annie?' the man asked just as Fern got to the door.

'Yes,' Annie replied with surprise. 'Have we met before?'

At this, the man shook his head slowly, cast his eyes down to the hands clasped tightly in front of him and said: 'Oh dear, oh dear . . .'

Fern was standing beside Annie now and as she laid eyes on the man at the door, her hand flew up to her chest: 'Oh my good gracious!' she said with real shock.

Annie looked at her mother, then back at the man.

She didn't know why, but she could feel the hairs rise up on the back of her neck.

'*Good gracious!*' Fern repeated.

Annie looked at the man very closely, scrutinizing the eyes beyond the crinkles and the mouth slightly upturned in a smile, which looked deeply apologetic.

'Mick,' Fern's mother said much more calmly now, 'I think you'd better come in.'

The man gave a nod and Annie felt both her eyes and her mouth widen in horror.

Mick?

Mick!

As far as Annie knew there had only ever been one Mick in Fern's life.

Could this really be him? No. Surely not.

Mick was long gone, had not been heard from in years and years. Mick was not expected to ever return again . . .

Chapter Thirty-Four

Totally sexy Sye:

White cotton button-down shirt (Brooks Brothers)
Beige multi-pocketed cargos (Patagonia)
Leather bracelet (Mom)
Multi-coloured fabric bracelets (a special ex)
Hiking boots (Hi-Tec)
Total est. cost: £210

'All yours, baby . . .'

In a cosy booth in an old-fashioned pub in Kensington, a very good-looking couple had forgotten all about the drinks on the table in front of them.

The blond girl had both her arms wrapped around the slim waist of the slightly scruffily dressed guy beside her. The guy, kissing her probingly on the mouth, wished only that there was somewhere more private where they could wrap their legs around each other too.

'Sye?' Elena asked when she finally broke the kiss off and came up for air. 'You can use the photo you took. I'll sign the form.'

Sye's green-brown eyes were fixed on hers. He didn't think he'd ever, ever felt more attracted to anyone in his whole life.

'Aha,' he murmured, just wanting the kissing to carry on again.

He was thinking about the logistics: he was staying on a fold-down sofa with a friend who had small children. There was no taking Elena back there. From what he could understand about her situation, she was living with her mother and stepfather, plus more children. So male visitors weren't exactly going to be welcomed there either, were they?

He was wondering if they could get a hotel room. But in Kensington? His eyes watered at the thought of how much that might cost.

'But then can I keep the photo after *Women's Wear Daily* has published it? Can it be mine?' Elena was asking him.

'Yeah,' he told her, 'you sign a release form for me, then I'll sign the rights over to you . . . so that when you've dumped me and made the photo into a billboard, twenty-four feet by twelve, I won't be able to claim a penny. Is that your plan?' he asked, kissing her neck.

'Yeah!' she teased. 'How did you guess?'

It wasn't a billboard she had in mind – well, not yet anyway, she just wanted to own that photo in case she needed an advertising shot.

'Happens all the time. Gorgeous but ruthless young businesswomen seduce photographers and steal all their copyrights,' Sye said.

'Poor, poor you,' Elena replied with a throaty giggle. 'How long are you in London?' she added, her lips pressed right up against his ear, which seemed to call every hair from the top of his neck to the base of his spine to attention.

'Two days,' he told her. 'And I have lots of work to do . . . unfortunately.'

'Are you working tonight?'

'Not until eight thirty,' he told her, hoping she was going to suggest where they could go to be alone together.

'Then we go to hotel,' she said, scrunching up the fabric of his shirt in her hand, because the thought of ripping it off was uppermost in her mind.

'I'm not sure if I can afford a hotel round here.' He wanted to warn her straightaway.

'No, I know somewhere . . . friend of friend . . .' she added, with something of a dark look.

Sye felt another surge of desire. There was so much to know about her, so much to find out. He didn't doubt for a moment that it was all intriguing.

'Let's go now,' he said, wrapping her hand in his, wanting to pull her away from the table and go immediately to wherever it was they were going.

'But first we need to sign,' Elena said, all business sense not quite forgotten. 'Later, we forget . . . or maybe fall out.'

Sye shook his head at the idea of arguing with her. 'I don't think so.'

Elena, head tilted flirtatiously, handed him a pen, and then from her mock-croc handbag she also brought out a form.

'You sign this to say photo is mine,' she insisted.

Sye reached down to the largest flap pocket on his trousers and brought out a rolled-up sheet of paper.

'Model release form,' he explained.

They exchanged papers, Elena found another pen and signed hers. Sye read over his typed sheets carefully, pushing his hair thoughtfully from his face.

For a moment his hand hovered over the page and she felt a little flutter of worry. Maybe he wasn't going to sign.

But then the pen hit the page and he signed with a flourish: 'All yours, baby. You're worth it. Perfect Dress is going to be big, better believe me.' He smiled at her and winked, delighted that he knew something about this that she didn't know yet. But she would. She was going to find out very soon.

'Now . . .' He rolled up his form, tucked it into his pocket and handed Elena hers, together with her pen. 'Formalities over, I think we should go to your friend's hotel and be very, very informal.'

Elena took the silver pen between her fingers. Sye leaned back, untucked his shirt and lifted it just far enough to reveal a glimpse of taut, tanned stomach. 'Could you sign just here as well?' he asked, pointing down to the gap between waistband and shirt.

'Oh yeah.' Elena smiled foxily at him and, reaching down with her pen, she too used the words: 'All yours, baby.'

Harry, home from work, had padded all over the four floors of Svetlana's Mayfair mansion in a bid to find his wife.

He'd seen Maria and the boys, who were very busy with their whole bedtime routine upstairs in the attic rooms.

Maria had been rubbing Michael dry with an enormous white towel as Petrov, in blue and white striped pyjamas, brushed his teeth.

'Mrs Roscoff downstairs, in the study, still working,' Maria had informed him with a shrug of her shoulders, as if she couldn't understand what all this working silliness was about. She still fully expected it to come to an end just like the other fads Svetlana had adopted and then abandoned: the all-raw diet, golf lessons, learning Arabic and so on.

'Mrs Roscoff?' Harry repeated with a smile. 'You know you are the only person who calls her that.'

'Is her name!' Maria said with some indignation. 'And you much nicer husband than last one.'

'Thank you,' Harry told her. 'Boys, I'll be up in ten minutes to read to you.'

This news produced two cheeky little grins, which Harry found exceptionally rewarding.

Entering the chic little study room all the way back down the stairs in the basement, Harry saw that Svetlana was sitting at the desk in front of the computer. Her back was to him and she was deep in conversation.

He couldn't resist the temptation of tiptoeing up from behind and wrapping his arms lovingly around her.

Unfortunately, this made her scream with fright. Mid phone call. 'Aaaargh!' she shrieked and dropped her handset.

She turned to see what was attacking her and when she saw her husband, she pulled a furious face at him.

Not exactly the welcome he'd been expecting.

'I'm busy,' she hissed. 'Very, very important call.'

'Sorry!' he whispered back and took several steps away from her, hoping she would finish soon.

Svetlana retrieved the handset and put it back up to her ear.

'Sorry, sorry . . . I just . . . ummm . . . spill my coffee . . . No, nothing serious. So? What do you think of our offer?'

Now Svetlana had to take a little breath and be quiet.

She had to wait. There was nothing more she could say and nothing more she could do.

She had the head buyer of Bloomingdale's in New York on the other end of the line. So far, Elena and Svetlana had sold a total of forty dresses in the UK. But this woman on the line from Bloomingdale's was wanting to buy fifty.

All in one single order. Provided she got a good price.

Svetlana felt the enormous pressure of making a good decision without her business partner. She wanted to do very, very well and go some way towards making up for the terrible disaster she had caused with Patrizio.

Bloomingdale's! Svetlana knew this was a great store to start in New York. From Bloomingdale's the American invasion of Perfect Dress could begin.

'What about your advertising campaign?' the buyer was asking. 'I take it you have an image we can use? For posters? Maybe even billboards?'

'Oh yes,' Svetlana answered without hesitation; in front of her on the computer screen was the breathtaking photo of Elena with the silvery-grey dress sliding from her shoulder. 'I have a fabulous image, I send it to you right now.' With that she attached the photo to an email and hit send.

'I'm going to say yes,' the buyer said. 'Congratulations, you've got yourself a deal.'

'Fantastic,' Svetlana breathed down the line. 'But how did you hear about the dresses?' she had to ask. 'Did my partner Elena contact you?'

'No, as a matter of fact I saw photos from the show. My son is a photographer, he was the one who liked the dresses so much and flagged them up to me.'

'And who is your son?' Svetlana asked, trying to remember some of the photographers she'd met on the day of the disaster.

'Sye Westhoven,' came the reply.

Chapter Thirty-Five

Mick at the door:

Thick blue cotton trousers (ship's chandler)
Blue cotton reefer jacket (same)
White shirt (tailor in Hong Kong)
Rubber-soled boots (Dr Martens)
Total est. cost: £120

'How are you doing?'

'*Come in?*' Annie hissed at her mother. 'Well, I don't think he can just come in!'

She stood sentry at the doorway to her mother's flat, one arm holding the door jamb, a barrier against this man.

'No, it's OK,' Fern said calmly, 'let him in.'

'No!' Annie insisted. 'He can't just turn up here and walk in.'

'Yes, I'm going to let him in.'

Annie turned and glared at her mother.

'Annie!' Fern said, glaring straight back.

Mick cleared his throat. 'Should I come back another time?' he suggested.

'Why didn't you phone? Or email? Or, you know . . .' Annie floundered, 'look us up on Facebook or something? I mean you can't just appear on our doorstep like this. I think you should make an appointment and . . . and right now you should go away!' She tried hard to sound as angry as she possibly could to disguise the turmoil in her mind.

She *was* angry; she was outraged, in fact. How dare this man just turn up without any warning? What was he trying to do? Shock them into some sort of forgiveness? He was a louse. A useless husband and a useless dad, who'd not been any good to any of them: his wife or his three daughters.

They'd kicked him out back then and they should just kick him out again, right now.

They should.

But despite her fury, Annie could feel all sorts of questions bubbling up in her mind. Where had he been for all these years? What had he been doing? Had he missed them? Had he even thought of them? What was bringing him back now? Was there something he wanted to tell them? Had he spoken to that magazine? Was he ill? Was he dying? Was he sorry?

Was he sorry? That question jammed in her mind.

Was he sorry that he'd been such a bad husband and bad father?

When Annie thought of how great Roddy had been with his children and how much effort Ed was putting in, her contempt for this man inflated again and she just wanted to slam the door in his face.

'Annie,' Fern said gently at her shoulder, 'let Mick come in.'

There was a calmness to Fern's voice that Annie found almost shocking. She looked at her mother and wondered for a minute if she was clouding over, but Fern looked totally alert and normal.

Finally, Annie stood back and watched as Mick came in through the door.

He held out his arms to Fern, and Fern, to Annie's horror, allowed herself to be hugged.

'How are you doing?' Mick asked Fern kindly.

'Oh, holding up. You must know how it is at our age.'

Mick gave a little laugh at this.

'Annie,' Mick held out his hand for Annie to shake, 'I'm pleased to meet you. It's been a long, long time. Too long, I know.'

Annie considered for a moment, then stuck her hand out stiffly. She certainly wasn't going to let him hug or kiss her. He didn't deserve that privilege.

'Tea, Mick?' Fern asked as she led them back into the sitting room. 'Or something stronger?'

'Oh, I brought something for the occasion . . .' he answered and lifted up the bag in his hand.

A few moments of awkward silence were filled with Mick searching through his shoulder bag and then bringing out an expensive-looking bottle and holding it up for approval.

'Madeira,' he said.

Annie insisted on going for the glasses because she didn't want to be left alone with him. She also wanted a break from scanning the brown, wrinkled face, looking for traces of the man she only so vaguely remembered.

The way memories were rising up to the surface of her mind was making her feel uncomfortable. There were unhappy memories of listening to her parents row but perhaps more unsettling were the happy memories, which Annie realized she had worked so hard to repress.

No one really gets over the disappointment of their darling dad turning out to be a big fat fraud: someone who makes your mum cry and cry, someone who doesn't come back for weeks, then months on end, someone who is finally sent away and doesn't make any effort to return . . . or even keep in touch.

He could have been dead! They could have been dead! And he wouldn't have known and he obviously wouldn't have cared, otherwise he might have made some tiny effort to keep in touch.

'How did you find us?' Annie demanded as she came back into the room with the glasses and watched Mick extract the cork from the Madeira bottle. 'Is this because I'm on TV now? Is this something to do with that magazine tracking you down?'

'What?' Fern turned to Annie. 'Why didn't I know anything about that?'

'Well, I don't know much about it myself,' Annie replied.

'I have seen you on television,' Mick admitted. 'I didn't know your new surname, but I had a feeling it might be you. Then a journalist tracked down someone I know, he put her on to me . . . I asked her for your address. I thought I should speak to you before you read about me.'

'You've cut it fine,' Annie exclaimed. 'Doesn't the piece come out in a day or two?'

Mick gave his apologetic smile once again. 'This has been a difficult decision,' he said. 'I kept changing my mind.'

'What have you told the journalist?' Fern asked with concern.

'Not a great deal,' was Mick's reply.

'So are you back in Britain, Mick? Or is the ship just in port? Sit . . .' Fern instructed and Mick perched himself on the edge of the armchair. Fern also sat down, but Annie busied herself with the pouring of two small glasses of Madeira.

She didn't want to join them.

As she handed the glasses out, she saw that her hands were shaking.

'Well, I'm thinking about retiring,' Mick began, 'from the full-time malarkey anyway. So I'm looking into maybe buying a place. Essex – that's where we always wanted to go, wasn't it?' He risked a smile. 'A bit of countryside, but not too far from the ol' smoke.'

Annie recognized his voice, she realized. But it had been so long since she'd heard him it was almost like listening to the dead speak.

'I live in Essex,' Fern said.

'Clever girl,' Mick told her.

'I'm just here temporarily,' Fern added. 'So you're going to retire?'

'Yeah, I think so, I've put a bit of money away—'

'That doesn't sound like you,' Fern said with a laugh.

'No . . .' Mick had to say.

For several moments they looked at their glasses, at each other, and didn't say anything.

It felt almost comfortable, Annie couldn't help thinking. How on earth could they be sitting there feeling comfortable? Fern was smiling, as if she was finding it amusing.

'So where have you been all this time then?' Annie heard herself snap.

'Working . . . travelling . . . living . . .' Mick replied slowly. 'Regretting some of my worst decisions.'

Annie didn't say anything; she just let his words hang in the air.

There was a rap on the front door. Annie's family was probably looking for her and she suddenly felt panicked about whether to let them in or not.

Did she want them to meet Mick? Instinctively, she felt *no*. She wanted to protect them from his callousness, his ability to walk away so easily from those he was supposed to be closest to.

There was another rap; then the door opened and Ed was in the doorway with a twin on each arm.

'Annie?' he asked, catching sight of her with her mother and this strange man in the sitting room. 'I saw you arriving and I just wondered if you were going to come and see us soon. Hope I'm not interrupting.'

'Ed . . .' Annie turned her face towards him and suddenly felt as if she wanted to cry.

He saw the look and hurried over to her. 'Are you OK? Is everything OK?'

To Annie, it all seemed too ridiculous, but she blurted out: 'Ed, meet my dad. Dad, meet—'

There was another silence. Annie found that her throat had closed up and she couldn't continue. Wordlessly, Annie held out her hands for her babies and Ed passed over Minnie.

Fern intervened. 'Hello, Ed, love, we've just had a bit of a shock here. This is my ex-husband, Mick Mitchell. He's just turned up out of the blue. He's Annie, Nic and Dinah's father.'

For a moment, Ed just stared as Mick got to his feet, said hello and offered his hand.

Ed moved Micky round to his left arm so he could shake the hand that was offered.

'So are these your children then, Annie?' Mick asked. 'They look very like you when you were . . .' He tailed off.

Annie felt relieved that he hadn't used the word grand-children. She didn't feel he was entitled to use that word. He'd done nothing to earn it.

'These are my two youngest,' she answered stiffly, 'my older children are upstairs.'

As no invitation to meet them followed, the room fell silent and awkward again.

Ed stood close to Annie, understanding that she needed him to be right beside her, supporting her and protecting her.

'Fern, I have something else for you,' Mick began. He started to pat down the pockets of his jacket to relocate whatever it was.

'Oh,' Fern said, taking a little sip from her glass and wondering what on earth was going to come next.

Mick finally found the relevant pocket and brought out a small velvet bag.

With a lurch of her stomach, Annie realized at once what this was. She could see the astonishment written across her mother's face as well.

'This is yours,' Mick said, handing the pouch over to Fern. 'I'm sorry I've had it for so long. I always meant to return it to you, but I never seemed to find . . . er . . .' He cleared his throat. '. . . the right moment.'

Fern took the pouch from him, loosened the drawstring at the top and pulled out a beautiful, heavy gold bracelet. It was woven into a chunky chain pattern and as Fern wrapped it tenderly around her wrist, Annie could see the obvious quality of the piece.

'Oh . . .' was all Fern could manage as she fastened the bracelet into place. 'Oh, I've spent so long . . . I've wondered where this was for all this time. I hoped so much I would have it again.' She brought her wrist up to her face to look at the bracelet more closely. 'My freckly old arm looks just like I remember Mum's! Thank you, Mick. Thank you so much!' She gave Mick a smile much more kind, warm and generous than he deserved.

'He's just returning what was yours,' Annie pointed out angrily. 'If he hadn't taken it in the first place, you wouldn't have missed it for all these years! So you were finally able to get it back from the pawnshop, were you?

I've never heard of any pawnshop keeping anything for twenty-five years.'

'I've had it for a while,' Mick had to admit sheepishly.

'Mum isn't well,' Annie blurted out. 'She forgets things, she gets confused. She's spent entire days recently looking for that bracelet because she remembers that it's missing but she can't remember why.'

'I'm very sorry, Fern,' Mick offered.

'I'm just glad to have it back,' Fern said with a contented smile that Annie wanted her to wipe off. Why was she being like this? Why wasn't she much, much more angry with him?

Mick turned to Ed, hoping to move the conversation away from the bracelet. 'So what are these little people called?'

'This is Minnie, short for Minette and this is Micky—'

'Short for Michael, just like Mick,' Mick jumped in, smiling with obvious pleasure.

Annie could have kicked him.

'Ed's dad was called Michael too,' Annie pointed out. 'He was a lovely family man and Ed always wanted to name his son after him. Your name is an unfortunate coincidence,' she added.

Mick's eyes were cast down. 'Well, yes, I can see that would have been awkward. Your husband wanting to use the name and you wanting to use anything but . . .'

'Not really,' Annie told him defiantly. 'I'd so nearly for-gotten about you that I didn't think it would matter. And Ed is not my husband. I had a husband but . . . oh never mind!'

Now Annie could feel tears choking the back of her throat and stinging behind her eyes. She was just so furious with this stupid man. He'd missed whole chunks of her life. Huge things had happened since she was thirteen.

Wouldn't it have been wonderful to have had a great dad by her side through some of those times? Someone to talk her through teenagehood from a dad perspective. Someone to teach her how to drive, or help her pick out her first car. That was the kind of thing dads were good at.

An elderly uncle of Fern's had walked Annie down the aisle towards Roddy, not her dad. And when she had buried Roddy, she should have had a great, strong dad standing right beside her, someone whom she could have leaned against in her terrible grief.

Instead this stupid, bloody man had never had the courage to stand by them or learn anything about fathering.

'Mum isn't well,' Annie blurted out, 'you really can't stay.' She took the glass from his hand. 'I think we'd all prefer it if you just went away. If you want to talk to us again, we'll give you the number and you can . . . make an appointment.'

She bent her head to scribble a phone number on to a piece of paper, biting her lip hard to stop the scalding tears from spilling out. There was no way she was going to let this stranger see her cry.

Chapter Thirty-Six

Roadtrip Lana:

Skinny black top (Dorothy Perkins)
Skinny black jeans (Diesel)
Dark green tunic top (Auntie Dinah)
Black lace-up baseball boots (Converse)
Total est. cost: £90

'I will have to KILL you!'

' "We're all going on a summer holiday, no more working for a week or two . . ." ' Owen sang loudly for about the fifty-seventh time from his seat in the back of the Sharan.

Lana was staring out of the window. She didn't think she could take it any more, not one more verse, not one more time, not one more bloody note. 'OWEN!' she shrieked. 'If you don't stop singing, I will have to KILL you!'

'But if I don't keep singing, the babies will cry again,' Owen pointed out.

No one could take any more of that: two babies bawling in unison as the Sharan lumbered up the road mile after mile.

This was their ninth hour of Sharan travel and tempers were fraying. No, make that tempers had frayed, snapped, been repaired and were fraying and snapping all over again.

' "We're all going on a summer holiday . . ." ' Owen started up again. Lana jammed her fingers furiously into her ears.

She'd not asked to come on some stupid trip to stupid Scotland anyway. No one had asked her. She'd just been told: pack your bag, pack your books, there's a three-day trip to Scotland coming up . . . it's a treat! It's a holiday, oh and Mum – what a surprise! – has got to do some filming while we're there.

Wasn't it bad enough that everyone in her class had had to read the interview with her mother's long-lost sailor dad in *Pssst!* magazine last week? Now Lana was being dragged up to Scotland along with all her revision. Fingers pushed hard into her ears, she looked out of the window at the damp green scenery passing by the window. Trees, hills, trees, hills, more trees, more hills . . . some bloody exciting place this was.

Annie's phone burst into life. 'Stop singing for a minute,' she instructed Owen as she picked it up.

'Dinah!' she exclaimed on answering. 'No, I'm not driving, Ed's driving, so we might die any moment now. Have you just come back from Mum's?'

'Yeah, everything's going really well,' Dinah assured her. 'How is she?'

'She's fine, she's really fine. Normal, Annie, with just the odd little senior moment, and I'm really liking Stefano. And apparently Mick is taking her out to lunch tomorrow.'

The noise Annie made on hearing this could only be called a harrumph.

'They're talking about having a sort of family

get-together. He wants to meet you again, me and my family and Nic, of course.'

Their older sister Nic had been kept fully up to speed about the return of Mick and, just like Annie, she had many reservations.

Dinah and Fern were the tender-hearted family members who seemed a little too ready to give Mick the benefit of the doubt.

'He's getting on,' Dinah reminded Annie, 'I think he just wants to make some reconnection with us before . . . it's too late.'

'Ha! Just like he said in the magazine. It is too late,' Annie said sternly, 'he should just have stayed away.'

'Where are you?' Dinah asked.

'On the west coast of Scotland with just another thirty minutes to go, Ed promises.' She looked over to the driver's seat where Ed nodded at her more in hope than with firm conviction. 'If he's not right, there's probably going to be a mutiny,' Annie added, casting a glance towards the back of the car, where the babies looked grumpy, Lana looked furious and even Owen's usual cheeriness seemed to be wearing thin.

'And what are you doing up there?' Dinah asked, struggling to remember.

'A bit of filming and lots of lovely family time,' Annie answered, hoping she would get away with this.

'This hasn't got anything to do with the jokes you made on TV about hillwalking in heels, has it?' Dinah asked suspiciously. When there was no immediate reply from Annie, she went on: 'You're not actually going to do it, are you?'

'Don't worry about me, girl, we're going to have a proper guide with us and we're only going for a short, glorified walk . . .' Annie tried to reassure her sister. 'It's really about having a bit of family time.'

She didn't like the way Ed looked as if he was trying to suppress a laugh.

'We?' Dinah asked. 'Who else is doing the walk with you? Not the crazy Russian lady? Things always seem to go completely haywire whenever she's around.'

'Yeah, Svetlana, and she's Ukrainian,' Annie countered. 'It'll be fine,' she said down a line which was beginning to break up.

'I'm losing you,' Annie called.

'Welcome to the wilderness,' Ed announced, 'your mobile cannot help you now.'

Set well back from the narrow road, in front of a dense green forest, the cabin rose in an elegant triangle from the luscious lawn before it. Built of dark wooden planks, with an enormous triangular glass window at the front, it looked surprisingly sleek and stylish.

'Good old Tamsin,' Annie said as the Sharan turned down the grassy driveway towards the cabin. 'She wouldn't let us slum it.'

It took almost forty-five minutes to fully unpack the Sharan. There were clothes, there were shoes, there were hiking things, then baby beds, baby seats, baby plates, baby cups, baby bottles, followed by Lana's book bags, then all of Owen's hiking and generally-mucking-about-outdoors equipment.

Also, of course, there were the Everest things which the mountaineer was going to wear and sing the praises of: a special pair of hiking boots, an anorak, longjohns and waterpoof trousers.

As Ed, Owen and Lana humped things back and forth from the car to the house, Annie sat outside on the lawn watching her twins crawl joyfully about the grass, delighted to finally be free.

Minnie crawled a good 10 feet or so away from Annie; then she stopped and carefully raised herself up on her knees and looked back, just checking, to make sure she was still within range of Mummy.

'Hello, Min!' Annie cooed and gave a wave. Minnie lifted her hand into the air and turned it several times with a bubbling giggle.

Micky stopped crawling and sat down with a thud on his big, padded nappy-bottom. After several attempts, he managed to get hold of the buttercup he was aiming for, plucked it and, after a moment of examination, stuffed it into his mouth.

Annie leaped up from the bench and went over to extract the buttercup. Then Minnie nosedived into a deep clump of grass and began to wail for rescue.

Now Annie had a baby under each arm and she decided she would sit down on the grass with them to guard against further disasters. No sooner had she sat down and released the babies than she felt a tiny prick on her face, quickly followed by another, then one on her hand and one on her neck.

'Ouch!' she exclaimed, smacking against the pain on her hand. The high-pitched whine in her ear told her that she and probably the babies were being eaten alive.

'How's it going?' Ed shouted from the cabin door.

'Mosquitoes!' she shouted back.

'You'll have to come in anyway,' he called. 'The twins need food and you have to get Owen to explain to you how your camera works!'

Annie groaned to herself. She was a TV personality who needed her thirteen-year-old son to talk her through the basics of making a video diary. It was embarrassing. Totally embarrassing.

*

'So here I am in the Scottish Highlands, miles from civiliz-ation, watching you have an outfit crisis,' Ed teased as Annie fussed in front of the dressing-table mirror in their bedroom the following morning. 'This is surreal. The only things it's safe to wear out there are hiking boots, an anorak and—'

'A mosquito net!' Annie snarled. 'Look at those' – she had two enormous zit-like eruptions on her face – 'some turbo-charged, burly, porridge-eating mosquito gave me those. No amount of concealer is going to hide them. They're so itchy!'

'They're called midges,' Ed said helpfully as he saved Micky from diving head-first off the bed. 'Scottish mosquitoes are called midges. And you look lovely,' he approved.

'You always say that!' she huffed.

'Because you always look lovely,' Ed soothed.

Annie, in her full 'ladies who lunch' hiking outfit, tried to look herself over in the tiny mirror. From the selection of high-end outfits she'd crammed into the back of the Sharan, she'd chosen a beautiful silk dress, ivory-coloured with big red poppies strewn across it. Then came a snappy trenchcoat worn with the sleeves pushed up and the collar turned high. On her feet were an ever-so-slightly cheating pair of red high heels. They were just under three inches, very comfortable, well worn and, most importantly of all, they had a chunky rubber sole. When she stepped into the shoes, her sense of confidence returned. These were old favourites. She felt totally at home in them and suddenly the possibility of managing a hillwalk in high heels didn't seem so remote.

She picked up the soft red bag she'd selected and slung it over her shoulder.

'Ah, a shoulder bag,' came Ed's comment. 'Good idea.'

'Why?'

'You'll need your hands free.'

'Why?' she asked again.

'To break your fall,' he replied with a wink.

'Ed?' Annie walked over to the bed and sat down. 'You would tell me, wouldn't you, if this was going to be totally stupid, or dangerous? I mean . . . I know accidents can happen.'

Ed, one hand on Micky, put his other arm around her.

'It's up to you,' he said finally. 'Only bite off what you can chew out there. Even if you only manage ten minutes, that's probably all the footage they'll use anyway.'

'Ten minutes!' Annie protested. 'I'm being sponsored by the mile. Anything less than two miles is going to be total and utter humiliation.'

'Don't do anything silly,' Ed warned. 'If you feel it's too high or too steep or too difficult, give up!' Putting his forehead against hers, he added: 'It's about time you got it into your stubborn little head that not everything can just somehow be willed into the way Annie wants it.'

'I don't think that. Ed . . .' She let out a long sigh before breaking the news: 'I might not get signed up to do the next series.'

'Of course you will!' he replied. 'The show's doing great . . . isn't it?'

'Yes, but they think it might do even better with a celebrity in my place.'

'What?' Ed said, astonished. 'But you *make* that show. You are the celebrity.'

'No, a real celebrity. A big name,' Annie explained. 'Tamsin wants me to stay on, so the last episode of the series has to be unforgettable.'

'Good grief . . . so, no pressure then,' Ed said. He hugged her tightly with his free arm and kissed the top of her head.

'Try not to worry. Whatever happens, we'll deal with it, we'll be OK.'

A loud honk outside the window alerted Annie to the arrival of a taxi.

She ran over and spotted the blond sweep of hair in the back seat that let her know Svetlana had arrived.

'Isn't she early?' Annie asked Ed.

'It's eleven forty-five,' he replied. 'Aren't you supposed to meet your guide at twelve? He'll be hoping he'll be back at base in time for lunch,' Ed teased.

'Oh, very funny. Is that seriously the time?' Annie looked at her watch.

With a quick kiss for Ed and each of her babies and an instruction to 'Please get the other two out of bed, OK?' she snatched up her video camera and hurried down to greet Svetlana.

When Svetlana stepped out of the taxi, Annie felt a fresh burst of hope at the genius of this idea.

Svetlana looked so dazzling that she almost lifted the gloom of the grey and drizzly day.

She'd managed to make it from Mayfair to the Highlands in a single morning, in high heels and a blow dry that still looked perfect. No doubt it had been chauffeurs and first class all the way, which could only have helped. Still, a hairdresser must have been summoned before dawn to lacquer the Svetlana locks.

Annie looked at her friend in wordless admiration: immaculate blond hairdo – check. Perfect Dress with maximum cleavage – check. Towering heels which made Annie's look wimpy – check. Raincoat in defiance of the drizzle – check. Unbelievably stunning crocodile Zagliani bag – check.

Annie stared at the bag. Only Svetlana could risk taking a seven-thousand-pound piece of real croc up a mountain.

'Annah!' Svetlana thrust a wad of twenty-pound notes at the driver and then moved in to give Annie a hug.

'Hello, babes, you look beyond beautiful. How is business?' she wondered.

'Business is fantastic. More orders in Britain, a new order from Holland and an amazing order from New York. It is so exciting. I never thought making money could be as much fun as spending money. But it is! Where we meet our mountain guide?' she asked as she brought her phone out of her handbag.

'Forget it,' Annie warned her, 'the last signal I got was on the road. Since then, dead as a doornail. The guide's coming here any minute to pick us up.'

Svetlana stared at her phone in disbelief. 'No phone?' she said sounding horrified. '*Nothing?* No email? How I stay in touch with Elena? How I get my urgent calls for today? If I knew this, Annah, I would not have come.'

'Of course you would have come,' Annie reminded her. 'This is fantastic publicity for the dress. Show me today's number.'

Svetlana unbuckled her YSL raincoat. Underneath was a bright violet dress with a net petticoat underneath to make it as girlie and frilly as possible.

'Stunning,' Annie had to agree. 'I think I need to invest more money with you. This is going to be huge.'

'Ya,' Svetlana confirmed with a nod.

As the taxi reversed down the narrow driveway, it met a dark blue Land-Rover trying to turn in. There was a moment of cars backing up and giving way. Then the blue Land-Rover began to rumble up the driveway towards them.

There was a young woman behind the wheel. When she parked up and stepped down from the car, Annie and Svetlana were left in no doubt that this was their guide.

'Hello there, I'm Morven,' she began and tried to clear the look of astonishment from her face.

Annie and Svetlana tried to do the same.

It was as if two different species of female were meeting. On the one hand: Annie and Svetlana, fully made up, glossy, *soignées*, dressed with the greatest care and attention to the smallest detail. On the other: Morven, a twenty-something dressed for the hills and for total practicality. Clumpy hiking boots poked out from underneath baggy cord trousers. On top, a great thick fleece top swamped a frame that may actually have been quite dainty – it was impossible to tell. She could have been pretty, but her brown hair was scraped back in a ponytail / bun / scrunchie situation and there wasn't the slightest trace of anything, not even lip balm, on her rosy-with-weather face.

'Nice to meet you,' she said and held out her unadorned, slightly rough hand for them to shake.

Annie had kept her hands simple with just a French manicure, whereas Svetlana was sporting long pink talons and two astonishingly large diamond rings.

'You must be Annie, I recognize you from the TV.'

'Oh, have you seen the show?' Annie asked.

'Yes,' Morven replied.

Annie waited for the compliment to follow: 'I love your show', or 'It's great', even just a little 'It's fun'. But none came.

Obviously Morven had watched for research purposes only and was far too serious to have actually enjoyed it.

Annie and Svetlana exchanged a glance.

It occurred to Annie that Morven may have been one of the many women who had taken personal offence at her declaration of war against the clumpy shoe and anorak.

'Well, I can see you're a girl who dresses for action,'

Annie said, trying to make it sound nice, although really she would love to take Morven aside and make a few significant tweaks to her work uniform. If her fleece was just a bit tighter and brighter . . . if she had a nice haircut instead of the scrunchie . . . at least some lip gloss and a touch of concealer as well as the midge repellent.

'So,' Morven said, 'I hope you're covered in Jungle Juice. The cloud's low and the weather's mild, so the beasties will be out in force. But then' – she gave a questioning look at their outfits – 'we'll not be going far today, will we? That's why I've been given the job,' she added. 'The two other guides are looking after a Scout troop.'

'I don't know,' Annie countered. 'We're being sponsored by the mile. I thought we could do at least five miles or so.'

'Ten!' Svetlana laid down the challenge.

Morven looked dubious. 'Have you got the stuff you need me to wear?'

Annie held up a bag full of the Everest camping clothes.

'Well, get into the car,' Morven instructed. 'I've been told it's got to look like proper hill-climbing; there can't be a path or anything too easy.'

'Ya!' Svetlana said, urging her on. 'We are two very, very tough women. Trust me. We do ten, twelve miles and raise thousands of pounds for charity.'

But as Annie watched Svetlana struggle to climb into the Land-Rover, all of a sudden she wasn't so sure.

This was a woman who couldn't even open doors for herself. What was she going to make of a mountain?

Chapter Thirty-Seven

Action girl Morven:

Base layer (Patagonia)
Wicking fleece (same)
Technical anorak (Everest Camping)
Longjohns (same)
Waterproof trousers (same)
Hiking boots (same)
Total est. cost: £350

'Then we start heading down on the north side.'

Three entire hours had passed. Only three hours! It was barely believable. Annie felt as if she had been watching Morven's easy strides marching ahead of them for an eternity. All talk and jolly chit-chat had run dry ages ago. Now the walk was just about marching and hoping: hoping that the madness would end soon.

It had taken some time for the over-dressed walkers to get into any sort of stride, to work out how to negotiate soft Scottish grass, slippery pebbles and rocky outcrops in the shoes and dresses. Not to mention balancing the handbags.

Annie had a large, humiliating grass stain on her raincoat where she'd fallen on her bum in about the fourth minute of the walk.

She'd screamed too – and Morven had looked at her in total exasperation. Plus she'd dropped the video camera and it had been making an odd buzzing noise ever since, although it was definitely still recording.

Occasionally, Annie would manage to say something slightly upbeat into the camera, such as: 'OK, I think we've got the hang of this now. We have to sort of tiptoe forward, especially on the pebbly bits.'

Truthfully, she and Svetlana were hobbling forwards yard by tricky yard and making slow and painful progress. More times than she would like to have admitted, Annie had said to herself: *Why, oh why did I ever mention hillwalking on air? I should just have kept my big trap shut!*

But Svetlana was determined not to give in until they'd covered a reasonable distance and Annie wasn't going to give in first.

Every now and then, Morven would try to cheer and chivvy them along, promising smoother ground ahead or a fantastic view just half a mile from here . . . but it was obvious she was finding them slow and she certainly didn't think they'd hit their target of 5 miles, let alone 10.

The last time Svetlana had asked, it turned out they had covered just over 2 miles. This news had been so deeply disappointing that neither Annie nor Svetlana had had the heart to ask again.

They were walking, er, stumbling along side by side with Morven way ahead of them now. She had wound them slowly up a disconcertingly high hill and now they were coming to an edge. A surprisingly sheer and rocky edge.

'How your feet?' Svetlana asked.

'Not so good,' Annie decided to admit. From what she could feel in her shoes, she guessed she'd shredded through her tights. The raw edges were chafing against her toes. The wet, sticky sensation suggested that blisters had burst and bleeding had begun. She'd already decided she didn't want to take the shoes off and look, because then she'd just feel worse.

'I think I pull muscle in calf,' Svetlana admitted. 'But you and I two tough girls, Annie. We not give in yet. Ten miles,' she said through teeth that were slightly gritted. 'How much money we make if we walk ten miles?'

It was an easy enough calculation. The current phone-in pledges worked out at £5,400 per mile.

'Fifty-four thousand,' Annie answered.

Svetlana gave a little whistle. 'That's good. Come on.' She put her arm through Annie's. 'We soldier on. Maybe we over halfway already.'

'Are your parents still alive?' Annie wondered. It seemed a good moment to ask while they were cosied up together with hours of walking and talking still ahead of them.

'I don't know,' Svetlana replied casually, 'they not very interesting, I never try to find them, they never try to find me . . .'

'I thought my dad was probably dead,' Annie confided, 'then he just turned up on my doorstep, like Elena turned up on yours.'

'Tcha. Is surprising, no? Take some time to get used to. The first two times I see her' – Svetlana stuck two fingers up for emphasis – 'I want to kill her! I want to shout, I don't want to know her or anything about her. This part of my life over. Finished! Now . . . I think one of best things ever happen to me is Elena.'

Annie shook her head thoughtfully; she could not

imagine anything about Mick's return working out so well for her.

'Now I'm worried she fall in love with this American man and leave London for him,' Svetlana admitted.

'I thought Elena was in love with business and had no time for men?' Annie said.

Svetlana smiled. 'Elena think this too. Is biggest surprise for her.'

Morven, still a good 400 metres or so ahead of them, had come to a standstill. She was on the very edge of the hill, looking out over a view that even Annie and Svetlana, dedicated city-dwellers that they were, could recognize as inspiring.

Much, much higher hills surrounded them here, looming over them with a wild and majestic presence, every slope a slightly different shade of grey, purple or green.

Annie was overcome by the sense of immensity. She felt so small in her little heels with her tiny video camera, which, even when she waved it about the landscape, couldn't begin to capture the scale. The three of them standing here seemed so insignificant and so alone. There was not another soul to be seen. Annie scanned the hillsides and couldn't spy another house, cottage or any sign that human beings had ever set foot here at all.

'Wow!' she said to Morven. 'I've never been anywhere so wild and so . . . remote ever before.'

'Is like the Ukrainian steppe,' Svetlana said, not sounding as impressed as Annie. 'Wild and bare. In Ukraine, very dangerous: bandit-country.'

A huge white and black bird flew overhead; with each wing beat, a creaking noise filled the air.

'Have you ever heard anything like that?' Annie asked in surprise. 'It's so quiet out here, we can actually hear the sound of a bird flying.'

'That's an osprey,' Morven told them, an excited edge to her voice. 'Those great big black and white wings, you don't see them often. You should also know that we've done six miles,' she added with an encouraging grin. 'You should be very proud. You've already gone much, much further than I thought you would. *Much* further. I thought I'd be back at base by two p.m. at the latest. We're going to go round the hill here' – Morven pointed out the route they were about to take – 'then we start heading down on the north side. It's nearly four miles from here back to where we started.'

'So we will do ten?' Svetlana asked, sounding pleased.

'Fingers crossed. Take care on this next bit though, it's quite rocky.'

Morven was warming up, Annie couldn't help thinking; underneath the serious front was a quite friendly person just waiting to be teased out.

'What's that?' Annie's attention was caught by a column of dark and brooding cloud over to the far west which seemed to be scudding towards them in a hurry.

'Oh . . .' Morven had looked over to where Annie had pointed and sounded a little surprised. 'We need to get a move on. Rain was forecast for late afternoon and that looks like very heavy rain. Unless the wind changes direction, it's headed straight for us.'

Annie took another look at the cloud. She couldn't think when she'd ever watched weather approaching so fast or so obviously. She'd never been so aware of the weather before. It was fascinating to stand here, almost above the clouds, and watch them moving around like this.

Down on the valley floor below them, the shadow of the clouds chased the sunlight away, plunging the valley into shade.

The thought of donning real hiking clothes and coming

out on a proper walk with Ed and Owen, who both loved to camp and hillwalk, didn't seem so utterly bizarre as she'd once thought. Maybe it would be interesting to go out with them.

Ed hadn't been out with Owen to commune with the great outdoors since the babies were born. Today was going to be their first trip out, each carrying a baby in a backpack. Annie suddenly realized she would have liked to be part of that trip.

'C'mon,' Morven instructed, 'the shower might not hit us quite so hard round this corner of the hill.' Nevertheless, she was unrolling the hood from the collar of the seriously technical and entirely waterproof anorak she was wearing. The best Svetlana and Annie could do as the shadow of the clouds began to catch up with them was button up their trenchcoats, tie the belts tightly and turn up the collars.

'We should have brought umbrellas,' Svetlana said. Annie didn't think she was joking.

As they rounded the hill and hit the bare and rocky-looking ground on the other side, it went dark, as if the lights had been turned off; then rain, the like of which Annie had never endured before, began to lash down on them.

'Aaaargh!' Svetlana cried in dismay as her bouncy blow dry was washed clean away and soaking wet hair began to stick to her face in lank rats' tails.

As Annie tucked her handbag under her coat to protect it from the downpour, Svetlana actually put her crocodile beauty on top of her head to protect her face from the rain!

Not that the bag was going to help much. The rain had all the force of a cold power shower. Within seconds, it had totally soaked them through. Annie could feel water running in cold rivulets down her neck, her back and her legs, which now felt as exposed as if they were bare.

'Eurrrgh!' she complained, huddling up against Svetlana. Once again Morven was striding ahead of them, but not so far in front now. She wasn't enjoying the cold rain lashing against her face either; in fact sometimes she even walked backwards to keep the water from hitting her so hard on the cheeks.

'Careful, careful,' Annie warned Svetlana after slipping slightly on the now treacherously wet, bare stone face.

The two women clung to each other for support as they tiptoed over the stone.

The rain and the cloudy gloom made it hard to see very far ahead and all three had their eyes down searching for sure footing.

'This not so good,' Svetlana told Annie. 'We need to get back to grass, if we fall on the rocks . . . tcha!' She gave her Ukrainian noise of universal disapproval.

'Just take it easy,' Annie encouraged her, moving forward on tiny baby steps. She felt vulnerable too. Maybe they should have doubled back and gone home the way they'd come, but it was 6 miles back the other way and only 4 miles this way.

'Is OK to hold you?' Svetlana asked, as she was now clinging on to Annie's arm. 'You not worried I bring us both down?'

'No,' Annie told her as confidently as she could.

More than anything, Annie wanted the rain to stop. She was sure everything would seem much better and more manageable just as soon as needles of icy cold water stopped hitting them in the face.

With a lurch of panic, Annie felt Svetlana stumble. Her heel had wedged in a crevice between two rocks and, with a small cry, she wobbled on her left leg.

But just as Annie thought she couldn't hold her friend

up, Svetlana's heel flew out again and she managed to remain upright.

They both giggled with relief.

'That was close, watch it!' Morven instructed. She was walking backwards again, keeping her face out of the oncoming gusts of rain.

As Annie's soaked raincoat flapped about her wet legs, rain poured down her neck and she chilled to the bone. She looked at Morven's sturdy hiking boots, Morven's legs encased in dry, cosy waterproofs, Morven's hair tucked out of the rain in a snug hood. Annie didn't think she had ever coveted someone's outfit more.

She would have stripped down naked right there and then to change clothes with Morven.

And just as that thought formed in her mind, that was when it happened.

Morven stepped backwards and seemed to skid awkwardly. Her left foot buckled over and her arms flailed at her sides in a sort of windmill way. Her right leg shot forwards high up into the air, as if she was trying to score a major premiership-winning goal. Then she fell flat on her back and her head bounced once, sickeningly, off the rocks.

'Jesus!' was Annie's stunned reaction.

Heels or no heels, both she and Svetlana rushed forward to help.

Chapter Thirty-Eight

Hiker Ed:

Blue T-shirt (M&S)
Blue longjohns (M&S)
Black waterproof trousers (Sprayway)
Black waterproof anorak (Trespass)
Blue hiking boots (Hi-Tec)
Baby backpack (Outward Bound)
Baby (Micky)
Total est. cost: £160

'No sign of your mum then?'

'Tired?' Ed asked Owen as they walked the pathway towards the cabin.

'Exhausted!' Owen admitted with a roll of his eyes. 'Minnie weighs a total ton. What did she have for lunch? A brick?'

Both babies, each in a backpack strapped to Owen and Ed's backs, had fallen asleep on the home stretch of the hour-long walk they'd just done.

Ed had kept it nice and easy. They'd walked 3 miles

along flat, woodland paths, Ed checking all the time that he wasn't going too far or too fast for Owen. He was well aware that a twenty-pound baby was a heavy load for a young back.

Ed looked at his watch and saw that it was 5 p.m. already. His schedule was totally off. Never mind.

'We'll put the babies in bed, fire up the kettle and dig into the ginger cake that I know is safely stored at the bottom of the food box. Your mum's bound to be back by now,' he told Owen.

'You don't think there's any chance Lana could have eaten it?' Owen worried. 'You know what she's like when she's supposed to be studying. She'd eat the entire contents of the fridge if we let her.'

'No, I think the cake is safely hidden,' Ed reassured him.

As they went in the cabin door, it seemed so quiet that, were it not for the sleeping babies, Ed would have called out a 'hellooo!'

Instead, he and Owen took off their muddy boots and headed upstairs to slide Micky and Minnie into their beds. Then Ed padded off to look for any other signs of life in the cabin, while Owen headed for the kitchen.

After knocking on one of the small bedroom doors, Ed was told to come in by Lana, who lay on her bed surrounded by books with a scowl on her face.

'You OK?' he asked.

'Suppose so,' came the sulky reply. 'It's not exactly fun though, is it? Being stuck out here with nothing but studying to do?'

'You should have come for the walk and had a break. Just a few more weeks,' Ed tried to reassure her. 'Think how much you'll enjoy your summer holiday after all this.'

'Huh,' came the response, 'stuck hanging around my family with no money. Great.'

'We'll help you to find a job, Lana,' Ed said, trying to be as nice and understanding as he possibly could. 'I'm sure you could do some babysitting, for a start.'

'Boring!' came the response. Lana turned her head away from him.

Ed gripped the door handle tightly. Saying any of the things on his mind right now, like: 'Why are you always so negative about my children?' 'Why have you taken the birth of the twins as a personal insult?' 'Why don't you just try and bond with them a tiny bit?' wouldn't be helpful. He was going to have to talk to Lana about this some time when she was calm, when she had less work to do and when they were both in a happy place.

'Would you like to come down and have a piece of cake? I've got ginger cake in the kitchen . . . and butter,' he coaxed.

'Oh, all right then,' Lana replied and gave almost a hint of a smile.

'No sign of your mum then?'

'No, not heard anything.'

Ed glanced at the window; outside, grey clouds were gathering. It looked as if it was going to be a damp and dreary evening.

Annie had been gone for over five hours; a bubble of worry surfaced in his mind at this thought. But then he told himself they were with a mountain guide who was sure to know exactly what she was doing. They would be fine. They would be absolutely fine. Any moment now, he would hear the Land-Rover rumbling down the driveway and all would be well.

As he made for the kitchen, he thought about how battered and blistered Annie would probably be and felt sorry for her.

'Have you got the kettle on?' he asked Owen, who was

already spreading a wedge of cake 2 inches thick with a layer of butter. 'And have you even washed your hands?'

When Owen looked at him in surprise, Ed sighed. 'Owen! Go, find soap, now.'

Once Owen was out of the kitchen, Ed made tea, slowly. He cut and buttered his cake, slowly. He wanted to be busy so he didn't have to think about the time. He sat down at the table to eat the cake . . . and then realized he wasn't hungry any more.

He wondered at what point he should worry properly and do something. Should he wait until 6 p.m.? Then what should he do? Should he phone mountain rescue? Just to see if they had heard anything? Or should he go and look for her?

Oh, good grief! He told himself off. They were probably all in some cosy little pub drying off and drinking a hot toddy and of course, normally, she would have called to let him know, but the signal was so bad that she couldn't.

He looked around the cabin and realized there was a landline. Why had he not thought to give Annie that number? Then if she was in a pub, she'd have been able to phone the cabin on a payphone.

He would eat the cake and start to worry properly when he had finished, he told himself.

'Morven? Morven? Are you OK?' Annie asked.

'Morven? You feel sick?' Svetlana added.

Annie and Svetlana, despite heels, snagged stockings and the rain, were crouched down beside their guide, desperately hoping this was not as serious as it looked.

Morven's eyes remained shut and Annie could feel panic rising up in her chest. Not just because she had no idea how to get back or how to get help but because of what had happened to Roddy.

He had slipped, rolled down a slope and suffered a blow to the head from which he'd never recovered.

These things happened. They really did happen.

Why the bloody hell did anyone even go near a hillock without a crash helmet, ropes and a walkie-talkie? What the hell was she doing up here? This was all her fault! If it hadn't been for her boasting about her heel-walking skills none of this would have happened. Morven wouldn't be up some godforsaken bloody Scottish mountain in a rainstorm, living out the last few moments of her precious life, Annie panicked.

'Morven!' she wailed, not knowing whether to move the guide's head into her lap or not. 'Morven, please!'

Much to Annie's astonishment and relief, Morven's eyes opened at this and seemed to focus easily enough on her.

'What on earth . . . ?' Morven began.

'You fall,' Svetlana told her bluntly.

'How do you feel?' Annie asked, still feeling panicky. 'How's your head?'

Slowly, Morven raised herself up on to her elbows. 'I think my head's fine,' she replied, 'but my ankle is agony.' With that she tried to lift her left leg, but from the expression on her face, it was obviously too painful.

'What do we do?' Svetlana asked. 'Who we call?'

Morven slowly moved her hand to the zip of her anorak, pulled it down, and then rummaged in the inside pocket. She brought out a big black walkie-talkie.

'Thank God for that,' Annie said. Relief flooded her as she pictured burly rescuers in bright yellow oilskins carrying Morven down the mountain in a fireman's lift.

Svetlana was imagining a helicopter. She loved to go by helicopter. It was her favourite way to travel. Especially if champagne was involved.

Morven switched on the walkie-talkie. It made a crackling noise followed by heavy static.

'Lima Hotel calling base,' Morven said into the walkie-talkie. 'Lima Hotel calling base.'

'Hotel?' Svetlana asked.

'I think it's a codename,' Annie whispered.

There was no reply.

'Two other guides work around here, we have a little office . . . but we're not in the office very much,' Morven informed them. 'They were looking after some Scouts today.'

'Can't you phone them directly on that thing?' Annie asked.

'No, that's not how a walkie-talkie works.'

'Can you leave them a message?'

'That's not how it works either,' Morven repeated. 'We'll just have to sit tight and keep trying.'

Svetlana and Annie exchanged a look. Sit here on this bloody hillside in the pouring rain! With someone who might have a broken ankle and maybe even concussion and just wait on the off-chance that someone might wander into the office and hear them?

Both were thinking exactly the same thing: *No way!*

A glance at the darkening sky told them that there was only another hour or so of daylight left.

'We look at ankle,' Svetlana instructed and she moved down towards Morven's foot. 'I take off boot, very gently,' she added before Morven could protest.

Svetlana's long pink fingernails began to work at the bootlaces. Only when the boot had been fully opened did Svetlana gently and gingerly lift out the injured foot.

'Easy, easy!' Morven instructed, clenching her jaw in pain. Supported by Annie, she sat up again to take a look at the damage she'd inflicted on her own foot.

With Morven hissing and wincing all the time, Svetlana rolled up the waterproof trouser leg and then eased down the thick cotton hiking sock.

The foot looked awful. It dangled slightly at an angle, and was already puffing and swelling right before their eyes.

'A little broken, I think,' came Svetlana's verdict, 'but no bone through skin. This is good. Less chance of infection.'

Annie looked at Svetlana with renewed respect. 'How do you know about ankles?' she asked.

'Oh' – Svetlana gave a shrug – 'I train to be army nurse. You know, before Miss World.'

Although the pain in her foot was making her feel sick, Morven still had to ask: 'You were Miss World?'

'No, Miss Ukraine.' Summoning up her usual disdain for the result, Svetlana spat out, 'Midget Miss Thailand win.'

'You were *in* Miss World?' Morven had to ask again. 'That's pretty impressive.'

At least this was taking her mind off the broken foot.

'Won't anyone be expecting you back?' Annie wanted to know. 'Won't someone in your office notice you're missing?'

'I didn't think you two would last a mile,' Morven had to admit. 'I mean, who can hillwalk in heels? And it's Saturday. The guys probably think I went out with you for half an hour, then clocked off early and have been lying low since then.'

'But it's a mountain!' Annie exclaimed. 'Surely you're supposed to tell someone when you go up a mountain and when you get back so they can look out for you?'

'It's a hill,' Morven corrected her, 'and what about you? Isn't someone looking out for you? Won't someone miss you?'

Well, what big fat help would that be? Ed only vaguely knew where they were headed, he couldn't phone her or anyone else on his out-of-signal phone and he had four children in his care. He wasn't exactly in the best position to launch a rescue effort, was he?

'It's a bit difficult for him . . .' Annie began.

'We are only three miles or so away from Land-Rover,' Svetlana began. 'We have to carry you down the hill. One arm over each shoulder, you hop on good leg. We get there.'

The way Svetlana said it, it sounded reasonable. Only 3 miles. They'd already managed 7, hadn't they?

'But first we need bandage for the foot. Annie, your dress best,' came Svetlana's instruction.

'Huh?' It took Annie a good moment to understand what was meant here.

Meanwhile, Svetlana opened her croc bag and brought out a sturdy-looking folding knife.

'What's that?' Annie asked.

'Ukrainian hunting knife. Always in bag, very useful,' came the reply.

She opened it up and began to close in on Annie's silk Prada dress.

No!

Oh, no!

After several deft slices, Annie was wearing a Prada micromini and Morven's foot was being bound up in a very, very expensive silk bandage.

Extremely carefully, Svetlana and Annie lifted Morven up on to the foot that could support her weight.

With Morven's arm and weight around her neck, Annie immediately felt thrown off balance. She and Svetlana were taller than Morven, so the injured guide pulled them down and forwards. Plus, Annie had both a handbag and a video camera to manage, not that she'd been doing much filming lately.

The exposed stone on the hill face was still slippery and,

with every step she took, Annie felt her footing skid. She felt Svetlana slipping about too. This was too dangerous. Whenever Morven felt them slip, she let out a little moan of fear, because the thought of being dropped on her broken ankle was horrible.

'Why don't you take off your shoes?' Morven asked in a voice that sounded frightened.

'Walk barefoot?' Annie asked in astonishment. 'But it's freezing and it's really hard and rocky.'

'One of you could have my boots,' Morven suggested.

'Stop,' Svetlana commanded, so they came to a halt and gently set Morven down again.

Svetlana also sat down and took off her shoes. 'We break heels off shoes,' she said calmly and then began to bash her beautifully made Italian stiletto against a rock in an attempt to dislodge the heel.

Several forceful strikes achieved absolutely nothing.

'Give me that,' Annie said and took the shoe from her friend's hand. After a brief examination, she said: 'It's a metal heel, welded into the sole. It ain't coming off, girl. Same as mine.' She took off one of her red shoes and struck it against the rock to demonstrate.

Morven's voice sounded small and scared when she said, 'It's going to be dark in half an hour.'

Annie looked up at the greying sky above them. This was, it had to be admitted, an additional complication.

'I don't feel well,' Morven added and with that she twisted to the side and vomited, hitting mainly grass, but also a corner of Svetlana's YSL raincoat.

'Sorry,' she mumbled once she was done.

'No problem,' Svetlana assured her.

Now Annie felt sick too because she knew that someone who'd banged her head and begun to vomit needed urgent medical attention.

'We have to get her down; you take the boots and I'll go barefoot,' she said grimly, taking the second shoe from her foot.

'No,' Svetlana said, 'you take boots, I make my own,' and with that, she opened up her magnificent handbag. From inside she pulled out the folding knife again.

Annie wasn't quite sure whether she was going to laugh or cry; it felt as if it could go either way. 'What the bloody hell are you going to make shoes out of?' she asked.

Svetlana held up her fabulous crocodile masterpiece to demonstrate.

'No!' was Annie's immediate response. 'You can't do that! Not the Zagliani!'

'Ya,' Svetlana insisted, almost enjoying the horror on her friend's face. 'Get camera, Annah, you film.'

Chapter Thirty-Nine

Babysitting Lana:

Multi-coloured top (Miss Sixty)
Blobs of gunge (Sudocrem)
Skinny jeans (Topshop)
Fluffy slippers (Christmas)
Total est. cost: £70

'WHAT?!'

'If you're going to go out to look for Mum, then I'm going to come with you,' Owen said, appearing in the doorway of the cabin.

'What?' Ed asked as he laced up his hiking boots, carefully tucking his waterproof trousers into the waterproof gaiters round his ankles.

It was horribly wet out there. If Annie and Svetlana weren't tucked up in a cosy little pub, they were going to be totally soaked through and freezing, which is why he'd packed a flask of tea and spare waterproof cagoules into the little backpack he was wearing.

'Owen,' Ed said urgently, 'I need you to stay with Lana.'

When the babies wake up, she won't know what to do. You'll have to show her where I've left the bottles and the food and how to do it. She's never fed them before.'

'You've left it all in the fridge,' Owen said. 'I'll go and tell her right now. How hard can it be? I have to come with you.'

There was an edge to Owen's voice that Ed had heard only a handful of times before. It was angry insistence . . . laced with fear. He made one last effort to put Owen off. 'I'll probably be back here in twenty minutes. I'll probably meet them on the road . . .'

'Fine,' Owen said, shoving his feet into his boots, 'then we'll both be back to help Lana with the twins.'

With a sigh, Ed realized he would have to give in. 'OK, OK. You'll need your proper waterproof jacket and maybe put your torch into your backpack. It's getting dark out there and I don't know how long my batteries are going to last.'

It was a much cheerier Owen who answered, with a grin: 'No problem.'

He disappeared back into the house. As well as getting the things Ed had asked him for, he went to Lana's room with the message he couldn't wait to deliver.

Sticking his head round his big sister's door, he said: 'Ed and I are going out to find Mum. The babies won't be asleep for much longer and when they wake up, you'll have to warm up their bottles and give them supper.' Casually, he added: 'They'll probably need new nappies too.'

'WHAT?!' Lana exclaimed.

Lana was sure that Owen slammed the cabin door extra hard just to cause trouble. Because no sooner had he and Ed left, the bang reverberating right around the building, than

Lana heard the little wail of distress from the main bedroom.

For several minutes, she tried to ignore it, hoping that somehow whichever baby it was would settle down again and fall back to sleep.

Lana knew *nothing* about babies. For all the time she had lived in a house with two babies, she had done her utmost to avoid them. She'd never wanted the babies. No one had asked her. She resented every moment Ed and her mother spent with those children. Really, hadn't her mother been busy enough without stirring twin babies into the mix?

The twins were like the central magnet in the house now. Everyone and everything fixated on them. She and Owen were in orbit around the twins and Owen was definitely on a much closer orbit than she was.

Lana felt like a distant star who might quite like just to drift off into another galaxy.

Preferably a galaxy inhabited by Andrei.

She shook her head to dislodge the thought and got up from the bed. She felt stiff. Unlike the boys, she hadn't even been outside today. She'd just been lying here, looking out at damp scenery and trying to read boring books written in the eighteenth century. Good grief. As soon as this A level was over, she was never going to study English again for as long as she lived.

She crossed the corridor and stepped into the main bedroom. Both Micky and Minnie were awake now and, Lana realized nervously, they were relying on her to look after them. They were sitting up in their travel cots facing the door with anticipation.

As soon as they saw her face, they began to smile and giggle.

Lana looked at them nervously. Minnie put her hands above her head, wanting to be picked up.

'Hello,' Lana said, reaching down to get her.

Immediately Micky began to protest, lifting his arms too, desperate not to be forgotten.

'C'mon, Micky,' Lana said and bent over the second cot. Minnie was tucked up in her right arm, now she struggled to hoist Micky up with her left.

They were heavy, these babies!

Only when she was sure she had a tight hold of them did Lana slowly begin the walk out of the room and down the stairs towards the kitchen.

Food?

That's what Owen had told her to do next, wasn't it?

Minnie took hold of Lana's hair and curled it round in her fist. She smiled charmingly at Lana, said 'Baba' adorably and then yanked viciously hard on the hair.

'Ouch!' Lana exclaimed, not able to stop herself.

Micky, shocked, burst into tears. Minnie joined in.

They were so loud!

'It's OK,' Lana soothed, 'it's OK, really. It's fine.'

Halfway down the stairs she suddenly remembered about nappies. Wasn't she supposed to change their nappies before they ate? Or would it be after they ate?

She tried to crane a look at Minnie's behind. There wasn't any terrible smell coming from either of the babies but those bottoms looked big, as if the nappies were swollen with wetness.

Yes. She would do nappies first, and then maybe, by the time she'd done that, everyone would be back to rescue her from the terror of trying to give the twins a meal.

Back in the bedroom, Lana mentally ran through a nappy-changing plan. OK, she would put Minnie back in her cot and change Micky first.

No, she would put both babies in the cot and arrange the

changing mat, wipes, nappies and cream all together on the floor before she got the first baby out.

As soon as she put the babies into their beds they began to wail, so now she was working in a stressed and panicky way, wanting everything to be sorted out as quickly as possible so she could get this over with.

Changing mat down, wipes, nappies, cream . . . OK. She hadn't actually done a nappy herself yet, but if Owen could do it, how hard could it be?

Lana brought Micky out first, because he seemed to be crying the loudest, but as soon as she did that, Minnie set up an outraged, ear-bursting protest which almost made Lana change her mind.

'C'mon, it's OK,' she tried to soothe them both. 'I'm just going to do Micky's nappy and then I'll do yours, Minnie.'

She laid Micky down on his back. He promptly rolled over on to his front. She tried to roll him back, but he resisted with surprising force.

'C'mon, Micky, where's your nappy?' she said, handing it to him as she wrestled with the poppers on his sleep suit.

His great big soaking nappy was finally off. She wiped him clean, applied cream and then tried to wrestle the nappy out of his hands. He wouldn't give it up.

'Lana needs the nappy,' she told him. 'Yes she does.' She leaned her face a little closer and felt a jet of warm wetness hit her in the face.

No!

Her baby brother had *not* just peed in her face. NO!

But there was the little willy waving from side to side like a miniature hose, soaking not just Lana but the changing mat, the new nappy and his outfit.

'Micky! Oh Micky,' she complained.

She picked him up and grabbed at the towel hanging over the end of the bed.

'Stop crying, Minnie, please,' she begged the distraught twin imprisoned in the cot.

With the towel, Lana dabbed at her face, the mat and everything else caught in Micky's range.

Then she took off Micky's sleep suit and looked about for something else to change him into. Only one of Min's little pink Babygros was within reach. Oh, it would hardly matter, would it? Lana thought to herself as she ham-fistedly bundled Micky into his nappy and then, limb by protesting limb, into the little pink suit.

There.

She put him into the cot, where he promptly burst into tears, and she took Minnie out.

This nappy change went a little more smoothly. Well, Minnie somehow got hold of the nappy cream and had it on her fingers, her hair, the mat and Lana's top before Lana had even noticed, but apart from that . . .

Once both babies were back in her arms, Lana was astonished to see that it was 6.30 p.m., it was almost dark outside and, since no one had bothered to come back and help her yet, she was going to have to attempt to feed the babies by herself.

Ed didn't know whether to feel relieved or worried when he saw the blue Land-Rover sitting in the car park at the start of the route he guessed Annie had been taken on.

'Isn't that the guide's car?' Owen asked. 'They must still be on the hill.'

'Well, I think so,' Ed began carefully, 'but we don't know for sure. Someone else might have given them a lift. I keep thinking that your mum is probably in a pub somewhere, drinking a second glass of wine to ease the pain of her blisters.'

Owen gave a tense smile in reply to this.

They got out and went over to look in the car window. Ed could see a few belongings on the back seat: cords, an orange fleece and a pair of shoes. At a guess, these were the clothes the guide had left behind after changing into her Everest outfit. So, probably, they were all still out on their walk . . . maybe.

Owen and Ed looked at the great brooding hill in front of them. The gloomy grey light was fading fast, a chilly wind was blowing and, although it had stopped raining, there was a cold, damp feeling to the air. Annie was in a raincoat, dress and thin tights. If she was still out here, she would be soaked and completely freezing.

Ed looked at the map he had brought with him. There was a clear 10-mile walk marked around this hill. It was steep in the middle, he noticed.

If they had been out this long, they must surely have passed the mid-point and be heading back by now? But would they have done the loop and be walking home on the north face? Maybe they had decided to give the steep bit a miss and had doubled back, returning once again on the south path?

The thought that something might have happened out there on the steep part, 3 or 4 miles away from here, he didn't want to dwell on. But it kept pushing its way to the forefront of his mind.

'What if they've had an accident?' Owen asked. He was clearly not pushing the thought away at all.

'Owen, we're going to switch on our torches, take our map and go and have a look for them. OK? Try not to worry,' Ed added, giving Owen a reassuring squeeze on the shoulder. 'This is your mum we're talking about. She is the toughest old boot on the planet. I promise.'

Owen didn't laugh, he just gave Ed another of his tense little smiles.

'North face,' Ed decided, mainly because this would take him and Owen to the tricky bit of the walk as quickly as possible. If something had happened, Ed was almost certain it might have happened there.

It was 3 miles or so away. He looked at his watch. If they went at a really brisk pace, they could be there in about forty minutes.

'Quick march,' he instructed Owen.

'Yessir,' Owen replied.

For about fifteen minutes, they walked quickly, saying very little. Well, Owen said very little; Ed tried to make cheery, light-hearted conversation.

The ground beneath their feet was wet and squelchy and Ed wondered how Annie, in heels, had coped. Every step must have been an effort.

'No camping or hillwalking since the babies were born, now two walks in one day,' Ed said to Owen jokily.

'Hmmm,' was all the reply that Owen made.

Owen didn't like the fact that all he could think about was the first hillwalk Ed had taken him on. That had been a soft, rolling strollable hill, just like this one. A big green chunk of hillside with big views out over the landscape just like this one. On that very first walk together, they'd been looking for the place where Owen's real dad had fallen.

His dead dad.

'I wonder how Lana's getting on,' Ed said next. 'I just hope it's not a complete disaster. Imagine if we come back and she's fed them all . . .' Ed trailed off. The jokes just wouldn't come. He was suddenly feeling choked with anxiety about not just Annie but the babies too. There was so much that Lana could get wrong. What was he thinking? She wasn't even a safe person to leave two babies with, let alone a capable one.

He looked round at Owen, who was walking a pace or

two behind him. He was distraught to see, even in the pale light of his torch, that Owen was struggling not to cry – and failing.

A tear was slipping down his cheek and his face was horribly pale.

'Owen!' Ed stopped immediately and put an arm around him. 'Hey, Owen, try not to worry.'

But it was impossible not to worry. It was also impossible for either of them not to think about how Owen's father had died.

'You should at least have got married!' Owen blurted out angrily. 'What if Mum's dead too? You're not even my real stepdad! They might not let me stay with you and the twins! There was this guy at school and when his mum died, he had to go off and live with some aunt he'd never even met before!'

'Hey, hey,' Ed soothed, holding his arm tight around Owen's shoulders. Ed felt his throat squeeze. It was fear, yes, definitely. What the bloody hell had Annie gone and done now? But it was love too. He absolutely loved Owen, just as much as his own children. 'I'm your legal guardian,' he reminded Owen, 'but just as soon as we find your mum, which will be any moment now, you make sure you tell her that she *has* to marry me. OK?'

Chapter Forty

Svetlana on the hill:

Purple dress, very wet (Perfect Dress)
Soaked beige raincoat (YSL)
Crocodile slippers (DIY Zagliani)
Diamond rings (husband Harry)
Total est. cost: £25,800

'This is a terrible song.'

'Morven, wakey, wakey. We need you to tell us which direction we should be going in!' Annie tried to sound cheery, but Morven had been sick again and was now far too drowsy for Annie's liking.

Annie hobbled along in the hiking boots. Her red stilettos had been abandoned somewhere on the hillside along with Svetlana's Louboutins. The boots were too small and crushed her toes almost as badly as the heels, but she did appreciate their infinitely superior gripping power.

Poor Morven was barefoot, apart from her Prada bandage, as Svetlana had had to use her hiking socks to keep the crocodile DIY moccasins on her feet.

The croc had proved its quality by being a very, very tough bugger to cut. Even if Svetlana had been carrying a needle and thread, the leather would have been impossible to sew. So Svetlana had surrounded her feet with the DIY croc sole, then pulled the socks on top to keep it in place.

Morven was finding it hard to hop now and Annie and Svetlana were dragging her down the hill, her weight a heavy load between them.

'Come on, Morven,' Annie encouraged. 'Is this the path? We're going downwards. Down is good. I'm sure we'll be back at the car park soon.'

It was Annie's small, unspoken fear that in the gloom they would miss the car park and be left wandering around this bloody hillside for the whole night.

She kept telling herself that she was a strong person and she could cope, but she was soaked to the skin, chilled to the bone, and totally exhausted with the walk and the weight of Morven on her shoulders. The cold wind blowing on to her wet hair was giving her a headache of monumental proportions and, worst of all, she was frightened for Morven. She needed to be seen right now by a doctor, or preferably a team of highly trained specialists, who could put her through all the tests and make sure she was going to be OK.

Little flashes of Roddy on life support kept appearing in Annie's mind, making her so frightened that she just wanted to sit down and cry.

'I have feeling someone will notice very soon and will come and help us,' Svetlana said with determination.

Svetlana's wet hair was clinging to her head, but her make-up was unmoved. Clearly she always applied the waterproof kind, and lashings of it. Whenever Annie glanced over at her and saw the determined chin pointing ahead, the clenched hand with the mega-diamonds powering on, she took courage.

Ed knew hills and hillwalking, Annie told herself, he would know they should have been back ages ago. Surely he would do something?

But then there was no mobile phone signal, he might think she was sitting in a pub somewhere celebrating. Just the thought of this brought tears of frustration to the back of Annie's eyes.

Good grief!

She didn't want to feel sorry for herself, she wanted to pull herself together. 'I think we should sing,' she suggested out loud.

'Ya. What songs you know?' Svetlana asked.

For a moment, Annie's mind was blank, and then she realized there was a tune which she had been humming in her head all day long, despite her best efforts to forget it.

Taking a deep breath, she began to blurt out: ' "We're all going on a summer holiday, no more working for a week or two . . ." '

When she had finished a verse of it, Svetlana's verdict was harsh.

'This is a terrible song,' she declared. 'I will sing Ukrainian song for you now. Will be much better.'

She was so competitive, it occurred to Annie. It didn't matter what the arena was – best outfit, slimmest waist, richest husband, brightest child – Svetlana always wanted to come first. Now here she was on a mountain in the dark in this horrible situation and she wanted to sing the best song.

Svetlana began to belt out some marching anthem in her native tongue. It sounded great; she had a beautiful voice – was there no end to her talents? – and best of all it seemed to rally Morven a little.

'We must be getting close,' Annie encouraged the guide. 'How are you feeling?'

'My foot is killing me.'

'I know how you feel,' Annie couldn't help agreeing.

Svetlana finished the song. Annie gave a little cheer, then decided to sing a fresh round of 'Summer Holiday' again, in the hope of jollying Morven along a little.

She was just reaching the end of the chorus when she thought she saw it. Just the merest flicker, but still – and there it was again.

She was still singing, but her mind was on this little flicker of light.

She was screwing up her eyes to concentrate on it. She didn't want to lose it.

Maybe it was a car headlight, way in the distance; maybe someone was in the car park looking for them?

If that was a headlight in the car park, they didn't have far to go.

But maybe it was a cottage window?

She didn't like that thought so much. If that tiny dot was a cottage window, they were still a mile or two away from it. Every step was making her wince and she had been wondering for some time how much further she could go.

For several moments, Annie wasn't sure whether to mention the light or not, she didn't want to get anyone's hopes up too soon, but then Svetlana blurted out: 'I see a light.'

'Yes,' Annie agreed. 'I think I see it too. It's still small and far away, but it is a light, isn't it?'

'We need to be careful,' Morven told them in a faint voice. 'Parts of the hill drop away really steeply into the valley down here. We need to go very carefully.'

'Is it a house?' Svetlana wondered.

Morven shook her head. 'No one lives round here,' she told them.

'Maybe a car?' Annie offered. But she could see now that it was only one very small flickering light. Not car headlamps.

It was still a good thing though. Light meant there was someone there . . . didn't it?

'I thought I heard something!' Owen said all of a sudden. 'Shhhh,' he ordered Ed. 'I'm sure I heard something.'

They both stood still and strained their ears to listen.

Apart from the sound of the wind – or the mountains breathing, as Ed liked to call it – they couldn't hear anything.

'What did it sound like?' Ed asked.

'Ermmm . . .' Owen considered. 'I thought it sounded a bit like . . . ermmm . . .'

'What?' Ed asked in exasperation.

'All right, I just thought it sounded like someone was singing the Summer Holiday song – you know. I've probably just got it in my head. I was singing it in the car,' Owen tried to explain. He was feeling stupid. Everything about this was annoying him, especially the fact that he'd burst into tears. Even if Ed had been really nice about it, he still felt embarrassed.

'Annie!' Ed was saying more to himself than out loud or to Owen. 'Maybe it's Annie, maybe she can't get that bloody song out of her head either! ANNIE!' he suddenly shouted without warning at the very top of his voice, 'ANNIE!'

'There's someone there!' Annie exclaimed, sure now that she had heard something coming from the direction of the light.

'Yes!' Morven agreed. 'I heard something too.'

'Hello!' Annie shouted and felt a renewed surge of energy help her on down the hill towards the light.

'We are here!' Svetlana shouted, also managing to pick up the pace in her Zagliani slippers.

'I think it's a torch!' Annie exclaimed as the flickering light seemed to turn in their direction. 'I think someone's down there with a torch! HELLOOOO!' she shouted out, causing her head to throb violently.

It must be one of the mountain guides. Finally, someone must have noticed that Morven was missing!

But then Annie heard something which made her heart thud in her chest with joy.

First came the voice she knew so well calling out her name. *Ed was here! He had come to look for them! He was going to help them get Morven off the mountainside.*

Then came the second voice, the one which was questioning and a little anxious: 'Muuum?' it asked.

Owen! she thought with a ridiculously happy smile. *Owen's come to get us too.*

'We're up here!' she shouted, hoping to speed them up, desperate to see them as soon as possible.

Now the light of the torch was growing closer and clearer; now she could make out the two shapes behind it: one taller, the other a little smaller, following on behind.

'Ed!' she shouted. 'Owen! I can't believe you've come to get us! I can't believe you're here.'

'Whoa!' Morven urged as she felt herself being carried slightly too enthusiastically downhill. 'Whoa, there are steep stone slopes round here. I don't want to fall again.'

Within a few brief minutes, Annie was somehow, without letting go of Morven, in a bear hug. Two sets of arms were around her and she felt as if she was in danger of having the life squeezed out of her.

'My darlin's,' she managed to croak, feeling tears of relief squeeze from the corners of her eyes. 'It's very nice to see you.'

Finally, she could feel Owen's smaller, slighter arms letting go of her, but Ed was still holding tight. It felt as if he didn't want to lose his grip on her.

'Of all your ideas,' he was saying against her ear, 'of all your daft and crazy ideas, this was the most daft and crazy of them all. I am not going to let you go . . .'

Ed had thought he was going to say 'hillwalking' or 'rushing off on another daft adventure'. But instead, he ended the sentence there.

'I'm not ever going to let you go . . .' he repeated and that sounded exactly right.

Then Owen remembered what Ed had told him and came out with his own version of it: 'Ed said once we found you, Mum, that he was going to marry you. Gretna Green,' he added, 'I noticed we passed it on the way up from London. It's like Las Vegas. You can just turn up there and get married. Just like Las Vegas.'

Svetlana gave a little whoop of approval. 'I be brides-maid,' she decided straightaway. 'Maybe Morven too . . . We get Morven nice dress. Shame about the foot, but we cut off in the pictures.'

Chapter Forty-One

Owen on the hill:

Waterproof anorak (Trespass)
Waterproof trousers (same)
Hiking boots (Timberland)
Torch (Tiso's)
Swiss Army knife (same)
Total est. cost: £120

'See you, Mum.'

The babies had eaten the vegetable goo and the yoghurt goo. The babies had each had their bottle of milk. The babies had been played with extensively, exhaustively, until Lana didn't think she wanted to do another 'Round and round the garden' ever again. For as long as she lived.

It was fun though. It was actually lovely to make them laugh at her. But Lana was exhausted. She wanted to lie down on the sofa and watch TV until she fell asleep. This babysitting stint had felt like almost as much work as trying to read her way through *The Romantic Poets* from cover to cover.

Lana was beginning to get just a tiny inkling of why her mum and Ed were so busy and so preoccupied with their twins.

Surely someone should be back *soon*? Lana had to wonder. Surely they weren't going to leave her to bath the babies and put them to bed? She didn't know if she could do it. She imagined slippery, soapy babies sliding around the bathtub as she fumbled about for towels, sleep suits and whatever else they might need.

She'd already endured the horror of changing the post-supper nappies. How could such small people produce such an enormous amount of waste product? And all at the same time? It had been unbearable, a nightmarish experience. At certain points, when wipes had not been able to contain the situation, when she'd felt *stuff ooze* in behind her fingernail, she'd not been sure if she would be able to pull through. But somehow she'd managed to focus and find her inner strength and afterwards, it was amazing how clean, how fresh and renewed the babies seemed.

It felt as if they were grateful to her. Well, it just couldn't in any way be pleasant, crawling about with some great, warm, steaming, stinging dump strapped to your bottom.

'Please, somebody, come home soon,' Lana said out loud. She was flat out on the sofa now, the babies on top of her, gurgling, pulling at her hair and, in one instance, drooling right into her eye.

For a few minutes, it crossed Lana's mind to worry but she dismissed the anxiety quickly. No, her family was probably hiding out somewhere warm, laughing at the thought of her coping with the twins.

'Nana,' Minnie said, throwing herself down on to Lana's chest and burrowing up against her.

'Yes, I'm a good big sister, yes I am.' Lana stroked the silky hair on Minnie's head. 'I'm going to spend lots of time looking after you both.'

Lana looked down and saw that Minnie had snuggled right down on her chest. As Lana's breath rose and fell, Minnie's body rose and fell too. Micky was still sitting up, in between Lana's knees, making funny little sounds to himself and chewing on his fingers with a very drooly mouth.

Lana looked back down at Minnie and could see that her eyes were growing heavy, her lids were sinking and she was about to fall asleep in Lana's arms.

Lana felt completely charmed.

Owen held the torch and walked beside his mum; the very faint beam of light not providing a great deal in the way of guidance.

With Ed's help, Svetlana soldiered on under the weight of Morven. Annie had offered to stay in position, but Svetlana had insisted.

'How far is it to the car park?' Annie decided to ask.

'Roughly two miles,' Ed said. 'Maybe less,' he added quickly when this news produced a demoralized sigh from Annie.

'We only managed two miles! With the DIY Zagliani shoes and everything!' Annie was horrified. 'Just two miles!' she repeated.

'By the time we get back, you'll have walked ten whole miles though,' Ed told her proudly.

Before Annie could even remind herself about how much money this would raise, she felt the ground under her boots turn crunchy.

'Loose gravel,' she warned the others; she didn't want Svetlana in her homemade moccasins to land in any trouble.

All of a sudden Annie pitched violently to the side. She grabbed at the air with her hands and let out a cry which seemed to disappear into a gurgle.

In the darkness, she could make no sense of what was happening, but the rushing in the pit of her stomach let her know she was falling.

Before she could even think about where she might be falling – or why? How far? Or form any sort of question at all – she landed, hard.

In a crumpled heap, in disorientating darkness, at first all she could feel was pain: sharp, piercing pain travelling up through her stomach and into her lungs; low, grumbling pain in her knees, her elbows, her hands and a great burning pain right across both buttocks.

For several stunned moments, Annie didn't move at all. She didn't dare to. She waited, trying to gather her thoughts and wondering how the pains were going to develop.

Nothing seemed to be getting worse. Things were bad . . . but nothing seemed to be deteriorating, which was surely good.

Annie had landed on her bum. That's why it was so sore. Her increasingly padded derrière had probably saved her from a really bad injury.

She sat up a little, breathed in carefully and realized that the pain in her stomach had a lot to do with being winded and with the video camera which was in her lap.

With growing waves of relief, she wiggled her fingers and her toes, then moved her knees, ankles and elbows. Nothing seemed to be broken. There must be huge grazes on her burning elbows and hands and her bum was going to be black and blue. But nothing was broken.

Now she just had to worry about the next thing: where the bloody hell was she? And how the bloody hell was she supposed to get out?

It was too dark to make sense of her surroundings. Looking up, all she could work out was that it was slightly lighter above her.

Taking a deep breath, she shouted out: 'Heeeeel-looooooo. I'm here. Heeeeellooooooooo!'

For a long, worrying moment, Annie heard nothing in reply. Then finally, from up above came the shout.

'Annie!'

'Ed!' she shouted back.

She looked up and thought she could make out the outline of a head. Then came the beam of light from the torch.

'Are you OK?' he called down. 'Are you hurt?'

She could hear the anxiety in his voice.

'I don't think so, I landed on my big bum,' she called up towards him.

'Why on earth did you . . . ?' he began but seemed to think better of the question.

'Where am I?' she shouted back.

'I think you're in a stream bed. Are you wet?'

Now, come to think of it, yes, she was.

'Are you safe? You can't fall any further?'

'I don't think so,' she replied.

She looked up and couldn't see the outline of Ed's head or the torchlight any more.

Then, several moments later, they were back in place: 'Here's the plan,' Ed called down. 'We'll take Morven down and get help. Morven has to go to hospital and . . . I'll need help to get you out.'

Annie considered this. It was what Ed had to do. Get Morven down and then come back for her. It would take at least an hour . . . maybe more. She would have to sit in a stream on her bruised bottom in the pitch dark for an hour or more.

She wasn't exactly overjoyed at the prospect.

'Annie?' Ed called down, wondering if she'd heard him.

'Could I have the torch?' she asked, sounding embarrass-ingly wimpy.

'Annie, I'm sorry but we need the torch.'

'Could Owen stay and talk to me?' was her next request.

'We need Owen to carry the torch, and I don't want him to fall in too,' was the perfectly sensible reply. 'You'll be OK. I'll see you very, very soon.'

'See you, Mum,' Owen called out a little too cheerfully. He was obviously enjoying every moment of this adventure.

'I love you,' she shouted back.

'I'll be right back,' Ed promised.

And with that, they were off.

For some time, Annie sat in the pitch black listening hard as the little group went away from her.

Finally, she couldn't hear their voices any more. Then all sorts of thoughts came to her in the lonely darkness. She remembered the time when Owen and his little cousin Billie had fallen into a dry well in Italy. Hours they'd spent in there, chatting, trying to coax a lizard to come out, eating the pears they had on them and never doubting for a moment they'd be found . . . while she, Dinah and the rest of the holiday party tore around the hillside like maniacs looking for them.

Annie wished she was in a nice warm well in Italy instead of a cold and soggy stream in the dark in Scotland.

Finally, she remembered the video camera in her lap. Feeling her way around the buttons, she switched it on. The lights came on and, although she couldn't see the digital display, she hoped this meant that she'd broken the camera's fall and everything was working fine.

She pointed it at her face.

'Hello, it's me, Annie. I just want you to know that I've

fallen off the mountain, but I was wearing *hiking boots* at the time. So there! If you hillwalk in heels, bad things can happen. If you hillwalk in hiking boots, bad things can happen. Best stick to the pavement, if you ask me.'

She paused and then started up on a different tack.

'I've fallen down into who knows what, who knows where, just as the man I love asked me to marry him . . . again. This time, I should definitely have said yes. This time, I think he got me when I was almost ready.

'Now I am ready but I'm stuck down at the bottom of some horrible drop, sitting on my big sore wet behind in a stream, waiting for them to come back and rescue me.

'Maybe this was Tamsin's plan all along,' Annie added with some bitterness. 'She's my boss, by the way. She sent me up the mountain in my heels, hoping I'd fall off somewhere, and she's probably going to leave me here at the end of the series. If enough of you vote for me, they'll come and get me out; if no one cares . . . then I'll just be left here and you'll get Myleene Klass instead.'

Chapter Forty-Two

Annie resting:

Pink vest top (Topshop)
Pink cropped PJ bottoms (M&S)
Witch hazel (First Aid box)
Bandages (same)
Total est. cost: £32

'It was a nightmare, babes.'

Annie lay back on the small double bed she and Ed were sharing in the cabin. She was looking at her feet. Once Lana had heard all the hillside adventures, after the twins had been put to bed, once Owen had been washed, warmed and filled with cocoa, once Annie had showered and changed, finally she had been able to tend to her poor, battered feet and all the rest of her scrapes and bruises.

Well, Ed and his first-aid wisdom, not to mention kit, had helped. He'd dabbed witch hazel on to the burst blisters and deep, oozing cuts. He'd padded them with soft, sterile dressings, then wrapped both feet tenderly in bandages.

She looked at the feet now, down there at the end of the bed.

'Shame about the red shoes,' she said to Ed ruefully.

'Some hillwalker's going to get a bit of a surprise, coming across one battered red pair of heels halfway up there.' He was sitting on the other side of the bed, in a makeshift T-shirt-and-boxers version of pyjamas.

'Yeah, plus Svetlana's Louboutins!' Annie reminded him. 'Not to mention cuttings from a coral-coloured crocodile masterpiece.'

'You were all out of your minds,' Ed said.

'What else could we do? We couldn't have left Morven up there. There was no way of getting help and we couldn't walk another bloody step in our shoes, not with her hanging on to our necks. It was a nightmare, babes,' she said, sighing with relief that she was actually back in a bed, warm and dry, with her feet off the ground. 'Do you think I meant to fall down a fifteen-foot drop?'

The phone on her bedside table bleeped.

'Flipping heck,' she exclaimed, 'a signal! The cloud cover must have cleared, or maybe the large deer standing next to the transmitter has moved.'

'You're not really a country girl, are you?' Ed had to point out.

'Not likely,' was Annie's decided response. 'You've seen what people have to wear out here – and they still break their legs.'

She picked up the phone. She had a text. Opening it, she read out loud: '"Head fine, ankl brokn. Thnks 4 yr help. Lk forward to seeing it on TV. Morven x".'

'The final episode of the series?' Ed smiled. 'That is going to be a lot of fun. How much filming did you manage to do?'

'Oh, I have all the crucial moments, don't worry,' Annie

assured him. 'I think I even got when Morven fell and I definitely got the cutting up of the bag. That was class. Svetlana broke a nail … it was a moment of very high drama. She cut up the bag with a hunting knife! It was terrible, women all over the country will be covering their eyes. They won't be able to watch. She stuck her knife right in and made this terrible ripppppp noise, and that was it, seven thousand pounds' worth of craftsmanship gone with a single stroke.'

Ed took hold of her hand and held it in his. 'So are we going to stop off in Gretna Green on the way home then?' he asked softly.

For a moment there was silence in the room; then Annie turned to face him. 'Ed Leon!' she exclaimed. 'Is that seriously your idea of a proposal?'

'Annie Valentine!' he exclaimed right back. 'Is that seriously your idea of an answer?'

She rolled on to her back and crossed her arms: 'First of all, I'm not going to talk to you about anything wedding-related unless you ask properly.'

Ed paused for a moment and began to blush. He got out of the bed without saying anything and, for a moment, Annie thought she had gone too far. Maybe she had refused once too often. As she watched him walk round the bed towards her side and in the direction of the door, she knew immediately that she'd changed her mind.

Up until today, she'd thought that getting married would be too complicated and just unnecessary. And there was, deep down in her heart, the thought that getting married might somehow bring them bad luck. She had once buried her husband.

She knew it was irrational, but she couldn't help thinking that if she didn't marry Ed, nothing bad could happen to him. If he wasn't her husband, she could never be his widow.

'Ed?' she asked with a voice which felt tight.

Ed didn't make for the door, he turned, as he'd intended to turn, and knelt down on the floor beside her.

'Annie,' he began, scooping up her hands and holding them firmly in his, 'let's get married . . . and not just to make Owen happy. Let's get married because we want to and because it's not such a big deal. We're committed anyway: we have Lana and Owen, our babies, the house.'

She loved that he had put Lana and Owen first. That was very important to her.

'Gretna Green would be fine,' Ed assured her. 'If you can just turn up, I have no idea, but if we can, let's go there, sign some papers and we'll be done.'

He was playing it down. He didn't want to make it too romantic, too over the top or too momentous, because he was frightened that she would shy away.

'Ed?' she asked again. She propped herself up on her elbow and put her hand against this very kind face.

'Shhhh!' he insisted, perhaps wanting to stop her from refusing him again. 'It's OK, please, don't worry about it.' He put his hand over hers. 'I know you're worried, but I promise, it's going to be fine. I'm going to live for a very, very long time. Probably outlive you by years and years,' he twinkled, understanding and addressing her deepest fear. 'Gorgeous young girlfriends will be swanning around me in the contents of your wardrobe when I'm very old.'

'Shut up!' she told him with a grin. 'Have as many girlfriends as you like once I'm gone but the wardrobe goes to Lana and Minnie.'

The thought of Minnie being old enough to parade about in Annie's Versace numbers made both of them laugh.

'C'mon,' Ed urged, 'we'll just stop off, sign the papers and it will all be done.'

'No,' she said gently.

His face fell instantly.

'No, not no,' she backtracked, confusing him now. 'Just no to Gretna Green, babes. If I'm going to marry you . . . and I think I am . . .'

There was a pause here.

She looked right at him and let it sink in a little. She heard Ed's sharp intake of breath.

'If I'm going to marry you, then Dinah, Billie, Nic, Mum, Connor, your sister, Hannah, her little Sid . . . all the girls from The Store . . . everyone has to be there. Svetlana and her boys, Elena – I couldn't get married without them. I just couldn't. They'd never forgive me. And what about my girls? The regulars. The ones who watch the show every week, who email me and tell me the truth. Tell me if I've made a total pillock out of myself or not. They have to at least know that I'm planning to get married.

'I'm not saying they have to be there, *watching*,' Annie went on quickly, to Ed's relief, 'but they have to know about it. They'll have to help me choose my dress . . .

'Babes,' she said finally, 'if I'm going to get married again, then it has to be in a totally amazing dress. And look at my feet! I can't hobble down to Gretna Green tomorrow and tie the knot in a pair of hiking boots or a pair of those terrible tragic hiking sandals! It wouldn't be right! Would it?'

Ed shook his head. 'No,' he agreed, 'it wouldn't be right.'

'I won't be Annie Valentine any more!' she said, the realization dawning.

'Of course you will,' Ed assured her.

'No,' she told him with a shake of her head, 'that's Roddy's name. I can't keep it.'

'Well, you could be Annie Mitchell.'

'God no,' was her verdict on this, 'that's Mick's name.'
Running her hand slowly and fondly down his cheek, she

tried out: 'Annie Leon. That's nice. We'll all get used to it. I want to take your name. It's not PC, it's not cool, it's downright old-fashioned. But I want everyone to know just how much you mean to me.'

'Thank you,' he said and moved her hand to his lips so he could kiss it. 'You can be the one to tell Owen though,' he warned.

'What do you mean?'

'You can tell him that we're not getting married at Gretna Green. I think he's going to be gutted.'

The phone on the bedside table began to bleep again, but before Annie reached over and looked at the screen, she held Ed's searching look.

'You've not actually . . .' he began.

'Said yes?' She understood. 'Yes,' she told him but couldn't help adding, 'but don't be thinking this is a guaranteed-sex situation. I am un-bloody-believably tired.'

The phone bleeped again.

'OK.' Ed smiled at her. 'See who it's from. You know, it's just a proposal we're doing here, nothing urgent, we can do this again some time.'

'Sorry,' she said, but reached over for the phone.

'It's from Tamsin,' she began and read it first of all to herself with an increasing smile. Then she read it out to Ed: ' "Hv shown big boss yr Paris footage. He loves. Think u will be star of series 3. Txx". What do you think of that?' she asked him.

'I'm very proud of you,' he replied. 'You so deserve series three.'

'Yes, I'm very lucky. I'm about to get everything I always wanted,' she said, feeling slightly shocked at the idea herself. '*More* than I always wanted, babes. I didn't know how much I wanted the twins until I had them. And I didn't know how much I wanted another . . . *husband*.' She said the word carefully. It was still a loaded word for her. It was going to take a long time to be able to think of Ed as her husband, not Roddy.

'Annie Valentine gets everything she's always wanted,' Ed said with his eyebrows raised. 'It's not possible!' He bumped his nose gently against hers. 'Within twenty-four hours, Annie soon-to-be-Leon will want something else. I promise you, at least a second cupola or maybe your own range of shoes.'

'No!' she insisted. 'I have more than I ever wanted. This is all enough. Totally.'

She kissed him on the mouth, put her arms around his neck and suddenly felt that maybe the hours of trauma on the hillside might not have used up every last tiny bit of her energy.

Chapter Forty-Three

Connor economizing:

Blue T-shirt (Topman)
Blue V-necked cashmere sweater (Uniqlo)
Dark straight jeans with turn-ups (Lee)
Black baseball boots (Converse)
Total est. cost: £140

'I've been a prat.'

Annie wound her chair back just a little and shut her eyes. The four hours they'd spent in the car already had exhausted her. Babies had cried, babies had filled nappies, spilled milk, required the in-car stereo to play the theme tune to *The Teletubbies* so many times than both Lana and the ever-tolerant Owen had threatened to jump out.

The babies were now asleep, Owen and Lana had iPods on, Ed was concentrating on driving, so maybe Annie would manage to catch just a moment or two of shut-eye.

She liked the way Lana and Owen had responded to the wedding news. Owen, although intrigued by the idea of Gretna Green, had decided it would be OK to wait a bit longer, especially as Ed had taken him to one side and asked him if he'd like to be best man.

Owen had beamed a yes in reply, but he'd not been able to resist the cheeky: 'Is this because you haven't got any friends?'

Lana's happiness for the couple was quickly over-shadowed by one important concern: 'Am I going to be a bridesmaid?' she'd asked immediately.

'Only if you want to be,' had been Annie's reply.

'What will you make me wear?' had come the dark question.

'That's my girl,' Annie had told her proudly.

Just as Annie felt the deeply sleepy sensation of her thoughts merging and melting together, the phone in her handbag began to ring.

'For goodness' sake!' she said grumpily, sitting up in the car seat and coming abruptly round from the doze.

After a quick fumble through all the things in her bag, the phone was retrieved and Annie answered, surprised to see the name on the screen.

'Hello!' she said warmly. 'It's been ages.'

'I know,' Connor told her. 'I've been a prat.'

'Oh, me too. That's what happens when you're on TV, huh?'

'Yeah,' Connor agreed. 'I think I should come on your show, then we can at least be prats together.'

'Good idea,' Annie told him. 'I've told Tamsin all about you; she's trying to work you into the schedule.'

'Aha, and I know just what that means, babe, I've been in the biz long enough.'

'Huh?'

'That means: how the hell do we tell this wanker to get lost?'

'No!' Annie insisted.

'It's OK, I've got a good angle for you: from gorgeous to hideous. Cute Connor goes from sexy policeman to the Elephant Man.'

'No!' she said, shocked. 'Have you put on weight? We'll get rid of it together. Honestly, I need to go to the gym and you can show me the way.'

'No.' He was laughing at her. 'I'm going to play the Elephant Man. It was either that or sell my flat. And I keep telling you, when you're ready to commit to a personal trainer, I have the man. But you've got to commit to exercise, he won't train the weak.'

'You're going to play the Elephant Man?' Annie asked with astonishment – ignoring all the stuff about personal trainers. The idea appalled her.

'Oh yeah,' Connor replied, 'it's a great part. BBC Four, great director, plus there's talk of making it into a West End musical after the TV series ends.'

'No! You're going to be loaded!' Annie enthused.

'If I can just pay the mortgage and put something away for the next career downturn, I'll be happy. How about you? Are they signing you for a new series?'

'I don't know yet, but I think it looks OK. I've got other news, babes. Ermmm . . . Ed and I are going to get married,' she announced proudly, but suddenly feeling a slight choke in her throat as she said the words. Here she was telling not just one of her oldest friends, but also Roddy's best friend, that she'd moved on. Finally, she was ready to leave Annie 'Valentine', and all that it meant, behind and start a truly new phase.

'Really? You and Ed are finally going to tie the knot?'

'Yes,' Annie replied. She looked over at Ed, who glanced at her from the driver's seat and winked.

'That's fantastic! Brilliant! Can I walk you down the aisle? Because that way I'll definitely get into the *Heat* photo shoot with you. "Here is Annie Valentine's best friend Connor McCabe walking her gracefully through the church and down towards the man of her dreams,"' he intoned in best Royal Wedding commentator style.

It made Annie laugh. 'Register offices don't have aisles,' she warned him.

'For us, darling, they will make an aisle. Leave it to me,' he insisted.

'Connor?' She sounded serious now. 'Are we friends?'

'Of course we're friends.' He tried to wave the question away. 'We'll always be friends, even if you stand me up on lunch dates in the most crowded industry restaurants all over London.'

'I'm sorry, it was just a diary mistake. There was no need to take it so personally.'

'But, darling, I am an actor!' Connor camped it up. 'I have a very, very heightened sense of sensitivity.'

'Oh dear,' she began.

'What?'

'Oh dear, because I have another call coming in. Can you cope? You're not going to go all huffy and rejected on me just because I'm going to dump this conversation for another one?'

'It is going to take me weeks and weeks to recover,' he told her. 'Bye bye, bridie – but I can give you away, can't I?' he pleaded.

'Yes, all right. Well, we'll see . . .' Annie tried to stall him but she heard his little cheer at the other end of the line before he hung up.

Then Svetlana was breathing into her ear.

'Hi,' Annie said, 'so you got home OK and everything?'

'Ya, and claim for the bag and the shoes. My insurance broker laugh at me. Laugh but pay up.'

Insurance broker. Everyone else bought insurance online

and then made claims via some interminable call-centre line, but Svetlana had a broker, who had time for a laugh and a few jokes.

'I have to tell you more news—' Svetlana began.

'Me too!' Annie countered. 'But you first.'

'Ya! Elena has made magic in New York!' Svetlana began, her voice high with excitement. 'She over there, she have meetings, she sell, sell and wonderful result . . . Annah!' Svetlana paused before delivering the *coup de grâce*: 'We open office in New York, Perfect Dress going to be huge there. Maybe bigger in America than in Europe! I stay in London, Elena go to New York, she need partner over there to help her build this business and we both think of you!'

Svetlana stopped it there.

For a moment, Annie thought she could hear ringing in her ears. A sort of radio silence. As if she couldn't take any more in.

Ed's proposal . . . the probable third series . . . and now this.

She held her breath and gripped the phone tightly in her hand.

Moving to New York. Being a partner in a wonderful new fashion label. Making big, serious money. Being a mogul. Risking it all for the potential success and riches.

Moving to New York.

Running a business.

It was a wonderful, wonderful, fabulous opportunity, and it was being offered to her. On a plate.

Elena would be sensational to work with. Just to meet her was to know that she was really going to be something. Svetlana with knobs on. Svetlana but in charge of her own future, her own business, her own fortune and her own destiny.

Annie would love to see that.

Would love to get involved in that. Maybe even have her own children involved in it.

Build a business.

She ran the tip of her tongue over her lips just with the sheer anticipation of it all.

'Huh?' Svetlana was asking. 'Annah, is fabulous, fabulous offer. We only offer because of all you do for us. You dress me for my weddings, you find me my wonderful divorce lawyer and husband. When I want to throw my daughter out, you make me realize she is amazing girl. Annah . . . you my best friend in whole world.'

Now Annie's eyes began to blur. 'Thank you,' she managed.

But she looked over at the man who had just told her he wanted to marry her and spend the rest of his life with her. She glanced to the back seats and the two sleeping babies they'd made together. And then to her two older, wonderful children, both so happy at school, so settled in their London lives. They'd lost their dad and several family homes. But they were very happy now. Secure and contented.

Ed was going to go back to work, back to the school and the job he loved.

Hadn't she told him just last night that she had everything she'd ever, ever imagined wanting and so much more besides?

And hadn't he promised that she would want something else within twenty-four hours?

She had to smile at this.

He knew her so well. Too well. He knew her so thoroughly inside out but he *still* loved her and wanted to be with her.

'Annah?' Svetlana asked. 'Just say yes. We work everything out. You can rent out your house; we find you wonderful apartment. Just say yes and we make it all happen. TV is nice salary, but is not a business, not a label, not a career for ever. TV drop you after year or two because someone new come along. This how it works on TV. Always. You know this.'

'It's a wonderful offer,' Annie told her friend.

Her friend. No longer her client, no longer someone she was in awe of and took orders from: Svetlana, her friend.

'It's a truly, truly amazing offer and maybe sometime in the future . . .'

'Ah no, Annah, if not you now, then we have to choose someone else. This is your chance.'

'Maybe sometime in the future I can work with you and Elena,' Annie went on steadily, trying not to be put off by the siren call of Svetlana and her wonderful offer. 'I would love that. I would absolutely love to work with you. But just now, I have to be in London, with my family, in our home . . . with my great job.'

'What was all that about?' Ed wanted to know when she'd finally put away her phone.

'Connor's offered to walk me down the aisle,' Annie began.

This made Ed laugh.

'And Svetlana's offered me a business partnership in her new fashion company. In New York.'

Ed turned to look at Annie.

'Eyes on the road,' she instructed him, mainly because his driving made her nervous, but also because she didn't want him to read any trace of sorrow, or doubt, or regret in her decision.

'I told her it was a very nice offer, but that of course I couldn't accept,' Annie said quickly, 'because I'm very happy in London. And besides' – she put her hand out and squeezed him on the arm – 'didn't I just tell you I've got everything I ever wanted and more?'

Ed, who immediately understood what a big decision she had made for them all, said gently: 'Thank you. You won't regret one moment of staying in London with us. It's going to be brilliant. Anyway, you're only filming for twenty-five weeks of the year; plenty of time to go out to New York, help Elena arrange shows, plan advertising campaigns, look at dress fabrics . . . be a roving consultant for them. Get involved with them. I know you would love that.'

'Really?' she said, gasping in surprise at the possibility. 'You'd let me go off to New York? You'd let me help them out? Spend time over there?'

'Yeah,' he agreed. 'There are some great, great concerts to go to in New York. I could keep myself and the rest of the family very busy. We wouldn't come out every time,' he added with a wink, 'just every now and then, you know, so you didn't get lonely . . . or miss us too much. Just in the school holidays, obviously . . .'

Spotting a service station up ahead, Annie instructed Ed to pull in. Suddenly she felt the need of a break; there was too much going on, too much to think about.

She needed a packet of tissues and some extra-minty chewing gum. She had to have those things. If she had those in her hand, she'd be able to think straight and cope.

'Anyone else want anything?' Annie asked her fellow passengers.

Lana shook her head.

'Can I come in?' Owen wondered.

'So you can look at the latest camping-stroke-Dr-Who bits and pieces for sale?' Annie said with fond exasperation.

Owen shrugged and looked at her pleadingly.

'Oh, all right then,' she agreed, 'but quietly, don't wake the twins or I will personally murder you. I'd drug them and make them sleep all the way to London if I could.'

Owen slid the car's passenger door open and stepped out.

He strode across the forecourt ahead of his mum. She watched the jaunty little stride he was developing. He'd once been so shy; he'd not even been able to speak to anyone who wasn't a member of the family. Now look at him, swaggering towards the garage, probably about to wheel and deal his way into her purse, persuading her to part with some obscene amount of money for a bizarre little piece of plastic nonsense.

But no, his hand went into his jeans pocket and he brought out his small black wallet.

He'd come prepared; he'd armed himself with his pocket money.

Her cash was safe.

When she returned from the ladies', she found Owen browsing the many shelves of strange service-station merchandise with interest.

If the glamorous fashion mecca, The Store, where Annie had once reigned on the second floor as Head Personal Shopper, had been retail heaven, this service station had to be retail hell.

Who made the stock decisions here? Someone who had never been to another shop before? Annie cast her eye over the terrible joke mugs next to the boxes of Kendal mint cake, the hideous cuddly kittens, the Abba DVD box sets and the England football strips. Who shopped here? Who decided that these were good things to buy?

There were even bunches of fake flowers – who bought those? Who thought: I know, I'll give my wife / girlfriend / auntie / grannie/ mum a lovely bunch of fake flowers?

'I don't think you're going to find anything to burn your money on in here, babes,' Annie told her son.

Owen saw it first – well, he saw the label; he didn't register what it was attached to, he just saw a photograph of his mother sticking out from one of the shelves and instinctively moved in for a closer look.

Only a split second behind him, Annie saw it too. But she saw the whole package and understood at once what this was.

'Oh no!' she gasped. 'It can't be . . . oh NO!'

Owen's hand was already on the label with the photograph; he tugged at it to understand more.

A hideous, bright, shiny pink handbag slid out into his hands. It was so plasticky and stiff, it didn't yield to his touch in any way at all. It smelled like a new Barbie in her new box. It did in fact look like some sort of Barbie carry-case.

Annie wanted to snatch it out of his hands but she couldn't bring herself to touch it.

Owen held the label between his fingers and read out: ' "The Annie Bag. TV's Annie Valentine says: 'Think pink, you foxy girl.' Made in Taiwan. 100% polypropylene, £6.99." '

'Oh my God,' was Annie's whispered reaction, 'I can't believe this. How has this happened? I mean I saw a drawing . . . it looked fine in the drawing.'

Annie looked at the shelf. There were four Annie Bags – *Annie Bags? Could it get more hideous?* – in there. Should she buy them all? Then at least they would be out of here – but what if there were more in the back? And there must be many, many more in service stations up and down the motorway, in terrible tat-filled gift shops up and down the country. This was hideous! Horrible! It had to be stopped.

She stuffed an Icy gum into her mouth and tried to blink away the tears. Hadn't Tamsin warned her to leave the tie-ins alone? This was the worst. This was total humiliation.

Chapter Forty-Four

Bedtime Billie:

Fairy-print pyjamas (The White Company)
Pink bobbles for plaits (Boots)
Spritz of rose water (Neal's Yard)
Bunny slippers (a present)
Total est. cost: £45

'Awwww!'

Dinah ushered Annie into her little flat, poured her a glass of wine and made her sit down on the sofa.

Dinah's daughter Billie sat down on the sofa beside her auntie and tucked in under her arm.

'Hello, baby,' Annie said, kissing Billie on the nose, 'you're in your nightie already.'

'I know, it's ten minutes past my bedtime,' Billie informed her with a cheeky smile which showed her huge front teeth already halfway grown in.

Billie didn't look like a chubby-faced little girl any more, she suddenly looked older and Annie felt the stab of panic at how quickly time passed and children grew up. It was almost as if you turned your head for a few minutes and when you looked back, they'd sprouted up another bit. She noticed it much more with Billie, whom she saw only every few weeks, than with her own children.

'Very nice of you to fit me in after how many hours of filming?' Dinah asked.

'Ten and a half,' Annie replied and sprawled across the upholstery. 'I'm cream-crackered, but a sip or two of this and I'll be feeling much better. So show me the dress!'

'It's not finished yet,' Dinah protested.

'I know but I'm desperate to see it. Do you love it?' Annie asked Billie.

Billie laughed and nodded her head.

'Are you going to look totally unbelievably fantastic for Auntie Annie's wedding?'

'Yes,' Billie confirmed.

'Auntie Annie's wedding,' Dinah repeated, 'I can't believe it! I still can't believe it. It is so great. Have you got a dress yet?'

'No. I've got some time in the diary though, to go trying . . . and I've been doing just a little bit of research.'

'I bet you have.' Dinah turned and went out of the room to fetch the bridesmaid's dress that she'd been working on.

Annie had given her bridal party a simple brief: they could wear whatever they wanted to wear, as long as it was pink. Any style of outfit; any shade of pink. She wasn't going to make everyone line up in identical dresses looking like a bad assortment of shop dummies.

Dinah walked into the room holding a pale pink froth of chiffon in her hands; she shook it out so Annie could see the delicate little bell sleeves, the careful rows of beading and all the lovely little details Dinah was so busy making for her darling little girl.

'Oh my goodness, that is absolutely beautiful, you're doing such an amazing job. Isn't your mummy so clever?' Annie directed at Billie.

Billie nodded and smiled. 'I chose the material and the beads,' she pointed out.

'I know you did, you are so, so good at fashion, Billie. You're going to come and work for Auntie Annie one day, aren't you?'

Billie nodded proudly.

'Will you make Lana a dress?' was Annie's next question. 'She's in a total tizz, doesn't know what she wants. She definitely doesn't want to wear pink, in any shade at all . . . which I'm trying to be OK with. Instead, she wants to wear black. *Black?* I've told her everyone will think she disapproves if she turns up in black.'

'Oh dear,' Dinah sympathized, 'that is a little tricky.'

'She asked Ed if he would mind and he's told her as long as she's there, she can turn up in tartan pyjamas if she wants to.'

'Well, that's nice . . .'

'But not very helpful.'

'Maybe if I take her to a fabric shop,' Dinah suggested, 'she might see something she likes that isn't too heavy.'

'Even a steely grey or a blue,' Annie suggested. 'She always looks brilliant in blue.'

'Roddy's eyes,' Dinah pointed out.

'Penny's going to come. Have I told you that?' Annie said in response to this comment.

'Is she?' Dinah understood the mixed emotions at once.

Penny was Roddy's mother. When Roddy was alive, she had been close to Annie and her children. But after his death, she'd decided to move to France, so now they only saw her once or twice a year. Each and every visit was very emotional.

'Have you spoken to her?' Dinah asked.

'Yes – on the phone,' Annie replied. 'She sounds good. She's really pleased to be invited and be part of it. Missing her grandchildren.'

'Your wedding's going to be a big thing,' Dinah sympathized. 'C'mon, Billie, bedtime.'

'Awwww!' came the complaint.

'Sit!' Annie patted the cushion beside her when Dinah came back into the room after putting Billie to bed. 'I take it Bryan's working late?'

Dinah shook her head. 'Thursday night is now squash night. He plays with a friend and they treat themselves to one beer afterwards. Welcome to middle age.'

Annie gave a little grimace.

'How's your whole gym and personal trainer thing coming on?' Dinah asked, trying to suppress the smile that the thought of Annie in any sort of gym situation brought on.

'Just shut up,' was Annie's response. 'My viewers like me real. They don't want another aerobicized babe preaching to them from the small screen. Tamsin agrees.'

Dinah leaned back in her chair. 'Quite right.'

'But what with wedding dress angst, I've done a bit and the gut is receding.'

'Good,' Dinah encouraged.

For a moment there was a comfortable silence between them; then they both started talking again at once.

'Have—' Annie began.

'The—' Dinah started. 'You first,' she insisted.

'Well, I was just wondering if you'd thought about making bridesmaids' dresses – you know, for a living,' Annie said. 'You're brilliant and there must be so many brides in north London who'd love a really chi-chi, specialized service.'

'Oh no.' Dinah dismissed the idea. 'I really miss going to work, being somewhere else and having the company.'

'But when you're well known for bespoke bridesmaids' dresses, you hire a little premises, you employ some lovely other people and all those problems are solved,' Annie was quick to point out.

'Annie the plannie!' Dinah laughed. 'Did you know that's what Nic and I call you? You've always got a plan.'

'Well, I want everyone to enjoy life, live life, grab it by the balls. I don't like the thought of you sitting about at home feeling sad and not having enough cash. And what about trying for babies again?' Annie asked gently. 'You've not said anything for a while. You know that you are supposed to come to me and off-load any time. Sound me out about anything.'

Dinah took hold of Annie's hand and gave it a squeeze. 'Yeah,' she said, 'except when you're so busy you put me on hold, cut me off and then can't find the time to call me back for days.'

'Sorry,' Annie told her.

'Actually I do have a plan,' Dinah began. 'I'm not doing any more IVF. I can't take it. Not physically or emotionally . . .'

Annie squeezed Dinah's hand hard.

'But,' Dinah went on, feeling her voice choke a little, 'I have a plan which involves employment, filling the baby-shaped hole in my life . . . and you.'

Annie gazed at her with a puzzled look on her face.

'You know Ed's going back to work . . . ?' Dinah said, hoping Annie would catch on.

'Yes?' Annie was still in the dark.

'You'll need childcare and I think you should hire me.'

Annie's eyebrows shot up into her hair: 'Would you like to do it?' she asked, thrilled at the idea.

'Yeah, I'd totally, totally love to. You'll have to pay me the going rate, obviously.'

'Obviously,' Annie agreed.

'But I think I'd be excellent.'

'So do I. You're a much better mother than me.'

'Don't say that!' Dinah protested. 'Your kids are all fantastic and they think the world of you.'

'And Billie is brilliant,' Annie added quickly.

It was always so lovely to have someone tell you how fantastic your children were and what a good job you were doing. It was what sisters were for. Well, one of the many, many things sisters were for.

Once they had excitedly talked the nanny plan through, Dinah braced herself for a change of subject.

'Have you invited Mick to your wedding?' she asked her sister bravely, knowing perfectly well this was a difficult subject for Annie.

A sort of garrumphing harrumphing noise came from Annie's direction.

'Maybe you should speak to Mum about it,' Dinah added. 'If she wants him there . . .'

There was more garrumphing and harrumphing.

'I really do think he wants to get to know us again,' Dinah said gently.

'Get to know us at all,' Annie corrected her. 'Did he ever really know us before? All I know about him, I read in *Pssst!*'

'Luckily, he didn't say much to them. He did sound quite sorry about it all, though. Well, you're up at Mum's this weekend,' Dinah added. 'I bet he'll come round, it sounds as if he likes to pop round once a day to check up on her. And you have to admit that is a good thing.'

'She has Stefano,' Annie pointed out, 'and her neighbours, and one of us every weekend. It's not as if she needs Mick.'

'I think she likes Mick pottering about. He helps her in the garden; they drink vast buckets of tea and have a little reminisce about the time they spent travelling together. I think that was their happy time. Before any of us turned up.'

'Yeah. He was a rubbish dad.'

'He was,' Dinah agreed. 'Maybe we'll hear more about why one day.'

'D'you think he's got a Thai bride somewhere? I keep expecting some teeny little oriental woman to pop out of the woodwork. He looks the type: Captain Mick. I mean he was so completely, unrelentingly unfaithful to Mum . . . you remember all the things we only found out about once we were teenagers. After a dad like that in our lives it's a blooming miracle we all ended up with such good men,' Annie pointed out.

'Well, Mum's never found anyone else and Nic married a stinker first time round,' Dinah pointed out. 'Plus, for some reason I can never understand, you still don't like Bryan.'

'Oh . . .' Annie felt caught out, like a rabbit in the head-lights. 'I used to not like him. But . . . I'm mellowing, I'm actually really quite liking him now.' She wanted Dinah to know this was the truth. 'I'm seeing his many qualities. In another fifteen years or so I'll love him. It's just jealousy,' she added. 'You're my best friend and I don't like to share.'

'That's nice,' Dinah told her.

'What were you going to say?' Annie asked next.

When Dinah looked confused, Annie tried to jog her memory: 'When we both started talking at once. What were you about to say?'

'Oh . . . oh!' Suddenly a very mischievous look crossed Dinah's face. 'The bag!' she blurted out. 'I've seen the Annie Bag!'

Chapter Forty-Five

Personal Shopper Paula:

Multi-print silk blouse (DVF, store discount)
Blue wide-leg trousers (Chloé, store discount)
Blue patent ballet flats (French Sole)
Mustard-yellow nails with diamanté (Blaxx Salon)
Total est. cost: £390

'Give yourself time.'

Annie squeezed Paula tightly in her arms for a long time, even though hugging Paula always made Annie feel like a big, squidgy oink oink. Paula was so long and so lean and so lithe. To add insult to injury, she existed on chocolate brownies, hot chocolate with cream on the top and never lifted one perfectly manicured talon to do the slightest bit of exercise. She didn't even do stairs! She always took the escalators! It was so stinkingly unfair.

'It's my genes,' Paula would say casually.

Annie would kill, would actually hunt, stab or garrotte, for genes like that. Instead, she was stuck with genes which thickened her middle a little bit more every day, despite the sit-ups and all the other humiliations of the gym.

Annie was back at The Store for only the fifth or sixth time since her leaving party over two years ago now. It felt both strange and ridiculously familiar. Maybe what was strange was that it felt so familiar.

She'd come in through the beauty department, noticing how many counters and faces behind them were still the same.

'Oh Annie! I watch your show every single week. It's brilliant!' Sandra in handbags shouted over to her.

Annie immediately had to go over and have a little discussion about how good this season's Celines were looking before Nina at Bobbi Brown stole her away for a brisk mini-makeover.

'I have to go upstairs,' Annie had insisted, once Nina's dabs and touches were nearing an end. 'I have an appointment with Paula, because ... she's been looking out wedding dresses for me!'

This started up a whole hum of excitement on the ground floor.

'When's the wedding?'

'Where is it?'

'Will it be on TV?'

'What're you wearing?'

To which Annie had answered in turn: 'In six weeks' time. Register office. No, definitely not on TV, are you mad? And I don't know yet. That's why I need to go up and see Paula now.'

Once their greetings were over, Annie asked Paula: 'Have you got in the one that I'm really thinking about?'

'Oh yeah, girl, and in a twelve.'

Annie sucked in her stomach. 'Do you really think I can squeeze back into a twelve?'

'You'll have to, they don't make it any bigger,' Paula

warned, 'but I've lined up a whole rack of other possibilities, plus you can go out there and search the rails, see what else you like.'

'Yeah,' Annie agreed, fingers almost itching to go out on to the second floor and look around the clothes rails she once used to lord it over, 'but let's go and take a little peek' – her voice dropped almost to a reverential whisper – 'at the Williamson.'

Together they walked through the Personal Shopping suite where Annie had once reigned. The carpet had been replaced since she was last here; it was now a rich, royal purple, but still lusciously deep pile and spoiling. The fuchsia velvet curtains hanging in front of each changing room were still the same though, along with the pink velvet sofa in the middle of the space.

The huge white-framed mirror, where she'd stood for year after year admiring her transforming handiwork with her clients, was also still there.

But now she was going to be the client standing in front of it. This was such a strange, strange new thing.

'This is so exciting,' Paula began, 'the TV show and now the wedding – and how are the babies?' she asked.

'The babies are fantastic,' Annie told her. 'Oh my holy sainted hallelujah . . .' she gasped. There it was, the dress, hanging on the rail in the central changing room, waiting for her.

It was absolutely breathtaking. Unbelievably beautiful. Much lovelier in the flesh than it had looked on the internet.

Deepest, loveliest fuchsia satin, hanging in ripples from just below the bust to ankle. Well, she didn't want to go long, otherwise how would anyone see the knockout shoes she planned to be wearing?

A band of multi-coloured beading, reds, oranges, greens

and golds, circled the empire line, then the deep pink flowed up into a halter neck anchored with another collar of the amazing beads.

'Oh, it's so beautiful,' Annie gasped.

'You are going to look like a total peach in that, I just know it,' Paula assured her.

There was nothing else on the rail Paula had set out that would do for Annie at all. Everything else was white or pastel pink, peachy or mint green, nothing had the jaw-dropping verve of the Williamson.

'That's the one that I want!' Annie exclaimed, pointing at the gown. 'Let's get it on. So this is definitely the biggest size?' she asked, looking at the narrow empire line with some concern. 'Do you think I'll get in?'

'Only one way to find out,' Paula told her. 'Do you want me in or out?'

'Stay in,' Annie instructed, 'and we can laugh at my tummy disaster together. I'm going to New York in a couple of months,' she added, taking off her shoes and unbuttoning her blouse. 'Have you heard about Svetlana's new label, Perfect Dress? Of course you have, you're going to be selling some very soon.'

'Oh yeah, I'm liking the Perfect Dress,' Paula replied. 'I think I'm going to get one in orange.'

'Do that,' Annie told her. 'I'm now making . . . ummm .03 per cent of every Perfect Dress sold because I invested early.'

'So what are you doing in New York?' Paula asked, busy-ing herself with taking the Williamson off the hanger, unzipping it and getting it ready for the try-on.

'I'm going to be the Perfect Dress roving consultant,' Annie said with a smile of glee, but trying to sound casual. 'So I'm just flying over to New York in between shooting schedules to go to a fabric fair with Elena. We're looking at material for the new range. Get me!' she exclaimed, casualness forgotten. 'My life has suddenly got so glamorous it's unreal . . . but I still look like this!'

Both Annie and Paula considered Annie's reflection in the mirror. She was down to her bra and support knickers now.

'It's not right,' Annie added.

The arms and legs were fine, the boobs more luscious than they'd ever been in Annie's entire life, bar pregnancy. But the stomach . . .

'I think you need to up your crunches, girl,' was Paula's matter-of-fact advice.

'Yeah,' Annie agreed, thinking: *Oh God, it's hopeless. How many crunches would you need to do to shift a mountain of marshmallow like this? Ten thousand a day, probably.*

'C'mon,' Paula soothed, 'give yourself some time. You'll get there. I see it all the time. You've been in my job, you know mummies take a lot longer than a year to get their groove back.'

'Some of them never do,' Annie warned.

'And we dress them beautifully, just the same,' Paula reminded her. 'Come on, get this baby over your head.'

Annie held up her arms and Paula slid the dress over her head. They smoothed it down into place and Annie breathed in as the zip was pulled up.

Then they both looked in the mirror to study the result.

It was beautiful. It looked just as fabulous as Annie, in her wildest dreams, had hoped.

'Here comes the bride,' Paula said.

'Oh my,' Annie sighed, 'that is stunning. Just stunning.'

She turned to the left, and then to the right, taking in all the angles in the changing room's clever mirrors.

The dress draped over the troublesome tum. It stopped just below her calves, making her legs look as slim and shapely as possible. It did something very clever and flattering with her boobs and the beading round her neck was just delicious.

She thought of all the shoe possibilities. Red? No, gold? Even orange? Or green?

There was just this tiny little twinge . . . something was threatening to rain on her parade.

'It's perfect,' Paula told her.

'Annie! Are you in here?'

Annie recognized the male voice straightaway: it was Dale, from Menswear.

'Hi!' she called out. 'Open the curtain, Paula, we'll get a second opinion.'

When Dale saw her, he fell down on to his knees and pretended to cry. 'Oh my gosh,' he blubbed, 'it's too much. It really is her and she looks divine!'

Then Sandra and two other assistants from the second floor were in the room as well. No one seemed to be able to resist coming to have a look at Annie's new dress.

'Oh Annie,' Sandra blurted out, 'that's amazing! You look really beautiful. And I have a gold clutch downstairs made for that dress. Absolutely made for it . . . YSL,' she added.

All of a sudden, Annie felt it was too much. Too much approval, too much pressure, too big a decision and possibly – her eye caught the dangling tag – too big a price.

'OK, guys, I'm closing the curtain, I need to think about this on my own,' she told them.

She swished the curtain shut, leaving even Paula on the outside now.

Alone in the changing room, she tried to work out what it was that was bothering her.

She'd known the dress was very expensive before she'd tried it on. But it wasn't the most expensive dress she'd ever bought. She held the tag in her hand and looked at the eye-watering four-figure price. She earned a lot of money now, though, she could afford it.

But . . . but . . . The 'but' was this: on her wedding day, her second wedding day, she wasn't sure if she wanted to be swanning about in a three-thousand-pound dress. She wanted to be able to hug people, laugh and cry, spill champagne, hold the babies, be squeezed to death by Ed and not worry about the designer-label dress. She didn't want the day to be all about the dress.

Plus, wasn't she always telling her loyal TV fan base that you didn't need to spend thousands of pounds to look fantastic?

Well then, wasn't she just going to be a big, fat fraud if she bought this dress?

And somehow, she wanted her fans to be involved in choosing the dress . . . and Lana . . . and Dinah and even Billie too.

'Paula,' she called from inside the changing room, 'I'm about to turn into your nightmare customer.'

'What do you mean?' Paula asked, more than a little concerned.

Annie stuck her head out of the curtain and gave it to her straight: 'Babes, I'm going to ask you to put this on hold.'

'NOOOOOO!' Paula exclaimed. 'You can't! I won't let you.'

'But, Sandra,' Annie added, 'I'm definitely coming downstairs to talk to you about the gold clutch.'

Chapter Forty-Six

Visiting Nic:

Pale green linen dress (Phase Eight)
White leggings (Tesco)
White flip flops (Birkenstock)
Sunglasses (Zara)
Total est. cost: £140

'I didn't fling my arms around him . . .'

In the warm sunshine, Annie scraped the last crumbs from her plate and wondered if *two* slices of chocolate cake could form part of an acceptable diet for a bride just weeks from her wedding day.

'That was fantastic, clever Nic.' She winked at her sister, her other, older sister, sitting on the opposite side of the garden table from her. 'Isn't Mummy clever to make such a delicious cake?' she asked her adorable little niece, Tara, who was sitting on Nic's lap.

The toddler with the tumble of brown curls giggled and clapped in response. She was the only child currently in Fern's garden because Ed and Owen had wheeled the babies off for a walk and hopefully a snooze.

Ed had another reason for wanting to be out of the garden: Mick was due to pay a short visit at 3 p.m. and he had a feeling that maybe Nic and Annie should get on with this without him.

Annie had eaten the second slice of chocolate cake out of sheer anxiety.

'How did it go yesterday, when you first met him?' Annie asked her sister.

Although the question was out of the blue, Nic didn't need Annie to explain whom she was talking about.

'Well' – Nic gave a shrug – 'what can I say? I didn't fling my arms around him and scream: "Daddy, you're back."'

'No.' Annie's foot was tapping restlessly and she was seriously considering a third slice. 'I think it would be easier if he just went away,' she said. 'You know, he was in a box in my head and I don't want him out, running about here wanting me to deal with him, but Mum . . .'

'Mum seems quite pleased to see him,' Nic finished her sentence.

'I think she's forgotten to be angry with him, she's forgotten about every horrible thing he ever did and she just seems to want to reminisce about the good old days.'

Whatever Nic might have wanted to say to this was silenced by the sound of the garden gate opening.

The sisters shot each other a look, and then their eyes travelled to the far side of the garden where Mick was at the gate, waving at them.

Nic waved back.

'Hello,' Mick said as he came over the freshly cut grass towards them. 'Lovely weather.'

He had a white baseball cap pulled down over his eyes against the sunshine and this cap, more than his face, was setting off an uncomfortable train of memories in Annie's mind once again.

He'd always worn a cap of some sort. It had been his thing, his *signature look*, Annie thought with a trace of bitterness.

'Hello again, Tara . . . and Annie, how are you?'

'I'm fine, thanks,' came her stiff reply. 'Mum was having a nap, but she's probably up now. I was just going to go and check on her.'

'Right.' Mick put his hand on the back of one of the chairs but hesitated, he obviously didn't want to sit down until he was invited to do so.

'Would you like a cup of coffee?' Nic gestured to the pot in the middle of the table. 'And some cake? Take a seat,' she said hospitably.

Annie watched as he pulled out the chair and sat down.

As Nic busied herself pouring out the coffee, Annie struggled for something to say. It wasn't exactly easy making small talk to a complete stranger who also happened to be your father.

'I hear you're getting married,' Mick began. 'Congratulations.'

'Thank you,' Annie managed.

Mick bent down from the table and picked up the small canvas bag he'd been carrying. 'I have a little wedding present for you, and something for Nic too,' he said as he lifted the bag on to his knees.

'Oh!' Nic protested. 'You shouldn't have . . .'

Annie's toes curled up in her shoes because she felt so embarrassed. Embarrassed for him, embarrassed for herself. What could he possibly give her that would be a good present? He didn't know anything about her or her family.

She didn't want to sit beside him. She couldn't just have cosy chats as if nothing had happened. As if twenty-five-odd years without a word from him could just be erased and they could somehow pick up from where he'd left off without anyone noticing or wondering where he'd been all this time.

She felt a blush of sheer awkwardness tingle up from the base of her neck to her cheeks.

But Mick was busy rummaging in his bag and out came two clumsily wrapped parcels; one was handed to Nic, and then Annie was given hers.

It was a small packet in layers of plain paper, which looked as if they had been wrapped around this object for some time. Annie began to unwrap the paper slowly, trying to prepare herself for whatever this gift was and find a suitable reaction.

'Oh!'

She heard Nic's surprised response.

'That's lovely,' Nic added, as kindly as she possibly could about her gift.

Annie peeled away the last layer of paper and a small, hard cameo brooch was in her hand. An antique one, she realized, looking at the tarnished silver all around the carefully carved piece of shell. Annie didn't own a cameo brooch, she'd always thought of them as old-fashioned and stuffy – jewellery that looked like a stamp. But this one was sweet. The face inside the brooch was delicate and she liked the worn silver frame.

'This is very pretty,' she told Mick.

She looked over at her sister, who was holding up a small tarnished silver bracelet with a miniature padlock as a clasp.

'I've got something for Dinah too,' Mick said. 'These all belonged to your grandmother. I know you didn't meet her; she died young. And what with being at sea and my dad being at sea, we didn't have many of her things. But you're her granddaughters, she'd have wanted her little bits of jewellery to go to her granddaughters.'

Annie suddenly felt a prickle of teariness start up at the back of her throat. She knew nothing about Mick's family. Fern's family had been very small, so there was only the one relative, elderly Auntie Hilda, left on that side.

But now she was faced with a grandmother and grandfather she knew nothing about – and did Mick have brothers and sisters? Vaguely stirring at the back of her mind was the memory of an uncle.

'You have a brother, don't you?' Annie asked sharply.

'Yes. Pat,' Mick replied.

'Uncle Pat,' Annie remembered, and then felt embarrassed for remembering. 'Well, he didn't make any effort to stay in touch with us either. Does he have children?' she asked. 'Are there whole tribes of cousins and relations we don't know anything about?' came her accusation.

'Ermmm, he does have two children, yes,' Mick answered. He picked up his cup of coffee, holding it in front of him defensively. 'I don't think Fern wanted to hear from any of us after I'd . . . well, after she'd told me—'

'We get the picture,' Annie snapped.

'This is a lovely little bracelet.' Nic attempted to inject a note of calm.

Annie looked back down at the cameo in her hand. She wondered what her long-gone granny would have thought of her son. Maybe Mick's father had been just the same . . . being at sea. It wasn't an occupation exactly suited to homebody types.

Maybe seamen became seamen because they knew at heart they were suited for roaming and roving, not parenting.

'What do you want from us?' Annie asked her father.

'We're not going to forgive you. There's no hope of you suddenly being part of this family again. In fact, we don't want you in this family,' she blurted out, sensing her pulse race, her cheeks burn and her throat constrict with the effort of this.

'Annie,' Nic warned gently.

'No, it's all right,' Mick said, 'I understand you're upset. We're all upset. It's difficult to come back to you. It would have been much easier to carry on ignoring you all, but I'm retired. One day I'll be dead and it didn't seem right not to find out how you were and let you know a bit about me. I wasn't expecting much back.'

'Oh . . .' was all Annie could manage.

There were a few more awkward moments of silence, spoiling the lovely afternoon in this beautiful garden. A blackbird was trilling in the hedge and Fern's heady pink roses were just coming into flower. But that didn't do anything to relieve the churn of feelings, the emotional mess playing out over the garden table.

'I've not cut you that slice of cake,' Nic remarked. She was falling back on her manners. When nothing else was working, it seemed to make sense to Nic to do manners.

'No thanks.' Mick waved the cake away. 'I think I'll get back home. I'll drop in on Fern another time.'

Annie didn't even want to stay to watch his awkward goodbyes, so, jumping up from the table, she told them: 'I think I'll just go in and check on Mum. Er . . . see you,' she said to Mick lamely.

'Yes,' he replied.

It felt cool and shady inside her mother's comfortable house after the sunshine in the garden. Annie walked quietly to the sitting room, where Fern was snoozing.

For a few minutes, Annie stood at the doorway and watched her beloved mum. She was still asleep, her head slightly tilted, her feet up in the air in her recliner chair.

Annie tiptoed over to stand right beside her and couldn't resist running a soothing hand over her hair. It felt warm and bouncy, not smooth and slippery like her children's hair. This was older hair, a little rougher and wiry under the highlights and careful blow-drying.

Her mum. So much, much more important to her than her father. How dare he come back now, when Fern wasn't well, and think he could play some part in looking after her? Annie was sure that if only Fern weren't feeling so vulnerable, she'd have told Mick to get lost and never darken their doorstep again. No matter how nice and generous he thought he was being these days, he didn't deserve a family.

Fern deserved her daughters and all their love and affection and all the love and affection of her grand-children. She'd earned it. She'd put in the hours and the effort. She'd cared for them every day of her life. Not a day passed when she didn't think of them all and speak to at least one of them.

Mick couldn't just turn up here and expect to get any kind of respect or affection from total strangers who just happened to be related to him.

Fern's eyes opened and she lifted her hand to the fingers in her hair.

'Is that my Annie?' she asked in a voice that still sounded far away and sleepy.

'Yeah,' Annie whispered her reply. 'Are you back with us then?'

'Oh yes, back again,' Fern said sleepily. 'I hope I haven't missed anything good? That is going to be the absolute worst thing about being dead. I am going to miss all the good stuff.'

Annie squeezed hard at the fingers entwined with hers: 'Shhhh!' she said to try and banish this thought from both of their minds.

Chapter Forty-Seven

Bridesmaid Billie:

Pale pink chiffon dress (by Dinah)
Pale pink tights (Ballet Supplies)
Sparkly pink sandals (Lelli Kelly)
Pearl bead bracelet (Claire's Accessories)
Pink pearl tiara (same)
Total est. cost: £80

'It is so pink!'

Annie was taking her time in the changing room. This was the third shop and she was about to put on the fourth dress here.

It wasn't that nothing had been good. It was just that nothing had been WOW, nothing had really wooed her the way that Matthew Williamson's pink slice of genius had. The tempers of her fellow shoppers were holding up admirably but she sensed that if nothing worked in this shop, they were going to have to have lunch and rethink the strategy.

She slipped off the third dress which had just been too . . .

sigh . . . well, just too this and too that and not at all right. She turned her attention to the fourth and final frock. Secretly, she was hoping that this one would work. This was why she'd saved it for last. She'd wanted to rule out the other contenders in the hope that they would make this dress look like the best possibility.

It was a pink silk halter-neck dress. It was perfectly plain. No beading, so satin, no slithery on-the-bias cut, but it was a deep and vibrant shade of screaming pink.

Not millions of miles from the Williamson in shape and colour.

She looked at herself briefly in the mirror. In the pink lace bra with the beige tummy-hugging knee-to-waist pants and strappy high pink heels, she looked quite something. Like Vivienne Westwood about to go to the Palace and meet the Queen, maybe.

'D'you need a hand in there?' Dinah wondered from the other side of the curtain.

'No, no, I'll be fine,' Annie assured her. 'I'm just getting the last one on. I'll be out in a second.'

She slipped the dress from its hanger and slid it down over her head. She tied the straps into a bow at the nape of her neck, smoothed it down over her corseted contours and only then allowed herself to look in the mirror properly.

A little smile formed at the sight. This was not bad. This was not at all bad. Maybe a big blowsy pink flower at the front, where the cleavage slipped a little too low? Pearls, she thought. Big chunky pearls. The shoes looked fantastic. The dress was a great length for leg flattery and it fitted well round the body.

She took another glance at the price tag: £75! Seventy-five pounds! It was really a stunning dress for that money. She could squeeze people and be squeezed all day long in a dress that cost £75. Really, even if it took a red wine or baby sick direct hit, she wasn't going to mind too much. Maybe she should buy two, she thought wildly. Have a spare in case of a red wine or baby sick direct hit?

'Come out!' Dinah instructed. 'You've found a good one, haven't you? It's the bright pink one, isn't it?'

That girl could read her mind. She really could.

Annie pulled back the curtain with a flourish and stepped forward in her shoes.

'Always, always take the shoes you want to wear with your outfit,' she said out loud for the benefit of the camera. Because this wasn't just a quiet family shopping trip, Bob the cameraman was here too. The 'Scottish' final episode of *How Not To Shop*'s second series had revealed Annie's wedding plans, causing a fever of excitement amongst her viewers. Tamsin had told Annie there was no way on earth she could choose a wedding dress without them, so this footage was being shot for episode one of series three.

The cameras were going to catch up with Annie on her wedding day too, but only at the reception and only for a brief filming session.

'Oooh, Mum!' Lana said. 'That looks really nice.'

'Really?' Annie turned this way and that in front of both the mirrored wall and her little audience.

'It's not too . . . ?' she began.

'No,' Dinah answered firmly, 'the only thing it is "too" is too lovely. Look at your lovely shoulders and your *hot* legs,' she added, encouragingly.

'It is so pink!' Billie added, approvingly. She was dressed in her bridesmaid's dress, just as Auntie Annie had instructed: 'So as to make sure we match.'

Annie understood that when you were a little brides-maid, there just weren't enough opportunities to wear your fabulous dress, so some had to be created.

'Will you come and stand beside me?' Annie asked Billie and held out her hand to her.

'Awwww,' was Dinah's reaction when her little girl in pale pink chiffon and sparkles went to stand beside her sister, 'that looks really good.'

'And Lana,' Annie encouraged, holding out her other hand to her daughter.

'I'm not in my dress!' Lana protested, but came over anyway.

'I had noticed,' Annie told her, 'but you're wearing black, so I can get an idea of how we're all going to look together.'

'Who says I'm wearing black?' Lana challenged her.

'You know my new motto, babes: "Hope for the best, prepare for the worst." '

This made Dinah and Lana giggle. They exchanged conspiratorial glances.

'Have you got her to change her mind about the black?' Annie asked her sister. 'Really?'

'Shhhh!' Lana insisted.

'Just a clue?' Annie begged. 'One teeny, tiny little clue? That wouldn't be asking too much, would it?'

'Yes, it would,' Lana told her.

'Is this the one then?' Annie asked all three of them, plus the camera in turn.

All three heads, plus Bob's, nodded solemnly.

'You sure?' Annie looked at herself in the mirror again, critically, appraisingly. 'I was going to do pearls, plus a big pink flower in the cleavage. Maybe one of the assistants can get something like that for me ... We can have a little try-out?'

When the flower and a chunky messy necklace of several strands of pearls were wrapped around Annie, she looked hard in the mirror and then really loved what she saw.

This was really her. Home accessorized.

This was her, much more than the Williamson with its beaded neckline already in place and it's terrifyingly expensive folds. This was going to be the dress she could relax and say her vows in, relax and enjoy all the cuddles, hugs, sweat stains and tears of the day.

Now that she'd added the flower and the necklace and the shoes, she'd made it look just the way she wanted it to look.

'It's great,' she told the camera with a wink, 'perfect. Now just don't let Ed see it before the big day.'

'What about your bag, Mum?' Lana reminded her and went into the changing room to get the divine little gold YSL clutch out of Annie's larger handbag.

As soon as the clutch was in her hand Annie was almost complete. 'I just need my little bouquet of pink roses,' she told her helpers.

Dinah pointed to the gold clutch: 'Now that was totally not from the high street, was it?' she asked.

'Well, no.' Annie tipped her head towards Bob's camera lens again. 'I know, I know, it's not from the high street . . . but everyone needs a little touch of luxury on their wedding day and, darlin's, this is mine. YSL,' she added in a whisper.

Chapter Forty-Eight

The registrar:

Light grey skirt suit (MaxMara)
Pale pink silk blouse (Mango)
Black stockings (M&S)
Black slingbacks (Salvatore Ferragamo)
Total est. cost: £550

'Are we all set?'

Micky and Minnie were squirming in Ed's arms.

'Is Dinah here yet?' he asked, trying not to make the question sound too agitated.

'I haven't seen her, but she'll be here any minute.' Annie was frantically trying to sound calm herself. 'Give me one,' she instructed.

Dinah had promised she would be here early and be chief babysitter for the entire day.

Ed passed Minnie, in a pink frilly dress with tiny ribbon roses embroidered round the neckline, over to the woman who, in just another twenty minutes or so, would be his wife.

'I am dying to see what's under there,' Ed said, looking at his about-to-be-wife's tightly belted raincoat.

'Well, hold that thought,' Annie told him with a tense attempt at a smile.

She, Ed and the babies had come in the first taxi. The registrar, smartly dressed in a grey skirt suit, ushered them from the waiting room into her office where she shook their hands and welcomed them.

'OK, we're just going to go over a few final details and then it will be time,' she told them happily.

Annie smiled back and tried to look like a relaxed and joyful bride but she felt the most terrible jangle of nerves.

'I haven't looked through the vows,' she hissed urgently at Ed.

'Yes, you have,' he reminded her, 'the last time we were here, plus I gave you a printout.'

She shook her head. 'I can't remember,' she told him.

Really what she now desperately needed to know was that she wouldn't have to say: 'Till death do us part.' It was suddenly obsessing her: if she had to say those words to him, knowing it had happened to her before, she wouldn't be able to do it. Her knees would buckle and she would just drop to the ground and howl. She knew it. It was making her feel panicky.

'Here are the vows, Ms Valentine.' The registrar calmly handed her a plastic sleeve with several sheets of typed white paper inside.

Despite Minnie squirming in her arms and trying to wrench off her pearl earring, Annie managed to scan the words.

It looked OK. She couldn't see any sign of the dreaded phrase. It was going to be OK.

Ed put a hand on the back of her waist. 'It's all right,' he told her, 'you don't have to promise to share your wardrobe with me, or the proceeds of any eBay fire sales, and there's no clause about you having to have a savings account or anything like that.'

'Right.' Annie tried to smile. Normally she would have laughed, but she was far too anxious.

They did all the official bits and pieces the registrar wanted them to do and then it was time.

'There's a little holding area for the bridal party if you want to use it,' the registrar offered. 'Turn left, second door down. I take it you're going to the room, Mr Leon, to meet and greet.'

'Yes . . . Annie, give me Minnie and I'll . . .' He paused. 'I'll see you soon.' He bent over and kissed her gently on the forehead. 'I can't wait,' he whispered.

She took one last look at his broad, navy-suited back, a baby poking over each shoulder, and then he was gone.

Annie stepped out into the corridor and headed for the little waiting room. As soon as she opened the door, Dinah, Billie and Lana, who were already inside, jumped up excitedly.

'Where's Owen?' was Annie's first question.

'Meeting and greeting,' Lana informed her. 'He's taking his duties very seriously.'

'Hello, Annie,' Dinah said and hugged her sister hard.

'You look gorgeous,' Annie told her, taking in the sophisticated deep pink and white tea dress slithering round Dinah's whippety form. A white flower clip held one side of her bob behind her ear and she looked totally foxy.

'Good,' Dinah smiled. 'It is your wedding – style event of the decade!'

'Billie,' Annie instructed, 'come here and let me squeeze the life out of your gorgeousness.'

Billie, resplendent in not just the pink chiffon cloud but also a white down shrug and pink sparkly shoes, obliged.

Finally, Annie turned to Lana: 'OK, baby, time to unzip your parka and show me what you've got under there.'

'I will if you will,' Lana said with a smile.

Annie had almost forgotten she was still under her coat. She turned from Lana, then undid her buttons and put the coat on to a chair.

She smoothed down her dress, adjusted the slightly crushed flower at the cleavage, then turned to see her daughter's dress, which had been kept totally secret from her until now.

As soon as Annie set eyes on Lana, she gave a little scream of delight, then hugged her tightly.

Instead of something slinky and soberly dark, Lana was wearing an iridescent purply-pinky-violet dress, its bodice with delicate straps set on top of a surprisingly full and frilly skirt. Lana wore her dark, fringed hair up at the back, showing off her pretty white shoulders.

'Oh, look at you!' Annie exclaimed. 'I can't believe you! You look like Lily Allen's beautiful little sister. Dinah! You are so talented.'

Lana smoothed over her ruffled skirt shyly. 'We only picked the material once you'd got your dress, so we knew it would go really well.'

'Photo,' Dinah commanded.

Annie stood in the middle with little baby-pink Billie tucked under one arm and lilac Lana under the other.

'Smile!' Dinah demanded.

As soon as the flash had popped, Dinah realized the flowers, all heaped on to the chair behind her, were missing from the shot.

'Flowers!' she instructed and handed each of them a bunch. 'I have to go, Ed will be frantic for his babysitter!' She added, 'Break a leg, everyone!'

Suddenly Annie found herself gazing into Lana's eyes.

'You look amazing,' Annie told her.

'So do you,' Lana replied. 'I'm so happy for you.'

'I'm so happy for you and Owen and the babies,' Annie said and rubbed against Lana's cheek with her finger. 'We're already a family, this is just a . . . rubber stamp. And a lovely party to celebrate the fact.'

'It's great.'

'And it was all Owen's idea!' Annie added.

'It was a good idea.'

'I hope . . .' Annie began, her voice a little unsteady, 'I hope your wedding day, if you choose to have one, is just as wonderful as . . . both of mine. I've been so lucky.' She felt a hard lump at the back of her throat.

The door opened once again and in came Fern in a lovely pinky-beige suit with a huge pink rose at the lapel. Now Annie knew she was going to cry. She rushed her fingers to the corner of her eyes and pushed away the tears.

'Darlin',' Fern began and wrapped her daughter up in a hug, 'I just wanted to say hello before kick-off.'

'Thanks,' Annie croaked, staying in the hug. 'I feel all shaken up. I keep thinking of my first wedding . . . and two such fantastic men . . .' She stumbled. 'It's just hard to think that I wouldn't have met Ed if Roddy hadn't—' She broke off.

Fern hugged her daughter tightly and rubbed her back, as if she were soothing a baby.

'You were very happy with Roddy,' Fern said gently, 'so it's only natural you would want to find that again with someone else. You deserve this, Annie, you deserve this. Now, come on, blow your nose, chin up, fix yourself up. Time to look radiant, my girl.'

Fern's hand was under Annie's chin. She unclasped her handbag and brought out a pocket tissue from the inexhaustible supply kept in there.

'What a very different marriage I had,' Fern added, dabbing at the slight smudge under Annie's eye. 'Don't go thinking that anything Mick has told me has changed my mind about him. I'm not that dotty yet. I'm planning to keep him weeding and watering and taking out my rubbish for the next twenty years to atone for some of his sins.'

This made Annie laugh a little.

She looked her mother in the eye: 'I love you, Mum,' she said. 'Be right here with us for the next twenty years at least.'

'I'll try, darling,' Fern said and briskly dabbed at her daughter's eye again before there was time for another tear to fall.

There was a tap at the door: 'Are we all set?' the registrar asked.

'I've got to get to my seat,' Fern said and disappeared out of the door.

'All set,' Annie repeats, but makes one final press under her eyes. She picks up her bouquet with one hand and takes hold of Billie's toasty little paw with the other.

Lana's cool hand slips round the crook of her elbow on her bouquet-carrying side.

All three fall calmly in step behind the registrar.

Still there is a jangling of nerves and excitement: a great rushing mix of emotion in Annie's head and heart as the registrar opens the wood and glass door to the room.

Annie thinks of the little church lobby in Paris where the brides waited in turn, decade after decade, for the rest of their lives to begin.

There is music playing; she's left all the musical choices to Ed because he wants to surprise her. She recognizes this piece at once although she hasn't heard it for a long time;

it's an early recording of Ed and Owen on their violins: the very first duet they learned to play together all those years ago . . . when Annie first met Ed.

As Annie and her bridesmaids step into the room, there is a rustle as people murmur their approval and stand up.

At first Annie registers only a sea of faces; then she focuses in on friends and family in the crowd. There are Svetlana, Elena and Paula, the tallest women in the room, standing together under truly sensational hats. She beams at them. The flash which hits the corner of her eye must have been caused by Sye – the unofficial photographer.

Beautiful Amelia is in coral . . . and there's Tamsin, looking glamorously mumsy, with all three of her children around her.

It is something of a shock when Annie's eye falls next on Penny, Roddy's mother. Penny looks a little older, and somehow slighter, but her hair is in a very stylish pixie cut. She's chosen a bright blue linen jacket and on the lapel is a striking silver geometric brooch, picked out, many Christmases ago, by Annie and Roddy. She shoots Annie a bright and loving smile. Annie has to swallow hard. Chin up, she thinks. It's OK. It's really OK.

Connor in full kilt regalia risks a wave. The big show-off! Yes, persuading him not to walk her into the room was a very good decision. He'd probably have done a dance or performed a soliloquy. The handsome young man beside him? It's Andrei, Annie realizes . . . beaming at Lana.

Ed's sister Hannah and her little boy Sid; her wonderful sisters Nic and Dinah are all in the front row with their men beside them, a twin on each lap and their mother between them. Annie thinks she might cry at the sight of them all looking at her so very fondly and she presses her lips together hard. Dinah can tell, so she points down. Down at their feet are three (*three!*) of the grotesque pink plastic

Annie Bags. Three of those disgusting bags of horror! Dinah has done this especially to make her sister laugh, because she suspected Annie might get all teary and emotional right here.

Now Annie really wants to cry because she loves Dinah so much.

Instead, she turns to Ed, standing in front of the registrar's desk with his best man, Owen, upright and proud beside him.

They're both in such serious, dark blue suits, with pink shirts and blue ties. Owen looks gorgeous. He seems taller and more handsome and more grown up than Annie has ever seen him before. She flashes momentarily back to when Owen was a bright-eyed, happy baby, always so giggly . . . and flashes forward to the handsome, wonderful man he's going to turn into. She feels a rush of maternal pride. Somehow, she manages to shoot him a wink and he winks straight back.

Annie's eyes are now on Ed and, finally, she lets her eyes settle. No. Because one of the babies squawks, so both Ed and Annie look anxiously round.

Dinah rushes an emergency biscuit to each of the twins. Peace is momentarily restored.

Ed and Annie turn to face each other again.

This is big, Annie thinks, looking into his calm blue eyes.

Yes, comes the tiny distracting thought, that tie is just so perfect for those eyes.

This is immense, she reminds herself, *vastly important and monumental*.

Ed holds out his hand and Annie takes it. There is such calm and such love in those clear blue eyes, Annie knows that, whatever happens, it's going to be all right.

So long as Ed is right here at her side, Annie knows she is going to be just fine.

'Ladies and gentlemen, boys and girls,' the registrar begins, 'welcome to the marriage of Annie and Ed.'

Ed, never once taking his eyes from Annie's face, carefully repeats the words of the registrar and makes his vow to Annie.

Annie listens to every single word. She hears this fresh and different promise for the very first time. The different words make this not like a second marriage, but like a new and very different marriage. All at once, Annie feels as if she is absolutely overflowing with love. For Ed, for her children, for their children, for her family, her friends, for Roddy, for absolutely everyone she has ever met and will ever meet.

She feels as if she is full of an infinite capacity for love that could never possibly run dry. *Oh, babes*, she tells herself, *you're having a mystical moment*. She wishes she could rootle in her handbag for some extra-minty chewing gum to bring her round.

'*This* ring is a symbol of my love for you . . .' Ed says.

She hears the tiny stress on the word 'this'.

Owen steps forward, grins at his mum and hands Ed a ring.

Ed carefully turns Annie's hand in his, and then on to her fourth finger he slides a heartbreakingly perfect solitaire diamond that Annie has never seen before.

Together, they had tried on white-gold wedding bands, and she thought that was what he had bought.

This ring is not huge, it is not the kind of über-rock that Svetlana would sport, but nevertheless it is absolutely perfect. Annie has never owned a diamond before and doesn't think she has ever seen a more beautiful ring.

'Oh!' she exclaims. She has been buying fantasy diamond rings for so many years now that she knows all the terms and specifications but she's so overwhelmed that they all muddle in her head: *this is a flawless carat, D-cut, Tiffany weight, radiant . . . oh, whatever, absolutely gorgeous ring!*

She looks at Ed and gasps a little round: 'Oh!' at him once again.

He just tips her a wink and tries to rein in the smile about to burst over his face.

The registrar asks Annie gently if she is ready.

'Yes,' Annie replies.

Her hand, with its winking, blinking adornment is shaking slightly, even though Ed still holds it tightly.

'I, Annie Louise . . .' the registrar begins.

'I, Annie Louise,' she whispers.

Owen and Lana feel the enormity of the moment and instinctively move closer towards their mother. When she feels her children press in beside her, Annie finds her voice and the strength to make it through this wonderful promise.

Word by word she repeats it, until the registrar gives her the final phrase: '. . . to love and to cherish for the rest of our lives together'.

Before she can say these words, Annie swallows, she curls her toes and she wishes and wishes that they will all live long, very long and very happy lives together.

Then she looks at Ed and tells him with all her heart: 'to love and to cherish for the rest of our lives together'.

Carmen Reid is the bestselling author of the *Personal Shopper* series, also starring Annie Valentine.

She has worked as a newspaper journalist and columnist, but now writes fiction full-time. Carmen also writes a series for teen readers, *Secrets at St Jude's*. She lives in Glasgow, Scotland, with her husband and two children.

Visit www.carmenreid.com for competitions, exclusive content and Carmen's blog!